All they want for Christmas...

CHRISTMAS AFFAIRS

Kathie DeNosky and Christine Rimmer
will delight you once more with a
festive collection of sensual
and satisfying romances.

We're proud to present

December 2007
Desert Sheikhs by Susan Mallery
Featuring

The Sheikh & the Virgin Princess
The Prince & the Pregnant Princess

Christmas Affairs
Featuring

A Lawman in Her Stocking by Kathie DeNosky
Scrooge and the Single Girl by Christine Rimmer

January 2008
Crown & Glory
Featuring

The Princess Has Amnesia! by Patricia Thayer
Searching for Her Prince by Karen Rose Smith
The Royal Treatment by Maureen Child

The Bravos: Aaron & Cade
by Christine Rimmer
Featuring

His Executive Sweetheart
Mercury Rising

CHRISTMAS AFFAIRS

A Lawman in Her Stocking
KATHIE DeNOSKY

Scrooge and the Single Girl
CHRISTINE RIMMER

MILLS & BOON®
Pure reading pleasure

This collection is first published in Great Britain 2007
Harlequin Mills & Boon Limited,
Eton House, 18-24 Paradise Road, Richmond, Surrey TW9 1SR

CHRISTMAS AFFAIRS © Harlequin Books S.A. 2007.

The publisher acknowledges the copyright holders of the individual works, which have already been published in the UK in single, separate volumes, as follows:

A Lawman in Her Stocking © Kathie DeNosky 2002
Scrooge and the Single Girl © Christine Rimmer 2002

ISBN: 978 0 263 85690 3

064-1207

Printed and bound in Spain
by Litografia Rosés S.A., Barcelona

A Lawman in Her Stocking

KATHIE DeNOSKY

KATHIE DeNOSKY

lives in her native southern Illinois with her husband, three children and two very spoiled dogs. She writes highly sensual stories with a generous amount of humour. Kathie's books have appeared on bestseller lists. She enjoys going to rodeos, travelling to research settings for her books and listening to country music. She often starts her day at 2:00 am, so she can write without interruption, before the rest of the family is up and about. You may write to Kathie at PO Box 2064, Herrin, IL 62948-5264, USA or e-mail her at kathie@ kathiedenosky.com.

To Rox, Belinda and Ginny.
Thanks for sharing the laughter and fun.
Love you guys.

One

"Sheriff? Are you in here?"

At the sound of the female voice echoing through the cavernous firehouse side of Tranquillity's Sheriff's Office and Fire Department, Dylan Chandler's stomach twisted into a tight knot and the hair on the back of his neck stood straight up. He hated when a woman used that tone—fear tinged with indignation. In all his years as an officer of the law, he'd never seen it fail to be the prelude to big trouble.

He gripped the rafter with his gloved hand to steady himself, glanced down over his bare shoulder and stifled a groan. He'd been right in his assessment. Tranquillity's newest resident, Brenna Montgomery, looked like she'd seen a ghost, and it appeared that she'd been thoroughly pissed off by the encounter, too.

Dylan had only seen her once before, and that had been from a distance. He'd arrived late the night she'd shown up at the town council meeting to apply for a permit to open her craft shop, so they hadn't been formally introduced. And if her expression held any clue to the nature of her visit now, he didn't think he'd be able to work up much enthusiasm for getting acquainted.

Maybe if he remained silent, she wouldn't notice him dangling from a rope high above her head and wander back into the adjoining sheriff's office. At least long enough for him to climb down and put on his shirt.

But sure as shootin', she spotted the end of the rope dangling close to the wall, her gaze following it to his less than dignified position among the rafters of the firehouse. He groaned. Nothing left to do now but introduce himself.

"I'm Sheriff Chandler. What can I do for you, ma'am?"

He braced his feet against the wall, rappelled down to where she stood, and grabbed his shirt. Shrugging into it, he jammed the tail into his jeans as he waited for her to say something.

When she remained silent and continued to stare at him, he decided she probably thought he was some kind of a nut. Either that, or his fly was open. He made a show of glancing at his boots. His zipper was closed, but he still wore the climbing harness around his waist and upper thighs. Snug as it was, the webbed straps pulled his jeans tight and brought the male parts of his anatomy into stark relief.

"What did you need, Ms. Montgomery?" he

prompted as he hastily removed the nylon straps and tossed them on the chair where his shirt had been.

The dazed look in her pretty blue eyes suddenly cleared and her cheeks colored a rosy pink. Averting her astonished gaze to the rafters, she asked, "Why on earth were you hanging from the ceiling?"

Hot damn! She'd been checking him out.

In an effort to hide the grin pulling at the corners of his mouth, he used the cuff of his sleeve to buff a spot of imaginary dust from the silver star pinned to his chambray shirt. "I had to test some new climbing equipment for the Search and Rescue Team."

She nodded, but kept silent as she glanced around the firehouse. He almost laughed out loud. It seemed the lady was having trouble looking him in the eye.

After several moments of awkward silence, Dylan placed his hand at her lower back and guided her through the door into the adjoining sheriff's office. Walking behind the desk, he flexed his hand in an effort to stop the tingling that ran the length of his arm and spread throughout his torso. He'd probably been gripping the rope too tight, he decided. It was just plain ridiculous to think it had anything to do with feeling the warmth of her skin through the crisp fabric of her blouse.

"Now, why don't you tell me what's bothering you, Ms. Montgomery?" he suggested, removing his wide-brimmed Resistol from a hook on the wall. He jammed it onto his head before turning to face her.

While he waited for her to collect her thoughts, his gaze traveled to her copper-colored hair. For the life of him, he couldn't figure out why she'd piled it on top of her head in that god-awful knot. It looked like a baseball plopped down in the middle of a bird's nest.

"I want to report an elderly gentleman—" She stopped abruptly. "Sheriff, are you listening to me?"

She'd planted her fists on her shapely hips, drawing his attention to her feminine form. She expected him to listen with a distraction like that?

"Now what was that about an old man?" he managed to ask.

"I said there's an elderly gentleman accosting women on Main Street."

"Here? In Tranquillity? Are you sure?"

Dylan watched her cheeks flush with indignation at his dubious questions. The color highlighted the few golden freckles sprinkled across the bridge of her nose. Her big blue eyes and perfectly shaped lips made him think of long winter nights snuggled beneath the covers of his king-size bed.

He shook his head to dislodge the wayward thought. She'd said something else, but he'd missed it again. *Damn!* He'd better get his mind off the woman's looks and back to the business at hand.

"What was that?"

"I told you the old guy just grabbed me and kissed me," she stated, her patience clearly wearing thinner by the minute.

Dylan heaved a sigh as he looked over the top of her head to stare out the plate-glass window of his orderly office. What had happened to the pleasant lady who charmed the socks off the all-male town council? All the mayor and town council members had been able to talk about for the past week was what a sweet little gal that Montgomery woman was.

He shook his head. It never ceased to amaze him how a female could be so amiable when things went her way and how quarrelsome she could get when they didn't.

Turning his attention back to the woman standing on the other side of the desk, he silently cursed. He could deal with her insistence and tone of voice easy enough. It was the way she looked that made sweat pop out on his forehead and upper lip. Why did Brenna Montgomery have to be so darned...cute?

But what was up with her clothes? he wondered when her long skirt rustled. Her white, ruffled collar went clear up to her chin and her black skirt just barely cleared the floor. Dressed as she was, she reminded him of the schoolmarms in the old, western movies he'd watched as a kid.

"That's all there was to it?" he finally asked. "Just a simple kiss?"

"Wasn't that enough?" When he remained silent, she looked incredulous. "Surely you don't think I'd make up something like this?"

"No."

His stomach did a back flip. It didn't matter how her hair was styled, what kind of clothes she wore, or how kissable her lips looked; he'd always been a sucker when it came to redheads and ladies in distress. And Brenna Montgomery was both—all wrapped up into one neat little package.

Brenna felt a shiver slither up her spine and her tendency to crave chocolate whenever she became nervous rushed forward as the sheriff's brilliant, green gaze narrowed on her upturned face. She'd been so shocked to find the man shirtless and dangling from the firehouse ceiling, she hadn't noticed anything about him beyond his various muscle groups.

And what impressive, well-defined muscle groups they were, too. Bulging biceps, a ridged stomach and all that masculine bare skin had taken her by surprise. But the sight of the webbed harness pulling the denim tight across his impressive attributes had struck her absolutely speechless.

Sheriff Dylan Chandler certainly wasn't the average, run-of-the-mill, civil servant. In fact, she couldn't find one darned thing average or ordinary about the man.

His badge certified he was supposed to be one of the good guys. But didn't they wear white hats? His cowboy hat was outlaw-black, and combined with the lock of ebony hair hanging low on his forehead and the five o'clock shadow covering his lean cheeks, he appeared a little wild, relatively dangerous and totally fascinating.

Irritated with herself for giving the man's rugged good looks and bulging muscle mass a second thought, she took a deep breath, shored up her courage and asked, "What do you intend to do about this?"

Dylan pushed back the brim of his Resistol with his thumb, then folded his arms across his chest. He'd stopped several barroom bawls before they ever got started with that narrow-eyed stare he'd just given her. And for a second or two, he'd thought she might back down. But it was clear she wasn't intimidated by him. Nope. Not even a little bit.

He almost smiled. For the first time in six years,

his bluff had been called. And by a cute little redhead with freckles, no less. Amazing!

"Do you want to file a formal complaint, Ms. Montgomery?"

When she carefully avoided his gaze, he decided that he might not be losing his touch after all.

"No, I'm not going to file a complaint," she said, brushing imaginary lint from her skirt. "The old guy didn't exactly threaten me." She squared her shoulders and finally met his gaze head-on. "But I don't want it to happen again. I found it very frightening to have a total stranger grab me in a bear hug and kiss me. Even if it was on the cheek."

"I understand, Ms. Montgomery. Did the old gent hand you a rose just before he kissed you?" When she nodded, Dylan grinned. "I have a good idea who you're talking about, and believe me, you were in no danger. I'll ask him about it, but it's my bet you've just been officially welcomed to town by Pete Winstead."

"I don't care who he is," she said. "The man scared the bejeebers out of me."

Dylan frowned. "It was only a little peck on the cheek."

"Yes, but you have no idea how frightening something like that can be for a woman." She seemed to be gathering a full head of steam as she stared at him, and the heightening color on her pale cheeks fascinated the hell out of him. "Where I come from, his actions might even be considered an…" She paused as if searching for the right word, then glaring at him, finished, "…an assault."

Dylan couldn't help himself. He laughed out loud.

"Did the old geezer say anything during this alleged *assault?*"

The glare she sent his way was so heated it could have fried bacon. "Yes, but I was so frightened, I didn't understand what he said." She wrinkled her cute little nose. "Besides, he smelled like beer."

Dylan's grin instantly disappeared. "You have something against a man drinking a beer after a hard day's work?"

"Well...no—"

"Then let me clue you in on the way things are around these parts, Ms. Montgomery. Nearly every man in town stops by Luke's Bar and Grill after work for a beer and the latest gossip. It's a tradition—drink a beer, swap a story or two and go home." Dylan shrugged. "Pete's no different than the rest of us. He goes to Luke's regularly. But I've never known him to drink more than two beers at one sitting."

"I realize this is a tight-knit, little community and, believe me, I want to be a part of it just like everyone else." Her ankle-length skirt rustled like a bed of dry leaves when she tapped her toe. "But Pete Winstead's drinking habits aren't the issue here. When a stranger grabs a woman and kisses her, it can be very frightening. It's your job to prevent things like that from happening."

Dylan's arms dropped to his sides, his hands flexing in frustration. He was good at his job and he didn't need a high-strung, big-city female telling him how to do it. He'd had that happen once, he wasn't going to allow it to happen a second time.

He leaned forward and braced his hands on the polished surface of the desk. "I said I'd talk to him.

Now, is there anything else you feel the need to complain about, Ms. Montgomery?''

''It wouldn't do me any good if I did, now would it, Sheriff?'' She'd managed to make his title sound like a dirty word.

Before he had a chance to respond, she turned on her heel and slammed the door behind her so hard that the plate-glass window rattled ominously.

Shoving his hands in the front pockets of his jeans, Dylan silently watched her march across the street, gather the yards of her ridiculous skirt into a bunch around her knees and stuff it all into an aging Toyota.

He didn't doubt for a minute that the incident with Pete had scared the hell out of her. Her pale complexion and the tremor in her voice when she walked into the firehouse had been quite genuine.

But he'd dealt with Brenna Montgomery's brand of trouble before and wanted no part of it. Her kind moved in and started trying to change everything in sight. Her complaint was proof enough of that. She hadn't even been a resident of Tranquillity two full weeks and she was already trying to stop his uncle Pete's friendly tradition.

Dylan shook his head. No doubt about it. That little lady was going to be trouble with a great big, capital *T*. Unfortunately, even in those weird clothes Brenna Montgomery had to be the best-looking trouble he'd ever laid eyes on.

And he had a feeling if she stayed in town, Tranquillity would never be the same.

''Get a grip, Brenna. The sheriff's probably right about old Deke,'' Abigail Montgomery said.

"Pete," Brenna corrected her grandmother. "The old man's name is Pete."

Abigail waved her hand dismissively. "Whatever. I'm not interested in the old goat. I want to know more about the hunk wearing the badge."

Brenna sighed. She and her grandmother had been down this road before. "What's to tell? He listened to my complaint, then gave me his biased opinion."

Abigail's bright orange curls danced as she shook her head. "You know what I mean. What color are his eyes and hair? How tall is he? Is he a super stud or a major dud?"

Exasperated, Brenna stared at the woman. Since her retirement a little over a year ago as a high school guidance counselor, Abigail had made it her sole purpose in life to find Brenna a husband. She'd even gone so far as to sell the house she and Brenna had shared since the death of Brenna's parents ten years ago to move to Tranquillity, Texas, with Brenna in order to keep up the pressure.

"Granny, every time I meet a man, we go through this same inquisition. Aren't you getting a little tired of it?"

"Brenna Elaine Montgomery, you're almost twenty-six years old and the only thing you've had that even resembles a serious relationship was a college fling with that jerk, Tim Miller."

"Tom Mitchell," Brenna said, making a face. "And he taught me a valuable lesson—men use women, then cast them aside when they're done."

"If you'll remember, I told you from the beginning he reminded me of a weasel. And when he talked you into helping him get through law school, I knew I was right.'' Abigail shook her head. ''But don't judge all men by that loser.''

Brenna felt her cheeks heat with embarrassment. ''Well, I haven't seen a man yet who could tempt me into finding out if my first assessment was wrong.''

Abigail gave her a knowing look. ''Maybe old Devin—''

''Dylan.''

''Whatever. Maybe he'll prove you wrong.'' Her grandmother's gray eyes twinkled merrily. ''You know, that's probably why you're so uptight all the time. You need a man like Darwin in your life and a little hanky-panky to help you unwind.''

''Granny!''

''I just call it the way I see it.'' Abigail pushed the sleeves of her hot-pink, nylon warm-up jacket to her elbows and leaned forward in the ladder-back chair. ''Now, tell me about Sheriff Chancellor. You know I never get tired of talking about good-looking men.''

''His name is Chandler.''

''Whatever.''

Brenna frowned. ''You're not going to let this go, are you?''

''Absolutely not.'' Abigail winked. ''I'll bet my new Reeboks this guy is a real stud. Probably better-looking than Mel Gibson and muscled up like Ronald Schwasenhoofer.''

''Arnold Schwarzenegger.''

''Whatever.''

Brenna rose from the table to place her plate in the dishwasher. She was only delaying the inevitable. Abigail Montgomery could have been a top-notch interrogator for the CIA.

"Just how did you arrive at your conclusion that the sheriff had to be something special?"

"I didn't deal with teenagers for over forty years and not learn to recognize a hedge job when I see one," Abigail shot back. "You think he's a hunk."

"I do not."

"Do too. Now spill it."

Brenna threw up her hands, as much in exasperation as in surrender. "He's tall—"

"How tall?" Abigail pressed.

"I'd say he's a little over six feet tall and has black hair and green eyes." When her grandmother frowned at the lack of information, Brenna tried to sound indifferent. "He looks to be somewhere in his early thirties. Now, that's all I know about the man. And all I care to know."

"Uh-oh! He must have a spare tire around his waist." Abigail shook her head. "Don't worry. The way you cook, the extra weight will drop off the poor man like leaves from a tree."

Brenna ignored the remark about her lack of cooking skills as she remembered the sheriff's assortment of lean muscles. Her mouth went dry. "His stomach is actually quite flat."

"No teeth?"

A picture of his devastating smile flitted through Brenna's mind. "He has beautiful teeth."

"Got a real honker, huh?"

"Granny, will you stop?" Brenna placed her hands on her hips as she fought back a smile. "He doesn't have a big nose. And even if he did, I doubt that it would detract from his good looks."

"Ah-ha!" Abigail cried triumphantly. "Now we're

getting down to the nitty gritty. He's *that* good-looking, huh?'' She gave Brenna a wink and a wicked grin. ''I'll bet he's a hell of a kisser, too.''

''Granny—''

''Are you going to need the car tonight?'' Abigail asked, suddenly.

Dazed at how fast her grandmother had changed subjects, Brenna shook her head. ''No, I can walk to class. Why?''

''I wanted to drive down to Alpine with one of my new friends.''

''That will be nice,'' Brenna said, glad her grandmother had made friends so soon after their move to Tranquillity. ''What do you have planned?''

Abigail's grin turned wicked. ''We're going cruising for a stud muffin for you. Any preferences?''

''Granny, please don't start in again with the you-need-a-husband routine.''

''Oh, lighten up,'' Abigail said, rolling her eyes. ''We're just going to a movie. Want me to drop you off at the town hall?''

Brenna breathed a sigh of relief. She was never quite sure when the woman was serious and when she wasn't. ''No, thanks. It's not far, and I need the exercise.''

Her grandmother shook her head. ''I can't figure out why you're so concerned about staying in shape if you aren't interested in attracting a man.''

''Granny—''

''Okay. I'll shut up for now,'' Abigail said, glancing at her Mickey Mouse watch. ''Time to pick up my friend.'' She propelled herself from the chair and started into the living room. Turning back she shook her finger at Brenna. "Just remember I'd like to have a great-grandchild before I'm too senile to appreciate it. And that Sheriff Antler—"

"Chandler."

"Whatever," Abigail said, waving her hand. "He sounds like a great prospect for the father."

With that parting shot, Abigail breezed from the room in a flurry of hot-pink nylon and orange curls, leaving Brenna to wonder what sort of ridiculous fantasies her grandmother would start weaving about the town's insufferable sheriff.

Enjoying the mild, southwest Texas weather as she walked the short distance to the center of town, Brenna admired the rugged Davis Mountains a few miles away. Draped in the purpled shadows of early evening, the view was breathtaking and she forgot all about Abigail's matchmaking attempts as she focused on the nervous anticipation filling every cell in her body.

She took a deep breath to help settle the butterflies in her stomach and tamped down the need for something chocolate. She was going to do this. She was going to dig down deep inside and find the courage to share her love of handmade crafts with the women of Tranquillity. It was a big part of her plan to reinvent herself and she wasn't going to wimp out now. Besides, Tom had told her several times in the course of their four-year relationship that her dream of starting her own business and teaching Folk Art was silly and unprofitable. Brenna clenched her teeth. She had come a long way in the year since Tom decided that he had more in common with a woman in his law class than he had with her. But she still had a few things left to accomplish. She had every intention of proving him wrong about her teaching Folk Art, as well as his prediction that she'd never break her habit of reaching for something chocolate whenever she became nervous or upset.

By the time she reached the community room in the town hall, more than two dozen women milled around the display she'd set up earlier in the day, while others had already found a place for themselves at the work tables. Thrilled by the number of people in attendance, Brenna smiled as she walked into the room. Her only regret was that Tom wasn't around so she could tell him how wrong he'd been.

"My dear, this is the best thing that's happened to Tranquillity in decades," Mrs. Worthington said, stepping forward. "I just know you'll help add culture to our little community. It's something I've sorely missed since I married Myron and moved from the East."

Brenna smiled. Cornelia Worthington was the mayor's wife, chairwoman of the Beautification Society and self-appointed matriarch of Tranquillity. Her approval could make or break Brenna's classes.

"Thank you, Mrs. Worthington," she said slowly, searching for the most tactful way to explain that Folk Art painting wasn't in the same category with Rembrandt or van Gogh. "But I'm afraid this class will fall short of the benefits you have in mind. It's considered more of a craft than fine art."

"Oh, what a dear," Mrs. Worthington said, turning to the ladies behind her. "She has such a modest attitude for someone so immensely talented. I'm so glad

I discovered her and persuaded her to instruct this class.''

Brenna barely managed to keep her mouth from dropping open. She practically had to beg the woman for the use of the room, since it was overseen by the Beautification Society.

''Ladies, if you'll please take your seats, we'll get started,'' she said, shaking her head and walking to the front of the room.

''Mildred, what took you so long?'' she heard Mrs. Worthington call to a late arrival.

''My car broke down on the way home from work,'' the woman said, sounding flustered. ''Fortunately, Dylan passed by on his way to the poker game over at Luke's and offered me a ride.''

''Dylan!'' Mrs. Worthington's voice turned to syrup. ''It's simply marvelous to see a man take an interest in the arts.''

At the mention of the sheriff's name, Brenna cringed and slowly turned around. Sure enough, there the man stood, leaning against the door frame, a self-assured smile plastered on his masculine lips. His confidence grated on her nerves and reminded her of their earlier confrontation.

But they were on her turf now. Things were going to be vastly different from the first time they'd met.

Dylan swallowed hard when he noticed Brenna moving toward him. He was having the devil of a time accepting the way she looked now, as opposed to earlier. If he'd thought she was cute then, in that hideous, old-fashioned get-up, he'd sadly underestimated her attractiveness.

He no longer had to wonder about the curves hidden by yards of fabric, or the length of her hair. Hell's bells, he almost wished he did. It would definitely be easier on him than the reality he faced now.

Her light blue shirt loosely caressed high, full breasts, while her faded jeans outlined nicely shaped legs and hips that swayed slightly as she walked. Her copper hair, shot with gold, brushed her waist and looked so soft, his fingers burned to thread themselves in the silken waves.

"Dylan, dear, you look a little feverish." Mildred patted his arm sympathetically. "Are you feeling all right?"

Hell no! He felt like he'd just been run down by a herd of stampeding longhorns. He had to swallow hard to get words to form in his suddenly dry mouth. "Uh…sure. I'm fine."

He quickly looked around to see if anyone else detected his discomfort. Noting several curious stares, Dylan cursed his luck.

The room boasted the largest collection of gossips he'd seen since arresting Jed Phelps for getting drunk and crashing Corny's Tupperware party. And that had been three years ago. If the old hens thought there was even a remote possibility that he found Brenna Montgomery attractive, they'd be like sharks in a feeding frenzy.

He glanced over at the woman standing beside him. Mildred Bruner was the county clerk and responsible for issuing all the marriage licenses in the county. It was common knowledge she was an incurable romantic and carried her book of forms everywhere she went just hoping someone would stop her and ask to apply for a ticket to wedded bliss.

He shifted from one foot to the other. If he didn't leave, and damned quick, Mildred would start digging around in that suitcase of a purse she carried, trying to find her license book, and by sunrise the rest of the busybodies would have everyone in town taking bets on when the wedding would take place. He silently ran through every curse word he knew. He wasn't looking for a wife, and even if he was, Brenna Montgomery wasn't likely to ever be a candidate.

"I'll be over at Luke's if you need a ride home, Mildred."

His cheeks burned as he watched several of the women smile knowingly. If they hadn't noticed he was having a problem before, they sure as hell would now. His voice hadn't sounded that uneven since puberty.

"You aren't staying for class, Sheriff?" Brenna asked when he headed for the door.

Dylan stopped dead in his tracks. He couldn't believe his ears. Brenna Montgomery wanted him in her painting class about as much as a poor, lost soul wanted to see a heat wave in hell.

He turned to face her, his scowl deepening. "No."

"That's a shame. Some of the most talented crafts-people I know are men."

She took a step in Dylan's direction. He took a step back. What was the woman up to now?

She thoughtfully tilted her head, her blue eyes dancing. "Of course, some men lack the patience and coordination it takes to learn the techniques."

Her challenge punched him right square in his ego.

When she took another step forward, Dylan stood his ground and reaching out, took her hand in his. "Oh, I'm sure I could master *any* technique, Ms. Montgomery. And I'm *very* patient."

The moment their fingers touched, a tingle raced the length of Dylan's arm, making his blood pressure skyrocket. But pride wouldn't allow him to back down. "I've never had any trouble getting my hands to do what I want," he assured. Letting a provocative drawl warm his words, he smiled suggestively. "Nor have I ever had anyone complain about their ability to obtain a satisfying result."

She jerked her hand out of his so fast, he thought she might have sprained her wrist.

"It was nice of you to stop by, Sheriff, but you'll have to excuse me. I need to start my class. I'm sure you can find your way out."

Dylan knew for sure he'd turned the tables. He could tell Brenna had been as affected by the touch of his hand as he'd been by hers. And, she was trying to give him the bum's rush.

But he'd be damned before he let it happen. She'd started this confrontation. He intended to finish it.

"Where do you want me to sit?"

Her eyes grew round. "You…you don't mean you're staying?"

"Yep." At her stunned reaction, he didn't even try to hold back his satisfied smile. "That's exactly what I mean."

"Oh, this is wonderful," old Corny said, clapping her pudgy hands to gain the women's attention. "Now that Dylan's taking the class, we shouldn't have any trouble convincing our men they could use a measure of culture, too. I intend to speak with My-ron about it this very evening, and I encourage every one of you to do the same with your husbands.''

Dylan's triumphant grin evaporated, and he barely controlled the urge to squirm when several of the women bobbed their heads in eager agreement. He'd forgotten all about the guys over at Luke's. Once they got wind he was taking an art class, he'd never hear the end of it. Now, short of humiliating himself in front of the entire room full of world-class busybod-ies, there wasn't any way out.

Every Tuesday night for no telling how long, he'd miss the poker game over at Luke's. He'd be forced to listen to Brenna's soft voice as she instructed the class. He'd have to watch her silky, red hair brush the top of her shapely rear—

His body tightened noticeably, and muttering a curse, he removed his Resistol, lowered it to zipper level and took a seat. As he sat watching Brenna, his mood lightened and he fought back a grin. If any good came out of this mess, it had to be the dazed look on her face.

Brenna Montgomery looked like she'd just sat down on a bumblebee.

Two

Dazed, Brenna turned and slowly walked to the front of the class. What had she been thinking? The sheriff had been ready to leave. And he would have, if she'd just kept her mouth shut.

But, no. She couldn't leave well enough alone. She'd tried to get even for this afternoon's disagreement—tried to practice being assertive—and ended up making a mess of everything. Becoming a stronger, more self-assured woman was a balancing act. And she'd just proven she was tilting a little too far to one side.

"Okay, ladies...and gentleman." She purposely avoided looking at the man as she handed out the supply lists. "These are the items you'll need for the course."

"What's the difference between Folk Art and

painting a landscape or a portrait?'' one of the women asked.

Brenna perched on the edge of the desk as she tried to organize her tangled thoughts. The sheriff's presence was playing havoc with her already jangled nerves and had her ready to kill for a Hershey bar.

''Originally the label Folk Art was given to all forms of art created by people who knew little, if anything, about method or design. A folk artist 'created' without knowing how or what they'd done. Fine art requires more disciplined techniques.''

''How did it get started?'' Mildred Bruner asked.

''You could say it evolved out of envy,'' Brenna answered, trying her best to ignore the man sitting in the back of the room. He was grinning like the Cheshire cat. ''In Europe, peasants wanted to simulate the expensive furnishings of the noble class, so they used Folk Art to paint their furniture, dishes and pottery. They even used it on store signs.''

Mrs. Worthington frowned. ''Store signs?''

Brenna nodded. ''Around the seventeenth and eighteenth century, the craft was used for practical, as well as decorative, purposes. Most of the common people were illiterate. But by having signs painted with bright colors and bold designs, shopkeepers could effectively advertise their product.'' She paused as she searched for an example. ''Let's say Luke's had a wooden sign with nothing more than a large beer stein with suds running down the side.'' She smiled. ''I don't think any of us would be left to wonder what Luke sold, would we?''

''Oh, how quaint,'' Mrs. Worthington said, her face brightening with a wide smile.

By the time Brenna went over what the ladies and Sheriff Chandler could expect to learn, it was almost time to dismiss the class. "Are there any more questions?" When no one responded, she smiled. "Then I'll dismiss class early. I have all the supplies at my shop. Stop by and I'll help you find everything you need so we can start painting next week."

On their way out, several of the ladies stopped to tell Brenna how enthusiastic they were about the class and to inquire about her new craft shop. Her spirits soared and the incident with the sheriff was all but forgotten as she closed the door to the community room and stepped out into the late-November night.

She'd accomplished two very important goals tonight. She'd generated a lot of interest in her new business, but more important, she'd found the courage to stand in front of a class to teach. She only wished Tom had been around to see just how far she'd come in the year since he'd dumped her, and how wrong he'd been about her ambitions.

Thinking about the man who'd taken her to the cleaners, both emotionally and financially, she cringed. How could she have been so naive, so blind about his self-centeredness?

"Ms. Montgomery, could I have a word with you?" a male voice asked from behind her at the same time a hand came down on her shoulder.

Her surprised cry echoed through the deserted streets of Tranquillity as she spun around and swung her tote, her aim directed where it would hurt the most—her assailant's groin.

"Take it easy, lady," Dylan said, quickly turning his body to protect himself. "It's just me."

"Sheriff Chandler!" She placed her hand over her heart as she glared at him. "Do all the men in this town get some kind of kick out of frightening women?"

Dylan stepped closer and hooked his thumbs in his belt loops. He couldn't understand why she'd been so upset about the incident with Pete. If the way she swung that bag was any indication, she could easily take care of herself.

"I didn't mean to scare you," he said, thankful that he'd been quick enough to side-step her blow. If he hadn't, he'd be writhing around on the sidewalk right now, feeling as if death would be a blessing. "I was just trying to stay out of the way until I could talk to you in private."

"Do you want to withdraw from the class?" she asked, sounding hopeful.

Nothing would make him happier. But he'd be damned before he gave her the satisfaction. "Nope. I think I'm going to enjoy learning to paint," he lied.

Her hopeful smile vanished. "That's nice, Sheriff. Now, if you'll excuse me, I need to be going."

Dylan frowned. That was the second time this evening that she'd tried to dismiss him. And it didn't sit any better this time than it had the last.

"Not so fast, Ms. Montgomery. We need to talk about what happened this afternoon."

She shook her head as she stared up at him. "I really don't see the need, Sheriff. I told you what happened. And you made it quite clear that you thought I was overreacting to the situation."

Dylan studied her upturned face for several long seconds. She really was the best-looking trouble he'd seen in years. Her guileless blue eyes held an intelligence that he found sexy as hell and her perfect cupid's bow lips were just begging to be kissed.

The ridiculous thought caused his stomach to twist into a tight knot. Thinking along those lines could get a man in serious trouble. He'd been there once and he had no intention of ever going there again.

Taking a deep breath, he nodded in the direction of the restaurant across the street. "Let's talk this out over a cup of coffee."

"But aren't you supposed to give Mildred Bruner a ride home?" she asked, looking around.

"Corny...Mrs. Worthington, whisked Mildred away about ten minutes ago, along with the rest of the class." He chuckled and shook his head when he thought of the flurry of flowered polyester as the women crowded into Corny's pink Cadillac and Helen Washburn's old Buick. "They mentioned something about an emergency meeting of the B.S. Club."

Brenna arched a perfectly shaped brow. "B.S. Club?"

"Uh...Beautification Society."

Way to go, Chandler. He'd just slipped up and told her the men's secret name for the town's only women's organization. A name that the men knew better than to mention in front of any of the club's members.

He cleared his throat. "They...uh, get together once or twice a month and share the latest gossip."

"I get the distinct impression that secrets aren't kept for very long around here," she said.

"Everyone knowing your business is one of the

hazards of living in a small town,'' he said, relieved that she'd let his less than flattering reference to the organization pass. He placed a hand on her back to usher her across the quiet street and felt a jolt travel up his arm and spread across his chest.

''Just a minute, Sheriff,'' she said, stiffening beneath his touch. ''Why can't we talk right here?''

A slight tremor coursed through her, and he knew it had nothing to do with the chill of the autumn evening.

Good. At least he wasn't the only one affected by the contact.

''I wouldn't be much of a gentleman if I asked you to stand out here in the night air.'' He did his best to suppress a knowing grin as he added, ''You're already shivering.''

He almost laughed out loud when he had to trot to keep up with her as she marched across the street to Luke's.

Brenna had only been in Luke's Bar and Grill twice in the two weeks she'd been in Tranquillity, but both times she felt as if she'd taken a step back in time. Wanted posters from the late 1800s decorated the walls, along with cow skulls, branding irons and various pieces of old, leather harness. Shiny, brass spittoons were placed on the floor at either end of the bar and the room's muted light filtered down from suspended wagon wheels with antique lanterns converted to accommodate electricity.

Sheriff Chandler must have noticed her curiosity as he led the way to an empty table on the far side of the room. ''Luke's granddaddy opened the saloon around the turn of the century and Luke is pretty sentimental about the place." He held a chair for her. "How do you take your coffee?"

"With cream."

She watched his long-legged stride carry him to the bar. Sheriff Chandler was as good-looking from the back as he was from the front, she decided. He had the widest shoulders, longest legs and the tightest butt—

Stunned by the direction her thoughts had taken, Brenna quickly looked away. Had she lost her mind? She had absolutely no interest in Dylan Chandler. No way. None.

"Here you go," he said, returning with their coffee. He placed two mugs on the table, then seated himself in the chair opposite her.

Taking a sip of the steamy liquid, Brenna listened to a country ballad playing on the jukebox as she waited for him to tell her what was on his mind. She wanted to get this over and put some distance between them. Something about the man made her insides quiver and her nerves tingle. And she was mere seconds away from going in search of the nearest candy machine for a chocolate fix.

Unable to stand the tension any longer, she cleared her throat and asked, "What was it you wanted to talk about, Sheriff?"

He smiled at her over the top of his cup, making her heart skip a beat. "You got the wrong impression this afternoon and I'd like to set things straight." She started to interrupt, but he held up a hand. "I wasn't making light of the situation. But this is a small town, with small-town ways. When someone moves in, most everyone tries to do the neighborly thing and welcome the newcomer with open arms." He chuckled. "I'll admit most folks are a little more subtle than Pete, but believe me, he has the best intentions. After you left the office, I talked to him and it was just as I thought—he was only trying to make you feel a part of the community."

Brenna set her cup down and tried to ignore the tingling sensation skimming up her spine from the sound of his smooth baritone. "Before today, I'd never laid eyes on the man. How was I to know about his neighborly tradition?"

"I'm sure it was unnerving," he said, nodding. "But that's not why I wanted to talk to you."

"If that's not it, then what's the purpose of this?"

"I think you have the right to know why I was so defensive about Pete."

"Okay, I'm listening, Sheriff. Why don't you explain it to me?"

"Will you stop that?" For reasons he'd rather not dwell on, Dylan wanted to hear her velvet voice say his name. "Call me Dylan."

"Okay...*Dylan*. Why are you so protective of Pete?"

He slowly placed his cup on the table as he tried to collect his thoughts. Maybe it hadn't been such a good idea, insisting that she use his name. The sound had sent his blood pressure up a couple of dozen points and made his mouth go dry.

"If you'll remember, I told you I've known Pete all my life," he said, finally forcing words past the cotton in his throat. "In fact, he lives with me."

Dylan paused. This was the part he dreaded. But it

would be better coming from him than from someone else. And she'd find out soon enough anyway.

Clearing his throat, he met her expectant gaze head-on. "Pete Winstead is my uncle."

Her expressive blue eyes widened. "No wonder you were so adamant about him being harmless. Why didn't you tell me this afternoon?"

Relieved she wasn't throwing something at him for withholding that bit of information, Dylan grinned. "To tell the truth, I was pretty frustrated about the whole thing. I've warned him for years that something like this might happen." He shrugged. "Anyway, I think Pete will be a lot less enthusiastic about his greetings from now on. He was pretty upset that he'd frightened you and made me promise to talk to you the first chance I got."

"I can understand your frustration," she said, nodding. "I live with a pretty eccentric relative of my own. I hope Pete's not too upset."

Her lips turned up and Dylan felt as if he'd been kicked in the gut. Brenna Montgomery could drop a three hundred pound lumberjack with that smile of hers.

"Don't worry about Pete." Dylan cringed at the rust in his voice. Clearing his throat, he went on, "He'll get over it. Nothing gets him down for long."

"He sounds like my grandmother." Grinning, she shook her head. "On second thought, I don't think anyone's like Granny."

In spite of the warning bells clanging in his brain, Dylan grinned right back. "She's not your typical, rocking chair senior citizen?"

"No," Brenna said, laughing.

Dylan felt his gut do a cartwheel and sweat pop out on his upper lip. When Brenna Montgomery let herself, she could be downright devastating. She had the most delightful laugh. And her lips were just meant for kissing.

He frowned. What was wrong with him? She was too unpredictable, too anxious to upset the status quo. She'd not only complained about his uncle Pete's forty year tradition, she'd goaded him into taking her damned class and missing the Tuesday night poker game—a ritual he hadn't missed in the last ten years. Until tonight.

No doubt about it. The lady was trouble. And he'd do well to remember that. He suddenly looked around. The poker game would be breaking up soon. The last thing he needed was for the boys to come out of the back room and start asking why he'd missed the game.

"Is something wrong?" Brenna asked. "All of a sudden you look rather grim."

"Uh…no." Dylan glanced at his watch. "It's getting late. I think we'd better call it a night."

Rising from his chair, he offered his hand. But the moment she placed her hand in his, he knew he'd made a big mistake. Her tender flesh slid along his callused palm like a piece of fine silk, and it took monumental effort on his part not to groan aloud.

He said nothing as he released her hand and followed her out into the night. He couldn't. His mind and body were at war, and it took every bit of his concentration to keep from acting on his first impulse.

Trouble or not, Dylan wanted to take Brenna in his arms and kiss her senseless.

"Where's your car parked?" he asked.

"My grandmother borrowed it for the evening." She glanced at her watch. "But it's probably at home by now." She started down the street. "See you in class next week."

He caught her by the shoulder and turned her to face him. "You walked?"

Nodding, she shrugged out of his grip. "It's not that far."

"It's dark."

"It gets that way at night," she said, dryly. "And that's a problem, because…?"

"It's not safe."

She met his frown with one of her own. "You've just spent the last half hour telling me what a friendly place Tranquillity is. Now you're telling me it's not safe to walk the streets?" She folded her arms and glared up at him. "Make up your mind, Sheriff. What kind of place is this?"

"For the most part, Tranquillity is about as safe as any place can be," he admitted, trying not to stare at the way her full breasts rested on her folded arms. He focused his gaze on the safer area of her forehead. "But once in a while a cowboy from one of the ranches around here gets tanked up and starts to thinking he's Don Juan."

Taking her by the elbow, Dylan hustled her toward his restored '49 Chevy pickup parked across the deserted street. "I've already gotten one complaint from you today. I'd just as soon skip the second."

"No, thanks," she said stubbornly. "I'd rather walk."

He stared down at her. Damn, but she was a feisty

little thing. It was all he could do to keep from kissing her right then and there. Instead, he opened the driver's door, placed his hands at her waist and lifted her into the truck.

She let out an alarmed squeak. "What do you think you're doing?"

"Seeing that you get home safely," he said, climbing in beside her.

"This is totally uncalled for." Glaring at him, she slid over to the passenger side. "I can take care of myself."

"Yeah, sure."

"You can't do this."

"Watch me." He gave her a stern look in an effort to stop any further protest, but she completely ignored it. Blowing out a frustrated breath, he jammed the key into the ignition.

"Are you this controlling with everyone?" she asked.

Dylan tried counting to ten, then twenty. At thirty he gave up. "Lady, you could drive Job over the edge. You complain about an old man's innocent gesture of friendship and then go walking down a dark street at night, inviting all kinds of trouble."

"I do not."

"Yes, you do."

Gunning the engine, he spun gravel and squealed the tires as he steered the truck away from the curb. He cringed as he imagined the chips the rocks had made in the paint job. He and his dad had spent several years restoring the old Chevy, and Jack Chandler was probably looking down from heaven right now, ready to sling a couple of lightning bolts Dylan's way for treating the truck with such irreverence.

He glanced over at the woman beside him. And it was all her fault, too. She was making him crazy and causing him to do things he hadn't done in years. The last time he'd laid rubber had been when he was nineteen and full of more piss and vinegar than good sense.

Fuming, Brenna stared out the passenger window. Dylan was probably right about her walking home alone in the dark, but she'd be darned if she let him know it.

Why did men think they knew what was best for a woman? What made them think that a woman was incapable of making her own decisions?

Tom had always been that way, had always tried to tell her what she should do. And it appeared Dylan Chandler was cut from the same cloth.

When he pulled up in front of her house, she prepared to get out of the truck. "Thank you for the ride. But I have to tell you, your behavior borders on Neanderthal, Sheriff. I—"

"That may be," he interrupted. "But I'm proud to say this caveman can go to bed tonight with a clear conscience." At her raised eyebrow, he had the audacity to grin. "I saw that you got home safe and sound."

"Before you know it, you'll be spouting the code of chivalry, straight from the Round Table," she retorted.

As she reached for the door handle, Dylan caught her wrist and leaned close. "There's nothing wrong with a man protecting a woman from the dangers she's either too naive or too stubborn to recognize for herself.''

"The woman in question might just be a black belt in karate, and able to take care of herself,'' she bluffed, trying to ignore the tingling sensations from his touch, his nearness.

The close confines of the truck cab seemed to grow even smaller and a crazy fluttering started deep in her stomach. His lips were only a few inches from hers. She needed space.

"I appreciate your concern, but—''

"Hush,'' Dylan said, his deep baritone vibrating against her lips a moment before his mouth brushed hers.

At first he teased with featherlight kisses, nibbling, testing her willingness to allow the caress to continue. But when he traced her lips with his tongue, all thought of putting distance between them ceased. Her own tongue automatically darted out to ease the tingling friction of his exploration, but coming into contact with the rough tip of his, the flutters in her stomach went absolutely wild.

At the moment, it didn't seem to matter that she shouldn't be kissing him, tasting him with eager abandon. She was too caught up in the many sensations racing through her to even breathe. When she finally did, the mingled scents of leather, spicy cologne and Dylan caused her nostrils to flare. She didn't think she'd ever smelled anything quite so sensuous, so sexy, so wonderful as the man gathering her to him.

He pulled her unresisting body closer and, trapped between them, her hands clenched his shirt. The firm muscles beneath flexed and bunched at her touch, and his heart pounded against her fingertips. Heat and excitement simultaneously coursed through her when Dylan's tongue penetrated the inner recesses of her mouth. Exploring. Claiming.

Dylan Chandler was the very last man she should be kissing, she thought, her sanity intruding. He was arrogant, controlling and macho from the top of his handsome head, all the way to his big, booted feet. And he was kissing her like she'd never been kissed before.

The intensity of passion might have gotten the better of Dylan, had the steering wheel digging into his ribs not reminded him of where they were. He hadn't necked in the cab of a pickup truck since his senior year in high school. He briefly wished he'd driven the Explorer to town, instead of the truck. It had more room to maneuver. But then, Corny and her hens would have had a field day talking about the sheriff making out in the sheriff's patrol car with the new painting teacher.

Regaining control of his sanity, he leisurely broke the kiss. He'd kissed his share of women, but nothing in his past experience could compare with the wild, untamed feelings he had coursing through him now. He felt like pounding his chest and bench pressing a dump truck.

Hell, he just might have to in order to work off the adrenaline. There were kisses, and then there were *kisses*. And on a scale of one to ten, he'd have to rate this one a fifteen. Maybe even a twenty. Definitely an off-the-scale experience.

His hand shook slightly as he cupped the back of

Brenna's head and gently pressed her cheek to his shoulder. "Wow!"

"That shouldn't have happened," she said breathlessly.

"No, it shouldn't have," he said honestly.

What the hell did he think he was doing? The woman was trouble from the top of her pretty head all the way to her little feet. Hadn't he learned his lesson five years ago?

The best thing he could do would be to see that she got into the house, then get back in his truck and put as many miles between them as the old Chevy would take him.

"I'll walk you to the porch," he said, releasing her.

She reached for the door handle. "It isn't necessary."

But Dylan was out of the cab and around the front of the truck in a flash. When he opened the door and helped her down from the bench seat, he could tell she was going to protest again.

Placing his hand at her back, he ushered her toward the front porch. "My dad made me promise a long time ago that I'd be a gentleman at all times. And that includes walking a lady to the door when I take her home."

"But you were only giving me a ride."

"Doesn't matter," he said stubbornly. "You're a lady. I drove you home. I walk you to the door. It's as simple as that."

When they reached the porch steps, he glanced down at her and felt as if he'd had the wind knocked out of him. This was the way she was meant to look—soft, her hair slightly mussed from having his fingers tangled in the silky strands, a blush of desire coloring her porcelain cheeks.

He had to have lost every ounce of sense he possessed, but he wasn't one bit sorry he was the man to cause that look. His body tightened and he figured it was time to beat a hasty retreat before he did something stupid like kiss her again.

Just as he started to bid her a good evening, the sudden brightness of the porch light made him blink. "What the hell?"

"Brenna? Is that you?"

"You know darned well it is," she muttered, quickly stepping away from him.

An elderly woman around the same age as his uncle Pete, stepped out onto the porch. "Of course I do." The old gal winked at him. "But since it's obvious you aren't going to ask this handsome young man inside, I had to come up with an excuse to meet him."

Removing his hat, Dylan extended his hand. "Dylan Chandler, ma'am. You must be Brenna's grandmother. It's nice to meet you."

"I'm Abigail Montgomery. Won't you come in for a few minutes?" she asked, shaking his hand and treating Brenna to an impish grin.

Brenna gripped the strap on her tote bag so tight she was surprised it didn't snap in two. The smile on her grandmother's face and the delighted twinkle in her eyes promised days of questions, teasing and anything but subtle innuendo.

"Granny, I'm sure Sheriff Chandler has more important matters to attend to." She gave Dylan a pointed look. "Don't you, Sheriff?"

He nodded. "Maybe another time, Mrs. Montgomery."

"I'll hold you to that." Abigail smiled pleasantly. "Maybe Brenna can cook dinner for you some evening."

Brenna couldn't help it. Her mouth dropped open at her grandmother's ridiculous statement.

"Shut your mouth before you catch a bug, kiddo," Abigail advised.

"I'd better say good-night and let you ladies get inside," Dylan said, sounding anxious to make his getaway.

"Thanks again for the ride," Brenna said when her grandmother elbowed her in the ribs.

"No problem," he called, walking out to the truck. "Good night, ladies."

"Night," Abigail said. Once Dylan had started his truck, she steered Brenna through the door. "Let's go inside. You have a lot to tell me. And I'm warning you. This time, I want the straight poop."

"There's nothing to tell," Brenna said, closing the door to secure the lock.

"Oh, yes there is," Abigail shot back. "You told me you didn't like Darren Chancellor."

"Dylan Chandler."

"Whatever," Abigail said, waving her hand. "You told me you had no interest in him."

"I don't."

Abigail snorted. "Yeah, and the Grand Canyon is nothing but a big drainage ditch. Get real."

"Dylan just gave me a ride home." At her grandmother's dubious expression, Brenna added, "He's not my type."

"Sure looked like he is." Abigail laughed delightedly. "It takes some pretty heavy breathing to fog up windows that fast. And I don't blame you one bit. That man's the sexiest stud muffin I've seen come down the pike in a long time."

When her grandmother began humming "Here Comes the Bride," Brenna turned on her heel, walked into her bedroom and slammed the door. She sank down on the side of the bed, rummaged through the drawer of her nightstand and pulled the object of her search from inside. Peeling back the wrapper, she bit into the chocolate bar.

As the rich, smooth taste spread throughout her mouth, she sighed heavily. Life with her grandmother could be trying at best, but now that she'd met Dylan Chandler, it was going to be downright impossible.

Three

Dylan rested his chin on his palm and stared off into space. It had been four days since he'd agreed to take Brenna's painting class. Four days since he'd taken her home. And four days that he'd been useless to himself and everyone else.

Oh, he'd gone through the motions of tending to business. But more times than he cared to count, he found himself staring off into space. Like now.

When he'd kissed her, he'd only meant to silence her. But he'd been the one at a loss for words when the kiss ended.

He shook his head as he turned his attention back to the papers on his desk. The last time he'd made the mistake of letting his hormones overrule his good sense he'd come out looking like a complete fool. He had no intention of letting anything like that happen again. And the best way to see that it didn't would be to remove himself from temptation.

Next Tuesday night, instead of going to that damned painting class, he'd be over at Luke's with the rest of the guys doing what they always did—playing poker in the back room.

His decision made, Dylan settled down to the paperwork in front of him. He'd only gotten as far as the middle of the first page when Myron Worthington rushed into his office and plopped his bulk into the chair in front of Dylan's desk.

"We've got big trouble brewin', boy."

"What makes you think that, Myron?" Dylan asked calmly, accustomed to the mayor's excited outbursts.

"Cornelia and them hens of hers are up to somethin'," Myron answered. He fidgeted with his bolo tie every time he talked about his wife, but this time, Dylan thought the man might strangle himself with it.

"You mean the B.S. Club is discussing something more complicated than what refreshments to serve at their next meeting or who they'll get to help them decorate the community room for the Christmas Jamboree?" he asked.

Myron sat forward and nodded vigorously. "This mornin' at breakfast, Cornelia just up and tells me they're gonna redo Main Street in time for the Jamboree, then after that they're gonna do somethin' special for every holiday."

Dylan leaned back, clasped his hands behind his head and propped his boots on the edge of his desk. "Besides holding a weekly meeting, the B.S. Club hasn't done a single thing in the past twenty years besides make cookies and punch for the Christmas Jamboree and decide who they'll coerce into being elves when you play Santa Claus for the kids. What makes you think they'll get anything accomplished in the next month?''

"Because Cornelia told me they already decided to use that artsy-fartsy stuff they're learnin' on Tuesday nights to do it," Myron shot back.

Dylan's stomach clenched at the mention of Brenna's painting class. "Did she tell you what they have planned?"

"No. And that's what's got me worried." Myron removed his wide-brimmed Resistol and ran an exasperated hand over his bald head. "As long as Cornelia's talkin', she ain't doin'. It's when she finally shuts up that you gotta watch out."

"Did she tell you when they plan to get started?"

Myron shook his head. "That's where you come in."

"Me?" Dylan's boots hit the floor with a thud as he sat up straight. "What have I got to do with all this?"

"You're takin' that class ain't you?"

"No."

Myron glared at him. "Cornelia said you was. She even tried to get me to join in the damned thing."

Dylan felt heat begin to creep up his neck. "I was there Tuesday night, but I don't intend to go back."

"You have to," Myron insisted.

The heat spread upward to Dylan's cheeks. "Why?"

Myron rose from his chair to pace back and forth. "We have to find out what the B.S. Club's got up their sleeves. And when they plan to get started on it."

"Just ask your wife," Dylan said reasonably.

Myron stopped pacing to peer at him as if he'd sprouted horns and a tail. "You don't know one damned thing 'bout women, do you, boy?"

Dylan laughed. "I know enough to get by."

"I'm not talkin' about snugglin' up to a gal," Myron said, exasperated. He tapped his temple with his index finger. "I'm talkin' about the way they think."

"How *do* they think, Myron?"

The man splayed his pudgy hands. "Damned if I know. I've been married to Cornelia for thirty years and I still ain't got her figured out. But I do know when she's got her mind set on somethin', there ain't nothin' or nobody gonna change it. And she's fixed her sights on overhaulin' Main Street."

"Well, you'll have to get your information some other way," Dylan said firmly. "I don't get along with the teacher."

"That ought to make it easy then," Myron said, looking relieved.

"Forget it, Myron." Dylan shook his head. "I'm not going back to that class."

Myron gave him a measuring look. "I don't ever recall havin' to do this, boy. But it looks like there ain't no other way."

Dylan's stomach twisted into a knot. He knew what the man was driving at. But before he could stop him, Myron announced, "As the mayor, and your boss, I'm givin' you a direct order to stay in that class and find out what them hens are up to before they make

Tranquillity the laughingstock of the whole damned state.''

Having pronounced sentence, Myron plunked his hat on his shiny, bald pate and walked out of the office with all the authority of a rotund, little monarch.

Dylan propped his elbows on the desk and buried his head in his hands. He didn't like the turn of events one damned bit. The role of spy just wasn't his style. And seeing Brenna every Tuesday night for the next month wasn't going to help him forget that kiss, either.

But orders were orders. He'd always taken pride in his job, and short of resigning as sheriff, Dylan didn't see where he had any other choice.

Brenna took a deep breath, opened the back door and readied herself to face her grandmother once again. Since meeting Dylan four days ago, Abigail had dispensed with any pretense of subtlety and had even gone so far as to try to get Brenna to discuss the number of guests she'd like to invite to the wedding.

"I'm in the living room," Abigail called, when Brenna entered the kitchen. "Come and see who's dropped by for a visit."

Seated beside Abigail on the living room sofa, Pete Winstead treated Brenna to a big grin as he smoothed his mussed hair and replaced his battered cowboy hat. "Nice to see you again, Miss Brenna."

Brenna's eyes widened when her grandmother patted Pete's thigh. "He stopped by to apologize for frightening you the other day,'' Abigail announced. ''Didn't you, Pete?''

''Uh…yeah,'' he agreed. Brenna thought he looked anything but repentant when he added, ''I'm mighty sorry I scared you.''

Abigail rose and walked over to Brenna. ''I can't believe you thought this old goat tried to put the moves on you.'' Eyeing Pete up and down, she looped her arm through Brenna's and gave her a sly grin. ''It's my guess he's too old to have anything but fond memories.''

Brenna's cheeks burned. ''Granny!''

Pete got to his feet, his grin wide. ''Oh, don't you worry nothin' about it, gal.'' He turned his attention to Abigail, took off his hat and pointed to his thick white hair. ''Looks can fool you, sugar. There may be snow on the roof, but there's still one hell of a fire burnin' in the furnace.''

''I wouldn't know about that,'' Abigail shot back. ''I'm not that cold, yet.''

At a loss for words, Brenna looked at her grandmother. Abigail's wrinkled cheeks glowed and her eyes sparkled with mischief. She was having the time of her life.

Pete laughed. ''How 'bout goin' with me to Luke's this evenin', sugar? Some of the men get together on Saturday nights to play their guitars and fiddles. The music ain't too bad and it beats sittin' at home.''

''Doesn't that sound like a hoot?'' Abigail asked Brenna. Turning back to Pete, her voice took on a teasing note. ''We'd love to go. But we're modern women. We'll meet you there.''

Brenna felt like she'd just entered the Twilight

Zone. Not only had Abigail just accepted a date with Pete, she'd included Brenna as part of the package. "I don't think—"

"Hush, Brenna." Abigail hurried Pete toward the door. "If we don't let this old fossil go, we'll never get ready in time."

"Old fossil!" Pete laughed as he stepped out onto the porch. "I ain't much older than you, sugar. And just wait till tonight. I'll dance your feet plumb off."

"He'll probably stomp all over them," Abigail confided, closing the door. She breezed past Brenna on her way to the bedroom. "I wonder what the accepted duds are for a place like Kook's?"

"Luke's," Brenna corrected. "The place is called Luke's."

"Whatever."

Brenna followed Abigail down the hall. It was just as well her grandmother included her as part of the date. No telling what kind of trouble the geriatric duo would get themselves into.

"Pete thinks he's going to outdance me, but I've got news for the old buzzard. By the time I'm finished with him, his cowboy boots will be smoking." Abigail rummaged through her dresser drawers. "Have you seen my blue scarf?"

"No," Brenna said, distracted. She couldn't believe after twenty years of widowhood, Abigail had finally found a man she wanted to see socially.

A sudden thought had her smiling. If her grandmother's mind was on her own love life, she wouldn't have time to concentrate on Brenna's.

As if she could read minds, Abigail stopped searching for the scarf to give Brenna a wicked grin. "Maybe Stud Muffin will be there tonight."

"Give it up, Granny," Brenna said, refusing to believe the sudden flutter in her stomach had anything to do with Abigail's reference to Dylan. "I'm not interested in the man."

Taking a swig of his beer, Dylan listened contentedly to the band play an offbeat version of a George Strait song. Since his talk with the mayor, he'd had time to think, time to put things in perspective about the kiss he'd shared with Brenna. His reaction to her hadn't been all that unusual. It had been a while since he'd enjoyed the warmth of a woman's body, and given the same set of circumstances, a saint would have been tempted.

But the minute he saw Brenna walk through Luke's door, Dylan's mouth went as dry as a desert in a drought. Her pink sweater and designer jeans outlined a body made for sin. The way her hips swayed when she moved made his body tighten and his own jeans feel like they were at least two sizes too small.

Trouble had never looked so good or so tempting. And apparently he wasn't the only man to notice. Several cowboys at the bar nudged each other, their expressions changing from idle curiosity to open appreciation as they watched her cross the room.

Dylan had the inexplicable urge to punch something when one of the men grabbed her by the shoulder. But, bless her heart, Abigail took one look at the guy, whacked him across the knuckles with her handbag, then steered Brenna toward the table Dylan shared with Pete.

"Well, would you look who's here?" Pete declared, a grin spreading across his wrinkled face.

"Brenna, this table only has two chairs. Why don't you and Dillard find yourself one of your own?" Abigail suggested. Her eyes danced merrily as she pointed to the far corner of the room. "That one over in the shadows would give you two the chance to pick up where you left off the other night."

Dylan watched embarrassment stain Brenna's cheeks as several of Luke's patrons turned to openly stare at the old gal's outrageous statement. Something deep inside Dylan's gut twisted and made him want to shelter her from the prying eyes.

"You two kids have fun," Pete said, giving Dylan a meaningful look as he seated Abigail in the chair Dylan had been sitting in.

With the choice taken out of his hands, Dylan touched Brenna's elbow. "It's too noisy to talk here anyway. Let's find a table farther away from the dance floor."

He guided her through the Saturday night crowd and over to an unoccupied table in the corner. Holding the chair for her, he was aware that nearly every eye in the place watched them.

Apparently, the B.S. Club had activated their phone tree after class the other night and spread the word— the sheriff had shown an interest in the new painting teacher. Unfortunately, Abigail had just reinforced the erroneous rumors.

"Need another beer, Dylan?" a young waitress asked as she approached the table.

Dylan smiled at his deputy, Jason's, girlfriend. "I'm fine. Thanks, Susie." Turning his attention to the silent woman beside him, he asked, "Would you like something, Brenna?"

"A diet cola," she murmured quietly.

"Be right back," Susie called over her shoulder as she threaded her way through the tables.

Dylan waited until Brenna's drink arrived before he commented on her somber mood. "You might as well get over it. Your grandmother isn't going to change at this stage of the game."

"You're probably right," Brenna said with a sigh.

Dylan shrugged. "I have the same problem with Uncle Pete. He says what he damned well pleases and to hell with what other people think."

"Granny says it's one of the perks of being older," Brenna agreed. "But I wish she'd use a little more discretion."

He grinned. "I wouldn't count on that happening."

"I suppose you're right," she said, her smile resigned.

After several moments of awkward silence, the band began to play a ballad. Reaching for her hand, Dylan pulled Brenna to her feet. "Let's dance."

He couldn't dance worth a hoot to the faster songs, but he could sway in time to the slower ones. Besides it was better than just staring at each other for the rest of the evening.

But when they reached the dance floor, the crowd swelled and Brenna was pushed against him. Wrapping his arms around her to keep her from falling, Dylan gulped hard. Even though she was quite a bit shorter, she fit him perfectly and his body was already responding in a very X-rated way.

As he held her close, he tried to ignore the feel of

her soft breasts pressed tightly to his chest, the touch of her thighs as they grazed his own. The friction of her lower body rubbing intimately against his caused him to swallow convulsively. Pressed so closely together, there was no way he could hide the fact that he was harder than hell.

Brenna felt the butterflies in her lower abdomen go absolutely wild, and her breath came out in short, little puffs at the feel of Dylan's strong arousal pressed to her lower abdomen. His wide chest blocked out everything around her, and even though they were far from alone, she felt as if they were a million miles from the nearest living soul.

Her arms had automatically encircled his neck when she'd been shoved into him, and she couldn't seem to stop herself from threading her fingers in the thick, ebony hair at his collar. Her eyes drifted shut and she sighed as the soft fabric of Dylan's shirt brushed her cheek. His steely muscles quivered in response to the moist heat of her breath and the movement caused her legs to grow weak.

It would definitely be in her best interest to put some distance between them and seek out a candy machine. Having something chocolate was much safer than wanting to have the sheriff.

His hands caressed the small of her back.

She really should move away.

His lips grazed her temple.

In another moment or two, she'd—

The music stopped suddenly and the room became unnaturally quiet a moment before Pete Winstead's angry voice reverberated across the dance floor. "I said to leave my woman the hell alone, Ira!"

* * *

Dylan's muscles spasmed in protest as he released Brenna and shouldered his way through the crush of people. "What's up, Uncle Pete?" he demanded when he reached the elderly couple.

"This here dog-eared jackass won't leave Abby alone," Pete said, his doubled fist threatening the other man's nose.

"Granny, what's going on?" Brenna asked from behind Dylan.

Abigail's eyes sparkled with excitement. "Isn't this radical?"

"All I wanted was to dance with her," Ira said sullenly, his own fists held in a ready position.

"Then why did you go and call her an old biddy?" Pete asked, his voice accusing.

"I think you both had better settle down," Dylan advised. Mindful of the attention they were drawing from the crowd, he nodded toward the exit. "Let's step outside and see if we can get this straightened out. Ladies?" He held the door as Brenna, Abigail and the two old gentlemen filed past. Once they stood under the neon sign outside Luke's, Dylan turned to Abigail. "What happened, Mrs. Montgomery?"

Abigail pointed to Ira. "This man asked me to dance and I politely refused. When he wouldn't take no for an answer, I told him I preferred a man with a pulse and for him to buzz off. That's when he called me an old biddy."

For having been insulted, Dylan thought Abigail's voice sounded suspiciously pleased. He looked at Ira Jennings and his uncle Pete. Both were seventy and much too old to contemplate a fistfight. Yet here they were, ready to do battle over Abigail. And the old girl was as happy about it as a kid at Christmas.

Dylan's mouth twitched and he struggled to stifle his laughter. Clearing his throat, he tried to sound stern as he stared at the three septuagenarians. "I should probably run all of you in for disturbing the peace."

The guilty parties suddenly tried to speak at the same time.

"Now, Dylan, all I wanted was to dance—"

"Whoa, boy! Me and Abby—"

"Pete and I didn't start—"

Dylan placed two fingers to his lips and let loose with a loud, piercing whistle. When the three fell silent, he asked, "If I let all of you off with a warning, do you think you can go back in there and behave yourselves for the rest of the evening?"

Ira Jennings nodded and beat as hasty a retreat back into the building as his age and arthritis would allow.

Dylan leaned his shoulder against the side of the building and crossed his arms over his chest. "What about you two?"

Abigail reached for Pete's hand and pulled him along behind her as she headed toward Luke's parking lot. "We were about to leave anyway."

"Where are you going?" Brenna asked.

"Home." Abigail continued on to Brenna's car with Pete in tow. Handing him a set of keys, she turned back to wink. "We're going to make out on the couch."

"We are?" Pete asked, his step quickening. Not waiting for an answer, he opened the driver's door and slid inside with a speed that belied his age.

Abigail turned back to Brenna and grinned. "If there's a handkerchief tied to the front doorknob when you come home, drive around the block a few times."

"Granny!"

Dylan watched Brenna's cheeks turn a deep shade of rose as she looked around to see if anyone had overheard her grandmother's declaration.

When Pete popped the clutch on the Toyota and spewed gravel as they sped from the parking lot, Dylan pushed away from the building. "Don't worry. At their age, at least we won't have to worry about a shotgun wedding."

She stared in the direction the two had disappeared. "I guess you have a point."

"Let's go back inside," he suggested, holding the door for her.

They hadn't been settled at their table more than ten minutes when Susie tapped him on the shoulder. "You have a phone call."

He sighed heavily. The whole evening had been a comedy of errors from the very beginning. "I suppose Jason told you it was urgent?"

Susie shook her head. "It isn't Jason."

"This had better be important," Dylan grumbled, making his way to the bar. He covered one ear to block out the rowdy sounds and listened intently. A tight coil of fear twisted his gut a moment before he slammed the receiver back onto its cradle with a succinct curse.

"What is it?" Brenna asked when he walked back to their table.

"We have to leave." He took her by the elbow and ushered her toward the exit.

"What's wrong?" she asked once they were outside.

The brisk, night air whipped Brenna's hair around her face and she had to trot to keep up with his long strides. He slowed his pace a bit and helped her into the cab when they reached the truck. "You'll see when we get to your place."

Brenna sucked in a sharp breath. "Has something happened to Granny? Or Pete?"

"Yes."

"Which one?"

"Both. They've had a wreck."

"Oh, my God!"

"Pete said they're both all right."

Brenna held on tight as Dylan navigated the deserted streets as if the hounds of hell chased them, and in no time they were slowing down to turn into her drive. When he brought the antique truck to a sliding stop, she gasped at the sight in front of them. One side of the front porch sagged precariously over the crumpled front end of her Toyota.

"Where's Granny and Pete?" she asked, jumping from the cab of Dylan's truck. She reached for her grandmother when the elderly pair stepped from the shadows. "Are you okay?" She looked from Abigail to Pete. "Do either of you need to see a doctor?"

"We're both fine." Abigail hugged Brenna, then pointed to the wreckage. "The car is a little banged up and I think the porch will need a new support post, but it's nothing that can't be fixed."

"How did this happen?" Dylan demanded.

Pete shuffled his feet and stared off into the darkness. "Well...I...that is..."

Abigail winked. "I put my hand on his thigh, and instead of hitting the brake, he floored it. But it doesn't matter now. What's done is done." She looped her arm through Pete's. "We'll go make coffee, while you kids figure out what to do about getting the car off the porch."

"I'm real sorry," Pete said, his blue eyes apologetic.

When the elderly pair walked around to the back of the house, Brenna sighed. "What am I going to do with her? It's like dealing with a teenager."

Staring at the destruction, Dylan shook his head. "It's worse."

Brenna nodded. "I think you're right. It's not like we can ground them or anything."

"I wouldn't want to try." Laughing, he draped a companionable arm across her shoulders. "Let's see what kind of damage the two delinquents have left in their wake and what we'll have to do in order to fix it."

Four

Brenna had just put the finishing touches to the black Geisha girl wig when Abigail tapped lightly on the bedroom door. "Studly's here."

"Who?"

Abigail grinned. "Dylan."

"Why?"

Her grandmother walked over and plopped down on the edge of the bed. "It's my guess he has the hots for you."

"Please tell me you didn't ask him to give me a ride to the school," Brenna pleaded.

"Nope." Abigail smiled beatifically. "Bright boy, that Dylan Chandler. It was all his idea. He said since Pete wrecked your car it was only right that he drive you to work until it's repaired."

The thought of seeing Dylan again made Brenna's pulse quicken. And that wasn't good. Not good at all.

Since her ill-fated relationship with Tom ended almost a year ago, she'd been very careful to avoid becoming involved with another man. And especially one like Dylan Chandler.

His take-charge personality made her nervous and reminded her of why she'd moved to Texas in the first place. She was making a fresh start, becoming a new, self-assured woman who controlled her own life and made her own choices. Never again would she allow a man to manipulate her into doing what he wanted or what he thought was best for her.

Dylan's decision to drive her to the grade school for story hour might be a minor point, but it was an important one. Instead of asking her if she wanted him to give her a ride, he'd just assumed that she would go along with his plan.

"Tell him thanks, but I prefer to walk. I need the exercise."

"Oh, cellulite be damned." Abigail jerked her thumb at the window. "There's a good-looking man out there who obviously wants to be with you, and if you don't get the lead out, you're going to be late anyway."

Brenna glanced at her watch and cursed herself for hitting the snooze button on her alarm one too many times. If she didn't hurry, the Story Lady would be the second graders least favorite person in about ten minutes.

"Tell Dylan I'll be right out," she said, deciding that whether she liked it or not, accepting a ride to the school was the only way she'd arrive on time.

"Outstanding decision." Abigail smiled triumphantly as she headed for the door. "It's a relief to know I didn't raise a total ditz."

Brenna ignored her grandmother's comment and hurriedly gathered her bag of craft supplies and the book she'd chosen to read to the children. Glancing at herself in the mirror on the back of her closet door to make sure her kimono was straight, she shook her head. "It's no big deal. You're not interested in him. He's just giving you a ride to the school. Nothing more."

But when she stepped outside and spied Dylan leaning against the fender of a black-and-white SUV with Sheriff's Patrol painted on the sides, her pulse fluttered and she had an almost uncontrollable urge to dig through her handbag for a chocolate bar.

He was wearing aviator sunglasses and a black leather bomber jacket. Combined with his black cowboy hat and snug jeans, he looked better than any man had the right to look. And especially at eight in the morning.

As Brenna approached, Dylan unfolded his arms to point to her costume. "Why do you wear those get-ups?"

"The children enjoy seeing costumes that go along with the stories I read and the crafts we make afterward." Her eyes narrowed. "You have a problem with that...Sheriff?"

"None at all," Dylan lied, opening the passenger door. He couldn't tell her that whether she represented a truckload of trouble or not, he hated seeing her luscious curves covered up with the outlandish garbs. She wouldn't appreciate it one bit. Hell, he wasn't even comfortable with the way he felt about it himself. "What time do you close your shop this afternoon?"

"Five." She hitched her kimono up to her knees and climbed into the Explorer. "Why?"

When he caught sight of her shapely legs, he had to swallow several times before he finally managed, "I'll be by to give you a ride home." Walking around the front of the vehicle, he slid behind the wheel, then radioing his deputy that he would return to the office in a few minutes, signed off.

"Thank you for the offer. I really appreciate it. But I prefer to walk," she said, sounding quite firm about the matter. "I'm getting soft in my old age and I need the exercise."

"You're not old." He backed the SUV out onto the street, then let his gaze travel from her pretty face to her little feet. Before he could stop himself, he added, "And soft is nice. Real nice."

Her cheeks colored a pretty pink. "Dylan—"

The sudden crackle of the police radio, followed by his deputy's excited voice, intruded. "Dylan, Mayor Worthington is here to see you and he's as mad as an old wet hen."

Dylan cursed and reached for the radio's microphone. "Calm down, Jason. Get Myron a cup of coffee and tell him to relax. I'll be there in five minutes."

He replaced the handheld mike and drove the distance to the grade school in silence. What the hell had he been thinking when he told her he liked her softness? If Jason hadn't interrupted him, there was no telling what he would have ended up saying.

And why was he insisting on taking her home this

afternoon? Why did it bother him that she preferred to walk, rather than accept a ride with him?

He should be down on his hands and knees thanking the good Lord above that she had the good sense to turn him down. But the memory of how she'd felt in his arms when they'd danced at Luke's the other night, the taste of her sweet lips beneath his when he'd brought her home from painting class, had haunted him for the better part of a week. And whether it was smart or not, Dylan wanted to feel her soft curves against his body once again, wanted to kiss her until they both required oxygen.

"I'll see you at five," he said, pulling to a stop in front of the school.

"I'd rather—"

"This isn't negotiable. I'll take you home," he said. Unable to stop himself, he reached out to gently run the back of his hand along the side of her soft cheek. "Do you need a ride from the school to your shop after story hour?"

"No, it's only a couple of blocks," she said, sounding breathless.

Satisfied that she wasn't going to protest further, he smiled as she got out of the truck. "I'll see you this afternoon, Brenna."

Dylan watched Myron bluster and sputter about the Beautification Society's latest scheme to improve the town, and he had to admit the excitable little man had a valid point. "Myron, I agree with you one hundred percent. But I don't think you have anything to worry about."

Myron stopped his pacing to peer at Dylan as if

he'd sprouted another head. "Boy, ain't you heard a word I've said? Cornelia and them hens of hers are fixin' to turn this town into a laughingstock. Hell. We'll probably be the biggest joke in Texas."

Dylan calmly left his chair to pour himself and Myron another cup of coffee. "The only way it can happen is if they get the store owners to go along with the idea. And what chance do you think they'll have with Luke Washburn or Ed Taylor? Can you honestly say you think they'll replace their neon signs with painted, wooden ones?"

The rotund little mayor sat down heavily in the chair across from Dylan's desk. "I guess you're right. It's just that I know Cornelia. Once she sets her mind to something, ain't nothin' or nobody gonna change it."

"In this case, she'll have to." Dylan returned to his chair. Leaning back, he propped his boots on the edge of the desk. "If the store owners don't want to change their signs, there's no way the B.S. Club can force the issue."

"I sure as hell hope not." Myron thoughtfully sipped his coffee. "I noticed you and that little Montgomery gal were at Luke's Saturday night. Did you find out anything?"

Dylan shook his head warily as he watched the mayor take another sip. Myron's beady little eyes peering at him over the edge of the coffee mug made the hair on the back of Dylan's neck crawl and reminded him of the way a rattlesnake looked just before it strikes.

"You two seem to be mighty friendly," Myron said, giving him a smile that caused Dylan to grind his back teeth. "That might be a good way to find out what we need to know."

"You can forget that angle, Myron." Dylan narrowed his eyes to let the man know he meant business. "We both happened to be at Luke's and shared a dance. Nothing more. Besides, Brenna has nothing to do with the B.S. Club or any of their hare-brained schemes."

Long after the mayor left his office, Dylan stared off into space. He didn't like that Myron or anyone else would even suggest that he see Brenna in order to gain information about the B.S. Club. Dylan had something similar happen to him a few years back and he knew exactly how it felt to be used to further someone's cause.

Thinking back on that time, he still couldn't believe what a fool he'd been. He'd fallen hook, line and sinker for the beautiful young woman who had breezed into Tranquillity on the pretense of buying property to open a bed-and-breakfast. But he'd found out the hard way she was only using his attraction to her in order to gain information she needed about the town for a much bigger venture.

He'd quickly learned how much he meant to her when she showed up at a town council meeting and revealed that she'd been collecting facts and figures for a development deal that would have turned Tranquillity into a resort for the rich to "get back to nature." She'd thrown out statistics and talked about how the town should capitalize on its location at the base of the Davis Mountains. She'd pressed the councilmen to pass zoning laws requiring the shop owners along Main Street to upgrade their businesses or close their doors. And had she been successful, the cost of living in Tranquillity would have skyrocketed, making it impossible for the longtime residents to afford to stay there.

But the worst of it had been when she indicated that Dylan supported the changes and the new resort her development firm intended to build at the edge of town. She'd even gone so far as to pull out a nice, fat check for his part in the research and feasibility study, and tried to give it to him in front of Myron and the rest of the council. That's when all hell broke loose.

The council rejected her proposal outright and she'd left town without a backward glance. But the damage had been done. Dylan's reputation with the people of Tranquillity, not to mention his ego, had taken a hell of a beating that night. And for the first time in his life, his integrity had been thrown into question.

It had taken him months to regain the town's trust and respect, and there wasn't a snowball's chance in hell that he'd ever treat anyone to that brand of humiliation or betray their trust in such a callous manner. And especially not Brenna.

Dylan shook his head. It was a moot point anyway. She wasn't a member of the B.S. Club and had no knowledge of what the old hens were up to.

He reached inside his desk drawer to pull out the list of supplies for Brenna's class. He'd follow orders and go through the motions of learning to paint. If he overheard the women talking about the project, he'd tell Myron. And if he didn't, the mayor would just have to gain the information he wanted elsewhere.

But either way, Dylan had every intention of distancing himself from the whole situation as soon as possible.

Dylan entered Brenna's craft store about fifteen minutes before closing and stopped dead in his tracks. Several things about her seemed to register with him all at once. She'd changed from the Oriental costume she'd worn that morning into a pair of jeans and a long-sleeved, forest-green T-shirt. She'd taken off the Japanese-styled, black wig and her long copper hair hung in a single braid down the middle of her back. But most of all, he noticed how her little rump looked when she bent over to help old Mrs. Pennington with something on the bottom shelf of a wall filled with skeins of yarn. Damn, but Brenna had a fine-looking rear end.

The bell over the door had alerted her of his arrival, and looking over her shoulder, she smiled. "Is it five already?"

He shrugged as he tried to get his vocal cords to work. "Close enough," he finally managed. "Where would I find the supplies for the painting class?"

She pointed to a shelf filled with paints, brushes and wood cut into all kinds of shapes. "Everything you'll need is grouped together by project. If you need help, just let me know."

Dylan nodded, then forced his feet to move in the direction she'd indicated. He needed help all right, but not the kind she was talking about. The sight of her delightful bottom had his heart pounding against his rib cage like a jungle drum and had brought him to full arousal so fast he felt light-headed.

Picking up a basket, he held it in front of him and tried to will himself to calm down as he filled it with little plastic bottles of acrylic paint. If he didn't get hold of himself, and damned quick, he'd be a raving lunatic in short order.

"Are you finding everything you need?" she asked from beside him.

He looked around. Mrs. Pennington was gone and they were alone. Why hadn't he heard the bell over the door when the elderly woman left, or the sound of Brenna's approach?

"I'm pretty sure I have everything on the list," he said, holding out the basket for her inspection.

She gazed at the items, then smiled. "Looks like you're right."

When she reached out to take hold of the handle her hand brushed his and Dylan felt a streak of electricity run up his arm, then down through his chest and straight to his groin. It took every ounce of willpower he possessed to keep from dropping the basket, pulling her into his arms and kissing her as senseless as he felt.

They stared at each other for several long seconds before she took the basket from him. "I'll start totaling these so we can get out of here." She walked behind the counter to remove the supplies from the basket. "How was your day?"

Thinking of his meeting with Myron helped Dylan get his mind off the gentle sway of her hips and back to the reason he was buying painting supplies in the first place. "I've had better."

"I'm sure it couldn't have been all that bad," she

said, smiling up at him. "Things will probably look a lot different tomorrow."

That all depends on who's doing the looking.

"Maybe," he said, trying not to think about how pretty she was, or how soft and sweet her voice sounded. He reached into his hip pocket for his wallet, removed a couple of bills and handed them to her. "We've talked about my day. How was yours?"

"Pretty fantastic," she said, pressing the buttons to total out the cash register. "Mrs. Worthington came by this afternoon with the most marvelous idea. She and the ladies of the Beautification Society have asked me to join the organization and head the project to decorate Main Street for the holidays. Isn't that wonderful?"

Dylan felt like his heart landed on top of his boots. "Sure." It's just downright peachy, he thought sourly.

"You look awfully grim. Is something wrong?"

"No." He hadn't intended for the word to come out quite so quickly or with such force. But why did she have to go and join old Corny and her hens, and in the process, complicate his life that much more?

"I'm a good listener. Would you like to talk about what's bothering you?" she asked as she placed his painting supplies into a sack. "Sometimes it helps to get it out, put it behind you and move on."

"Not really."

If he told her about the mayor ordering him to remain in her class, in order to find out what the B.S. Club had up their sleeves, it would get things out and put something *behind* him all right—her foot behind him as she kicked his sorry butt *out* the door.

"If you change your mind, the offer stands," she said, with a shrug. She walked around the room, turning off lights over display cases. "Oh, by the way, Granny called this afternoon. She wanted me to tell you that she and Pete took your truck and drove down to Alpine for dinner and a movie."

"That's just great," Dylan said sarcastically. "It was Pete's turn to cook."

"I guess I could fix something for both of us," Brenna said, looking uncertain.

His mood lightened considerably and he smiled for the first time since entering her shop. "That would be nice."

He had no intention of questioning her. But if she volunteered information about the B.S. Club's plans, he could tell Myron, then drop out of her class with a clear conscience.

But watching Brenna gather her purse and tote bag, he felt as if a weight settled over his shoulders. Why did the idea of not seeing her every Tuesday night bother him?

"Do you need help?" Dylan asked when they entered the house Brenna shared with her grandmother.

She shook her head as she turned on the television. "Why don't you relax and watch the news while I get things started?"

When she left him alone, Dylan took off his hat and looked around the small, comfortably furnished room. From the ruffled curtains at the windows, to the lace doilies on the fragile-looking end tables, everything looked so feminine, he felt like a bull in a china shop.

Amused, he shook his head. Brenna's house was nothing like the rustic cabin he shared with Pete—a place where a man wasn't afraid to sit down.

A delicate, antique curio cabinet with a collection of porcelain cherubs, some of which looked quite old, drew Dylan's attention and he walked over to take a look. Nestled among the figurines a brass frame displayed the photograph of a man and woman, their arms around each other.

"My mother and father," Brenna said quietly, walking up to stand beside him. "That picture was taken shortly before their deaths."

"What happened?"

"They were killed in a car accident almost ten years ago. When I was fifteen," she said quietly.

His gut twisted into a tight knot at the haunted shadows clouding her wide blue eyes and the sadness in her soft voice. Without a second thought, he turned and took her into his arms.

He told himself he was only lending her comfort. But to be perfectly honest, he'd wanted to hold her body to his, to feel her breasts pressed to his chest since they'd danced together the other night at Luke's.

When she wrapped her arms around his waist, he rested his cheek against the top of her head and they stood silently for several moments.

"What about your folks, Dylan?" she finally asked.

The sound of his name on her velvet voice did strange things to his insides. "Mom died when I was in college and Dad passed away about five years ago."

"You're an only child, too?"

He nodded. "My mother found out she was pregnant with me on her fortieth birthday, right after they'd given up any hope of ever having kids."

Brenna pulled back to smile at him. "And look what they wound up with."

He understood her need to lighten the mood. "What they wound up with is getting hungry, lady," he said, laughing. He turned her loose, then stepped back. "When do we eat?"

Brenna took a deep breath. The moment of truth had arrived. She was going to have to go into the kitchen and give it her best shot. Or tell Dylan the truth and call for a pizza.

"I guess I'd better get started on dinner before you waste away to nothing."

"I'll help," he offered, following her.

Walking to the refrigerator, she opened the door and stared inside as if the answer to her dilemma would somehow magically be revealed. Nothing materialized. Spying a carton of eggs, she hesitated. Her grandmother had always said anyone could make an omelette. She sure hoped Abigail was right.

"How does an omelette sound?" Brenna asked, hopefully.

"Great." He rubbed his hands together. "Give me a knife and I'll dice up whatever you have for the filling."

"Filling?"

"Yeah, the stuff that goes inside, like ham, cheese, peppers...." He frowned. "You have made omelettes before, haven't you?"

"Uh...sure," Brenna lied. "Why don't you relax

and watch television, or read the newspaper while I whip these up?''

''Are you sure?''

''Of course.'' She had to get him out of the kitchen so she could search for her grandmother's cookbook. ''You've had a hard day and it won't take long for me to get these baked.''

He frowned. ''Baked?''

''Cooked,'' she said quickly. ''I meant cooked.''

A sudden wave of panic swept through her as she watched him shrug and walk back into the living room. Her culinary skills barely included boiling water to make a cup of tea. What on earth had she been thinking when she'd offered to cook for them?

She stood motionless for a moment as she stared at the cabinets. Then spinning into action, she searched first one cabinet, then another for Abigail's cookbook. Where had her grandmother put the darned thing?

When Brenna finally found the tattered book, she breathed a sigh of relief. ''Omelettes,'' she muttered, running her finger down the index. ''Where are the recipes for omelettes?''

Dylan listened to the sounds coming from the kitchen over the low volume of the television. It sounded like a small war had broken out. Pans clattered and cabinet doors banged as Brenna moved around the compact kitchen. A loud splat followed by a heartfelt *damn* had him rising halfway out of the chair.

''Are you sure you don't need help?'' he called.

''Everything's under control.''

Uneasy about the strange sounds coming from the kitchen, he settled back into the chair. If things were fine, why did she sound so flustered? And why was she making all that noise?

A panicked shriek, followed closely by the screech of a smoke detector, suddenly caused the hair on the back of his neck to stand straight up, and a chill to race the length of his spine. Bolting from the chair, he collided with Brenna as she ran from the kitchen.

"What the hell's going on?" he demanded.

"The kitchen is on fire!"

He pushed past her and into the dense smoke that was rapidly filling the room. Flames licked at the bottom of a small skillet and a dark cloud of smoke billowed from the top of the electric range.

"Do you have a fire extinguisher?"

She coughed and pointed to the cabinet under the sink. "In there."

Dylan quickly located the red cylinder strapped to the inside of the cabinet, jerked it loose, took aim and squeezed the handle. A cloud of white vapor instantly and efficiently put out the flame.

"Are you all right?" he asked when he turned to face her. His voice sounded more harsh than he'd intended, but the woman had scared him out of a good ten years of life.

His concern increased when Brenna stood silently in the doorway, tears streaming down her red face. Had she suffered a burn?

He walked over to her and searched for any signs that she'd been injured. When he found none, he took her into his arms. "How in the hell did you manage to set an electric stove on fire?"

"I have no idea." Obviously embarrassed to tears, she buried her face against his chest and wailed, "I don't know the first thing about cooking."

An empty pizza box between them, Dylan and Brenna sat cross-legged on the living room floor. They'd scrubbed down the range top and washed the skillet, but an acrid scorched scent still lingered throughout the house.

"I wish we could get the smell out of here," she said, wrinkling her nose.

She watched him move the box to the side, stretch his legs out in front of him, then lean back on one elbow. "That's going to take some time. You really had the smoke rolling in there, darlin'."

When she noticed his inquisitive look, she sighed. "I suppose you want to know why I didn't tell you I'm one of the cooking impaired."

He nodded and the corner of his mouth twitched suspiciously, as if he were trying to keep from grinning.

"I didn't think cooking an omelette would be *that* hard," she said defensively.

"It's not."

"And I suppose you know how to cook?"

"Sure do," he said, his grin breaking through.

"I might have known." She frowned. "And you're probably good at it, too."

"As a matter of fact, I am," he said, chuckling. He reached out and took her hand, then pulled her down onto the thick carpet beside him. "But I'm much better at other things," he said, his drawl so warm and sexy that a shiver slid down her spine.

Her breath caught at the smoldering look in his eyes. He was going to kiss her again, and the thought both thrilled her and scared her to death at the same time.

"Dylan, I don't think—"

He placed his index finger to her lips. "I'm not thinking right now either," he said, lowering his head.

She tried to remind herself he was all wrong for her, that he was too macho, too controlling. But the moment his firm lips settled over hers, none of that seemed to matter.

Caught up in the maelstrom of sensation, she decided that whether it was wise or not, she wanted his kiss. She wanted him to once again make her aware of the differences between them, the complementing contrast of man to woman.

She reveled in his strength, the feel of his strong arms cradling her to him, his muscular legs tangled with hers. As his lips leisurely caressed hers that fluttery feeling in the pit of her stomach took off at a gallop. But when Dylan parted her lips to deepen the kiss, the fluttering intensified, tightened and transformed into the sweet ache of pure desire.

Tiny jolts of electric current skipped along Brenna's nerve endings as Dylan's hands tangled in her hair. He pressed his hard length to her and the groan of pleasure rumbling up from deep in his chest, sent an answering need spreading throughout her body.

"Well now. This explains why the house smells like smoke, Abby," Brenna heard Pete say. "Looks like the kids are playin' with fire."

"Or Brenna's been trying to cook again," her grandmother said.

The sensual fog around Brenna disappeared in an instant.

"To tell you the truth, it's a combination of both," Dylan said, raising his head to look up at them.

Brenna pushed against Dylan's wide chest. Thank goodness, her grandmother and Pete had shown up before she did something stupid.

But the sight of the elderly couple's *we-know-what-you've-been-doing* smiles had her immediately trying to bury her face in Dylan's wide chest, and wishing with all her heart that she could get her hands on a Hershey bar.

Five

His mind occupied with the gentle sway of Brenna's hips as she moved from table to table around the community room, Dylan failed to catch what the woman next to him had said. "What's that, Mildred?"

She pointed to the streak of paint that looked like a big, fat comma on the wooden plaque he was painting. "I said, you do the brush strokes so well that you should think about helping the Beautification Society with our Main Street Project."

His left eyebrow twitched at the mention of the B.S. Club's project. "I don't think that would be a good idea, Mildred," he said, careful to keep his voice low. "The guys over at Luke's—"

"Oh, how silly of me," Mildred interrupted with a laugh. She placed her wrinkled hand on his arm, her expression sympathetic. "Of course, you wouldn't be able to help. The Beautification Society is a women's organization. I forgot about you being a man.''

Nodding, Dylan managed a smile that probably looked more like a grimace before turning his attention back to his painting. How much more was his ego supposed to endure for the sake of the town anyway? Not only had the guys over at Luke's given him a hard time about taking a damned painting class with old Corny and her hens, he'd just been neutered by a sweet little sixty-year-old lady he'd known all of his life.

''You're doing a wonderful job, Dylan. I'm very impressed with your progress.''

At the sound of Brenna's soft voice, he raised his head and anything he might have said about not giving a damn whether he was good at the technique or not, lodged in his throat. The smile she gave him was so encouraging, he forgot all about the guys over at Luke's or that he'd just been stripped of his gender by Mildred. All he could think of was how soft Brenna's lips looked and how he'd like nothing more than to taste them again, to feel them beneath his as he kissed her.

''Would you like to go over to Luke's for a cup of coffee after class?'' he blurted out without thinking of where he was, or that he had an audience.

The background buzz of female voices suddenly stopped as if they awaited Brenna's answer, and when he glanced around the room, Dylan barely controlled the urge to squirm. The knowing smiles on the women's faces sent heat creeping up his neck to spread across his cheeks. He'd just the same as announced an interest in Brenna to an entire roomful of world-class gossips.

But as the women continued to grin at him, he decided there was no sense denying it any longer—not to himself or anyone else. He *was* interested in Brenna and not because he'd been ordered to take her class, or for the information she might pass on about the B.S. Club project.

Whether he liked it or not, the more he was around Brenna, the more he wanted to know about her, and the more he wanted to explore the attraction that seemed to draw them together like a magnet. He'd just have to make sure he kept it casual. That shouldn't be difficult, he decided.

Coming to terms with the realization, and his decision, he grinned back at the roomful of women, not giving a damn what they thought. "So what do you say?" he asked, turning his attention back to Brenna. "Want to go for coffee after class?"

Her cheeks colored a pretty pink as she glared at him. "I don't think—"

Before Brenna could finish turning him down, old Corny came to his rescue by jumping to her feet and announcing, "Girls, it's time to quit for the evening."

He watched Brenna look helplessly around the room at the women gathering their painting supplies. "But class isn't over. We still have another fifteen minutes, ladies."

"Brenna, dear, will you be available tomorrow evening for a meeting of the Beautification Society's planning committee?" Cornelia asked as she hurriedly stuffed bottles of acrylic paint into a small box.

As Brenna's disapproving expression turned to anticipation, a tight knot formed in the pit of Dylan's belly and his eyebrow twitched. He could tell she not only looked forward to being part of the Main Street Project, she was eager to get started.

"What time should I be here, Mrs. Worthington?" she asked.

"Seven is our usual meeting time," Corny said, picking up the basket of painting supplies and heading for the door. The old gal stopped to send a wink his way. "The meeting will be over around eight-thirty, in case someone wants to give her a ride home, Dylan."

"I'll remember that," he said, grinning back at the older woman.

The women cleared the room in record time, and when the last one closed the door behind her, Brenna turned to glare at Dylan. "I hope you're happy, Sheriff. You've single-handedly destroyed my first Folk Art class."

"Nope." His unrepentant grin took her by surprise. "As far as I could tell, it was a huge success."

"How can you say that?" she asked incredulously. "Everyone left before they'd completed the project."

He stood, then rounding the table, stopped in front of her. "Anything that can keep Cornelia Worthington as quiet as she was this evening when she practiced the painting techniques you taught, is nothing short of miraculous."

His sexy smile and the rhythm of his deep voice made Brenna's heart skip a beat. But when he reached out to draw her into his arms, she shook her head to clear it. "Dylan, this isn't a good idea."

"What?" he asked, pulling her close.

"You. Me." His lips brushed hers, sending a wave of shivers coursing through her. "I don't think it's…wise."

"Darlin', whether it's wise or not, it's not going to go away."

He nibbled kisses along her jawline to the hollow of her ear, and instead of pushing him away, she wrapped her arms around his waist. "It might."

His deep chuckle caused her pulse to race. "I don't think so, Brenna. I've tried ignoring it for the past week and it's just gotten stronger."

"Try harder," she said, wondering if the community center had candy machines with a good selection of chocolate bars.

"Do you really want me to do that, darlin'?" he asked, nuzzling the sensitive skin along the side of her neck.

"Yes." Even she could detect the lack of conviction in her tone.

"Liar." He leaned back to look down at her and the heat in his gaze took her breath. "I'm going to kiss you, Brenna. And afterward, I want you to look me in the eyes and tell me you don't feel something drawing us together."

Before she could protest, he lowered his mouth to hers and she felt every ounce of her resistance drain away. Even the intense desire for something chocolate to sooth her jangled nerves faded to nothingness as she melted against him.

He caught her to his wide chest, then ran his hands from her back down to cup her bottom in his large hands. Lifting her to him, he let her feel his strong arousal at the same time he parted her lips with a thrust of his tongue. It felt as if a herd of butterflies were suddenly set free inside her lower stomach. As he stroked, tasted and explored her with a mastery that made her lightheaded, the fluttering tightened into a coil of deep need and Brenna had to cling to his strong biceps for support.

Dylan eased the kiss in slow degrees and by the time he lifted his mouth from hers, she felt as if her world had changed and nothing would ever be the same again. Whether she liked it or not, there was no denying the truth any longer. Maybe it was chemistry. Maybe it was magnetism. She wasn't sure. But whatever it was called, there was something between her and Dylan that was far more explosive than anything she'd ever shared with Tom. And it scared the daylights out of her.

"Now, tell me you didn't feel that, too," Dylan said, resting his forehead against hers.

"I...I'd be lying if I told you I didn't feel anything," she said shakily. "But I won't give up my independence or my identity for the opportunity to find out what it is. I won't give another man that kind of power over me ever again."

Brenna suddenly clamped her lips together and when she looked up at him, the shadows in her expressive blue eyes caused a knot to form in Dylan's gut. "Who did this to you, darlin'?"

Her gaze skittered away. "Did what?"

"Who gave you the idea that men want to control women, want them to be dependent?" he demanded. If he could get his hands on the man who gave her that impression, Dylan would cheerfully throttle the stupid jerk.

"It's…not important," she said, pulling herself from his arms. "Just suffice it to say, I learned my lesson well."

"Dammit, Brenna, it is important," Dylan said, reaching out to place his hands on her shoulders. "If I'm being compared to another man, I'd like to know why."

Just when he thought she was going to ignore his request, she took a deep breath. "I met Tom in my senior year in college. He was a struggling law student and I was well on my way to a degree in business administration. To make a long story short, we started seeing each other and fell in love." She shook her head. "That's not right. I thought I was in love and he thought that gave him the right to manipulate and control me."

"What do you mean?"

She sighed heavily. "Over time, he convinced me to dress a certain way, told me how I should wear my hair and when I should go on a diet." When she laughed, the self-deprecating sound caused Dylan to wince. "I was naive and wanted to please the man I loved, so I went along with the changes. Then after I graduated, he even talked me into helping him financially with his last year of law school."

Dylan felt his chest tighten. He had a good idea what was coming next and he didn't like it one damned bit. "How long before—"

"Before he dumped me?"

"I wasn't going to put it that way," Dylan said gently. She looked so vulnerable, he pulled her back into his arms.

"You might as well put it that way," she said,

shrugging. "Because that's exactly what happened—right after he passed the bar." She pulled back to look up at him. "I trusted Tom when he said the money I gave him for his schooling was an investment in our future."

Dylan's gut twisted into a tight knot at the pain and humiliation the conniving jerk had caused Brenna. If he could have gotten his hands on this Tom character at that very moment, Dylan would have made the bum sorry he'd ever been born.

Cupping her face with his hands, Dylan gazed into her pretty blue eyes. "Darlin', I promise you that's one thing you'll never have to worry about with me. I'm not a control freak. I like you just the way you are. And I don't want anything more from you than the pleasure of your company."

She stared up at him for several long seconds before she stepped back, then walked to the front of the room to pack her tote bag. They had more in common than he would have thought. Apparently he wasn't the only one with a past he'd rather not repeat.

Walking up behind her, Dylan wrapped his arms around her midriff, then leaned down to whisper in her ear. "Let's just take this one step at a time and see what happens."

"But—"

"One step at a time, darlin'." He turned her to face him. "But I think I'd better warn you. I have every intention of asking you to go with me to Luke's Saturday night." Smiling, he took a step back to keep her from feeling crowded. "You know, I think I'm going to live dangerously tonight and have a piece of apple pie with my coffee. How about you?"

She looked thoughtful for a moment before she finally asked, "Do you think Luke would happen to have a slice of chocolate pie in that pie case?"

The first Saturday in December, Brenna waited for the members of the Beautification Society to gather around her on the sidewalk in front of her craft store. Fortunately, winters in southwest Texas were very mild and today was testament to how beautiful the weather could be. The sun was shining brightly, the temperature was in the upper sixties and humidity was almost nonexistent—ideal weather for paint to dry.

"Okay, ladies, I think it would be best to work in pairs," she said, checking her list. She glanced up to count the number of women who had shown up for the first phase of the Main Street Project. "Mildred, you have a notation here that one side of Main Street has an extra hydrant."

Mildred Bruner stepped forward as she hitched up her patched blue jeans. "That's right. There's one on the west side that's stuck in the middle of the block." Her cackling laughter broke the early morning silence as she pointed down the street. "Right in front of the Fire Department and Sheriff's office."

Brenna laughed. "I don't guess it would do for the Fire Department to catch fire." She glanced at her clipboard again. "We have enough teams to do all of them, except for that one. I suppose I could paint it after I get everyone else started."

"Oh, that's a marvelous idea, since you and Dylan are courting," Mrs. Worthington said excitedly. "Don't you think would be appropriate to put a star on that one's chest and make it look like Dylan in a Santa suit?''

"I think that's a great idea," one of the women said, causing the entire group to nod their heads in eager agreement.

Brenna smiled wanly. If her grandmother's comments about her seeing Dylan weren't enough, now the women of Tranquillity were jumping on the bandwagon. But she was reasonably sure they wouldn't be taking it to the extreme her grandmother had. Just that morning, before Brenna left to start the first phase of the Main Street Project, Abigail had gone so far as to ask what flavor of punch Brenna preferred for the wedding reception.

"I think painting the fire hydrants like our men in Santa suits is a fantastic idea," Emily Taylor said. She gave Brenna a sly grin, then pointed down the block. "I intend to make the one in front of our hardware store look just like my Ed."

Helen Washburn nodded vigorously. "And I'll paint the one in front of our place to look like Luke." She glanced at her watch. "Brenna, do you really think we can get all these done today?"

"That's the plan," Brenna said, smiling.

"Oh, good," Helen said, clearly excited. "It being Saturday and all, everyone will be coming to the dance at our place tonight. It's going to be the perfect opportunity to show off the first phase of our Christmas project."

"Then let's begin," Cornelia said, grabbing a box filled with jars of paint and brushes. "Brenna, dear, how should we go about this?"

"Everyone choose a painting partner," Brenna instructed the eager women. "While one of you works on the front of the hydrant, the other should work on the back."

Brenna watched the ladies of the Tranquillity Beautification Society set to work with more enthusiasm than expertise, turning ordinary fire hydrants into works of Christmas art. After making sure everything was going smoothly, she picked up her own paint kit and headed for the hydrant in front of Dylan's office.

She worked quickly and, in no time, had the details roughed in. Her eyes held an impish gleam as she used the liner brush to add the finishing touches. It was an absolute shame she couldn't put a red fur Santa's hat on the little guy, instead of having to paint one on.

"Dear, you've done an excellent job of capturing Dylan's likeness." Cornelia pushed a strand of blue-gray hair from her eyes as she peered at Brenna's work, then glanced at the door of the Sheriff's office. "By the way, where is Dylan? Shouldn't he be on duty?"

"He's gone up into the mountains to help search for a couple of lost hikers," Brenna answered. She finished painting a silver star on the chest of the Santa Claus hydrant. "He probably won't be back until late this afternoon or evening. But Jason is in charge if you need something."

"No." Lowering her voice for privacy, Cornelia asked, "Has Dylan mentioned what he thinks of the Beautification Society's plans to decorate Main Street for the Jamboree?"

The tone in the older woman's voice caused Brenna

to glance up from her work. Seeing the woman's grave expression, Brenna rose to face her.

"He knows the Society have some improvements planned, but I haven't shared any of the details. Why?"

"I just wondered." Cornelia heaved a sigh. "Last night, Myron almost suffered apoplexy when I told him that the first phase would begin today."

Brenna smiled as she gazed down at the hydrant she'd just finished painting. "I'm sure he'll calm down when he sees how cute these little guys are. How could anyone not be charmed by fire hydrants painted to look like some of Tranquillity's most prominent citizens dressed up in Santa suits?"

Dylan steered his truck around the last curve on the road leading into Tranquillity. He was tired, his muscles ached and his mood had improved little since leaving the ranger station. He hated it when people who had no previous hiking experience, decided to test themselves on the trails in the Davis Mountains. Fortunately, the two lost hikers had been found, and although they'd been scared half out of their minds from spending a night on the side of a mountain without shelter, neither had suffered serious injury during their ordeal.

His thoughts on the teenage boys he'd helped find earlier in the afternoon, it took a few seconds for his mind to register what his eyes were seeing. He stomped on the brake to bring his truck to a crawl and stared openmouthed as he slowly drove down Main Street. Instead of plain red fire hydrants, a short, squatty, brightly painted Santa Claus stood on every corner.

He swore a blue streak. They had to be the most ridiculous-looking things he'd ever seen. They even beat that cheap toupee old Corny insisted Myron wear to Luke's every Saturday night.

Pulling into his reserved parking space in front of the sheriff's office, Dylan paid little attention to the Santa hydrant standing guard in front of the building. In a rush to find out what was going on, his leg bumped into it as he walked past and he instinctively reached down to rub his knee. His fingers stuck slightly and when he glanced, first at his hand, then at the red paint on his jeans, he rattled off a word that would have gotten his mouth washed out with soap if his mother had been alive to hear him.

"Jason, what the hell happened out there?" he bellowed as he shoved open the office door.

Startled out of his nap, the wide-eyed young man almost fell off the chair he had tipped back against the wall behind the desk. Jumping to his feet, he placed his hand on his service revolver. "Where's the disturbance? Should I call the auxiliary for backup?"

"No, dammit," Dylan said impatiently. He jerked his thumb toward the street. "What happened out there today with the fire hydrants?"

Jason visibly relaxed. "Did you notice the likeness?" he asked, his grin wide.

"Likeness?"

"This is gonna be priceless," Jason said, laughing as he rounded the desk. He motioned for Dylan to follow him.

"Dammit, Jason, I'm not playing games," Dylan growled. But he followed his deputy outside.

Choking on his laughter, Jason pointed to the hydrant Dylan had run into only moments before. "Look like anybody you know?"

Dylan walked around to the front of the hydrant. There stood a two-foot miniature of himself in a Santa suit, complete with green eyes and a star painted on his chest, grinning back at him.

"The B.S. Club kicked off the first phase of their Main Street Project today," Jason said. He shook his head. "First time I ever remember them doing anything, besides sitting around and swapping the latest gossip."

Dylan's left eyebrow twitched rapidly and his stomach clenched into a painful knot at the mention of the B.S. Club. Brenna had been head of the committee responsible for the fire hydrants. When the women finally stopped talking and actually started doing something, everything suddenly got a lot more complicated than it had ever been in the past.

"Has Myron called yet?" he asked. Dylan could just imagine the conniption the mayor had gone into when he found out about the hydrants.

"Nope." Jason chuckled. "But he's the only council member who hasn't."

Dylan's stomach churned like a cement mixer as he walked back into the office. "I'll call Myron, while you call Ed and Luke. Tell them I want to see them here in the office first thing Monday morning. No excuses."

"Won't you see them tonight over at Luke's?" Jason asked as he picked up the phone. "You could set up the meeting then."

Dylan shook his head when he thought of all the complaints he'd be getting from the men. "I'm not going to Luke's this evening. I'm not in a very sociable mood."

Two hours later, standing on Brenna's newly repaired porch, Dylan felt as if the sun had risen on a new day when she opened the door. Her smile, the sparkle of happiness in her eyes, made his heart race. She was genuinely glad to see him.

Reaching for her, he pulled her into his arms. "Do you mind staying here instead of going to Luke's this evening?"

"No. I don't mind at all." She looked concerned. "Is everything all right?"

Not by a long shot. "Yeah," he lied, shrugging out of his leather jacket. "Everything's fine. I'm just a little tired, that's all."

"Me, too." She hung his jacket and Resistol on the coatrack, then turned to wind her arms around his neck. She gazed up at him with a satisfied smile. "I helped paint—"

Dylan immediately fused his lips to hers. He didn't need to be told what she'd been up to. He'd seen the fruits of her labor firsthand and wanted to avoid having to make a comment.

He kissed her thoroughly, then lifted his head to gaze down into her startled eyes. "I've missed you."

"Pete, I don't know if we should go to Luke's or not. Looks like there's going to be plenty of action right here tonight."

Dylan looked up to see Abigail's approving grin as she and Pete strolled into the room.

"Yeah, but it's gonna be *their* action, sugar." Pete kissed Abigail's cheek. "I want some of our own. Now, let's get goin'."

Dylan watched Abigail's cheeks turn pink. He'd bet she didn't blush very often. "Have a good time," he said, biting back a grin.

Abigail winked at him. "We'd wish you the same thing, but it's obvious you will."

"We're takin' your Chevy, Dylan," Pete said, hustling Abigail toward the door. "Since Brenna's car is back from the body shop, you've got hers if you change your mind about comin' over to the dance." When he passed Dylan, Pete lowered his voice. "We'll be back around midnight. But if we decide to come home earlier, I'll call first."

Dylan laughed. "I'd appreciate that, Uncle Pete."

When Pete and Abigail closed the door behind them, Dylan placed his arm around Brenna's shoulders and steered her toward the couch. "You don't mind staying here to watch a movie?"

She shook her head. "Actually, I'm rather glad. I'm pretty tired from helping the Beautification Society paint the fire hydrants today."

Dylan's eyebrow started to twitch as he sat down. He had a sinking feeling he knew what was coming next.

"By the way, did you notice them when you got back this afternoon?" she asked, settling herself beside him.

Well, there it was. The question he'd wanted to avoid as long as possible. He had a sneaking suspicion that if he told her what he really thought of them, she'd never speak to him again. But his conscience wouldn't allow him to lie to her either.

Uncomfortable with the whole situation, he cleared his throat. "Uh...yeah, I saw them when I drove through town."

"Well, what do you think?" she asked, smiling eagerly. "Aren't they unique?"

So's a longhorn steer, but I don't want one of them on Main Street, either.

"They're definitely different," he said evasively. He jumped to his feet. "Do you have some popcorn? We can't watch a movie without popcorn."

Clearly confused that he'd changed the subject so fast, Brenna nodded as she rose from the couch. "Sure. Why don't you come in and talk to me while I put it into the microwave?"

Happy to be off the hook for the moment, Dylan teased. "Are you sure it won't catch fire?"

She made a face at him as they entered the kitchen. "Unless the microwave malfunctions, you should be safe." Placing the bag inside, she set the timer. "You never did say what you thought of the fire hydrants."

Dylan felt the twitch over his left eye go completely berserk. He should've known better than to think Brenna would be content with the noncommittal answer he'd given her. And her hopeful expression made him feel like a heel. It would take a blind man or a fool not to see how enthusiastic she was over the damnable things.

He gave her a sideways glance. He couldn't bring himself to tell her he thought they were uglier than a day old vulture, so he hedged, "I hadn't given them much thought."

"How silly of me. Of course, you haven't. You were searching for those two boys lost up in the mountains." She made him feel worse when she gave him an understanding smile as she removed the popcorn from the microwave and emptied it into a bowl. "I heard they found them safe and sound this afternoon."

He nodded. "They were both scared spitless from being out there on the trail all night, and hungry as hell, but none the worse for wear."

"I'm sure that was frightening for you, too," she said, her voice filled with compassion. "Not knowing if you'd find them hurt, or worse, had to have given you several anxious moments."

His spirits sank lower. Her compassion made him feel like a low-down, double-dealing snake, even though he hadn't done anything wrong. But not wanting to tell her how ridiculous those hydrants looked made him feel as if he had—or was about to.

He had to move. The more understanding Brenna became, the worse he felt. Grabbing the bowl, he spun around and left the room. "Come on, we'll miss the beginning of the movie."

Brenna stared in stunned silence as Dylan made a hasty retreat. Something wasn't right, and she had every intention of finding out what it was.

"Dylan, what's going on?" she demanded, following him into the living room. "You've acted strange ever since I mentioned the fire hydrants."

When he turned to face her, she could have sworn he winced. But just as quickly as the expression appeared, it vanished. "What makes you think something's going on?"

She might have been slow to catch on, but she had a good idea what bothered him. "Your mood has nothing to do with being tired, or with finding those two lost teenagers, does it?" Walking up to him, she laid her hand on his arm. "Why don't you just come out and tell me you don't like the Santa Claus hydrants?"

He sank down on the couch, leaned his head back and closed his eyes. "I didn't want to hurt your feelings."

"Since when has the truth ever been more hurtful than a lie?" she asked, planting her hands on her hips. "Now, tell me what you really think of them."

She watched him open first one eye, then the other to peer up at her. Taking a deep breath, he cringed. "To tell you the truth, I think they're tacky as hell."

"Now, that didn't hurt, did it?" she asked, seating herself beside him on the couch.

"You're not upset?" He looked and sounded incredulous.

"No." She reached down and picked up a kernel of popcorn from the bowl he held, then placed it to his lips. "You'll get used to them. Besides, they won't be so out of place when the second phase of the project is completed."

He placed the bowl of popcorn on the end table, then rubbing at his left eyebrow, asked, "There's a second phase?"

Brenna nodded. "We plan on—"

But before she could tell him about the next step in the Beautification Society's plans to decorate for the Christmas season, Dylan pulled her onto his lap, brought his mouth down on hers and kissed her with a passion that took her breath away.

Her eyes drifted shut and Brenna felt as if the world spun out of control as Dylan slid his tongue across her lips, once, twice, then slipped between them to trace the inner recesses of her mouth. Playing a game of advance and retreat, he coaxed her into following his lead and when she slipped between his lips, to learn the taste of him, a feminine power she'd never felt before swept through her. All thoughts of Santa Claus fire hydrants, Main Street and the town of Tranquillity faded to nothingness when his groan of pleasure vibrated against her mouth.

Encouraged by his reaction, she tangled her hands in his thick hair as she lost herself in the moment. Sparkles of light danced behind her eyelids, but the thrill of kissing him once again was nothing compared to the feel of his hands on her body as he slid his palms beneath her sweater to stroke the sensitive skin across her rib cage. At the feel of his hard arousal against her bottom, shivers of excitement coursed through her and headed straight for the pit of her belly.

The feeling was so poignant that it startled her with its intensity and allowed a degree of sanity to intrude. ''Dylan, what are we—''

Pulling his hands from beneath her sweater, Dylan's chest rose and fell against hers as he took several deep breaths. ''Don't worry, darlin'.'' He placed her on the couch beside him, then handed her the bowl of popcorn. ''I meant it when I told you we'd take this one step at a time.''

"I think we just skipped step one and moved right on to step two," she said, feeling as if she'd run a marathon.

His deep, sexy chuckle sent a fresh wave of goose bumps skipping over her skin. Without a word, she handed him the bowl of popcorn, then reached into the candy dish on the coffee table for a handful of chocolate drops. Having chocolate was much safer than having Dylan, she told herself as she hastily unwrapped the silver foil and popped a piece of candy into her mouth.

Six

When the mayor and councilmen arrived Monday morning for the meeting he had requested, Dylan ushered them into his office and slammed the door. "Which one of you gave the B.S. Club permission to paint the fire hydrants?" he asked, motioning for the three men to seat themselves in the chairs in front of his desk.

"It sure wasn't me," Luke Washburn said emphatically, plopping down in one of the chairs.

Ed Taylor shook his head as he and Myron took their seats. "It wasn't me either."

When they all turned to stare at Myron, he remained strangely silent, and Dylan thought the man just might hang himself if he didn't stop fingering his bolo tie.

"Myron, do you have any idea who gave the B.S.

Club permission to do this?'' Dylan asked, already knowing the answer as he sank into the chair behind his desk.

The rotund little man's face turned beet-red. "Cornelia said it would be done in good taste and—''

"Good taste?" Dylan and the other men shouted in unison.

Myron's shoulders sagged "—she threatened to stop cookin'.''

"Well, hell, Myron, you didn't have to let them vandalize the fire hydrants,'' Luke said, sounding as disgusted as he looked. "I run a restaurant. I could of fed you.''

Myron's expression conveyed his misery. "She said I'd have to sleep on the couch till I came to my senses, too.''

"I guess it would get mighty lonely sleepin' by yourself,'' Ed said, understanding written all over his face.

Myron snorted. "Aw, hell, Ed. I ain't worried about sleepin' by myself, or doin' without for a while. It's that damned couch that bothers me. There's a loose spring right in the middle of the blasted thing that pokes me in the butt every time I lay down.'' He rubbed his rump as if the thought of it caused pain. "I think she keeps it around just to threaten me when she wants her way.''

Dylan watched the exchange, then sighed heavily. "Giving them permission to paint the hydrants isn't the problem. What I'd like to know is whose bright idea it was to plaster my face on the one outside?''

"They painted every one of the danged things to resemble somebody,'' Luke Washburn complained.

"My wife, Helen, painted the one in front of our place and made me look like a damned Santa troll."

"Yeah, one that's been on a real bender," Ed chortled.

"If I were you, I wouldn't act too cocky, Taylor." Luke laughed. "Your wife painted yours with its eyes crossed."

"Isn't that the most pitiful-lookin' thing you ever saw?" Ed shook his head. "I told Emily she'd better buy herself a pair of specs or quit that damned paintin'. I know I ain't the best-lookin' man around, but I ain't *that* homely."

"Dylan, I don't know why you've got your shorts in a bunch," Luke said, turning back to face him. "Yours looks better than most."

"That's right," Ed chimed in. "At least that Montgomery gal can paint."

When Ed mentioned Brenna's involvement, Dylan's left eyebrow started twitching and his stomach felt as if little men in spiked shoes were doing an Irish jig in his belly. He didn't need the added complications of the B.S. Club project, on top of trying to deal with his feelings for Brenna.

"Dylan, you've been seein' that little gal pretty regular," Ed said thoughtfully.

"Yeah, and the women didn't get all fired-up about changin' the way things have always been until she came to town and started them danged classes," Luke groused.

"You gotta do somethin' about all this, Dylan," Ed said in earnest.

Dylan sat forward. "Now, hold it right there. It's *your* wives who came up with this hare-brained scheme. Besides, I can't, and won't, try to tell Brenna what to do, or not do. I'm not getting involved.''

''Oh, yes, you are,'' Myron said, jumping to his feet. He paced back and forth in front of Dylan's desk. ''You're gonna have to start snoopin' around more if we intend to stop this before they completely ruin the town.''

''That's right, Dylan,'' Ed added. ''Knowin' that bunch, if we don't stop 'em now, come this spring you'll be drivin' around in the sheriff's truck with pink and yellow daisies painted on the sides.''

''Since you ain't married, it won't cause you near the grief it could cause us,'' Luke said earnestly.

Dylan tasted defeat and it sat heavily on an already knotted stomach. ''What can *I* do? Brenna has a mind of her own. I can't tell her what to do, any more than you men can tell your wives.''

Myron looked thoughtful. ''We don't want you to tell her nothin', boy. Try askin' her what they have up their sleeves next. Then when you find out, let us know so we can head 'em off 'fore they do something else to make a mockery of Tranquillity.''

Ed Taylor stood up. ''Now that we've got that settled, I'm goin' by the drugstore to pick up a box of chocolates for Emily.''

''Why you doin' that?'' Luke asked.

''To make amends,'' Ed answered as he started for the door. ''Myron may not care about sleepin' all by his lonesome, but I do.''

''Me, too.'' Looking thoughtful, Luke followed him. ''I'm pretty sure Helen got offended when I told her the best thing she could do would be to throw them paints and brushes away and buy a dog to play with.''

''If you two are buyin' candy for your wives, I'd better buy some for Cornelia,'' Myron said, joining them. At their questioning look, he shrugged. ''I need some kind of insurance against that damned couch.''

Dylan watched the three men file out of his office. He was stuck between a rock and a hard place. No matter which way he turned, he couldn't win.

On one hand, he wholeheartedly agreed with the men. The women did have some cockamamie ideas. God only knew what they planned to do next.

But on the other hand, he couldn't forget the excitement in Brenna's eyes when she talked about her role in the B.S. Club's plans. She was genuinely thrilled to have been asked to join the women and become involved in the community so quickly. And he'd be damned before he did anything to take that happiness from her.

His gaze landed on the clock and he noticed it was already after lunch. He couldn't believe he'd wasted most of the morning listening to the council members' impotent complaints, then the rest of it trying to figure out what his own role was in the whole mess.

Shaking his head, Dylan made the decision to put it out of his mind. He had a feeling he could spend the rest of the day speculating on what he could do to resolve the matter and never come up with a solution. Besides, thinking about it just made his eyebrow twitch and his stomach churn.

Brenna shivered uncontrollably as she hurried down the sidewalk. Why had she opted to walk from her shop instead of driving the distance to the grade school? In the hour she'd been inside working with the fourth graders, the temperature had dropped a good twenty degrees and the cold rain pelting down on her felt like icy needles.

If only the storm had waited just a few more minutes, she'd have reached her shop before the downpour started. But it hadn't and instead of being dry and warm, she was completely soaked and chilled to the bone.

For the third time in as many minutes, she wondered what had possessed her to choose a Polynesian Christmas tale and a hula girl costume for today's story hour. The rain had quickly soaked the grass skirt, and besides clinging to her legs like pieces of limp spaghetti, it felt as if it weighed twenty pounds. She'd worn her hair down and the long, wet strands slapped her in the face with every gust of wind.

But if there was any part of her that felt more miserable than another, it had to be her feet. The flip-flop shoes she'd worn offered no protection from the weather at all. Her feet were drenched, extremely cold, and with every step the shoes slopped cold water up from the sidewalk onto the backs of her legs. Fortunately, she'd thought to throw a jacket in her tote bag and her hot-pink sports bra was blessedly dry. At least, for the moment.

Why hadn't she opted to wear mukluks and tell the story of *Nanook of the North?* she wondered as she plodded through yet another puddle. At least she'd be warmer than she was now.

Trying not to think about how miserable she was, it took a moment for her to realize that the sheriff's

SUV had pulled up beside her. When the power window slid down, Dylan was frowning. "Come on. Get in out of the rain."

Brenna was so glad to see him, she didn't think twice about accepting his offer, even though he'd told her to get into the truck instead of asking. Opening the door, she quickly slid into the passenger side of the nice, warm vehicle and closed the door.

"N-nice day…f-for ducks…w-wouldn't you say?" She shivered uncontrollably and her teeth chattered so badly they sounded like castanets.

"Damn, darlin', you're frozen," Dylan said, turning the heat to full blast. The warm air immediately washed over her and felt absolutely heavenly.

"Th-thank you…f-for the…r-ride," she managed to get out around her clicking teeth.

Shifting the SUV into park, he reached over to rub his hands up and down her arms. "Why didn't you drive to the school? Didn't you hear the weather report this morning about a blue norther blowing through?"

"I d-didn't listen to…t-the radio this morning. Besides, I th-thought I would be…finished before it started raining." The chattering began to slow down as she felt the heat from Dylan's hands flow through her. "I was wrong."

"Obviously." He reached over to help her out of her wet jacket, then slipped out of his dry, leather one and placed it around her shoulders.

His gaze leisurely traveled the length of her, stopping at her sports bra, then traveling down to her skirt. The wet strands of grass had parted so her thighs were mostly exposed. Her cheeks heated and, reaching down, she tried to arrange the strips to cover herself.

"I'm afraid this isn't very appropriate for this type of weather," she said, uncertain whether the shiver that snaked up her spine was due to the weather, or from his heated gaze.

His deep chuckle sent a fresh wave of goose bumps sweeping across her skin and she knew the tremor had nothing to do with the chilling rain. "I can honestly say this is the first Story Lady costume you've worn that I approve of," he said, his smile sending another shiver coursing though her. His smile turning serious, he asked, "Do you have another change of clothes at the shop?"

"No, but I have some in my tote bag." She pulled a soggy turtleneck sweater and a pair of equally wet jeans from the canvas tote. "Well, they were dry a few minutes ago."

"I'll take you by your place first, then drive you to your shop."

Shifting the truck back into drive, Dylan remained silent as he drove Brenna to her house. He hated that she'd gotten cold and wet, but appreciated the hell out of the fact that the rain had provided him with more than a fair view of her luscious body.

Her bright pink spandex sports top did little to conceal that her nipples had peaked from the cold, and the droplets of water from her wet hair sliding down into the garment had caused his mouth to go dry. But when he'd noticed the grass skirt had parted, revealing her smooth thighs, his body had hardened so fast that it had momentarily made him dizzy.

"It looks like Pete and your grandmother have

plans for the afternoon," he said, pointing to his antique Chevy truck pulling from Brenna's driveway. He watched Pete and Abigail wave as they drove past. "I wonder where they're headed this time?"

"Granny mentioned something about her and Pete spending the afternoon and most of the evening down in Alpine," Brenna said, rummaging around in the depths of her tote. "By the way, would you like to come over to watch a movie after dinner?"

"Sure. What time should I come by?"

"I have a meeting right after I close the shop, but I should be finished by seven," she added, dragging several items out of the canvas bag. She sighed heavily. "Well, that's just great. I must have left my house keys on the dresser this morning and I have no way of getting into the house to change."

"You don't have an extra key under the doormat or hidden in a flowerpot somewhere?" he asked, turning the SUV into the drive.

She shook her head. "Granny says that's the first place a burglar would look."

"I agree," he said, nodding. "But most people do it anyway. I advise having an extra key made and carrying it in your purse or wallet." He left the motor running as they sat staring out the windshield at the house. "I don't suppose you have an extra key at the shop?"

She worried her lower lip as she shook her head. "Afraid not."

He picked up the microphone to radio Jason that he wouldn't be back to the office until later, then backed the truck out onto the street. "Looks like I'll have to take you to my place."

"We can't go to your house," she protested. "I need to reopen my shop for the rest of the afternoon."

He continued to drive toward the cabin he shared with Pete on the outskirts of town. "I doubt you'll have that much business in this kind of weather, but after I loan you a pair of sweats, I'll bring you back to town."

The thought of her wearing his clothes sent his blood pressure soaring and made him harder than hell. If just thinking about her in his baggy sweatsuit aroused him this much, he was in bigger trouble than he'd ever imagined possible.

Steering the truck up the lane to his cabin, Dylan tried not to dwell on the fact that very soon he'd be inside his home with Brenna. Alone. And she'd be taking off her clothes and putting on his. Sweat popped out on his upper lip and he had to concentrate to keep from groaning out loud.

"I hope Granny and Pete make it to Alpine safely," Brenna said, bringing him back to the present.

"I'm sure they will." He pulled the SUV to a stop beside the front porch of his home. "Pete's seen more than his share of blue northers move through." Dylan opened the driver's door, then came around to help her from the passenger side. "Just be glad that this far south we get rain and not snow. It's my bet the Panhandle is knee-deep in it about now."

"It feels cold enough to snow," she said, shivering visibly.

"It's chilly and you're wet. It just seems colder than it really is." He placed his hands at her waist to lift her down from the truck and gritted his teeth at the feel of her satiny skin against his rough palms.

Her eyes met his and he could tell that she was gripped by the same tension he was. He quickly stepped back and waited for her to precede him up the porch steps.

Maybe this hadn't been such a good idea. He was trying his damnedest to be a gentleman, but it seemed everything was working against him. He was going to be alone with Brenna in his cabin, she had on an outfit that sent his temperature soaring and he was harder than he'd been in a month of Sundays. It was a lethal combination to his good intentions any way he looked at it, and not at all encouraging.

When he opened the door and they stepped inside the darker interior, he reached out to turn on a lamp and cursed vehemently. "It looks like the storm has knocked out the power. Stay here and I'll be right back."

Entering the kitchen area, he removed a kerosene lamp from one of the shelves in the pantry, lit the wick, then went back into the living room where Brenna stood looking cold, wet and more desirable than any woman he'd ever seen. "Let's get you something warm and dry to put on," he said, placing the lamp on the mantel over the fireplace.

He went into his bedroom to find her something to wear, but made it a point not to look at his king-size bed. No telling how many different scenarios his suddenly active imagination would conjure up.

A sudden flash of light and a deafening clap of thunder preceded a startled cry from the other room.

The hair on the back of his neck stood straight up and every nerve in his body came to full alert.

"Are you all right?" he asked, rushing back to where Brenna stood, staring out the picture window.

As she nodded, she pointed toward the lane. "I was startled when lightning struck that tree."

"This can't be happening," he muttered, his hand tightening into a fist around the sweatsuit and thick socks he'd retrieved from the dresser.

Looking at the smoldering tree stump, then at the live oak blocking the drive, he couldn't believe how fate had stepped in to make matters worse. They were trapped, and there was no way they'd be making it back to town until the storm moved on and he could use the chain saw to clear the lane. And, if the reports were accurate, that wouldn't be until sometime tomorrow afternoon.

Dylan swallowed hard. He and Brenna would have to spend the night in his cabin. Alone.

Sweat popped out on his forehead and his groin tightened predictably. Glancing down at his chest, he almost groaned. The star pinned to his shirt represented justice, integrity and honor—principles he'd tried his damnedest to uphold all of his life. But at the moment, he wasn't sure he'd be able to live up to the last part of the code.

He glanced down at the woman standing beside him. With each passing second, his thoughts were becoming increasingly less honorable and exceedingly more lusty.

Suddenly unable to stand still, he handed her the sweats and the thick socks, then turned to the fireplace. "Get changed and I'll see about getting a fire started.'' Without looking at her, he gritted his teeth and added, ''We're going to be here a while.''

''Is there something I can do to help?'' Brenna asked, watching Dylan place logs in the stone fireplace.

He shook his head. ''There's not much to do. We'll just have to sit tight and make the best of things until the storm lets up.''

She pushed up the sleeves of the oversize gray sweatshirt and reached for her tote bag. Please let there be something chocolate somewhere inside, she prayed. But the only thing she found that was even remotely related to her chocolate addiction was a crumpled wrapper and a coupon for fifty cents off her next candy purchase.

Sighing, Brenna put the canvas bag back on the cushion beside her and stared at Dylan's broad back. They were trapped in his cozy cabin and there wasn't any way out until it stopped raining.

She glanced out the window. It didn't appear that would happen any time soon.

''In case you're wondering,'' he said, sounding calm, ''we're probably going to be spending the night here.''

Turning back to face him, she nodded. ''I figured that would be the case.''

How had she managed to sound so matter-of-fact when her insides fluttered wildly and her pulse beat like a little miniature snare drum?

She knew she was grasping at straws, but she had to ask, ''You couldn't use the Explorer to pull the tree out of the way enough to drive past it?''

He shook his head. "Afraid not." His back to her, he continued to work at starting the fire. "And I can't saw the tree up and move it until the storm lets up." He chuckled. "I'm not real big on dodging lightning bolts at any time, but especially not when I'm holding a chainsaw with a twenty-inch steel bar."

"No, that wouldn't be a very good idea," she agreed, glancing back at the fallen tree. "I suppose I should call and cancel my meeting for this afternoon." She hated the fact that it would put the Beautification Society behind on their plans. Knowing she had no choice, she retrieved her planner from the tote. "Do you think your phone still works?"

Dylan rose to his feet and walked over to a desk in the corner of the room. Picking up the receiver, he listened, then set it back on its base. "It's out, too."

"How am I going to let the ladies on the Main Street committee know that I won't be able to meet with them?"

"I'll go out and use the radio in the cruiser to contact Jason. I need to let him know what's happened anyway. While I'm at it, I'll have him make the calls for you." Dylan started toward the door, then turned back. "Do you have a list of the members involved?"

She pulled a paper from her datebook, then handed it to him. "Please ask him to let everyone know we'll reschedule the meeting for next week. Do you think he would mind calling my house to leave a message for Granny and Pete, as well?"

"No problem," he said, walking to the door.

While Dylan went out to make the radio call to his deputy, Brenna curled up on the couch and stared at the blazing logs in the fireplace. When she left for the grade school just after lunch all she'd had on her mind was being the Story Lady for an hour, meeting with the Main Street committee to discuss the next phase to be completed before the Jamboree on Christmas Eve night, and asking Dylan if he'd like to come over for a movie. Now, she was having to cancel her meeting and planning to spend the night with him.

She shook her head. She wasn't spending the night *with* him. She was spending the night in his cabin and he just happened to be there with her.

She took a deep breath. Dylan's masculine scent on the clothes he'd loaned her assailed her senses and a tremor raced the length of her spine. She closed her eyes against the coil tightening in her lower belly. She'd tried to tell herself for days that she was spending time with him because it was preferable to spending time alone while her grandmother was out with Pete. But the truth was, no matter how hard she'd tried, she was falling head over heels for him. And it scared her silly.

Dylan cursed as he hung the mike back on the dashboard of the Explorer. He had the urge to punch something.

While he'd been giving Jason instructions about calling Brenna's place and the women on her planning committee, Myron had walked into the office. The man had been so excited about the fact that Brenna was having to cancel the meeting, Myron had told Dylan he intended to see that Dylan received a commendation for going above and beyond the call of duty in his effort to stop the B.S. Club.

Dylan had tried to explain that it was a bizarre act

of nature and that he had nothing to do with it, but Myron wasn't listening. All the man could concentrate on was the fact that future plans for the Main Street Project had been put on hold for a week, giving the men extra time to come up with a scheme to stop whatever the women had planned next.

Sighing heavily, Dylan got out of the truck and made a mad dash for the front porch. He was sick of hearing about the B.S. Club, the Main Street Project, and the men's desire to stop the women from making any further changes.

He stood with his hand on the doorknob. The way he saw it, he had a choice to make. He could either spend the rest of the day feeling guilty about his part in the men's attempt to stop the women of Tranquillity, or he could forget about the town and concentrate on enjoying Brenna's company.

For the first time in the past hour, he smiled. As far as he was concerned there was no contest. Myron, the B.S. Club and the Main Street Project be damned.

He was going to spend the rest of the day, and night, concentrating on the most exciting, desirable woman he'd ever met.

Seven

"**W**ould you like another s'more?" Dylan asked, pulling a long-handled barbecue fork with toasted marshmallows on it from the fireplace.

Sitting on the braided rug in front of the hearth, Brenna shook her head as she licked the sticky remnants of chocolate and marshmallow from her fingertips. His mouth suddenly felt as if it had been coated with cotton. But when her little pink tongue darted out to remove a graham cracker crumb from her index finger, sweat popped out on his forehead and upper lip.

"No, thank you," she said, smiling. "I've had my chocolate fix. I'll be fine for a while."

"I'm glad I found Pete's stash of candy bars," Dylan teased, in an attempt to keep things light. "I'd hate for you to go into chocolate withdrawal."

"Oh, that wouldn't be pretty," she said, shaking her head. She grinned impishly. "You should have seen me the day we painted the fire hydrants. I'd gone all day without something chocolate and by late afternoon, I was not someone you'd want to be around."

At the mention of the Main Street Project, Dylan felt his eyebrow begin to twitch rhythmically. If he never heard another word about the B.S. Club and their plans it would be all too soon.

"When we start on—"

He quickly broke off a small section of chocolate and placed it to her lips, effectively cutting off what she was about to say. "I don't want you getting cranky," he said, hoping his smile looked less forced than it felt. "And I don't want to discuss anything about the Main Street Project."

"Why not?" Her throaty laughter as she chewed the candy sent a shaft of longing straight through him. "We have the cutest Christmas—"

"I'd rather concentrate on you," he interrupted. He reached out to run his index finger along her soft cheek. "You're much more exciting."

Dylan watched her luminous blue eyes widen a moment before she broke off another piece of the candy bar and popped it into her mouth.

"You know what they say about chocolate, don't you?" he asked, breaking off another piece.

She shook her head.

"Studies have shown that eating chocolate creates the same chemical reaction in the brain that making love does," he said, reaching down to lace his fingers with hers.

"I think I've heard that, too," she said, her gaze reflecting the same awareness he felt.

The feel of her smooth skin and the sound of her sultry voice did strange things to his insides and sent his temperature soaring. When she glanced up at him from beneath her lashes, desire—urgent and hot—flowed through his veins.

The shadows cast by the kerosene lamp and the logs blazing in the fireplace lent an intimacy to the room that stole his breath. Bathed in the soft glow, she was the most beautiful woman he'd ever seen, and he wanted her more than he'd ever wanted anything in his life.

He tugged her forward. "Come here, darlin'."

"I doubt this is wise," Brenna said, her gaze locking with his as he pulled her onto his lap. She knew she should put up more than a token protest, considering their situation. But the truth was, she wanted Dylan to hold her, to once again make her feel cherished and desirable.

"It probably isn't wise," he agreed. He placed a piece of chocolate between his lips, then brushed it across hers. Kissing her, he gently pushed the candy into her mouth with his tongue, then drawing back, he smiled at her. "But what the hell. I've never been accused of being the sharpest knife in the drawer."

She closed her eyes as the rich taste of chocolate spread across her taste buds. "Dylan?"

His mouth touched hers again in a feathery caress as he licked the chocolate from her lips. "What?"

"Please kiss me." His tantalizing caresses weren't nearly enough.

A groan rumbled up from deep in his chest and he

pulled her close, but continued to tease her. "In a minute, darlin'," he whispered against her lips. "This heightens the anticipation."

She shook her head and put her arms around his shoulders to tangle her fingers in his thick, black hair. "No, it doesn't." She suddenly felt quite breathless. "It just makes me crazy."

He chuckled and the low sexy sound caused her heart to skip several beats and the butterflies in the pit of her stomach to flap wildly. She knew she was playing with fire. They were completely alone, with no chance of interruptions. But she didn't care. She wanted Dylan to kiss her. And more.

The thought should have sent her running as fast as her feet would carry her back to the safety of her shop in Tranquillity. But the fear of being intimate with Dylan, of holding his body to hers, and experiencing the contrast of a man and woman for the first time didn't frighten her nearly as much as the thought of never knowing the power of his love.

He barely touched her mouth with his, then gently sucked on her lower lip. "I want you to remember this kiss for the rest of your life, Brenna."

She would have told him there was no way she could ever forget it, but his tongue slipped inside to trace her teeth, then stroke the inner recesses, and Brenna lost the ability to think of anything but the man holding her so tightly against him. The hunger of his kisses, the taste of his passion, sent heat surging through her veins and made every cell in her body tingle to life.

"You taste like chocolate and sweet, sexy woman," he said, his low drawl sending quivers of delight shimmering through her. Her nipples tightened and she arched against him in an effort to get closer.

The hard muscles of his chest crushed her breasts as he lifted her, then stretched them both out on the rug in front of the hearth. Melting against him, she reveled in the rapid beating of his heart, his groan of pleasure when she traced his nape with her fingertips.

Brenna brought her hands down to his shoulders, then giving him a little push to create a space between them, she worked on the snaps of his chambray shirt. She wanted to feel the warmth of his skin, the steely muscles that she'd admired the first day they met.

"I want to touch you," she murmured.

Her heart stopped, then took off at a gallop. She couldn't believe the degree of passion in her tone, or that she'd spoken her thoughts aloud.

But before she had time to dwell on the admission, Dylan rose to his knees, yanked the snap closures of his shirt free and quickly shrugged out of the garment. Her breath caught at the sight of his well-developed chest and stomach. The man could pose for a calendar and easily sell a million copies, she decided as she reached up to trace the ridges of sinew with her fingertips. His sharp intake of breath encouraged her and she placed her palms over his pectoral muscles to feel his flat male nipples pucker in response.

"We're going to touch each other," he promised.

His dark green eyes held her captive as he took her hands in his. Pulling her to a kneeling position in front of him, he slipped his hands beneath the hem of the sweatshirt he'd loaned her to stroke the sensitive skin from her waist to the underside of her breasts.

The raw desire she saw in his heated gaze, the feel of his callused palms on her skin and the clean, manly scent of him, created a longing in her that she'd never known. It was as if he'd unlocked her heart, her soul. She wanted to make love with him, to have him become a part of her body as she would be part of his.

In that moment, she knew beyond a shadow of doubt that she was falling in love with Dylan. But before she had time to think of the implications of her discovery, Dylan eased his hands up to cup her bare breasts.

"You aren't wearing a bra," he said, smiling as he supported the weight of her with his palms.

"It was too wet from the rain," she said, her cheeks heating as she tried to explain why she wasn't fully dressed.

The smoldering look he gave her took her breath. "I'm glad." Leaning forward, he kissed her. "I want to see you, darlin'."

Unable to make her voice work, she nodded without hesitation.

He must have sensed her vulnerability because he gave her an encouraging smile a moment before he swept his hands upward and stripped her of the sweatshirt. When he tossed it aside, her first inclination was to cover herself. But she heard his sharp intake of breath, saw the spark in his eyes turn to flames of desire, and any lingering inhibitions she might have had melted away.

Smiling appreciatively, he took her hands in his

and placed them on his chest before cupping her breasts with his palms. "You're beautiful, Brenna."

He gently chafed the beaded tips with the pads of his thumbs, then leaning forward to kiss the hollow behind her ear, whispered, "I'm going to taste you."

As he nibbled his way down her neck to her shoulder, then her collarbone, her head fell back and she trembled at the feel of his lips on her skin. Delicious, honeyed heat flowed through her to form a heavy coil of need in her nether regions and she had to bite her lower lip to keep from moaning aloud. But when his hot mouth closed around her taught nipple and his tongue flicked over her tight flesh, she couldn't have stopped the sound from escaping if her life depended on it.

Dylan lifted his head. He didn't think he'd ever heard a sweeter sound than that of the pleasure he'd created in Brenna. "That's it, darlin'. Let me hear you. Let me know how I make you feel and what you need."

Rising to his feet he pulled her up with him, then placed his hands at her waist to dip his fingers beneath the elastic band of the sweatpants he'd loaned her. The discovery that she wasn't wearing panties sent a shockwave of heat straight to his groin and his straining body felt as if it just might bust the zipper of his fly.

"They were wet, too," she said, unable to meet his gaze.

He put his finger under her chin and tilted her head up so their gazes met. "Do you have any idea how arousing it is for me just knowing you were naked inside my clothes?" When she shook her head, he cupped her bottom and pulled her lower body to him. "Does this give you an idea?"

Her eyes widened at the feel of his arousal pressed to her lower belly and he watched with mounting satisfaction as the spark of awareness in her eyes changed to a smoldering ember of passion. Determined to fan the spark into the flame of unbridled desire, Dylan stepped back, then slowly, carefully moved his hands downward. The too-big pants fell away from her hips and legs to land in a heap at her feet.

Air seemed in short supply as he looked at her. Brenna was shaped the way a woman should be, with full breasts, soft curves and nicely rounded hips. She wasn't the fragile type that a man was afraid to love for fear of breaking something when he held her to him. No, Brenna was a woman who could hold a man captive in her softness as she drained him of every last ounce of strength he possessed.

At first, she looked a bit unsure as she kicked free of the gray pool of fleece. But when her eyes met his, Dylan forgot all about her hesitant expression. Desire, passion and need were reflected in her blue gaze, and his only thought centered around removing the rest of his clothes and feeling all of her delicious body next to his.

With a practiced twist of his fingers, he worked the button at his waistband through the opening, eased the zipper down over his insistent arousal, then quickly shucked his jeans and briefs. Reaching for her, he wrapped her in his arms and pulled her to him.

The feel of her satiny skin finally touching his hair-roughened flesh, the sweet, womanly scent that was uniquely Brenna enveloping him, and the sound of her soft sigh as she melted against him sent his blood pressure into stroke range and his heartrate into overdrive. Taking several deep breaths to slow his runaway libido, he buried his face in the red-gold cloud of her hair. He'd never in his entire life been as turned on as he was at that very moment.

Unsure of how much more of the sweet torture his body could withstand, Dylan swung her up into his arms and headed for his bedroom. He wanted to take things slowly, to make love to Brenna the way she was meant to be loved—slowly, thoroughly.

When he reached the side of the king-size bed, he threw back the comforter, lowered her to the pristine sheets, and stretched out beside her. Pulling her into his arms, he kissed her again with every emotion he felt, but wasn't ready to identify.

By the time he broke the kiss, Dylan felt as if he might go up in flames. Never had desire been so intense, or his need for a woman so strong.

"Dylan, there's something I need to tell you," she said, her lips skimming his shoulder and sending a shock wave of heat to every part of him.

"What's that, honey?" he asked.

He propped his elbow on the mattress and rested his head on his hand. Staring down at the most beautiful woman he'd ever known, he lightly traced his index finger between the valley of her breasts, down her abdomen to her navel. Rewarded by her soft sigh and the trembling of her body at his touch, he continued his exploration. But when he reached the nest of curls at the juncture of her thighs, her body stiffened.

"You wanted to tell me something?" he asked, slowing his exploration in order to give her time to relax.

The uncertain look she'd worn earlier returned and gazing up at him, she worried her lower lip a moment before she nodded. "I've...never done this before."

She made the announcement so softly, he wasn't sure he'd heard correctly. "You've never been with a man?" The vulnerable look in her guileless blue eyes when she shook her head, touched something deep inside of him. "Not even the jerk who duped you into thinking the two of you would get married after he got out of law school?"

"We..." She stopped and shook her head again. "*I* never felt ready."

Dylan's heart stuttered. "And you feel ready now? With me?"

"Yes."

The firmness he detected in her voice, the sincerity in her gaze, shook him to the very foundation of his soul. Brenna hadn't given herself to the man she'd thought to eventually marry because it hadn't felt right. But she was ready to give herself to him.

An admission like Brenna had just made should have doused all traces of his desire and sent him running like a tail-tucked coyote. But the thought that she felt ready to make love with him when she'd never felt ready to share herself with any other man made Dylan's heart swell and his body throb with an intensity that caused his head to swim. Unable to express the depth of his feelings with words, he gathered her in his arms and kissed her with a passion that he'd never believed himself capable of.

As Dylan's mouth moved over hers, the apprehension that had built inside Brenna melted away and was quickly replaced with the sweet tension of renewed desire. His tongue plunged between her lips to explore her inner recesses and a kaleidoscope of shimmering light danced behind her closed eyes. His tongue teased hers and an empty ache began to pool in all of her secret places.

When he slid his hand back down her body to touch her intimately, every muscle in her body strained to be closer to him. He must have sensed her need, and parting her, he teased the tiny nub of her femininity with gentle, easy movements that heightened her excitement more than she'd ever dreamed possible. She'd never before experienced the intense sensations coursing through her, but when he dipped his finger inside her dewy moisture to stroke her, Brenna felt as if something inside her ignited and she was sure she would go up in flames.

Moaning her pleasure, she writhed against him as ribbons of desire twined into a deep coil of need in the pit of her stomach. "Please, Dylan—"

"Feel good?" he asked, his lips leisurely moving over her shoulder.

"Y-yes."

Raising his head, his expression took her breath. "Brenna, I want you more than I've ever wanted any woman in my life and I need to be inside you. Are you ready for that?"

"Yes."

"Are you sure?" he asked as he continued to

heighten her passion by moving his finger within her. "I'll do everything in my power not to hurt you, but this first time might not be as good for you as I'd like."

She'd accepted the fact that there would be a certain amount of discomfort her first time with a man, but Dylan's words chased away any hesitation she might have harbored. "I've never been more sure of anything in my life. Please, make love to me, Dylan."

A groan rumbled up from deep in his chest, then kissing her briefly, he reached inside the drawer of the bedside table to remove a small foil packet. As she watched him arrange their protection, a tiny sliver of doubt returned to invade the sensual haze surrounding her. She'd never seen a man's lower body other than in anatomy textbooks in college, but something told her that Dylan wasn't a small man.

When she glanced up, he was watching her. "Your body was made to hold a man's like you're about to hold mine, darlin'." He moved to gather her into his arms. "Just relax. We're going to fit together just fine."

His gentle kiss erased her uncertainty a moment before he parted her legs and moved over her. Holding her captive with his passionate gaze, he reached for her hand and together they guided him to her moist heat.

Brenna tensed involuntarily when she felt her body begin to stretch to accommodate his entry. But the mixture of tenderness and hungry desire in Dylan's eyes, his gentle words of encouragement as he drew back, then carefully pressed forward, reassured her. His body continued the rhythmic movements and with each slow, forward thrust she felt him slide more deeply inside her.

He soon met the resistance within her and she braced herself for the discomfort she knew would soon follow. But his steady gaze told her without words that everything would be all right a moment before he hugged her to him, covered her mouth with his, then pushed past the veil and completely sank himself inside her. Her breath caught momentarily at the shock of holding all of him, but he remained perfectly still and the discomfort quickly subsided.

She felt his taught muscles quiver when he propped himself on his forearms to gaze down at her and she could tell he was giving her time to adjust to his size and strength. "You're so tight. I don't want to hurt you. But I don't think I can stand much more of this, darlin'."

His face reflected the toll of his restraint and in that moment, Brenna knew she loved him with all of her heart and soul. Reaching up to touch his lean cheek, she whispered, "Please make love to me, Dylan."

With a growl of satisfaction, he leaned forward to kiss the sensitive hollow of her throat at the same time he drew his hips back. Easing forward, he repeated the movement again and again, setting a slow steady pace. Very soon his movements renewed her passion and the coil inside her tightened to unbearable proportions. She sensed that she was on the verge of an awakening, a liberation from the tension gripping her as she moved in time with Dylan, but unsure of what was to come, she tensed.

Apparently sensing her readiness, as well as her confusion, he held her close. "Just let go, darlin'," he said, his voice rough with passion. "I'll take care of you."

Trusting Dylan as she'd never trusted anyone, Brenna gave in to the increased rhythm of his love-making and was immediately consumed by wave after wave of pleasure washing through her. A moment later, groaning her name, he thrust into her one final time, and she felt him join her in the realm of soul-shattering release.

When the last spasms of his climax subsided and his heartrate slowly returned to normal, Dylan moved to Brenna's side and pulled her to him. Nothing in his past could compare to making love with the woman he held. He felt as if he'd died and gone to heaven.

"Are you all right, darlin'?" he asked, kissing the top of her head.

Snuggling against his chest, she nodded. "That was the most beautiful experience of my life."

"I didn't hurt you, did I?" He didn't think it had been overly uncomfortable for her, but he needed to know.

"No." She leaned back in his arms to gaze up at him. "Thank you for making my first time wonderful, Dylan."

Her first time. The knowledge that she'd waited for him to be the first man she was intimate with made his chest swell and his gut burn with the need to be the last. The thought of Brenna in another man's arms, sharing her body as she'd shared it with him, sent a shaft of deep need coursing through him to once again make her his.

Turning her to her back, Dylan kissed her closed eyes, the tip of her nose and her stubborn little chin. "I want you again, Brenna."

Opening her eyes, her smile warmed him to the very depths of his being. "I want you, too."

"Are you sure?" he asked, concerned that making love again so soon might cause her more discomfort.

Nodding her head, she brought her arms up to encircle his shoulders. "I've never been more sure of anything in my life. Make love to me again, Dylan."

Eight

The next afternoon, after Dylan had dealt with the tree blocking the lane, he drove Brenna home. But instead of finding his antique truck parked in her drive, as he expected, there was no sign of the vintage Chevy. "I wonder where Pete is?"

"I don't know, but I'm sure Granny's with him wherever he is," Brenna said, laughing.

Her sweet smile, the light of having been well-loved in her pretty blue eyes, caused a tightness in his chest and had his body reacting in a very predictable way. Damned if the woman couldn't make him hard by doing nothing more than looking at him.

Leaning over, he gave her a quick kiss, then opened the driver's door. "Remind me to thank your grandmother for keeping Pete occupied."

When he rounded the front of the Explorer to help

her from the truck, she smiled. "I think I should be the one thanking Pete for keeping Granny busy. You have no idea how challenging she can be at times."

Taking her hand in his, Dylan walked to the door with Brenna. "Looks like they're gone again," he said, removing a piece of paper taped to the inside of the storm door. Scanning the contents of the note, he frowned. "Good advice, but I don't know why they would bother taping it to the door."

"Let me see." She took the paper from him, then read it aloud. "The real key to safety is watching what's under your feet. Step carefully kids." Laughing, she shook her head. "My keys are under the step."

"How do you know?" he asked, completely confused.

She bent down to reach beneath the wooden step, then straightening, held up a set of keys in a small plastic bag. "It's a game we used to play when I was a child," she said, fitting the key into the deadbolt on the door. "Pick out every third word."

Following her into the house, he stood, reading the note while she walked into the kitchen. "Key....is... under...step. Well, I'll be damned. You two have a very effective way of communicating without anyone knowing what the hell you're talking about."

"Dylan—"

Something in her tone made him glance up. Brenna stood in the doorway, her complexion a ghostly pale. Rushing over to her, he demanded, "What's wrong?"

"I don't believe it." Her hand trembled as she

handed him another piece of paper. "They've used your truck to elope to Las Vegas."

"They've done what?" Surely he hadn't heard her right.

Dylan read the note, then shook his head. He thought it was great that his uncle Pete and Abigail had found happiness together in their golden years, but he wasn't nearly so enthusiastic about them taking his vintage truck as their get-away vehicle. He unthinkingly uttered a word that, if his father had been alive, would have tanned his hide for saying in front of a lady.

"Sorry," he muttered.

Apparently, Brenna was still too shocked to notice his less-than-polite language. "I can't believe this is happening," she said. She walked over to sink down on the couch. "Granny is actually getting married and I'm not going to be there to see it."

"Oh, yes you are, darlin'," he said, making a snap decision. He pulled her into his arms. "We're going to follow them."

She brightened. "We are?"

"Yep. You'll get to see your grandmother get married, and I'll get my truck back."

"But they've gotten almost a full day's head start on us." She sounded doubtful.

"That's true," he admitted. "But if I know Pete, they'll stop for the night in Albuquerque. He has a friend up that way and I'm betting they stay there tonight." Dylan checked his watch. "If we take off within the next hour, we should catch up to them by midnight."

"I left my car at the shop yesterday, but we could go by and get it for the trip," Brenna offered.

Dylan nodded. "We'll have to. I can't take the Explorer for a personal trip." He gave her a quick kiss, then set her away from him before he delayed their departure by taking her into the bedroom to make love to her for the rest of the day and night. "Now, go throw some things in a bag while I call Jason and fill him in on what's going on."

Once she'd trotted down the hall toward her bedroom, Dylan took a deep breath and dialed the sheriff's office. He wasn't happy that Pete had taken his truck. That antique Chevy was his pride and joy, and about the only thing Dylan had left that belonged to his father.

But he'd have to thank his uncle when they caught up to the elderly duo. By choosing to elope, Pete had handed Dylan the perfect excuse for spending more uninterrupted time with the most alluring woman he'd ever known as they drove the distance to Las Vegas.

"Granny, I still can't understand why you couldn't have gotten married back in Tranquillity," Brenna said as she closed the door to the honeymoon suite behind them.

Tired from the long trip, she yawned as she and her grandmother walked down the long hall to the elevator. She and Dylan had caught up with the geriatric duo in Albuquerque late last night, just as he had predicted. Then, rising early to drive the rest of the distance to Las Vegas, they'd spent what was left of the afternoon shopping for something to wear to Pete and Abigail's evening wedding.

"We chose Las Vegas because we wanted some-one out of the ordinary to marry us," Abigail said as they stepped onto the elevator. Straightening her cream-colored suit, her eyes twinkled merrily. "Can you think of a more radical way of getting married than having the King of Rock and Roll officiate the ceremony?"

Before Brenna could tell her grandmother that it was indeed unusual, the elevator doors swished open and there stood Dylan and Pete. Her pulse quickened and her breath caught. She hadn't seen him since their shopping trip that afternoon when Abigail insisted that she and Brenna use the honeymoon suite to dress for the wedding, while Dylan and Pete changed in the room that Dylan had checked into.

She smoothed a nervous hand down the skirt of the dark green, midlength dress her grandmother had cho-sen for her as she watched Dylan walk toward her. She'd never seen him look more handsome in the dark blue western-cut sports jacket, powder blue shirt and black jeans he'd bought for the honor of being best man.

"Dylan is one hot dude, isn't he?" her grand-mother whispered.

"He sure is," Brenna agreed before she could stop herself.

"You know, we could make this a double cere-mony," Abigail suggested.

"Granny, don't start," Brenna warned. But a warmth filled her at the thought of marrying Dylan.

"Ain't those two the prettiest gals you've ever seen?" she heard Pete ask Dylan. Stepping forward, Pete tucked Abigail's hand in the crook of his arm.

"Ready to get hitched up all good and proper, sugar?"

"I sure am, you old goat," Abigail answered, her smile absolutely radiant.

Dylan's gaze held Brenna's captive as he stepped forward to take her hands in his. The appreciation in his brilliant green eyes sent heat coursing through her veins and caused her toes to curl inside her new pumps.

Bringing her hands to his lips, he brushed a kiss on her sensitive skin. "You look beautiful, darlin'."

"Thank you," she said, hoping she didn't sound as breathless as she felt.

Before she could tell Dylan how good he looked, Pete cleared his throat. "Are you two gonna stand there lollygagin' over one 'nother, or you goin' with us?"

Dylan never took his eyes from hers and she felt as if she might drown in their depths as he tucked her to his side. "Lead the way, Uncle Pete. We're right behind you."

An hour later, Dylan helped Brenna from the back of the limousine in front of the hotel. He couldn't believe how fast the wedding had taken place. They'd no sooner walked into the chapel that Pete and Abigail had chosen to exchange their vows, than an Elvis impersonator gyrated his way to the altar, asked the two seniors if they promised to "love each other tender" for the rest of their lives, then pronounced them man and wife.

"We want you two to come up to our suite for a

toast," Abigail said as they all entered the hotel lobby.

Pete nodded. "We have a couple of things we need to talk about with you kids."

"Of course, we'll come up to your suite," Brenna said. She turned to Dylan. "As best man, you should be the one doing the honors."

Glancing at her, Dylan felt his lower body tighten. He'd never seen Brenna look more beautiful. From the moment she'd stepped off the elevator, he'd wanted to be alone with her, to slide that dark green dress from her delightful body and make love to her until they both needed resuscitation. And if the looks she'd given him throughout the evening were any indication, she was entertaining similar thoughts about him.

Wishing he could bypass the toast in favor of taking Brenna to his room, he lied, "There's nothing that I'd like more than toasting your happiness."

When they entered Pete and Abigail's suite a few minutes later, an ice bucket of champagne sat chilling beside a table in front of the sliding patio doors leading out to the balcony. Two long-stemmed wineglasses and a bowl of chocolate-coated strawberries sat waiting for the newly wedded couple's celebration.

"You do the honors while I get a couple more glasses," Pete said, handing Dylan the chilled bottle.

Popping the cork, he poured wine into the two crystal champagne flutes, then into the water glasses Pete had retrieved from the wet bar. Taking one of the water glasses, Dylan proposed a toast to the happiness and longevity of Pete and Abigail's marriage. The melodic ring of glass touching glass sealed the good wishes a moment before they all took a sip of the expensive champagne.

"Now, before we run you kids off to pursue your own good time, we have a confession to make," Abigail said, looking smug.

"Yep, and a request, too," Pete added as he reached for Abigail's hand.

Brenna took another sip of champagne, then looked at Dylan. He knew she wondered what the pair were driving at; the same as he was.

"What is it you have to confess?" he asked, not sure he wanted to know.

He watched Pete and Abigail exchange a look, a moment before Abigail cleared her throat. "You two didn't meet by accident. We set you up."

"You set us up?" Brenna asked, placing her glass on the table.

"Pete and I met a couple of days after you and I moved to Tranquillity," Abigail said, nodding. "Once we started talking about our families, it didn't take us any time at all to know that the two of you would be perfect for each other." She laughed. "And we've been arranging for you to spend time together ever since. We even took Dylan's truck, instead of your car for this trip because Pete said Dylan would come after it, and I knew you'd come with him."

"I've gone to the movie theater down in Alpine more in the last few weeks than I have in my whole life." Looking at Abigail, Pete grinned. "But spendin' all that time in the dark with Abby caused our matchmakin' to backfire."

"It serves the two of you right for trying to meddle,'' Brenna said good-naturedly. "You can keep my car for your honeymoon and I'll ride back with Dylan.'' She turned to face him. "If that's all right with you?''

Dylan nodded as he watched her reach for a chocolate-covered strawberry. When she popped the morsel into her mouth, then licked the juice from her fingers, it took everything he had in him not to groan out loud.

"What was the request?'' he asked, remembering the second reason the senior couple had wanted to talk to them. He braced himself. No telling what the pair had up their sleeves this time.

"With Christmas only a couple of weeks away, we ain't gonna have time to find a place of our own until after the holidays,'' Pete said, kissing the back of Abigail's wrinkled hand. "We want you two to decide which one of you Abby and I are gonna live with until we move.''

"We don't want you to decide right now,'' Abigail quickly added. "Talk it over on your way back to Tranquillity, then when Pete and I return from our honeymoon you can let us know.''

Dylan glanced at Brenna, then back at the newlyweds. "I think it's safe to say you're welcome to stay with either one of us.''

"For as long as you want,'' Brenna added, reaching for another chocolate-covered strawberry. When she bit into it, Dylan had to glance away. The more he watched her lick her fingers, the tighter his body became.

"When we get back to town next week you can let us know what you've decided,'' Abigail said. She smiled at Pete. "As long as we're together, we don't care where we stay."

"Well, thanks for comin' to the weddin'," Pete said suddenly. "But it's time for you kids to skedaddle." He put his arm around Abigail. "Me and Abby ain't gettin' no younger and we got us a honeymoon to get started."

Brenna's cheeks turned beet-red and Dylan watched her down another strawberry before hugging her grandmother and his uncle Pete. "Congratulations. I'm very happy for both of you."

Dylan added his good wishes to Brenna's, then taking her by the hand, led her out into the hall and down the corridor. "Let's go see what's playing on the movie channels."

He glanced down at her as they waited for the elevator. With her alabaster complexion and copper-colored hair, Brenna looked utterly stunning in that dark green dress. But as good as she looked in it, Dylan knew beyond a shadow of doubt that she'd look better out of it.

When they stepped into the empty elevator and the doors closed, he pulled her into his arms. "I've wanted to kiss you ever since I saw you in the lobby," he said, brushing his lips over hers. "Do you know how beautiful you look tonight? How difficult it's been to keep my hands to myself?"

The smile she gave him damned near knocked his boots off. "Probably as difficult as it's been for me to keep my hands off you. Do you have any idea how yummy you look in black jeans and a sports coat?"

"Yummy?" He chuckled. "As yummy as chocolate-covered strawberries?"

She nodded. "Do you know why I kept eating those strawberries?"

"No."

The smile she gave him lit the darkest corners of his soul. "It was the next best thing to having you."

His blood surged through his veins and a spark ignited in his gut. "Darlin', if you keep saying things like that, I won't be held responsible for us missing whatever the movie channel is showing."

Grinning, she wrapped her arms around his waist and pressed herself against him. "Did I say I wanted to watch a movie? I'd rather watch you."

He felt his heart stop, then thump hard against his rib cage. "You're going to cause me to have a heart attack if you don't stop that."

"Stop what?" she asked innocently as they stepped off the elevator and started toward their room.

"You know what," he growled, digging in his jacket pocket for the card key.

"You don't want me to tell you how sexy I think you are?" she whispered close to his ear. "The other night at your place you said you wanted to hear me—"

"Not until we're in the room," he interrupted, fumbling with the key.

"Can I tell you how good it feels to have you—"

He placed his hand over her mouth, effectively cutting her off. "I've created a monster," he muttered, inserting the key into the slot.

She tickled his palm with her tongue and he damned near broke the card off in the lock. Pulling his hand from her mouth, he rubbed it against his thigh to ease the tingling sensation that sent his blood pressure skyrocketing and heat racing straight to the region below his belt buckle.

"Darlin', if you don't stop that I'm going to die of frustration before I get this door open."

"I was just going to tell you how good it feels to have you…"

He gave her a stern look.

She ignored it. "…here with me for Granny and Pete's wedding," she finished, her eyes twinkling mischievously.

"Oh, you're going to pay for that one," he promised as he finally opened the door to their room and turned on the lights. Pulling her inside, he took her into his arms as he kicked the door closed behind them. "Do you have any idea what that kind of talk can do to a man?"

"No." Her smile almost brought him to his knees. "Would you like to show me?"

At the sudden tightening of his groin, he sucked in a sharp breath. "You're determined to drive me out of my mind, aren't you?"

"I hadn't considered it," she said thoughtfully.

A spark of mischief lit her pretty blue eyes a moment before she walked over to the dimmer switch on the wall beside the door. Dimming the lights to a soft muted glow, she turned back to face him.

"But you drove me out of my mind last night in the hotel in Albuquerque, and the night before in your cabin, so I think it's only fair." Reaching up, she slipped the sports jacket from his shoulders and hung it in the closet. "Would you mind if I drove you a little crazy tonight, Sheriff?"

Dylan swallowed hard. "Not at all, darlin'."

She gave him a smile that caused his heart to stop, then take off at an alarming rate. "Tonight it's my turn to drive you to the brink."

His pulse thundered in his ears at the sparkling promise he saw in her determined gaze. Sensing that she needed to feel in control of their lovemaking, he forced himself to stand still while she worked at unbuttoning his shirt. Slowly easing the button below his open collar through the buttonhole, she trailed her fingers down his chest to the next button, then the next. He sucked in a sharp breath with each touch, and by the time she reached his waistband to tug the tails of his shirt from his jeans, he felt as if his lungs might explode.

Parting the fabric, she placed her hands on his stomach and lightly smoothed them up his abdomen to his chest. She teased his puckered nipples with her fingertips, then caressed his pectoral muscles with her soft, warm palms. Dylan exhaled the air trapped in his lungs in one big whoosh.

"Does that feel good?" she asked, glancing up at him from beneath her lashes.

He had to clear his throat to make his voice work. "If it felt any better I doubt I could stand it, darlin'."

She ran her hands up to his shoulders, then down his arms, pushing his shirt off as she went. "You have a beautiful body, Dylan."

Her softly murmured appreciation sent his temperature up several degrees. "I like yours a lot better," he said hoarsely.

The look she gave him when she tossed his shirt aside was filled with promise and he wondered what she'd do next. He didn't have long to wait. Taking him by the hand, she led him farther into the room, then walked over to turn on the clock-radio beside the bed. A slow romantic tune immediately surrounded them.

When she returned to stand in front of him, she bent to pull off his boots, then straightened to give him a look that made sweat bead on his forehead and his arousal strain against his fly. If the glint in her eyes was any indication, she fully intended to drive him stark raving mad with her exploration of his body before she once again allowed him a glimpse of her tempting curves.

Holding his gaze with hers, she ran her index finger down the narrow line of hair from his navel to his belt. Every muscle in his body tensed and he took a deep steadying breath. Standing still while Brenna had her fun just might prove to be the hardest thing he'd ever done. Her hands brushing his belly as she worked the leather strap through the metal buckle, had him placing his hands on her shoulders to steady himself. There was no question about it. It was *definitely* the most difficult thing he'd ever done.

He took several deep breaths in an effort to slow his body down. He'd be lucky if he had an ounce of sense left by the time she was finished undressing him, he decided.

She popped the snap on his jeans and toyed with the metal tab, causing him to swallow hard around the lump of cotton clogging his throat. He was aroused to an almost painful state and a zipper could be a lethal weapon to a man in his condition if it wasn't lowered carefully.

"Darlin'—"

Before he could warn her, she placed her finger to his lips, then slowly eased the tab down over the insistent bulge stretching his cotton briefs. He let out the breath he hadn't realized he'd been holding.

But when she touched the fabric covering his arousal, Dylan groaned and closed his eyes as the burning in his lower belly spread to every cell of his being. She was definitely driving him out of his mind. And heaven help him, he was loving every minute of it.

"Open your eyes and look at me, darling."

When he did as she commanded, she held his gaze with hers, placed her hands at his flanks, then slowly pushed his jeans and briefs from his hips and down his legs. Stepping out of them, he kicked them to the side and reached for her.

"Not yet." Her throaty whisper sent a wave of heat down his spine and he cursed himself for agreeing to let her play the role of seductress. He'd be lucky if he had a mind left at all by the time she finished with him.

She removed her shoes and panty hose, then arranging her long hair over one shoulder, turned for him to unzip the back of her dress. Aroused as he was, the simple task proved extremely difficult and he fumbled with the tab a moment before he finally managed to slide it open. His knuckles brushed her satiny smooth back and she trembled in response to his touch. She was as turned on as he was, and he took comfort in the fact that he wasn't the only one suffering from her loveplay.

Placing his hands on her shoulders, he turned her

to face him and started to take her into his arms. But she shook her head and stepped away from him.

He watched, mesmerized, as she slipped the dress from her creamy shoulders and let it fall into a dark green pool at her feet. Dylan swallowed hard when she reached up to release the front closure of her bra. The damned thing was so filmy he could see the deep rose of her tightly beaded nipples beneath the emerald-green lace.

She smiled as she unfastened the clasp, then slipped the straps down her arms, freeing her full, firm breasts to his appreciative gaze. He groaned. But when she hooked her thumbs in the waistband of her tiny panties, he thought his eyes would pop right out of his head. Besides her panty hose, all she'd had on beneath that pretty green dress the entire evening had been nothing but a wisp of lace that revealed more of her breasts than it covered, and a minuscule silk and lace thong. The knowledge caused the blood to roar through his veins and his body to jerk to full alert.

"I'm glad I didn't know about what you *didn't* have on under that dress, darlin'," he said, his voice sounding as if it had turned to rust.

Laughing softly, she walked toward him. "Why?"

"Because it would have been hard as hell to hide how much I want you," he growled. He held out his arms. "Come here, Brenna."

When she walked into his embrace, he pulled her to him and the feel of female against male, firm masculine flesh to soft feminine skin, had him feeling as if he'd been set on fire. He felt scored where her pebbled nipples pressed into his chest and his hard arousal nestled to her lower belly sent a rush of desire coursing through him that he thought might just take his head right off his shoulders.

"Dance with me," she whispered against his shoulder.

Dance? He was lucky he was still able to stand upright. But he'd walk through hellfire before he disappointed her, and when she began to gently sway against him, Dylan held her tight, gritted his teeth and fought to keep his sanity as he helped her play out her fantasy.

Tucking her long, silky hair behind her ear, he lowered his head and nibbled the sensitive skin along the column of her neck. Her moan of pleasure encouraged him and he slid his hands down her back to her bottom, then back up her sides to the swell of her breasts.

"Darlin', I want you more than I want my next breath."

She leaned back to look up at him, and the hunger he saw in her eyes sent a shaft of need straight to his groin. Taking his hand in hers, she led him to the bed. "Lie down, darling."

"Just a minute," he said, reaching for his discarded jeans. Removing a couple of the foil packets tucked in the back of his wallet, he placed them within easy reach on the beside table, then stretched out on the bed.

He expected her to join him, but instead she picked up one of the packets and tore it open. She hesitated, and he could tell she wasn't quite sure she had the nerve to finish the task.

"You're doin' just fine, darlin'," he said encouragingly.

His heart stuttered, then took off at a dead run when

her gaze met his a moment before she touched his fevered flesh and rolled their protection into place. He'd never had a woman do that and he found it more exciting than he'd ever dreamed possible.

He reached for her, but she shook her head. "Remember, it's my turn to drive you wild tonight, darling."

To his immense relief, not to mention the preservation of what was left of his mental health, she straddled him and without hesitation guided him to her moist heat. Closing his eyes, Dylan brought his hands up to hold her hips as her supple body consumed all of his. But Brenna's moan of pleasure as she completely settled herself on top of him almost proved his undoing and it took everything he had to keep what small scrap of control he had left.

"Darlin'…" He clenched his back teeth so tightly his jaw ached. "I'm not sure how much more of this I can handle."

"Open your eyes, Dylan," she said softly, repeating what he'd said to her the first night they'd made love.

When his gaze locked with hers, she began a gentle rocking that quickly had him racing toward the point of no return. Unable to contain himself any longer, he took control of the rhythm she'd set. Their bodies seemed to move in time with the music from the radio as he guided them to the pinnacle and he lost sight of where he ended and she began.

Seconds later, he felt her tighten around him, heard her brokenly whisper his name, a moment before she gave herself up to the culmination of pleasure. She collapsed on top of him and he held her trembling body until the storm was spent and she went limp with completion.

Only then did Dylan allow himself to succumb to the red haze of passion surrounding him. Every muscle in his body constricted as he sought his own fulfillment, and surging into her a final time, he groaned with the satisfaction of finding his own release from the tension holding him captive.

Time seemed to stand still as Dylan slowly recovered from the most soul-shattering climax of his life. He'd never experienced anything like what he'd just shared with Brenna.

"Dylan?"

"What, darlin'?"

"I love you," she said softly.

His heart skittered to a halt, then thumped hard against his ribs as he came to terms with Brenna's sleepy confession. Before he could form a response, her even breathing signaled that she'd fallen asleep.

Had he heard her right? She loved him?

Dylan gently moved her to his side, then turned to face her. Brushing a silky strand of copper hair from her porcelain cheek, he watched her sleep. His chest tightened and the spark of renewed desire began to burn at his gut.

Brenna loved him.

Three weeks ago, that thought would have scared him to death and sent him running in the opposite direction. But now?

She snuggled against him in her sleep and Dylan wrapped his arms around her to cradle her to him. A protectiveness he'd never felt before swept through him.

He took a deep breath, then another.

Five years ago, he'd made a fool of himself, and the fear of doing it again had kept him from getting involved with anyone since. But Brenna wasn't just any other woman. She was fast becoming an obsession, a necessity in his life that he hadn't known existed.

He gazed down at her. Somehow she'd gotten under his skin without him realizing when or how. And if the tender, protective feelings he had welling up inside of him were any indication, she'd be there for a good long time.

Nine

Four days after she and Dylan returned from Las Vegas, Brenna sat in the community room of the town hall, staring off into space. Her mind wasn't on the Beautification Society's committee meeting, the second phase of the project, or the complaints the women mentioned getting from their husbands about the Santa Claus fire hydrants. All she'd been able to think about for the past few days had been Dylan and where their relationship was headed.

After they'd made love the night they'd spent in Las Vegas, she'd inadvertently told him she loved him before she'd fallen asleep. She hadn't meant to let him know how she felt, but once the words were out, there was no turning back.

He'd remained silent, and neither one of them had mentioned it, even though they'd spent every spare minute of the day together, and every night entwined in each other's arms since being trapped in his cabin the day the blue norther blew through. And that bothered her. A lot.

When she'd been involved with Tom, he'd been the first to tell her how he felt. But Tom had turned out to be self-centered, and she'd learned the hard way that his feelings for her were as shallow as he was.

But Dylan was different. He didn't have an agenda, a scheme to further his plans at her expense. His career was secure and there wasn't anything he needed from her. She sighed. Unfortunately, that still didn't alter the fact that he knew how she felt about him, while she had no idea what his feelings were for her.

"Brenna, dear, are you listening?" Cornelia asked, interrupting Brenna's disturbing introspection.

"I'm sorry." Brenna sat up straight and faced the other ladies of the planning committee sitting across the table from her. "What was that you were saying? Some of the men are complaining about the fire hydrants?"

Emily Taylor nodded. "When I told my Ed that we intend to paint them for every holiday, I thought he was going to choke on his supper." The woman shook her head. "I can't understand what the men are so upset about. They're just fire hydrants."

"Have any of you told your husbands what we plan to do for the week preceding the Christmas Jamboree?" Brenna asked, feeling a tension headache coming on. She certainly didn't want to continue the project if the men were all opposed to more changes.

"No," Helen Washburn said, looking grim. "Luke

and I haven't been on real good terms since he told me to throw away my paints and buy a dog to occupy my time." She snorted. "He tried to get back in my good graces with a box of chocolates a couple of days later, but he never did apologize."

"Ed did the same thing," Emily said, frowning.

Cornelia's eyes narrowed. "Myron did, too."

Brenna rubbed the throbbing at her temples. "If it's going to be this much of a problem, maybe we should scrap the rest of the project."

"We'll do no such thing," Cornelia stated flatly. She rose from her seat to pace back and forth a moment before she stopped to plant her fists on her ample hips. "The men in this town have had their way and run things long enough. And it's time we put a stop to it."

"We're citizens of Tranquillity the same as they are," Emily said, nodding.

"That's right," Helen agreed. "My family's been here a lot longer than Luke's."

Brenna listened to the exchange with a growing sense of trepidation. It sounded like the women were planning to take over the town, instead of decorate Main Street for the community Christmas party.

"Girls, we're going to proceed as planned, and the devil take what the men think," Cornelia said, slapping the tabletop with the flat of her hand.

"Ladies, I'm not sure that's such a good idea," Brenna said, hoping to defuse the mutiny. "If the men don't want the Beautification Society painting new street signs and renaming Main Street 'Reindeer Way' for the next week—"

"Don't worry about the men," Cornelia interrupted, laughing. "They're not going to know anything about it until it's a done deal. Tomorrow's Saturday and we'll have all day to work on them. We'll meet here first thing in the morning, lock the doors and paint the signs, then we'll divide into teams and put them up simultaneously. By the time the men notice what we're doing, we'll be finished."

"I'm all for it," Helen said, looking quite pleased.

"Me, too." Emily clapped her hands excitedly. "Cornelia, you're a genius."

If the men were protesting the painting of a handful of fire hydrants, what would happen when the women painted wooden cut-outs of reindeer and tacked them over the existing street signs all along Tranquillity's main thoroughfare?

"But don't we have to have permission from the town council to implement a change like that?" Brenna asked, hoping that reason would prevail.

"Not as far as I'm concerned," Cornelia said confidently. She grinned wickedly as she added, "If Myron says anything about our putting the signs up, I've got a couch that he considers an instrument of torture. If he has to spend a night or two on it, he'll shut up soon enough."

"What's wrong, darlin'?" Dylan asked as he helped Brenna hang ornaments on the Christmas tree he'd helped her set up in front of her living room window. She'd been strangely quiet all evening and he could tell something was bothering her. Bad.

She sighed heavily and the sound caused his chest to tighten. He didn't like the idea of anything upsetting her.

"I met with the Beautification Society's planning committee this afternoon."

At the mention of the B.S. Club, Dylan's eyebrow started to twitch and his gut twisted into a tight knot. How the hell was he going to get out of hearing about the Main Street Project this time?

If he'd known Brenna was troubled by something the B.S. Club had up their sleeves, he'd have kept his mouth shut. The less he knew about their cockamamie schemes, the better. That way, the next time Myron asked if Brenna had divulged any information about the second phase of the project, Dylan could honestly say that she hadn't.

"Do you know why some of the men are so upset by the Main Street Project?" she asked as she hung ornaments that looked like little miniature lassoes on the branches.

The twitch in his eyebrow increased. "What makes you think they're upset?" he asked, positioning a gold star on the top of the tree.

She turned to face him and her worried expression tightened the knot in his stomach. "The members of the committee said their husbands thought the idea of painting the fire hydrants for different holidays was ludicrous."

He swallowed hard. What could he say? He thought the damned things were pretty ridiculous, too.

"Most of the men in Tranquillity have been here all their lives," he said, choosing his words carefully. "They like the way the town has always been and don't see any reason to change it."

He watched her digest what he'd said, then shake her head. "The women don't want to change Tranquillity's way of life. They just want to liven it up a bit by putting up a few seasonal decorations to make its celebrations more special.''

"Like the Jamboree?''

Hanging a tiny Christmas stocking on one of the branches, she nodded. "Painting fire hydrants and—''

Before she could finish telling him something he'd rather not know, Dylan reached out and pulled her into his arms. "Don't worry about it, darlin'. Everyone will have a good time at the Jamboree just like they always do.''

"But—''

He covered her mouth with his, effectively putting an end to any further talk of fire hydrants, the B.S. Club, or anything else. By the time he lifted his head, the worried expression on Brenna's face had disappeared.

Stepping away from her, he took a deep breath to slow his body's response to the kiss. The sooner they finished decorating the tree, the sooner he could do what he really wanted. And that was to carry her to the bedroom and make love to her for the rest of the night.

"Have you heard from the newlyweds?'' he asked, picking up a strand of garland that looked like a string of red peppers. He grinned. Apparently, Brenna wanted her tree's theme to reflect her recent move to southwest Texas.

Nodding, she pulled a sprig of fake mistletoe from a sack. "Granny called this afternoon to say they'd be spending tomorrow night in Albuquerque, then drive home the day after.''

"Have you thought about which one of us they'll stay with until they find a place?" he asked, draping the garland over the branches.

"Not really," she said as she looked around for a place to hang the mistletoe. "I wish they hadn't put the burden of making a choice on us."

"I guess we could take turns." He shrugged. "One week here. One week out at my place."

"That would work," Brenna said, sounding distracted.

Dylan glanced up to see her worrying her lower lip. "What's wrong?"

"I can't seem to find a place to hang the mistletoe," she said, frowning.

"Let me see what I can come up with." He took the sprig of greenery from her and held it over her head. Grinning, he leaned down to kiss her soft, sweet lips. "I like hanging it right here."

On Sunday afternoon, Dylan sat in his private office, staring at the three grim-faced men on the other side of his desk. "Myron, did you give the B.S. Club permission for this latest change?" he asked tiredly.

"Hell no!" Apparently unable to sit still, the mayor shot from his chair to pace the perimeter of the room. "The first I heard about it was when Luke called to tell me to look out my window at the street sign on the corner."

"Whoever heard of a town in southwest Texas with the main road runnin' through it named Reindeer Way?" Luke asked, sounding as disgusted as he looked. "Hell, unless they got one in the zoo in El

Paso, or up in Dallas, there ain't a reindeer within two thousand miles of here.''

Ed snorted. ''And the women have it in their heads they're gonna do somethin' like this for every holiday.'' His face reddened and the veins on the side of his neck stood out as his anger rose. ''Emily said they're already makin' plans to paint the hydrants to look like rabbits for Easter, leprechauns for St. Patrick's Day and cupids for Valentine's Day.''

''No tellin' what else they'll come up with,'' Luke said, groaning.

Clearly exasperated, Myron took off his cowboy hat and ran an agitated hand over his bald head. ''Knowin' Cornelia and that bunch, they'll end up callin' Main Street somethin' stupid like the Bunny Trail or Leprechaun Lane.''

Ed's face turned a deeper shade of crimson. ''Aw, hell. You don't think they'll try to put some kind of canopy over Main Street and call it the Tunnel of Love for Valentine's Day, do you?''

Dylan reached up to rub his twitching eyebrow as he listened to the men bluster about the street signs along Main Street. He'd thought the Santa fire hydrants were tacky, but they couldn't hold a candle to the painted, wooden reindeer street signs the B.S. Club had put up. The damned things had the sappiest grins plastered on their faces that he'd ever seen. He could only imagine what the women would do with bunnies, leprechauns and cupids.

''If you didn't give them permission to do this, Myron, then who did?'' Dylan asked tiredly.

''That's the real kicker in all this,'' Ed said, looking bewildered. ''They just up and did it without checkin' with any of us." He shook his head. "They've never done that before."

"You know, Dylan, most of this is your fault," Myron said, sinking back down in his chair.

"My fault! How do you figure that?" Dylan demanded, his gut feeling as if he'd been sucker punched.

Ed nodded. "We told you to spend as much time as you could with that Montgomery gal and find out what the B.S. Club was up to."

"Yeah," Luke chimed in. "You were supposed to let us know what the women had up their sleeves so we could stop it before it went this far."

"Take that little gal down to a movie in Alpine this evenin'," Myron said. "And while you're sittin' in the dark all cuddled up, find out if they're plannin' anything else."

"Yeah," Ed said, crossing his arms over his chest. "If my face ends up on a leprechaun or a cupid, your job just might depend on it."

Before he could defend himself, Dylan heard a quiet gasp. Looking up, his heart felt as if it dropped to his boottops. There stood Brenna at the open door of his office, her face ashen.

"I'm sorry...the door was open and I—" She stopped to take a breath. "I have to go now."

Her eyes met his then, and the shattered expression on her beautiful face tore at his insides. Jumping to his feet, he started around the desk. "Brenna—"

But she'd already whirled around and fled.

Brenna ran across the outer room of the sheriff's office, shoved through the door, then started down the sidewalk. Her heart pounded and her chest felt too constricted to breathe. Dylan had only been seeing her because he'd been ordered to discover what he could about the Main Street Project and report back to the town council.

Tears blurred her vision, but she kept on running. He'd followed the directive and spent as much time as he could with her in his effort to carry out his mission. And like a fool, she'd played right into his hand.

Pain as sharp as if a knife had been plunged into her chest made her stop to wrap her arms around herself. No wonder he hadn't told her he loved her. He didn't. Dylan had only been seeing her to ensure his position as sheriff was secure. Her breath caught on a sob. He'd used her, just as Tom had done.

Feeling as if she might be physically ill, Brenna started down the side street leading to her house. But she'd only gone a few yards when two strong hands clamped down on her shoulders to stop her.

"Darlin'—"

"Don't call me that," she said around the lump clogging her throat. Whirling to face Dylan, she gritted her teeth as she fought the emotions churning inside of her. "Don't ever call me that again."

"I need to explain about—"

"You don't have to justify yourself, *Sheriff.* You were just following orders." Squirming from beneath his tight grasp, she once again started toward home.

"Dammit, Brenna, be reasonable," he said, falling into step beside her.

"Go away."

"No. Not until you listen."

"There's nothing you can say that will make a difference," she said, fighting with everything she had not to cry.

When she reached her yard, she hurried toward the sanctuary of her home. Once she went inside and bolted the door, she could let her pent-up emotions break free without Dylan seeing how badly he'd hurt her.

But he stopped her by placing his hand flat on the door to hold it shut when she tried to open it. She struggled to pull it free, but no amount of tugging on her part would budge him.

"Dammit, Brenna, you're going to hear me out," he said, his expression a mixture of anger and frustration.

Turning on him, she shook her head. "No, I'm not."

"Yes, you are," he said, taking hold of her upper arms.

To her frustration, tears began to fill her eyes. She blinked them away. She would not let him see her cry. "What's the point, Dylan? Are you hoping to assuage your conscience? Do you think that will make you feel better about what you've done?"

"I haven't done anything," he insisted.

Emotional pain like she'd never known tore through her. "Oh, really? You didn't follow orders? You haven't been with me for the past four weeks, hoping to learn something the men could use to stop the Main Street Project?"

"It wasn't like that," he said, shaking his head. "Yes, I was told to find out what you knew about the women's plans. But if you'll remember, I never questioned you about it.''

''Because you didn't ask me about it, you think that makes what you've done all right?'' she asked incredulously. ''You kissed me, you made love to me only because you were ordered to spend time with me.'' Her voice shook, but she didn't care. ''Do you have any idea how that makes me feel? How much it hurts to know that I gave myself to a man who was only using me in order to keep his job?''

''Now hold it right there, Brenna,'' he said, looking angry. ''What we have between us is real and has nothing to do with the orders I was given, the B.S. Club or the town. I've been with you because I wanted to be, because I care for you.''

''I wish I could believe that, Dylan,'' she said, feeling as if her heart was being torn in two. ''But I don't.''

''It's the truth,'' he said stubbornly. ''And if you'll think back, every time you started to talk about the project, I changed the subject.''

She shook her head. ''It doesn't matter. The fact remains that you allowed those men to think your role in all this was the reason for our being together. Not because you cared for me. You used me the same as Tom did.''

''No, I didn't,'' Dylan insisted. ''What goes on between the two of us is none of the council's business.'' He took a deep breath. ''Five years ago, I started seeing a woman who used my attraction to her in an effort to turn Tranquillity into a resort for people who have more money than good sense. She made a fool of me in front of the entire town. And believe me, I'd never put you through that kind of hell.''

"But you just did," Brenna said, pulling from his grasp. She shuddered from the strain of holding back the torrent of emotions threatening to break through. "I'm sorry I stumbled onto the scheme before you had the chance to make sure that your job was secure. Maybe the council members will take that into consideration when it's time for your next evaluation.''

"Darlin'—"

"Please don't," she interrupted, opening the door. "There's nothing left to say." Brenna took a deep breath in an effort to hold back her tears. "Granny and Pete should get home from their honeymoon sometime this evening. When they arrive, I'll have Pete give you a call."

"This isn't over, Brenna."

"Yes, it is." She had to get away from him before she fell completely apart. "Goodbye, Dylan."

Her heart breaking into a million pieces, Brenna entered the house, closed the door behind her, then leaned back against it. Shaking uncontrollably, she sank to the living room floor and covered her face with her hands. But when she heard the sound of Dylan's footsteps as he walked down the steps, as he walked away from her, the last of her control snapped and she gave free rein to the flood of tears she could no longer hold in check.

Dylan slowly descended the steps and started walking the six blocks back to the center of town. Was he guilty of what Brenna had accused him of? In his effort to maintain their privacy, had he cheapened the relationship they'd developed between them with his silence? Had he betrayed her trust by not making it clear to Myron and the council members that he had been seeing her because he wanted to, not because he'd been ordered to?

Since that incident five years ago, he'd done his damnedest to keep his private life separate from his position as sheriff. And up until the last month, he'd been successful.

But that was before everyone he knew started meddling in his and Brenna's lives. At first it had been his uncle and her grandmother playing matchmakers in order to get them together. Then when the mayor's wife and a handful of her friends decided to make a few harmless changes around town, the town council had gotten in on the act and ordered him to find out what Brenna knew in their effort to stop their wives.

And despite all the interference, all the subterfuge, he and Brenna had managed to fall in love.

Dylan stopped dead in his tracks. He took a deep breath, then another. He knew she'd gotten under his skin. But when had he fallen in love with her?

He shook his head as he resumed walking. It didn't matter when he'd given Brenna his heart. He had. And he'd be damned before he let any more well-meaning souls destroy what they had between them.

He smiled determinedly. And that included Brenna.

Ten

On Christmas Eve, Brenna sat staring at the huge bowl of chocolate rum balls her grandmother placed on the table in front of her. For the first time in her life, Brenna wasn't even tempted by the taste of chocolate.

"Pete, cover that bowl with plastic wrap while I cut the fudge," Abigail instructed. Stopping to adjust her Santa hat, she turned to Brenna. "You'd better start getting ready for the Jubilee."

"Jamboree," Brenna corrected.

"Whatever," her grandmother said, waving her hand dismissively. "If you don't get the lead out you're going to be late."

Brenna shook her head as she rose to go to her room. "I'm not going."

"You have to go, Brenna," Pete said, struggling

to tear the plastic wrap from the carton. "If you don't, who's gonna read to the kids?"

"Anyone can read *'Twas the Night Before Christmas* and the children will listen," she said shrugging.

"But you're the Story Lady," Pete argued. Brenna watched him exchange a look with her grandmother, then place the box of plastic wrap on the table. "I think I'll mosey on into the livin' room to...to..." He paused for a moment, then grinned sheepishly. "Aw, shoot. I'll find somethin' to do."

Brenna watched him kiss Abigail's cheek, then saunter from the room. "You can save your breath, Granny," she said, anticipating Abigail's argument that she attend the community party. "I'm not going."

Abigail motioned for her to sit down at the table, then plopped down in the chair across from her. "Brenna, as long as you continue living in Tranquillity you're going to run into Dylan from time to time." Leave it to her grandmother to cut right to the heart of the matter.

"It's just..." Brenna took a deep breath. "It's too soon."

"I know it hurts, honey," Abigail said, reaching out to cover Brenna's hand with hers. "But you have to face seeing him sometime. And the longer you put it off, the harder it's going to be when you do."

Moisture filled her eyes, but Brenna blinked it away. She'd already cried enough in the past week to fill a river, and she was determined not to shed another tear. "Maybe I'll move."

Abigail snorted and said a word that under different

circumstances would have shocked Brenna. "I didn't raise you to run from your problems."

"I'm not running from them," Brenna said defensively. "I'm just trying to survive them."

"Then face them head-on, deal with what you have to and move forward," Abigail said staunchly. "Show this town what kind of backbone you have."

Brenna shrugged. "That's what Cornelia said when she stopped by the shop this morning to tell me how sorry she was for what her husband and the town council tried to do."

"How many times does that make?"

"Between Cornelia, Emily Taylor and Helen Washburn, I've been apologized to every day this week." Brenna shook her head. "How could something as harmless as painting a few fire hydrants and putting up a handful of decorative signs cause so many problems?"

"I don't know." Her grandmother shook her head. "When Pete dropped by Luke's yesterday afternoon, he said the men were all stopping in for their supper." At Brenna's questioning look, Abigail laughed. "Apparently Cornelia, Emily and Helen are getting even with their husbands by refusing to cook. And Myron Worthington is hobbling around, complaining to anyone who will listen to him about a loose spring in a sofa."

Brenna groaned. "This power struggle between the women and men just keeps getting worse."

Grinning, Abigail nodded. "I can't wait to see what happens tonight."

"Granny!"

"Nothing like a good feud to liven up a party,"

Abigail said, rising to her feet. "Now, go get ready or you'll miss the fun."

"I might as well," Brenna said, sighing heavily as she rose to her feet. "You're not going to let me alone until I do, are you?"

"Nope." Abigail shook her head so vigorously that her bright orange curls bounced beneath her Santa hat. "Besides, it would be a waste of a good elf costume if you don't go."

Brenna shook her head as she walked into her room. She should have known her grandmother would keep after her until she gave in and got ready for the party.

As she slipped into the short elf dress, tights and green high-heeled boots with white fur trim, one thing kept running through her mind. Dylan would be at the celebration.

She bit her lower lip to stop its trembling as she tied the big red bows at the top of her boots. In the past week, she'd thought a lot about what he'd told her after she stumbled across the meeting being held in his office.

It was true that he'd never questioned her about the Main Street Project. In fact, he had avoided any mention of it, unless she brought it up. And reliving every moment of their time together, she had to admit that he'd never allowed her to tell him what the women were planning. He'd either quickly changed the subject, or kissed her into silence every time she'd tried to talk about the project.

After thinking of nothing else for an entire week, she'd even come to terms with, and understood, the precarious position he'd found himself in with the town council. He'd been stuck in the middle of the whole mess and forced to walk a fine line in order to keep everyone happy. Not an easy place to be, nor was it an easy task to undertake.

On one hand, he'd been trying to placate the mayor and town council members in order to keep a job he loved. And on the other hand, he'd tried his best not to betray her faith and trust in him while sidestepping their directive.

And she'd even come to understand his not making the councilmen aware of his relationship with her. After suffering the public humiliation he'd been forced to endure five years ago, she couldn't blame him for wanting to keep that part of his life private.

But all of her realization had come too late. She hadn't seen or heard from Dylan in a week. If that didn't speak volumes about his reluctance to give their relationship another chance, she didn't know what did.

Her breath caught on a soft sob. There was no way she could spend the entire evening watching Dylan, loving him, and not humiliate herself by falling apart.

She felt a tear trickle down her cheek and impatiently wiped it away with the back of her hand. She'd appease everyone and attend the Christmas Jamboree tonight, but she wouldn't stay. She'd read a story to the children, help whoever played Santa pass out the presents, then leave.

Dylan stood on the far side of the community room, watching the door, and the minute Brenna, Pete and Abigail walked in, his body tensed. He damned near crushed his cup of punch. Brenna looked good in the little green elf dress with white fur trim. Damned good. But as far as he was concerned, she looked good in, or out of, just about anything she wore.

The skirt brushed the middle of her thighs and the fluffy white fur around the collar touched her satiny smooth skin like he longed to do. His body tightened. He'd like nothing more than to throw her over his shoulder, find a nice secluded spot and make love to her until she came to her senses.

He barely managed to swallow back the groan threatening to escape. He'd decided to give her some time before he tried to once again get through to her. But how was he ever going to get through the evening without holding her, loving her?

"How's it goin', boy?" Pete asked, strolling over to stand next to him.

"About the same." Dylan took a swig of punch from the bent plastic cup. "How are things with you, Uncle Pete?"

"Good." They stood in silence for several minutes before his uncle shook his head. "Dang it, why don't you come right out and ask?"

Dylan feigned ignorance as he watched old Corny and her hens surround Brenna, then usher her over to where they'd been sitting. "Ask what?"

Pete snorted. "Aw, hell, boy. We both know you're dyin' to know about Brenna. Why don't you stop pussyfootin' around and ask me?"

Unable to take his eyes off her, Dylan shrugged. "Then why don't you just tell me and save both of us some time, Uncle Pete?"

"All righty, I will," Pete said, sounding irritated. "She's about the most miserable little gal I think I ever did see. Abby had to talk herself blue, just to get Brenna to come here tonight.''

Dylan's gut twisted. Knowing that he'd been the cause of her misery just about tore him apart. ''She wasn't going to attend the Jamboree?''

''Nope.'' Pete rocked back on his heels. ''And in case anybody wants to know, it wouldn't surprise me if she don't hightail it out of here as soon as she reads to the kids and helps pass out presents.''

''Looks like the feud is still in full swing,'' Abigail said, coming to stand next to Pete. ''With the women on one side of the room and the men huddled up on the other, I'd say the battlelines are drawn.''

Dylan had heard, first hand, about all the trouble Myron, Ed and Luke had encountered when their wives learned of their plot to end the Main Street Project. All week long, he'd listened to Myron whine about sleeping on that damned couch, until Dylan had been ready to go out and buy the man another one just to shut him up. And when Ed and Luke arrived earlier in the evening with Emily and Helen, they'd immediately split up with the women going one way and the men another.

''Pete, let's grab those two chairs over by the punch bowl,'' Abigail said excitedly. ''Unless I miss my guess, something's about to pop loose and I want a good seat.''

As Pete and Abigail hurried across the room to the chairs lined against the wall closest to the refreshment table, Dylan watched Brenna and the women walk over to the punch bowl. Glancing in the opposite direction, he saw the men head straight for them. It looked like Abigail was right, he decided when Cornelia and her hens started bobbing their heads and pointing their fingers, while Myron, Ed and Luke wore deep scowls and shook their heads in obvious disagreement.

Dylan watched as Brenna stood in the middle of all of it, her head turning from one side to the other as the debate heated up. She looked helpless and on the verge of tears.

"That's it," he said, tossing the cup in the trash as he walked toward the gathering crowd and the woman he loved.

Brenna cringed as the knot of people gathering in front of the refreshment table grew. It seemed that everyone had an opinion about the fire hydrants and street signs.

"I like the changes," a woman spoke up from the edge of the crowd. "I can't wait to see what the Beautification Society does for other holidays."

"How in the name of Sam Hill can you say that?" a man's voice countered disgustedly. "They're the silliest things I've ever laid eyes on."

"Please don't argue," Brenna said, in an effort to stop the escalating debate. But her voice was lost in all the noise as everyone stated their feelings.

"It's all her fault," an angry male voice rose above the din. "If she hadn't got the B.S. Club all stirred up, this never woulda happened."

"Now, hold it right there!"

At the sound of Dylan's baritone booming over the bedlam, Brenna looked up to see him shouldering his way toward her.

When she'd first walked into the community room,

she'd seen him standing alone on the far side of the room. She'd noticed that he had on the blue sports jacket and black jeans that he'd worn for her grandmother and Pete's wedding. He'd looked so handsome that she'd had to look away.

After that, she'd carefully avoided looking his direction. It simply hurt too much to love him, knowing there was no chance for them to work things out between them.

When he walked up to her, the brim of his black Resistol dipped slightly as he gave her an almost imperceptible nod. Her heart skipped a beat. What was he going to do?

Turning to face the crowd, he shook his head. "Brenna Montgomery didn't start this fight by teaching the women how to paint, or by taking charge when they *asked* for her help." He glanced down at her and the intense determination in his green eyes stole her breath. He was coming to her defense. "The only thing she's guilty of is wanting to find her place in Tranquillity and trying to become one of us." He pushed the brim of his hat up with his thumb, then propped his fists on his hips as he frowned at the crowd. "Although judging by the way you're all acting this evening, it's a mystery to me why she'd even want to bother."

She watched in disbelief as he pulled the lapel of his sports jacket aside to remove the silver star pinned to his shirt. "Dylan?"

The smile he gave her brought tears to her eyes. "It's all right, darlin'." Turning to the mayor, Dylan tossed the man his badge. "I've been proud to serve Tranquillity for the past six years, but when the town becomes more important than the people in it, I'm done.''

Obviously dumbstruck, everyone fell silent as they awaited a reaction from Myron Worthington. The only sound in the room came from a group of small children playing in the corner close to the Christmas tree.

''Now, Dylan—''

Dylan shook his head as he put his arm around Brenna's shoulders. ''Myron, when it comes to a choice between this town and the woman I love, there's no contest. Tranquillity will come in a distant second every time.''

Brenna felt as if the floor had dropped from beneath her feet and she wasn't sure she'd heard him correctly. Had Dylan just admitted he loved her in front of the entire town?

But she couldn't allow him to give up his job as sheriff. It meant too much to him.

Reaching out, she took the badge from the mayor and handed it back to Dylan. ''I can't let you do this, Dylan.'' Her voice caught, but she pressed on as she turned back to face the crowd. ''I know how much Dylan loves Tranquillity. How much he loves all of you. And being your sheriff means too much to him for me to let him resign.''

''Darlin'—''

She placed her finger to his lips. ''I'll take full responsibility for the fire hydrants and street signs, and I'll even close my shop and leave if that's what it takes to restore peace to the town.'' She rose up on tiptoes to brush his lips with hers. ''But I can't let them accept your resignation. I love you too much for that, Dylan.''

''Oh, that's the sweetest thing I've ever heard,'' Cornelia said tearfully. Turning to her husband, she demanded, ''Myron, say something.''

''Now…now, see here,'' the man stammered. ''There's no reason for anybody to go quittin' their job or leavin' town.''

''No reason at all,'' Luke Washburn said, his eyes looking slightly moist.

''Put that badge back on, Dylan,'' Ed Taylor said, his voice hoarse. ''We'll work this out.''

Dylan pulled her into his arms. ''What do you say, Brenna? Are we going to be able to work all this out?''

Tears flowed down her cheeks as Brenna gazed up at the man she loved with all her heart. ''I think there's a good probability that we will,'' she said, smiling.

''Good enough for me,'' he said, his heated gaze sending a shiver of longing down her spine. ''Darlin', will you do me the honor of being my wife?''

If Brenna thought the room fell silent when Dylan handed the mayor his badge, it couldn't compare to the hush that fell over the crowd as they awaited her answer. Even the children milling around the Christmas tree in the corner seemed to pause as if they sensed something significant was about to take place.

Tears ran unchecked down her cheeks as she threw her arms around his neck. ''Dylan, if it were possible, I'd marry you right here, tonight. Yes, I'll be your wife.''

An immediate cheer rose from the citizens of Tranquillity and it took several minutes for everyone to settle down after congratulating the happy couple.

"Brenna?"

Turning at the sound of her name, Brenna watched Mildred Bruner come forward. "Did you mean it when you said you'd marry Dylan tonight if it were possible?"

Glancing up at his handsome face, Brenna turned back to Mildred. "Yes, I would."

"What about you, dear?" Mildred asked Dylan.

Brenna watched him nod without hesitation. "I wish we could get married tonight, Mildred. But as county clerk, you know there's a three-day waiting period from the time the marriage license is issued until a couple can exchange vows."

"That's true," the woman admitted. "But if a district judge waives the waiting period, a couple can get married right away."

His grin wide, Pete walked up to slap Dylan on the back at the same time Abigail hugged Brenna. "Judge Bertrand's ranch is only seven miles from here," Pete said thoughtfully.

"He owes me a favor," Myron said, looking pleased. "Me, Ed and Luke can take a run up that way and have him back here in an hour."

Dylan gave Brenna a look that curled her toes inside her green Christmas boots. "Do you still carry your book of certificates with you, Mildred?" he asked.

Mildred nodded. "A body never knows when it might come in handy."

His slow grin made Brenna's heart skip a beat.

"What do you say, darlin'? Would you like to get married tonight?"

"Yes," she said without a moment's hesitation.

Dylan gave her a quick kiss a moment before everyone seemed to start talking at once.

Cornelia stepped forward, and barking orders that would have made any wedding planner proud, took charge. Dispatching Myron, Ed and Luke to get the judge, she set the ladies of the Beautification Society to the task of turning the Christmas Jamboree into a wedding, while an ecstatic Abigail hustled Brenna home to change out of the elf costume.

An hour later, wearing the green dress she'd worn for Pete and her grandmother's wedding, and holding a bouquet of red and white silk rosebuds, Brenna stood in the hallway outside of the community room.

"Brenna, you make a mighty pretty bride," Pete said, his faded blue eyes suspiciously bright.

"Of course, she does, you old goat." Abigail placed a garland of white baby's breath on Brenna's head. "She's my granddaughter."

Pete chuckled. "And Dylan's a handsome young buck because he's my nephew."

"I can't believe this is happening," Brenna murmured, her head spinning from the events of the last hour.

The muted sound of "Here Comes the Bride" filtered from the community room a moment before Cornelia opened the door. "Your groom awaits, Brenna."

Abigail gave her a watery smile and patted her

cheek, then turned and slowly walked through the door.

"Ready, gal?" Pete asked, holding his arm out for her to take.

Tucking her hand in the crook of his arm, Brenna nodded. "I've never been more ready for anything in my life."

When Pete escorted her through the door, the citizens of Tranquillity parted into two groups to form an aisle. Brenna looked for, and found, Dylan standing next to Judge Bertrand on the far side of the candlelit room by the Christmas tree. Lights on the tree twinkled behind him, but she barely noticed. The glow of love she saw in his emerald eyes held her captive as she walked toward the man she loved.

"Are you ready to make this a Christmas Jamboree that Tranquillity will never forget?" Dylan asked as he took her hand from Pete.

"I've never been more ready for anything in my life," she said, tears of happiness blurring her vision. "I love you, Dylan Chandler."

"And I love you, darlin'." He placed a soft kiss on the back of her hand, then giving her a smile that warmed her all the way to her soul, he said, "Let's get married."

Epilogue

Christmas Eve, one year later

Dylan smiled fondly as he watched Brenna slowly lower herself into a chair beside the Christmas tree, then pick up the book she'd selected to read to the kids before Santa Claus made his big entrance at the Christmas Jamboree. He'd have never believed it possible, but he loved her more today than he had the day he'd made her his wife.

"Brenna looks very pretty tonight," Mayor Worthington said, coming to stand next to Dylan.

"Yes, she does, Cornelia," he said proudly. He glanced over at the first female elected to the position of mayor in Tranquillity's one hundred and fifty year history. "Where's Myron?"

"He's putting on his suit." Cornelia laughed. "He

complained that it's a tradition for the mayor to play Santa at the Jamboree, but the council members and I decided that it would be best if he continued, since I wouldn't be as convincing as he is.''

Dylan grinned. "I heard the women also voted to have Luke and Ed play Santa's helpers this year, too."

"Emily made the motion and Helen seconded it," Cornelia said, giving him a smug smile.

Cornelia moved on to talk to some of her other constituents and Dylan turned his attention back to watching Brenna. When she finally closed the over-size book she'd been reading, Santa Claus appeared at the back of the room, right on cue, and the kids turned their attention on Myron and his two disgruntled-looking elves as they carried brightly wrapped presents to place under the Christmas tree.

As Pete and Abigail passed him on their way to the punch bowl, Pete laughed. "Did you ever see a more bowlegged elf than Ed Taylor?"

Laughing Dylan shook his head. "In those green tights, he's a real sight, that's for sure."

"If you ask me, Luke's the one who's a sight," Abigail said, pointing toward the three men passing out presents. "There's a good two inches of his belly shining between the bottom of his green T-shirt and the top of his pants."

"What time is it?" Brenna asked, waddling over to join them.

Checking his watch, Dylan told her the time, then placed his arms around her shoulders. "Are you getting tired?"

She shook her head as she placed her hand over her swollen belly. "No. Just checking."

"This is a lot different than last year's Jubilee, isn't it?" Abigail asked, sounding disappointed.

"Jamboree," Brenna, Dylan and Pete corrected in unison.

"Whatever." Abigail waved her hand dismissively. "It's not nearly as exciting. Nobody's feuding and no one's getting married."

"It can't be excitin' every year, sugar," Pete said, kissing Abigail's cheek.

Dylan hugged Brenna close, then kissed the top of her head. "As far as I'm concerned, there will never be another Jamboree as special as that one."

"Never say never," Brenna said, laughing breathlessly.

"So what did the doctor tell you today?" Abigail asked. "Is my first great-grandchild going to be a Christmas baby or a New Year's baby?"

Smiling down at the woman he loved more than life itself, Dylan covered Brenna's hand where it rested over their child. "He said it could be any time."

Brenna nodded. "All we know for sure is that the baby is a little girl."

"A girl?" Pete grinned. "If she's as pretty as her momma and great-grandma, we'll be beatin' the boys back with a stick, Dylan."

Dylan's eyebrow began to twitch and his gut twisted into a tight knot. "I'm getting an ulcer just thinking about it."

"Have you picked out a name?" Abigail asked.

"We're leaning toward Noelle," Brenna answered. She rubbed her lower back before asking, "What time is it now, Dylan?"

He laughed. "It's five minutes later than the last

time you asked. Why? Do you have somewhere you need to be?''

Brenna nodded and the grin on her beautiful face made Dylan feel as if he'd been punched in the gut. ''The hospital.''

''Are you sure?'' he asked, feeling as if his knees might not support him.

''Yes, darling,'' Brenna said calmly. ''I've been in labor for the last two hours.''

''Hot damn! Get the car, Pete,'' Abigail said happily. ''Looks like we might have some excitement tonight after all.''

Four hours later, in the wee hours of Christmas morning, Noelle Dyanne Chandler was born and placed into her father's waiting arms. Staring down at the most beautiful baby he'd ever seen, Dylan's chest tightened and moisture filled his eyes. He'd always been a sucker for redheads, and now he had two in his life—Brenna and his new baby daughter.

''Is she all right?'' Brenna asked anxiously.

Kissing the top of his wife's head, Dylan grinned. ''She's perfect in every way. Just like her mother.''

Brenna gave him a watery smile as he laid the baby in her arms. ''It looks like we disrupted the Christmas Jamboree again this year.''

Happier than he'd ever been in his life, Dylan grinned. ''Your grandmother's already speculating on what we'll do for next year's party.''

''That figures,'' Brenna said, sounding tired. ''Are she and Pete still out in the waiting room?''

Dylan nodded. ''I think half of Tranquillity is out there with them, too.''

''Are you serious?'' she asked, obviously shocked.

"Yep." He smiled as he touched his baby daughter's soft cheek. "They all wanted to know that you were going to be all right, and to welcome the town's newest resident." Dylan chuckled. "They were in such a hurry to get here that Cornelia, Emily and Helen wouldn't even give Myron, Ed and Luke time to change clothes. They're still dressed like Santa and his elves."

"I can't believe they all came to the hospital to wait," Brenna said, laughing.

"Darlin', don't you know what you mean to all of them?" Dylan asked, brushing a strand of copper hair from her porcelain cheek. "They love you almost as much as I do."

He watched tears fill her pretty blue eyes. "I love you, Dylan."

"And I love you, Brenna," Dylan said, leaning down to place a tender kiss on her sweet lips. "With every breath I take, I love you."

* * * * *

Scrooge and the Single Girl

CHRISTINE RIMMER

CHRISTINE RIMMER

came to her profession the long way around. Before settling down to write about the magic of romance, she'd been an actress, a sales assistant, a janitor, a model, a phone sales representative, a teacher, a waitress, a playwright and an office manager. Now that she's finally found work that suits her perfectly she insists she never had a problem keeping a job – she was merely gaining "life experience" for her future as a novelist. Christine is grateful not only for the joy she finds in writing, but for what waits when the day's work is through: a man she loves, who loves her right back, and the privilege of watching their children grow and change day to day. She lives with her family in Oklahoma.

In loving memory of
the house my mother was born in, a house
we filled with our family memories,
the house we always called the
Old House.

Chapter One

Jillian Diamond left Sacramento at a little after two on that cold, clear Sunday afternoon in late December. She was barely out of town before the sky began to darken.

In the foothills, a light snow was falling. The fluffy flakes blew down, swirling in the gray sky, melting the instant they hit the windshield.

Jilly cast a quick glance at the seat beside her. "Voilà, Missy. Snow."

Miss Demeanor, a small calico cat with one mangled ear and an ordinarily pleasant disposition, glared at her mistress through the screened door of the carrier that held her prisoner. Missy did not enjoy traveling.

Jilly faced the road again and continued, as if Missy cared, "Snow is good, you know that. Snow is part of the plan."

The plan was this: Take one creative, contented single woman, add Christmas in an idyllic setting, mix well and come up with...a column. Or maybe an article, something suitable for the slicks. Options, at this point, were wide open.

And no, this was not to be your usual desperate, club-hopping *singleton's* Christmas, not your ho-hum lonely career girl wandering aimlessly in a coupled-up world, with humor. Not your predictable tale of meaningless sexual encounters with guys who have it all—except for a heart. That was only what Jilly's editor at the *Sacramento Press-Telegram* had asked for in the first place.

Jilly had told him no way. "Listen, Frank. I don't care if half the time it seems to me that that's my life, exactly. It's not going in the *Press-Telegram* for everyone I know—not to mention two hundred and fifty thousand strangers—to read about." She'd shot back a counter-proposal: the *happy* single girl's Christmas. That is, Jillian and her cat and a Christmas tree, perfectly content all on their own, in some quiet, scenic, isolated place.

Frank had had the bad taste to stifle a yawn. "On second thought, never mind."

So fine. Jilly decided she would do it on spec and sell it next year.

Which was why she and Missy were all packed up in her 4Runner, heading toward a certain secluded old house high in the Sierras, on the Nevada side of Lake Tahoe.

And the weather was cooperating nicely. Because, of course, for Christmas with the contented single girl, there should be snow, and it should be drifting attractively down outside a big picture window.

Too bad Jilly got going on this project a little late, thus necessitating settling for a setting a tad less than ideal. Most likely, there wouldn't be any picture windows in this particular house. But Jilly was okay with that. She'd have mountains and pine trees and lovely, sparkly white snow. For the rest, she'd make do. She fed a Christmas CD into the stereo, pumped up the volume good and high and sang right along with Boyz II Men.

"Let it snow, let it snow, let it snow...."

Which it did. The snow came down harder. Thicker. It was starting to stick, too. Jilly turned on the wipers and slid in another Christmas CD.

By the time she reached Echo Summit, she found herself driving through a true snowstorm. But the Chains Required signs weren't up yet. Traffic was still moving right along. And she had four-wheel drive, so she was doing all right. Night was falling. Her headlights, set on auto, switched themselves on.

It was after she left the highway, not too far beyond Tahoe Village, that things started to get scary. But not *too* scary. She was handling it. At first.

Caitlin Bravo, a stunning and frequently overbearing woman on the far side of fifty, owned the house Jilly was looking for. Caitlin had provided detailed instructions for finding the place. There were a number of small, twisting mountain roads to navigate, but Jilly had it all mapped out. It should have been a piece of cake.

It *would* have been a piece of cake. In daylight, minus the blizzard.

Jilly turned off the Christmas music and tried the radio, but almost ran herself off the road in her effort to tune in the weather and drive at the same time. And really, she'd gone a little past the point where a weather report would do her much good. The view out her windshield told her more than she wanted to know. She should have checked the forecast a little earlier— like before she left Sacramento. It was a problem she had and she knew it. Sometimes she'd forget to look into important details in her enthusiasm to get going on a project that enticed her.

"So shoot me," she muttered as she switched off the radio. She focused all her concentration on the snakelike, narrow road as it materialized before her in the glare of her low beams. She was deep in the forest now, pines and firs looming thick and shadowed on either side of the road.

She missed a turn and didn't realize it until five or six miles later. Slowing to a crawl so she wouldn't miss it again, she backtracked, searching. She found it. And then missed the next one, had to backtrack, found the turn at last, felt her flagging spirits lifting— only to realize she'd missed *another* one.

On the seat beside her, Missy was not pleased. Irritated whines had begun to issue from the cat carrier.

"Missy honey, I am doing the best I can, all right?"

The cat only meowed back at her, a petulant sort of sound.

"I'll get us there, I promise you. And then it's a nice, big bowl of Fancy Feast for my favorite girl."

Missy said nothing. Just as well. Jilly needed all her attention focused on the next turn—which, for once, she actually found the first time around. She drove on, winding her way up and down the sides of mountains.

At last, at a few minutes after six, a good hour past the time she should have reached it, she found the rutted, snow-drifted dirt driveway that led to her destination. Her stomach growled. She thought of the bags of groceries in back. They contained ingredients for a number of gourmet meals. Gourmet, after all, had seemed the best way to go for this project.

Too bad what she longed for right now was some Dinty Moore chili, or maybe a big can of—

Jilly let out a startled cry and stomped on the brake as a doe leapt from the cover of the trees and directly into her path.

Luckily, she managed to stop before she hit it. And then it did what a deer always does. It froze directly in front of her vehicle and stared into the beams of her headlights, an expression of total surprise and dumb-animal disbelief in those big, sweet, bulging brown eyes.

Jilly rolled down her window, stuck her head out into the freezing storm and yelled, "Go on, you! Get out of here! Get lost before I make a jacket out of you!"

The doe blinked and took off, disappearing into the leafless bushes and pine trees at the other side of the driveway. Jilly pulled her head back inside, rolled up the window and brushed the snow out of her hair. Then she drove on, straining to see, the snow hitting the windshield so hard and thick, there was nothing but whiteness three feet beyond her front bumper.

The driveway was very long. Or at least, it seemed that way in the dark, with near-zero visibility. Jilly rolled along with great care, hunched over the steering wheel, peering into the wall of white in front of her, trying not to run into a pine tree or another startled deer.

Okay, truth. She was getting worried. She could end up snowed in up here in the middle of nowhere, with nobody but Missy to turn to. "Oh, not good," she murmured under her breath. "Not good at all...."

But then she reminded herself that she did have her cell phone, that people knew where the old house was and knew she was headed there. She would be all right. She could call for help and get it eventually if it turned out she really needed it.

However, on the subject of the house, where *was* it? What if she'd somehow managed to miss it? What would happen if she—

And right then she saw it.

"Oh, thank you," she cried. "Thank you, thank you, thank you, God!"

Not twenty feet ahead, the driveway opened out into a clearing. And in the middle of the clearing she could make out the looming shadow of the old house, with its high-pitched roof and long, deep porches. Smoke trailed up from the chimney-pipe and the golden light inside shone like a beacon through the swirling, blinding—

Wait a minute.

The golden light inside?

The house was supposed to be unoccupied.

Jilly reached the clearing. She pulled in beside the vehicle already parked there. Then she turned off the engine and sat for a moment, staring at the lighted house as snow gathered on the windshield, obscuring her view. Who could be in there? What in the world was going on?

About then she turned her head and looked through her side window at the other car. The window was fogging up. She rubbed at it with her open palm and peered closer.

"Omigod."

It was Will Bravo's car. She was sure of it. It was a very distinctive car, the Mercedes Benz version of a sport utility vehicle. Silver in color. What did they call it? A G-Class, she thought.

Will Bravo's car.

Jilly shivered. Will was Caitlin's middle son. The *only* one of Caitlin's three sons who remained a bachelor, the other two having married Jilly's two dearest friends, Jane Elliott and Celia Tuttle.

Will Bravo's car....

Everything was starting to make way too much sense. "Caitlin, how could you?" Jilly whispered under her breath. She felt tricked. Used. Thoroughly manipulated.

She grabbed her purse from the floor in front of the passenger seat and fumbled through it until she came up with her phone. She'd stored Caitlin's number, just in case she might need it. She punched it up. But when she put the phone to her ear, instead of ringing at the other end, all she got was static.

Jilly yanked the device away from her ear and glared at it. Terrific. So much for being able to count on her cell.

Missy meowed.

Jilly shoved the phone back in her purse, stuck her arm over the seat and got her coat and hat. She pulled on the coat and jammed the hat on her head. Then she hooked her purse over one shoulder, grabbed the cat carrier, leaned on her door and climbed out into the raging storm.

Chapter Two

Will Bravo was just about to sit down to his solitary dinner of franks and beans, with a copy of *Crime and Punishment* for company, when someone knocked on the kitchen door.

What the…?

His grandmother's cabin was off the beaten path in every way. To get there, you had to have directions. Even when the weather was good, nobody ever just dropped in. Which was why he was here in the first place. He wanted to be left alone.

Whoever it was knocked some more.

Will went over and pulled open the door, and Jillian Diamond blew in on a huge gust of snow-laden wind. She was wearing a red wool hat, a big shearling coat, faded overalls, lace-up boots and a red-and-green striped sweater with a row of red reindeer embroidered on the turtleneck collar. In her left hand, she clutched an animal carrier from which suspicious meowing sounds were issuing.

Will couldn't believe this. "What the hell are *you* doing here?"

Now, wasn't that going to be fun to explain? Jilly thought. She caught the door and pushed it shut, then set Missy's carrier on the warped linoleum floor, sliding her purse off her shoulder and dropping it next to her unhappy cat.

"I asked you what you're doing here," Will demanded for the second time.

She didn't know where to start, so she countered provokingly, "I could ask you the same question."

He studied her for a moment, his head tipped sideways. And then he folded his big arms across his broad chest and informed her, "I'm here every year from the twenty-second or twenty-third until the day after New Year's."

Jilly swiped her hat off her head and beat it against her leg to shake off the snow. "Well, sorry. I honestly didn't know."

He grunted. "You could have asked anyone. My mother—" Oh my, Jilly thought, surprise, surprise. "—my brothers. Even, more than likely, your two best friends."

"Oh, really?"

"Yeah. Really."

"Well, this may come as a rude shock to you, but asking if you were going to be here never even occurred to me." Yeah, okay. Maybe it *should* have occurred to her. Given what she knew about Caitlin

Bravo, it all seemed achingly obvious now. But that was called hindsight and it and $3.49 would get you a *venti* latte at Starbuck's.

He was glaring at her, as if he suspected her of all kinds of awful things, as if he didn't believe a word she had said. She didn't even want to look at him.

So she didn't. She looked away, and found herself staring at the single place-setting and the thick hard-bound book waiting on the ancient drop-leaf table about three feet from the door. Delicious comfort food smells issued from the pot on the stove.

"Answer my question," he growled at her. "What are you doing here?"

From the carrier, Missy meowed plaintively. "Look," Jilly said with a sigh. "I'm sorry to have disturbed you. I swear I didn't have a clue that you were going to be here."

He made a low scoffing sound. Jilly could see it all, right there in his gorgeous, lagoon-blue eyes. He thought she was *after* him. He believed she *had* known that he was staying here, that she'd followed him up here to the middle of nowhere to try and hook up with him.

She threw up both hands. "Think what you want to think. The deal is, though I truly hate to put you out, it's very bad out there. I'm stuck here for the night and we both know it."

He did more scowling and glaring. Then at last he gave in and muttered grudgingly, "You're right. You're going nowhere tonight."

Oh, thank you so much for admitting the obvious, she thought. She said, "Right now, I need to get a few things in from my car." Missy meowed again. "Like a litter box and some cat food, for starters."

"All right. That's reasonable." Various coats and wool scarves hung on a line of wooden pegs beside the door. He grabbed a hooded down jacket. "Let's go."

Nothing would have given her more pleasure than to tell him she didn't need his help. But there was her pride—and then there were her suitcases, the cat supplies and the various exotic lettuces and veggies and the hormone-free fresh turkey she'd brought to roast for her happy single-girl's Christmas feast. And what about that bottle of good pinot grigio she'd bought to enjoy with her Christmas dinner, not to mention the pricey champagne she'd bought to toast the New Year? No way she was leaving them outside to freeze. If she trekked everything in alone, it would take two trips, maybe three. And it really was cold out there.

"Thank you," she said tightly as she stuck her hat back on her head.

Outside, even under the protection provided by the porch, the icy wind seemed to cut the frozen night like the blade of a bitterly sharp knife. Once they moved off the porch and into the open clearing, it got worse. They struggled against the wind, getting beaten in the face with freezing snow, finding no shelter as they passed beneath the single bare maple tree between the vehicles and the cars. It wasn't really all that far; it only felt like a hundred miles.

When they reached the cars at last, she went around to the rear of her Toyota and lifted the hatch. She passed him a twenty-pound bag of cat litter and another bag containing cat food and a plastic litter box. He managed to handle all that with one arm, so she also gave him the smaller of her two suitcases—it had her pjs in it, and a change of underwear, all she'd need for one night. Then, after giving him a backhanded wave meant to dismiss him, she turned to the bags of groceries and started going through them, consolidating the food items that had to go inside.

Will hadn't budged. "What the hell are you doing?" he yelled at her over the howling of the wind.

"Just go on inside!" she shouted back.

But of course, he didn't. What was it about some men? Congenitally incapable of following instructions.

"I asked you what the hell you're doing!"

So she told him. "Perishables!"

He didn't say anything after that. Just stood there, looking at her, eyes narrowed, mouth turned down at the corners, ice collecting in his bronze eyebrows, his ears and that handsome blade of a nose turning Rudolph-red.

Jilly turned back to her bags of groceries. It didn't take all that long to get everything that wouldn't hold up in a freezing car down to four plastic bags—one of them being the turkey. She hefted the bags out of the car and shut the hatch.

"Here," Will shouted. "Give me—"

"No," she hollered back. "I've got the rest. Let's go."

He gave her another of those dark, mean looks he was so good at. Now what? He was peeved because she wouldn't let him carry the heaviest load? Was there no end to reasons for this man to be mad at her?

She turned her back on him and started for the porch. He was right behind her when she got to the front door. She set down the bags in her right hand to reach for the knob—and his hand came around and grabbed it first. She resisted the urge to glare at him over her shoulder. He pushed the door inward. She picked up her bags again and stepped inside.

It only took a few minutes to set up Missy's comfort station in a corner of the bathroom, which was right off the kitchen. She let the cat out of the carrier as she dished up the Fancy Feast and filled a water bowl.

Once Missy was taken care of, Jilly joined her in the bathroom, shutting the door on Will, who was standing by the ancient drop-leaf kitchen table, staring bleakly at the bags of groceries.

Jilly used the facilities and washed her hands. When she entered the kitchen again, he'd moved her grocery bags to the long counter beside the darling, classic-looking round-sided Frigidaire. "What is this turkey doing in here?" he demanded.

"The rumba?" she suggested cheerfully.

He opened the Frigidaire and began stashing her lettuce and vegetables inside. "You know what I mean. You could have left it in your car."

"No way. If I'd wanted a frozen turkey, I would have bought one. That's a free-range, all-natural *fresh* turkey and it's going to stay that way."

He grumbled something under his breath. She couldn't make it out and decided it was probably better if she didn't try. He moved stuff around on one of the shelves in the fridge, then he picked up the turkey, stuck it inside and shut the door. "All right. Your cat is taken care of and the food's put away. I'm going to eat now. It's only franks and beans, but you're welcome to join me.''

Oh, how she longed to hold her head high and refuse. But Jilly really loved franks and beans. As far as she was concerned, franks and beans ranked right up there with Dinty Moore chili. With Kraft mac and cheese. With bacon burgers. With her hands-down favorite of all time: Cheez Doodles.

And speaking of Cheez Doodles, she had several bags of them stowed out in the 4Runner. She should have thought to bring some along when they were lugging everything else inside.

"Do you want the food or not?" her ungracious host inquired darkly.

"Yes," she said. "I do."

He got down a plate, dug a fork out of a drawer. "Milk?"

"Yes, please." She found a glass in a cupboard and poured it for herself. Then they sat down, put their paper napkins in their laps and dug in.

Oh, it was heaven. She hadn't realized how hungry she was. With effort, she restrained herself from making ecstatic groaning noises. At that moment, eating the hot, lovely food, she could almost be grateful that she'd found Will Bravo here, that she hadn't arrived to find it all dark and deserted, had to start the fire herself and worry about being all alone out here in this creaky old house while a blizzard raged outside and her cell phone was on the blink.

But then she looked up and caught him glaring at her and all her good will evaporated.

He said, "Now tell me. Why are you here?"

She shoved in another mouthful of beans, chewed them and swallowed. Then she gulped a little milk. Let him wait, she was thinking. It's not going to kill him. Outside, the wind wailed.

Will went on scowling. Good gravy. How could she ever have imagined she might get something going with him?

And okay, she'd admit it. At one time—up until just a couple of weeks ago, as a matter of fact—she'd cherished the doomed hope that she and Will might get it together.

They had seemed to have a lot in common. Both from the same hometown, which was New Venice, Nevada, in the Comstock Valley, about twenty miles away from this dreary old house, down a number of twisting, turning mountain roads. They had both settled, at least for now, in Sacramento. And then there was the most obvious connection: his two brothers had married her two best friends.

And also, well, she might as well admit it. She'd been blinded for a while there by the kinds of minor details that have made women fools for certain men since the dawn of time. Blinded by things like his good looks and his social veneer—okay, it was hard to believe, looking at him now, but Will Bravo could be a major charmer when he chose to be. And along with the charm, he had that slightly dangerous rep as one of those yummy bad Bravo boys. Oh, and she mustn't forget his impressive professional credentials: Will was an up-and-coming attorney on the Sacramento scene. For a while there, she'd dared to imagine that just maybe Will Bravo could turn out to be the man of her dreams.

But not anymore. Her eyes were wide open now. She saw him for what he really was: sour, sad and angry. Lost and alone—and determined to stay that way.

So let him. Tomorrow, when the storm was over, she'd pack up her Toyota, put Missy in her carrier and make tracks for home.

"Jillian," he said in a low, warning tone.

She set down her glass and wiped her mouth with her napkin. "All right. It was like this. I needed an isolated cabin for a holiday piece I'm working on."

He was staring at her, a sneering curl to his mouth. She knew what he thought of her. That she was shallow, one-dimensional, flighty in the extreme.

Far be it from her to disappoint him. "Originally, of course, I imagined a place with cable and central heat and a nice view of Lake Tahoe. One with a fully equipped kitchen and chef-quality appliances." She waved her fork airily. "Unfortunately, it's just been too crazy lately. One project after another, if you know what I mean. By the time I got around to making the arrangements, options were limited. More than limited. I couldn't find a place."

"So you called my mother."

"No. First, I called Celia."

He blinked. Then he gave out grudgingly, "Makes sense."

And it did. Celia Tuttle, who was now Celia Bravo, had spent most of her working life as a personal assistant, first to a television talk-show host and then to the man who was now her husband, Will's brother, Aaron. It was part of Celia's job to know how to find just about anything anyone might need on very short notice.

"Celia reminded me about this house," Jilly told him.

"And suggested that you give Caitlin a call." He was getting the whole thing into perspective now, she could see it in his face. He was accepting the fact that she had been tricked every bit as much as he had.

Caitlin Bravo was a hopeless matchmaker when it came to her sons. And Aaron and Cade were all taken care of now. Only Will had yet to find a wife.

The son in question nodded wearily. "Okay. You called Caitlin. She offered you this place."

Jilly nodded. "Your mother was smart. She played it just right. She told me all about how primitive the setup would be, reminded me of all the old stories about your grandmother." The house had once belonged to Caitlin's mother, Mavis McCormack, known to everyone in Will and Jilly's hometown as Mad Mavis. People whispered that Mad Mavis's ghost still haunted the old house. "But somehow," Jilly added, "your mother forgot to mention that you would be up here, too. Isn't that surprising?"

"Not in the least." Will stared at the woman across the table from him. She'd taken off her big coat and her funny hat, shoved up the sleeves of her red-and-green turtleneck and dug right into the food he'd offered her. She had wild brown hair with gold streaks in it and sparkly gray-blue eyes under thick, straight, almost-black eyebrows—eyebrows so heavy they should have bordered on ridiculous. Yet somehow, they didn't. Somehow, they looked just right on her.

Attractive? All right, he'd admit it. She was a good-looking woman. If you liked them slightly manic and obsessively upbeat. She had her own business—Image by Jillian, it was called. She counseled fast-track execs and other professional types on how to dress for success—business casual, with flair. She also wrote an advice column, *Ask Jillian*. The column had started out as a weekly, but recently it had gone to Monday through Friday in the *Sacramento Press-Telegram.*

Yeah, he knew all about Jilly Diamond. His mother had made sure of that.

"I'm here every year," he reiterated grimly. "And Caitlin knows it." He was thinking that he wouldn't mind strangling Caitlin as soon as he could get his hands on her. He was thinking that she *deserved* strangling. After all, he'd made it crystal clear to her that Jillian Diamond was *not* the woman for him.

The woman who wasn't for him said, "Well, Caitlin didn't tell me you'd be here, or I promise you, I wouldn't have come."

At first, he'd thought otherwise. The last time he'd seen her, at that party of Jane and Cade's a couple of weeks ago, he could have sworn she was interested. It hadn't been anything obvious. Just the feeling that if he looked twice, she would, too.

He didn't have that feeling anymore. Now, she looked no happier to be stuck with him than he was to have found her at his door.

And that was absolutely fine with him.

He heard a strange, soft rumbling sound and saw

something furry in his side vision. Her cat. It had emerged from the bathroom and was sitting beside his chair, looking up at him, eyelids lowered lazily, an expression of near-ecstasy on its spotted face, its orange, black and white tail wrapped around its front paws. The rumbling sound, he realized, was coming from the cat. The damned animal was purring so loudly, he could hear it over the howling of the wind outside.

Jillian said, "Okay, Will. Now *you* tell *me*. What are you doing up here all alone for the holidays?"

He turned from the scary look of adoration in the cat's amber eyes and gave it to her straight. "I hate the holidays. I want nothing to do with them. I accept the fact that there's no way I can avoid this damn jolly season altogether. But I give it my best shot. I decorate nothing. I don't send a single Christmas card. I shop for no one. And I keep my calendar clear from the twenty-second on. I come up here to my eccentric dead grandmother's isolated house. I remain here until January second, without television or an Internet connection, with only a transistor radio to keep up with the weather reports and my mobile phone in case of emergencies." He indicated the Dostoevsky at his elbow. "I catch up on my reading. And I do my level best to tell myself that Christmas doesn't even exist."

She stared at him, one of those too-thick eyebrows lifting. He waited for her to ask the next logical question, which was "Why?" When she did, he would tell her to mind her own damn business.

But she didn't ask. She only said, softly, "Hey. Whatever launches your dinghy."

They did the dishes together, not speaking. She washed and he dried.

As he hooked the dishtowel on the nail above the sink, he said, "There's a bedroom down here, off the living area. I'm in there. You get the upstairs all to yourself." He gestured at the door beside the one that led to the bathroom.

Jilly got her suitcase and her purse and followed him up a narrow flight of steps to a long, dark, spooky attic room. He flicked a wall switch at the top of the stairs. A bare bulb overhead popped on. In the hard, unflattering glare it provided, Jilly took it all in, from the single small window at the head of the stairs to the dingy gray-blue curtain in a pineapple motif at the opposite end.

Someone had taken the time to Sheetrock the slanted ceiling and to paint it and the low walls bubble-gum pink. Too bad they hadn't bothered to cover the nails or tape the seams. The floor was the same as downstairs—buckling speckled linoleum. Three single beds were arranged dormitory style, with their headboards tucked under the lowest line of the eaves.

Oh joy, Jilly thought.

"There's a double bed in the other room." Will gestured at the curtain. "You'd probably be more comfortable in there."

She went through, set down her things and turned on the small lamp by the bed. This area was pretty much identical to the one she'd just left: Sheetrocked and painted pink, with a single dinky window at the end opposite the curtain. The head of the bed butted up under the windowsill.

Will was standing by the curtain. "Everything okay?" He didn't look as if he cared much what her answer might be.

"Fine."

He left her, ducking back through the curtain. She heard his steady tread as he crossed the first room and went down the creaking stairs.

The bed, which was made up already and covered in a threadbare chenille spread, consisted of a set of box springs and a mattress on a plain metal frame. Jilly dropped to the side of it. The springs complained and the mattress sagged beneath her weight. Lovely. She looked at the window and saw her own reflection, ghostly, in the glass. Up here, under the eaves, the eerie sighing of the wind was even louder than downstairs.

She glanced at her watch. It was just seven-thirty. It would be a long, long night.

However. She did have her phone. And she had a few pointed questions for Celia. For instance, did Celia know that Will would be at Mad Mavis's old house? Was Celia in on the matchmaking scheme, along with the devious, domineering Caitlin?

Jilly had a hard time believing that. For one thing, Jilly had never so much as mentioned to either of her closest friends that maybe—just *possibly*—she *might* have considered dating Will Bravo. And she'd also been careful not to ask questions about him. She'd scrupulously avoided showing too much interest when his name came up in conversation.

She did know there was tragedy in Will's past. A few years ago, he'd lost a woman he truly loved. Her name had been Nora. But Jilly had only heard about her in passing.

"Poor Will," Jane had said a month or so ago. "He was so in love. Did you know? Her name was Nora. Cade told me he's still not really over her, even after five years...."

And about a week later, Celia had mentioned that Will and Nora had planned to be married. And that Nora had died before the wedding.

But Jilly never got the details. She didn't let herself ask for them. It had never been anything solid, anyway, those stirrings of attraction she'd felt for Will. And in the end, he'd squashed her feelings flat, leaving her exceedingly glad that she hadn't said a word.

Jilly dug her phone out of her purse and pushed the Talk button—and got the same crackling static she'd gotten earlier, when she'd tried to call Caitlin.

"Wonderful." She tossed the phone down on the bed and let out a groan of frustrated boredom.

She thought of the Cheez Doodles she'd left out in the car. A bag or two could really help to get her through the night. And while she was at it, she could also grab her boom box and CDs. Since Caitlin had warned her that the cabin had no television or stereo, Jilly had brought along the boom box and a thick black zippered folder full of tunes. And not only that. Now that she thought about it, she remembered she'd stuck a few intriguing novels in her overnighter. The evening didn't have to be a total bust, after all.

On the negative side, getting the snacks and the music would mean another freezing excursion out to her car. But not to worry. There *was* good news here. This time she could handle it herself in a single trip. No need to get the scrooge downstairs involved.

Her coat and hat were waiting where she'd left them, on the pegs by the door. She was pulling on the coat when Will said, "What's going on?"

She flipped her hair out from under her collar and reached for her hat. Only then did she bother to face him.

He was sitting in the easy chair in the living area, reading his big, fat Russian novel. He'd dug up an old radio from somewhere and had it tuned in to what sounded like it might be an NPR talk show, though he had it down so low, who could say for sure? Missy lay curled in a ball on the rag rug at his feet, looking as if she belonged there. The cat seemed to like him— a lot. While Jilly understood that cats were contrary by nature, the idea of her own sweet Missy developing a kitty crush on Will Bravo didn't please her at all. To Jilly's mind, it was carrying contrariness altogether too far, not to mention that it bordered on disloyalty, considering the way Jilly felt about the man.

"I'm going out to my car. I forgot a few things."

He frowned. "It's pretty wild out there. Are you sure you can't get along without whatever it is?"

"Oh, yes. Absolutely. We're talking utter necessities." She smiled brightly and gave him an emphatic nod.

He was slanting her a doubtful look. "You need some help?" He didn't sound terribly anxious to get up from that comfortable chair and trudge out into the freezing, windy darkness.

But at least he had offered. She said, more pleasantly than before, ''No, thanks. I can manage.''

He shrugged and went back to his big, boring book.

She pulled open the door and went out into the icy night. A huge gust of wind came roaring down the porch just as she stepped over the threshold, so she had to struggle with the door in order to get it shut. Then she wrapped her coat close around her, hunched her shoulders against the cold and headed for her car.

The snow was thicker on the ground than it had been the last trip out. And the storm itself seemed worse, the wind crueler, the snow borne hard on it, not falling at all, but swooping in sideways, stinging when it hit her cheeks. The branches of the pines that rimmed the clearing whipped wildly, making those strange, ghostly crying noises as the wind rushed between them. Jilly forged on to her car, passing beneath that lone maple tree, hearing those creepy crackling sounds, like bones rubbing together, as the branches scraped against each other.

At the Toyota, she hauled up the hatch and crawled inside. She got the boom box from the back seat, then climbed over that set of seats and got the CD folder from where she'd left it on the front passenger side. Then she backed out, grabbing a bag of Cheez Doodles on her way. She almost reached for her laptop, too. But it would just be something else to drag back outside tomorrow morning when she loaded up to leave, so she vetoed that idea.

Easing her boots down to the snowy ground, she got the hatch shut. She had the CD folder tucked under an arm and the boom box and the bag of cheese snacks in either hand as she started for the house.

She got as far as the big maple tree when a particularly hard gust of wind struck. She heard a sharp, explosive sound and glanced up just in time to see the heavy bare branch come crashing down on top of her.

Chapter Three

That cat of Jillian's got up and stretched. It had started purring again. Loudly. It sat and licked its right front paw for a minute or two, then swiped the paw twice over its tattered ear. And then it just sat there, looking up at him. Adoringly.

Will found the situation nothing short of unnerving. "Get lost," he growled.

The cat didn't move. The purring, if anything, seemed to grow louder. Mentally, Will drew the line. If that animal started rubbing itself against his leg, he was going to kick it. Firmly.

He didn't like cats. Or dogs. Pets in general left him cold. Strangely, most animals seemed to like him. He didn't get it. He just wished they would leave him alone.

The cat rose up on all fours and took a step toward him.

"Don't," he said loudly.

The cat dropped to its haunches again and went back to staring and purring with low, dreamy eyes. Will stared back for another two or three seconds, a hard stare, a stare meant to impart how unwelcome he found the attention of animals in general and raggedy-eared calico cats in particular. The cat stayed where it was. He began to feel it would be safe to get back to his book.

He had just lowered his gaze to the open volume in his lap when a particularly hard gust of wind wailed outside. Faintly, he heard that popping crack—like a distant pistol shot. He recognized the sound. A nearby tree had lost a good-sized branch.

He glanced up in time to see the cat blink and perk up its one good ear. Reluctantly, he thought of Jillian. Was it possible that she—?

Ridiculous. No way she could have managed to walk under the wrong tree at exactly the wrong moment. He was just edgy because it was Christmastime, and in his experience, at Christmastime, if something bad could happen, it would.

He shook his head and looked down at his book again. These interruptions were damned irritating. As if he didn't have enough trouble keeping all those Russian names straight even under the most ideal of circumstances.

He read on. One page. Two.

How long had she been out there, anyway? Five minutes? More?

He looked up again. This time he found himself staring at the door, waiting for her to come bursting through it, that mouth of hers going a mile a minute, her arms full of whatever it was she just couldn't last a whole night without.

But it didn't happen. The door stayed closed.

So what? he tried to tell himself. She *was* Jillian, after all. Who knew what went on with a woman like that? She was probably only dithering as usual, fiddling with all those grocery bags, deciding she needed this or that, then changing her mind.

He tried to go back to his book one more time.

But it was no good. She'd been out there too long.

He swore and slammed the book shut.

Jilly blinked. For some strange reason, she was lying down, looking up through the bare branches of a tree at the stormy night sky. The wind was blowing hard and the snow was coming down and it was very cold. Also, she had a doozy of a headache.

She moaned and put a hand to her head, felt something warm and sticky. "Eeuu," she said. "Ugh."

Really, it was too cold to be lying around in the snow.

With effort, she turned over and got up on her hands and knees. From that position, though she found she swayed a little, she could see the tree branch that had hit her. It was directly in front of her. The memory of that split second before impact came back to her. She supposed it was a good thing she'd looked up when she did. As a result, it hadn't landed right on top of her but had only kind of grazed her forehead. She touched the tender, bloody spot again. A goose egg was rising there. Now, that was going to be really attractive.

And wait a minute. Her hair was blowing into her mouth, plastered against her cheeks. Which meant her hat was gone. Now, where could it have—?

"Whoa," she said as she realized she was listing to the right. She put her hand back down on the freezing snow. It sank in about five inches, all the way to the hard, rocky ground below.

Better, she thought—if, in this situation, there was such a thing. At least on all fours, she could keep her balance.

She turned her head—slowly, since it did ache a lot—to the right. Through the blowing tendrils of her hair, she saw a bag of Cheez Doodles and a tree trunk. She looked the other way, saw her boom box and CD folder and beyond that a ways, an old house.

Ah. She remembered everything now. That was Mad Mavis's house. She was staying there. Just for the night, as it had turned out. Will Bravo was in there, reading *Crime and Punishment,* listening to National Public Radio, and, she hoped, beginning to wonder why she hadn't come back in yet.

But no. Forget Will. He didn't like her. He didn't want her here. It would be a big mistake just to lie here, waiting for him to put down his book and come out and rescue her.

And besides, she was an independent, self-reliant woman and that meant she could take care of herself. She'd got herself into this jam and, by golly, she'd get herself out.

Could she stand?

Carefully, she lifted one hand again—and almost pitched sideways. She put the hand down.

"Ho-kay," she muttered to herself. "Standing up goes in the Doubtful column."

She glanced with regret at her Cheez Doodles. But there was no hope for getting them—or the boom box or the CDs—inside. Not this trip. She needed both hands in order to crawl.

So she started moving, slowly, with difficulty, more dragging herself, really, than crawling. She was thinking that if she could just make it to the porch, she could pound on the wall and Will would come out and help her the rest of the way. He might be a jerk, but he wasn't a total monster. Maybe she could even convince him to go get her Cheez Doodles and her tunes—not that she was counting on that. Oh, no. Just hoping.

She was perhaps a quarter of the way to the porch when she started thinking that maybe she could force herself upright, stagger forward for a while and then go ahead and continue crawling when she fell down again. Yes. That would probably work. She really was feeling less dizzy by the second, which was a very good thing, as the less dizzy she was, the faster she could get herself back inside and out of this bone-chilling cold. She levered up onto her knees.

Miracle of miracles, she stayed there. Her teeth were chattering harder than ever, but she didn't think she was going to fall over just then. She shoved at her unruly, wet hair, pushing it out of her eyes. Next step, bring one foot forward and—

But she didn't get to that, because right then,

she noticed that Will was striding toward her through the snow.

In no time at all, he was looming above her. "Damn it, Jilly." The wind was making a lot of noise, and he spoke softly, for once. But still, she made out what he said.

Hey, she thought. Jilly. For the first time, he'd called her Jilly. Was this progress—or just a wild hallucination brought on by a blow to the head?

She didn't much care. "You know, I have to admit it. I'm really glad to see you."

He didn't reply to that. She wondered if she'd even managed to say it aloud. And then she forgot to wonder as he knelt down and scooped her up into his strong arms, pulling her close to his hard, warm chest. She hooked an arm around his neck and buried her face against his shoulder with a sigh, all the reasons she disliked him for that moment forgotten.

Her head throbbed as he rose to his feet again, but the pain hardly registered. She was just so grateful he had come out and found her. She snuggled closer as he carried her into the house, stopping to stomp the snow off his boots before he went in, kicking the door closed with great authority once they'd crossed the threshold into the warmth and the light.

He took her to the narrow iron bed that served as a sofa and gently laid her down. He tucked pillows tenderly beneath her head. With care, he smoothed her snow-wet hair away from her face, frowning, looking at the goose egg swelling at her temple.

"Is it bad?" she asked.

"I've seen worse." He patted her arm in doctorly

fashion. He'd been such a complete crab since she'd knocked on his door that evening, it came as a pleasant surprise to learn that he could drum up a very respectable bedside manner when he had to.

Her booted feet, still encrusted with snow, hung over the side of the couch. He dropped down there and undid the laces and slid them off. She went ahead and straightened herself out on the couch as he stood.

"Right back," he said, and left her. She watched him set her boots by the door and then, still wearing his jacket, he disappeared behind the half-wall that marked off the living area from the kitchen.

She groaned and felt the bump at her temple. Her fingers came away smeared with blood. But it wasn't too bad. She strained to look down at herself. Everything in the right place, it seemed to her. And there wasn't that much blood. She could see a few drops on her coat, but nothing to get too worried about.

He returned with an ice pack and a damp cloth, sat down beside her and oh-so-gently began dabbing at her temple.

She winced. "Let me..."

He gave her the cloth. She cleaned herself up. Then he passed her the ice pack. She set the soiled cloth on the table beside her and pressed the ice pack over the bump. It felt good. Soothing.

He peered more closely at her, his brow furrowed. "Do you know who I am?"

That made her smile. "As if I could ever forget."

He actually smiled back—well, almost. There was a definite lift at the corners of his mouth. "Tell me."

"Your name is Will Bravo—and thanks. For coming out and checking on me."

"No problem. Are you hurt anywhere else, except for that bump on your head?"

She considered a moment. "No. Nowhere. Everything's fine."

"Did you lose consciousness?"

"For a minute or two, I think."

He got up again and went through the curtain at the end of the makeshift sofa. He came out with a cell phone, punched a button on it. But when he put it to his ear, he shook his head.

"Not working, huh?"

He turned the phone off and set it down. "I'm afraid you're right."

"I tried mine earlier. It didn't work either."

"The storm, probably—not that cell phones ever work all that well up here."

"How comforting."

"I was going to call 911." His mouth twisted ruefully.

"It's all right. I'll be fine. Though I could use an aspirin or two."

He frowned. "Better not."

She dragged herself to a sitting position. "Because?"

He looked at her for a long moment. "You *are* feeling better."

"I am. Better by the minute." She slipped off her coat, one arm and then the other, switching hands to keep the ice pack over her injury. "If I could just have that aspirin. Or Tylenol. Or—"

"No. You should wait, I think. See if you develop any symptoms." He took the coat from her and went to hang it by the door.

She asked, "Symptoms of...?"

"Serious brain injury."

She pulled the ice pack away from her forehead and gingerly poked at the goose egg. "My brain is fine." He turned toward her again, clearing his throat in such a way that she knew just what he was thinking. "Don't go there," she muttered.

"I don't know what you're talking about—and keep that ice pack on that bump."

"Right. Tell me more about these possible symptoms."

"Things like nausea, disorientation, seizures, vomiting..."

It wasn't going to happen. As she kept trying to tell him, she was just fine. "And if I do develop those symptoms, then what?" He was back to his old self again, glaring at her. She told him what. "Nothing. Because there's nothing we *can* do. We can't call 911. The phones don't work. We can't get out of here because of the storm. We're not going anywhere until tomorrow, at least."

"And your point is?"

"There's nothing to wait for, no medical professionals to consult. What happens, happens—though, as I keep telling you, I'm going to be fine. So could I *please* have a couple of Tylenol?"

He disappeared into the depths of the kitchen. He was back maybe two minutes later, with a glass of

water and the pills she'd asked for. She took them.
"Thank you."

He waited until she'd set the empty glass on the
little table beside the sofa bed and then he asked,
"Where are the things you went outside to get?"

She confessed, "I left them where they fell, under
that tree out there. I couldn't carry them and crawl at
the same time."

"And what, exactly, are they?"

Reluctantly, she told him.

He grunted. "Absolute necessities, huh?"

"So I exaggerated—and don't worry, I don't expect
you to—"

But he was already turning for the door again. She
let him go. It wasn't really dangerous out there, between the house and the vehicles—as long as you
didn't have the misfortune to be under a tree when it
lost a big branch. And what were the odds of that
happening again?

No worries. He'd be fine.

And he was. He came back in the door a few
minutes later. He had her boom box and her CDs and
even her hat. "Your Cheez Doodles must have blown
away."

It could have been worse. She thanked him again.

He set her things on the kitchen table and then
turned to find her starting to stand. "Stay there."

She made a face at him—but she did sit back down.

He shrugged out of his jacket. "Just lie back and
relax for a while."

"I told you, I feel—"

"Jillian. Humor me." He hung the jacket on its peg.

''For an hour or so, just stay there on the couch where I can keep an eye on you.''

She didn't like the way he said that. As if she were some spoiled, undependable child who might get into all kinds of trouble if left to her own devices.

Not that she could completely blame him for seeing her that way. After all, she *had* gotten herself into trouble and she was very lucky he'd been around to help out. She had no doubt she would have made it back inside on her own, but it would not have been fun crawling the rest of the way, and her boom box and CDs would still be out in the snow.

So okay. She owed him. She'd do what he told her to do—for an hour. She glanced at her watch—8:05— and then slanted him a look from beneath the shadow of the ice pack. ''I'll lie here till five after nine, and that's it.''

He said nothing, just went back to his chair, picked up his book, sat down and started reading again.

Jilly plumped up the two skimpy throw pillows and stretched out once more on the creaky old sofa bed. She readjusted the ice pack so it would stay in place by itself, which meant her right eye was covered. She folded her hands over her stomach and stared, one-eyed, at the ceiling.

Like the walls, the ceiling was paneled in wood. What kind of wood, she had no idea. It had all been painted in high-gloss white enamel long, long ago. The enamel was yellowed now and cracked in places.

For a while, as she studied the ceiling, she strained her ears to hear the radio. But he had it turned down so low, all she could make out were two voices speaking with English accents—maybe about world hunger, though there was no way she could be absolutely sure. What in the world, she wanted to ask him, is the point of listening to the radio if you have it down so low, you can't hear what they're saying?

But she didn't ask him. Who cared? She didn't. Let him read his big, fat, pretentious book.

He turned a page. The propane-burning wall heater not far from the kitchen door came on—a click, followed by a rushing sound as the gas was released and set alight by the pilot. Outside, the wind went on howling away.

Jilly sighed. She glanced at her watch—8:17. At this rate, she'd be an old woman by the time the hour was up.

Yes, she knew it. A total inability to lie still and do nothing unless she happened to be asleep was another of her faults. But she would do it. She would keep her agreement with him. Forty-eight more minutes of staring at the ceiling coming right up.

Missy, who'd apparently taken it upon herself to wander into Will's bedroom, came sliding through the split in the curtain—this one printed with palm trees—that served as his bedroom door. She strutted across the black-and-red spotted linoleum, tail held high.

Jilly couldn't resist. She lowered her left hand close to the floor and gestured to Missy to come over and see her.

Will looked up. "Problem?"

"No, not at all." Jilly folded her hands on her stomach again and made herself stare ceiling-ward. But a

CHRISTINE RIMMER   45

minute later, she couldn't resist a glance in Missy's direction.

The traitor. She'd found a seat near Will's feet and was looking up at him as if she understood the true meaning of love at last.

Jilly lifted the ice pack briefly in order to check out the bump on her head. It didn't feel all that bad. And her headache really was better. There was no reason at all for her to lie here one minute longer.

Except that she had said she would, *and* that she owed Will and this was what he wanted from her, so that if she went into convulsions or started imagining that she was Napoleon, he would be right there to...what?

To nothing. As she'd kept trying to tell him, if brain damage was in the offing, there wasn't a thing he'd be able to do.

He must have felt her exasperated stare, because he looked up again. "What?"

"Nothing." She carefully set the ice pack back in place, stifled a sigh and took up staring at the ceiling once more.

Decades later, it was 9:05. Jilly set the ice pack on the side table, and swung her feet to the floor.

Will glanced up from his book. "How do you feel?"

"Good. Fine. Incredible."

"Maybe you ought to—"

She put up a hand. "Don't. I did what you wanted. I'm feeling great. May I please be excused?"

He grunted. "All right, Jillian. Go."

I am dismissed, she thought. At last.

She stood. There was a slight throbbing in her temple, but nothing to worry about. Very manageable.

She headed straight for her coat.

She was just reaching to lift it from the peg when he demanded from behind her, "What in hell do you think you're doing?"

Lord, give me strength, she thought. Let me get through this night without murdering this man. She calmly took her coat off the peg.

"Jillian. Are you completely insane? You almost got yourself killed once tonight. You're not giving it another try."

The pure disgust in his voice really got to her. She had a powerful urge to start shouting rude things. But somehow, she managed to keep her cool as she faced him, holding out the coat. "See that? Bloodstains. Once they're set, they're almost impossible to get out. I'm taking this coat in the bathroom and I'm getting to work on these spots."

He blinked. "You're not going outside."

"No. I'm not."

"You're going to spot-clean your coat."

"That's what I said."

"That is the most ridiculous thing I've ever heard."

There was something about the way he said *ridiculous*. She knew what he meant by it. Oh, yes. She did. He meant that *she* was ridiculous.

"Will Bravo. You are pushing me. You are pushing me too far."

"Just put the damn coat back on the peg. Go upstairs and lie down."

"You are so hateful. So bitter. So mean."

"Jillian—"

"It's not my fault a tree branch fell on me. I'm very sorry you had to come out and rescue me."

"I didn't say—"

She waved a hand. "I don't care what you said. *I'm* saying that I wish you'd just stayed in here by the fire with that damn book of yours. I would have made it in on my own."

"You were barely—"

"I was getting there. All right, it wasn't pretty, but I was managing."

He dared to open his mouth again.

She didn't even let him get a word out. "I want you to listen. I want you to hear me. I am sorry to be here, sorry to disturb you. I was tricked into being here. I swear if I'd had even a suspicion, even a scintilla of a notion that you might be here, I never, ever would have come within a hundred miles of this place."

"I don't care what—"

"I'm not finished. I'm not even close to finished."

He raked a hand back through his hair, and he glared at her good and hard.

As if she cared how hard he glared. He had pushed her too far and he was going to get it.

She hit him with the one thing she would have sworn, until that moment, that she would never, ever have revealed to him. "I heard what you said about me two weeks ago at that party at Jane's."

He actually flinched. Good. He *should* flinch.

"I was right around the corner in the front hall when your mother suggested you ought to go and say hi to that 'sweet little Jillian.' Tell me, Will. Do you happen to remember what you said then?''

''Jillian, I—''

''Oh, no. Please. Wait. Don't tell me. Let me tell you. You said that if you were looking for a woman—which you were not—the last woman in the world you'd go after would be me. Because you find me flighty. That's right. Flighty. Flighty and…how did you put it? Ah. I remember. I'm 'A silly woman with a silly job. A woman of absolutely no depth, a slave to fashion, the kind of woman who would jump over a dying man on the street in order to be at the head of the line when they unlock the doors for Nordstrom's after-Christmas sale.'''

Chapter Four

Jilly noticed with a high degree of satisfaction that Will didn't seem to have anything more to say. There was a long silence, one that crackled with mutual hostility.

Finally, he muttered, "Are you through now?"

"Oh, absolutely. I am done, concluded, finished in the truest sense of the word—and may I please go take care of my coat?"

"Be my guest."

Her head high and her shoulders back, Jilly headed for the bathroom, shutting the door good and hard when she got in there, and then catching sight of herself in the cracked full-length mirror on the back of that door. What she saw was not encouraging. Her hair gave new meaning to the words *matted* and *stringy*.

The knot on the right side of her forehead was turning a very unflattering shade of magenta.

Jilly wished a lot of things right then, as she stared at her pitiful reflection in the mirror on the back of the bathroom door. She wished she'd just written the piece Frank had asked for in the first place. Certainly wandering the club scene, guzzling Cosmopolitans, listening to tired pick-up lines couldn't be worse than this. She wished she'd never called Celia about finding a cabin, wished she'd taken a pass on the suggestion that she get a hold of Caitlin—and yes, she *had* been reluctant, after what she'd heard at Jane's party. She wished she'd gone with that reluctance and never picked up the phone.

As a matter of fact, she couldn't wait to get home, to spend Christmas with her own family, after all. Next to what she'd been through up here at Mad Mavis's ramshackle old house, she was actually looking forward to having her mother and her two very married sisters sending her the usual pitying looks, dropping subtle hints about how much happier she'd be if she found someone special, had a baby and did something *worthwhile* with her life for a change.

But wait. What was this?

Looked like a serious case of Poor Me, oh yes it did. And though Jillian Diamond had a number of faults, wallowing around in self-pity was not one of them.

Jilly straightened her shoulders again and carefully smoothed a few straggling strands of hair away from her injury. Okay, it was ugly. But it could have been much worse. And her hair would look a hundred percent better once she'd taken a brush to it.

Too bad her brush was upstairs....

But later for that. First things first. Her coat required attention.

The bathroom lacked the usual white porcelain sink. Instead, two deep concrete laundry sinks lined the outside wall, a long window above them. Jilly turned to the sinks and flipped on the cold water.

As she moistened and blotted the soft suede of her stained coat, she decided that she didn't feel so low, after all. There was something about telling a person the one thing you would have sworn you'd never confess to them that was very freeing. Somehow, it didn't even matter that he hadn't apologized. His response wasn't important.

Jilly bent over her coat, dabbing and blotting. To be fair, she would have to say that he had looked just a little bit embarrassed at what a complete jerk he'd been. She found that appropriate. He *should* be embarrassed.

"There," she said under her breath, holding up the coat and examining her handiwork. "Best I can do until I can get it to the cleaners."

She took the coat back out through the kitchen and hung it at the door, taking scrupulous care not to look in Will's direction. Next, she padded over to the little table by the sofa bed and collected her empty water glass, the bloodstained cloth and the ice pack. She washed the glass, rinsed out the cloth and hung it over one of the bathroom sinks. She emptied the ice pack, leaving it, with the glass, in the dish drainer to dry.

Oh, what she wouldn't give for a long, hot soak in that clawfoot bathtub. But it *was* Will's house—more or less. Somehow, she felt it would be nothing short of rude just to get out her bath salts and fill up the tub without asking him first. And since the last thing she wanted to do was speak to him again, the bath was out. She carried her boom box and CDs upstairs and came back down with her vanity kit. She cleaned her face, brushed her teeth and did what she could with her hideous hair.

Finally, there was Missy to deal with. Jilly carried the litter box and water bowl upstairs. Then she went to get the cat.

As Jilly had feared, Missy was reluctant to leave the newfound object of her inexplicable devotion, but Jilly tempted her with a few cat treats and that was the end of that. She closed the door to the kitchen before she carried the cat up the stairs.

As soon as Jilly put her down, Missy took off. Jilly shrugged and got out her lovely soft micro-fleece pajamas with the blue and yellow stripes on the bottoms and cheerful daisies on the top. She was pulling them on when Missy started crying from the foot of the stairs.

Too bad. She'd get over it.

Jilly slid her Ray Charles *Spirit of Christmas* CD into the boom box, turned the volume low enough that it wouldn't disturb the Grinch downstairs, and got out the three novels she'd brought.

There were two juicy romances and a nail-biting thriller. She chose the thriller. She had no desire at all to read about men and women working out their problems, enjoying great sex and finding lasting love. Not tonight, anyway.

Jilly got under the covers, plumped the pillows against her back and started reading. Eventually, Missy quit meowing pathetically at the stairway door. She appeared at the side of the bed, jumped up next to Jilly, curled in a ball and went to sleep. Outside, the wind wailed and the snow blew against the window, making a sound like someone tapping to get in.

The CD ended. Jilly hardly noticed. The thriller certainly did deliver the goods. It was a tale of a serial killer who murdered young women in various gruesome ways. He broke in on them late at night—they all lived in isolated houses—and no one heard their terrified screams.

The book was probably a bad choice, in hindsight. One of those books that shouldn't be read at night, in the dim attic bedroom of a house rumored to be haunted, with the wind howling outside and a view of a dingy curtain with pineapples on it—pineapples that, somehow, had begun to resemble ghostly faces, grinning malevolently.

"There is nothing to be afraid of," Jilly whispered aloud as she marked her place in the book and set it aside for the night. She was safe in a warm bed. No deranged serial killer lurked outside—and if one did, he certainly should be frozen to death by now. The pineapples in the curtain were not evil faces. Mad Mavis was long gone. And Jilly did not believe in ghosts.

But just to be on the safe side, she left the lamp on. She turned away from the light and snuggled down with Missy purring at her back.

Her headache, she realized, was completely gone. She allowed herself a smug little smile. Take that, Will Bravo. No brain damage for this girl. She yawned.

It wasn't long at all before she drifted off to sleep.

Jilly woke some time later. She was lying on her stomach with her face buried in the pillow.

She lifted her head, blinked, and looked out the window above the bed.

The clouds had cleared. The storm was over. A full moon shone in on her, casting a magical, silvery light through the narrow attic room.

And wait a minute. The lamp was off. Odd. Hadn't she left it on?

Jilly pushed herself to her knees and brushed her sleep-tangled hair from her eyes. She picked up her watch from the nightstand and peered at it.

Midnight, on the nose.

Jilly set the watch down and turned over, dragging herself up to a sitting position. She saw Missy, then. The cat was sitting at the end of the bed, golden eyes gleaming eerily in the moonlight, watching her. Jilly stretched out a hand.

And Missy vanished—or rather, she faded away, first becoming transparent and then, poof, gone. Just like that.

Jilly pondered her cat's Cheshire-like disappearance. All was not as it should be.

And who was that skinny old woman standing at the foot of the bed, the one in the quilted blue bathrobe and the ruffled hairnet, the one with the face that vaguely resembled Caitlin Bravo's? The one with Will's blue, blue eyes?

"Mavis?"

The old woman nodded. Imagine that. First, her cat literally faded away. And now she was being treated to a visitation from Mad Mavis McCormack.

"This is a dream, right?"

Mad Mavis smiled. For such an old, wrinkled woman, she had surprisingly white, straight teeth. She stepped forward—right *through* the bed—and held out her hand.

"Oh, I don't think so," Jilly said.

But Mavis just went on standing there, her lower half disappearing into the bed, holding out that bony hand until Jilly looked down and discovered that she'd taken that hand, after all.

The walls around them were melting, the bed disappearing. Jilly closed her eyes.

When she opened them, she and Mavis still held hands, but now they stood side-by-side. There was another bed in front of them. A man lay sleeping on that bed, facing away from them. Jilly knew who the man was even before she noticed the curtain on the other side of the bed—the one that led to the living area and was printed with palm trees.

"Mavis, I am begging you," Jilly whispered. "Don't do this to me. Okay, maybe for a minute or two, for a fraction of a nanosecond, I *might* have been attracted to him. But not anymore. It's really over, you know? I mean, it never even got started. I don't want anything to do with him. I just want to forget he even exists. And I most certainly don't want him taking up space in my dreams.''

Mavis began fading backward, her skinny old hand passing out of Jilly's grip without either of then actually letting go. She floated toward the corner of the room, drifting past the ladder-back rocker under the window, insinuating herself between the far wall and an old dresser with a yellowed lace runner and a streaked mirror in a heavily carved frame.

''Mavis,'' Jilly hissed. ''I am *so* not happy about this.''

From the shadows between the dresser and the wall, Mavis gazed at Jilly, mournful reproach in those big, blue eyes.

''Mavis. Let me make myself perfectly clear.'' Jilly raised her voice to a shout. ''Get me out of here!''

But Mavis only stood there—well, hovered there, really. Her pale, bony toes—just visible behind the dark shape of the dresser—didn't quite seem to be touching the floor.

Jilly looked at the dream-Will, lying there on the bed, sound asleep. Her shouting hadn't disturbed him in the least. He turned over with a sigh, but didn't open his eyes.

Okay. She'd admit it. With his eyes closed, not scowling, Will Bravo was a hunk and a half. In this dream of hers, he slept nude—or at least, nude from the waist up. She couldn't tell about the rest of him. The blankets covered that. He had shoulders for days. And beautiful, muscled arms...

''No. Not. No way.'' Jilly blinked furiously in an effort to make the sleeping, too-tempting Will vanish.

He didn't. She insisted, as if anyone was listening, "I said I'm not interested, and I am a woman who says just what she means." She whirled toward the corner where Mavis should have been hovering. "You had better get me out of—"

But the old woman was gone.

"Jilly." The deep, lazy voice came from behind her.

"Oh, no. Forget it. I am not turning around."

"Jilly…"

"I am not going to look. I am not even going to…" Well, all right, maybe just one little glance.

She sneaked a quick peek. He was sitting up, holding out his fine, long-fingered hand to her, looking at her tenderly, pleadingly. "Jilly."

She gave in and faced him fully. "All right, what?"

He wiggled his fingers at her in a come-hither gesture.

"You can't be serious."

He stared deeply, meaningfully, into her eyes as the sheet, of its own accord, slithered back from his fabulous naked body. Jilly tore her gaze away from those pleading blue eyes and looked lower. Wow. Some dream.

She looked up again, into those tender, pleading eyes and a disembodied voice from somewhere near her left ear said, "Why not?"

"Why not?" she cried. "You've got to be kidding. He doesn't like me. I don't like him."

"Jilly," said the disembodied voice. "Don't you get it? This isn't real. It isn't happening. So what if you hate each other in real life? This isn't real life. This is only a dream."

Jilly considered. While she did that, the dream-Will conveniently froze in place—with his hand out and the covers down to his muscular thighs, looking at her longingly, his manliest attribute pointing proudly ceiling-ward.

"Hmm," said Jilly. It was clear that in this dream he found her overwhelmingly attractive. And she had to admit she really did enjoy having him look at her that way.

Why not just go with it? Why pass up a chance to have him falling all over her for one magical night? Why deny herself? This was one situation where she could do anything she wanted, let this fantasy spin out wherever it wanted to go, and suffer absolutely no consequences after the fact.

There was no "fact." She wasn't here. She was upstairs, sound asleep, dreaming all this.

"Okay," she announced. "I've decided. I'm going with this."

Nobody answered. And Will continued to sit there, still as a statue.

Jilly cleared her throat. "Uh. Hello? Will?"

But he didn't move. He didn't even appear to be breathing. She clapped her hands. Twice.

Nothing.

Terrific. What fun was this going to be?

But wait. This *was* her dream. There had to be some way to—

And it came to her. She put her hand in his.

The room faded and reformed and she found herself on the bed with him, wrapped in those big arms of his.

"I've been waiting for you," he whispered. "For

so long.'' Jilly thought that was carrying the fantasy a little too far, but before she could tell him so, he asked, ''You'll help me out, won't you?''

She pulled back a little and peered up at him. ''Uh. Help you out, how?''

He didn't answer her question, just gathered her close again, rested his cheek against her hair, and repeated what he'd said before. ''Help me, Jilly.''

''But—''

''Help me out. God, do I need it.''

She pulled back again, intending to explain to him that he really had to get a little more specific or she didn't see how there was much she could do. But before she could say anything, he lowered his mouth to hers.

Good googly-moogly, what a kiss!

He almost burned her lips off. It honestly felt as if steam was coming out of her ears.

When he finally let her come up for air, she realized that her pjs had melted away. She was every bit as naked as he was.

Only a dream, she reminded herself. Only a dream. Enjoy, enjoy…

He guided her back onto the bed, kissing her as they went down. Somehow, it seemed he was kissing her everywhere, every part of her body, all at the same time—her mouth, her neck, lower, and lower still.

Omigoodness. Yes, yes, yes!

His lips were everywhere, all at once. And his hands, well, they were magic hands. He touched every inch of her, found all her most secret, most vulnerable places.

She moaned and she cried out, closing her eyes....

When she looked again, they were joined together. The bed, the room, everything was gone—everything but the two of them. They moved as one, floating in some warm, soft, enveloping space in the middle of nowhere, all wrapped up in each other, arms and legs entwined. She felt stunned by her own intense pleasure. Everything in that warm place seemed to glow. *They* glowed, Jilly and her fantasy lover, rolling and rippling, rising and falling, forever and ever....

Jilly closed her eyes again.

And they were back in his bedroom, lying contentedly side-by-side. He captured her hand, brought it to his mouth and pressed those wonderful lips of his to the back of it. She actually felt his breath on her skin.

Without stopping to think, she did it again, let her eyes drift shut.

And that time, when she opened them, she found herself lying in the bed upstairs, dressed in her fuzzy pjs once more.

Will had not come with her. Sweet old Mavis was tucking her in, bending close, smiling slightly, blue eyes mysterious and maybe a little bit sad.

Jilly certainly felt sad. "Oh, Mavis. Why do the good dreams always have to end?"

Mavis spoke for the first and only time in Jilly's beautiful, bittersweet almost-Christmas dream. "The dog was named Snatch."

"Huh?"

But nobody answered. Mavis was gone.

Chapter Five

Jilly woke to daylight.

She opened her eyes and stared at the pink ceiling and remembered the strange, lovely dream she'd had the night before. She let out a big sigh. Wouldn't it be something if—

But no. Jilly knew dream from daylight. In the real world, nothing had changed between her and Will Bravo. They disliked each other intensely. They'd been tricked into being here in this house alone together.

And this morning, she would pack her gear and hit the road.

She sat up. And there was Missy, perched in the same spot as last night in Jilly's dream. This morning, however, the cat showed no inclination to begin fading away.

"Rreeow?" Missy rose on all fours and strutted toward Jilly across the chenille spread.

Jilly laughed and caught the cat in her arms. Missy consented to be held. She even purred and reached up a paw to bat Jilly's nose.

Jilly giggled. "Oh, sweetie. Happy Christmas Eve and I love you, too. And you're forgiven your flirtation with Mr. Personality downstairs. Just tell me it's over between you."

Missy was admitting nothing. She continued to purr, looking up at Jilly through those lazy amber eyes.

"Listen here. You might as well start getting over him, because you and I are outta here as soon as I can pack up the car."

Missy had heard enough. She squirmed. Jilly let her go and turned to the window.

It didn't look too promising out there. The storm had passed, yes. But the sky was a threatening gun-metal gray that seemed to warn of more bad weather on the way. Jilly got up on her knees and peered down at the snow on the ground.

It looked...deep. Maybe a foot. Maybe more. From that angle, she couldn't see the vehicles, just the slope of the porch roof, a patch of sparkling-white ground, a lot of pine trees and the snow-covered, evergreen-blanketed mountains all around.

Jilly sank back onto the mattress and bit the inside of her lower lip. Was she snowed in here?

She refused to believe that. Surely the county snowplows would have been at work for hours by now. Maybe the long driveway would still be snowed over, but if she could make it to the road, she should be fine from there.

She had chains—and she knew how to put them on. In spite of what *some* people thought, she was a capable woman who could do what she had to do to get herself out of a jam.

And being snowed in with Will Bravo definitely qualified as a jam. Jilly shoved back the covers. Time to get up and get going.

"How are you feeling?" he asked when she came downstairs. He was scowling when he said it, which kind of ruined the effect of showing concern for her health.

"I'm fine, thanks."

"There's cereal," he said. "And instant coffee."

He'd set his radio on the kitchen counter, turned up a little higher than last night and tuned—surprise, surprise—to NPR. "Winter came a little late to the Sierras this year," said a voice from the radio. "But no one would argue that it's finally here. Reports are that—"

Jilly tuned it out. The cereal was Froot Loops, and the instant coffee was Belgian crème Cappuccino, and it was as eerie as her dream last night how closely Will Bravo's taste in food paralleled her own.

They sat down at the drop-leaf table. Jilly poured milk on her Froot Loops and stirred her instant cappuccino and told herself she was going to eat quickly, get packed and get out.

Still, as she chewed her cereal and sipped the steaming chocolate-flavored coffee, she just couldn't help shooting sideways glances at her surly host, wondering how any one person could be so utterly awful in real life when just last night, in her dreams, he'd been the sweetest, most tender man in the world—not to mention one heck of a kisser, the kind of lover who never tired, who could kiss every part of her body simultaneously, a man who literally glowed in the dark.

She was about halfway through her cereal when he fisted his spoon and hit the base of the handle twice—hard—on the tabletop, startling her so that she almost choked on a Froot Loop. "What?" he growled, and then, "*What?*" again, as if there was some chance she hadn't heard him the first time.

When she finally managed to swallow and could breathe again, she shouted, "What?" right back at him.

"You keep...looking at me." Those lips that looked just like the wonderful, sensual lips of her dream-lover were curled in disgust—and she *had* to stop thinking about that silly dream.

Right now was what counted. And right now, in the thin light of a cold winter's morn, she could easily toss her instant cappuccino right in his snarling face. "Well, excuse me for breathing. I certainly have no intention of—"

"Just stop it, okay? Just knock it off."

"Fine. Gotcha. No problem at all." She shoved another spoonful of cereal in her mouth and stared with bleak determination into her bowl. She honestly, sincerely intended not to so much as glance in his direction again.

But she couldn't help herself. He astonished her, he truly did. How could anyone be such a complete and total—

She realized she was looking at him again.

He realized it, too. And he was not happy. He muttered something incomprehensible, grabbed his empty cereal bowl and shoved back his chair.

Missy was under there.

She let out a horrible, injured yowl, followed by an angry hiss. Then she took off, so terrified she ran right into the wall.

"You've squashed her tail!" Jilly leapt to her feet. Missy shot off again, this time in the direction of the sofa bed in the living area. "How could you? Poor Missy. She's hurt."

He could not have cared less. He turned for the sink, grumbling roughly, "Keep that animal out of my way."

"Oh, shut up," she cried to his broad back. "Just shut your mean mouth."

Missy had disappeared under the sofa bed. Jilly went after her, getting down on her hands and knees and calling softly, "Missy, come on. Come on, Missy honey..."

But Missy wouldn't come out. She had backed herself way into the far corner among the dust balls and she glared out at Jilly, not budging an inch.

Jilly considered crawling under there and trying to get hold of her, but she didn't want to traumatize her further by grabbing her and dragging her out. Better to get ready, get everything out to the 4Runner, then come back for the cat. She pulled her head out from under the sofa bed and got to her feet again.

In the kitchen, she cleared off her place, washing out her bowl and mug, scrupulously ignoring Will. Once she'd cleaned up after her breakfast, she spent fifteen minutes in the bathroom, brushing her teeth, washing her face, pulling her hair back into a ponytail and applying rudimentary makeup. She indulged in a minute or two of studying the purple knot on her forehead, deciding it didn't look much worse than last night and telling herself to be grateful she didn't have a big shiner to go along with it. It was throbbing just a little.

She found the Tylenol on the shelf above the toilet and shook a couple into her hand. Then she bent over the faucet and gulped enough water to wash them down. That should get rid of her headache—and if it didn't, she knew what would: to get the heck out of here and away from Will Bravo.

When she left the bathroom, she went straight upstairs. She made the bed, packed up her suitcase, grabbed her CDs and her boom box, and marched down the stairs. She'd paused at the door to pull on her boots and get into her coat and hat when Will spoke again.

"What the hell do you think you're doing?"

"Leaving." She crouched to tie her laces.

"Jillian." He let out a very weary breath. She would happily have thrown her boots at him if they weren't already on her feet. "You're not going anywhere."

"Watch me."

"Didn't you hear the radio?"

"I don't care what the radio said."

"Then look outside. It's snowing again. It's going to snow all day. We are snowed in. And we're going to stay that way at least until tomorrow—and very likely until the day after that. The highways are closed. All the roads are impassable. You'll never get ten yards down the driveway."

"I'll manage." She stood and grabbed her coat.

He set his huge book aside and rose from his easy chair. "Jillian. Listen. I'm sorry about your cat."

"Tell that to Missy. She's the one whose tail you crushed."

"Get it through your head, will you?" He spoke quietly—but she could hear the strain in his voice. He was exercising considerable effort not to start shouting again. "We're going to be here, alone together, for a couple of days at the very least. We're going to have to find a way to get along with each other."

She reached for her hat. "A minute ago, you said you were sorry for what you did to Missy. Did you really mean that?"

"I want that animal to stay away from me, but I didn't mean to injure it."

"You're sorry."

"That's what I said."

"Well, I'm sorry, too. But I will go stark, raving out of mind if I don't get out of here and away from you." Jilly jammed her hat on her head, picked up her suitcase, her CDs and her boom box and stomped out the door.

Will winced as she slammed it behind her.

Damn. What the hell was her problem? She would not hear the truth.

So all right. Let her try to leave. It wasn't going to happen. She'd be back inside, driving him nuts with her incessant chatter, her sneaky oblique glances and that irritatingly arousing perfume of hers, within minutes of the time she climbed behind the wheel.

At least it wasn't dark out there. And the wind wasn't blowing that hard yet. She *should* be able to find her way between the house and her vehicle without having something else fall on her.

And on second thought, why not just sit back and enjoy the five minutes she was away? He sat down in his chair and picked up his book.

His enjoyment didn't last long. About ten seconds later, there she was again, bursting in the door, headed for the kitchen this time. He heard her banging around in the fridge.

She went out again, arms full of grocery bags. He'd read maybe three pages when she returned *again.* That time when she headed back out the door, she was trying to manage both that big bag of cat litter and another bag with God-knew-what in it.

He should have stayed out of it, especially considering that the whole thing was an exercise in purest futility, but somehow he couldn't stop himself from offering, "Look. Do you want some help with that?"

"I can manage, thank you." She set the bag of litter down, opened the door, picked up the bag and went through. The door stayed open for several drafty seconds, no doubt while she juggled the litter and whatever she had in her other hand. Finally, she reached inside and yanked it closed.

Maybe a minute and a half later, it blew open.

Will swore. At length. He started to stand, then dropped back into his chair.

He'd be damned if he was going over there and shutting the damn door for her. She'd be back soon enough. She could shut it herself.

The voice of reason—in general, Will liked to think of himself as reasonable man—whispered in his ear that he was being every bit as foolish and pigheaded as she was. But there was something about having that woman underfoot round-the-clock that brought his worst qualities to the fore. He started reading again, concentrating fiercely, trying to keep all those Russian names straight, resolutely ignoring the icy wind that was blowing in the door.

And then, out of nowhere, her cat landed on his lap, between his belt and his book.

He reacted on instinct, shouting ''No!'' raising his book and giving the animal a firm shove off his lap.

Maybe firmer than he should have. The cat went flying. But it landed on its feet. And it ran off into the kitchen, fast, using all four legs, not limping in the least. He was sure he hadn't hurt it—that time, or earlier, when he'd caught its tail under his chair. From what he'd just seen, its tail looked fine.

And where in hell, he wondered, had that woman gotten herself off to?

Outside, he heard engine noises.

What the hell? She shouldn't be trying to drive off yet. Her cat was still in the house with him.

It flew in the face of good sense to pay the slightest attention to what she was up to, but he did it anyway. There was a window about three feet from his chair. He got up and went over there and peeked around the edge of the blind.

The snow was coming down pretty thick by then, but even through the veil of white, he could see the vehicles—and Jillian. She was putting on her chains. Surprisingly, she seemed to have a clear grasp of the process. She'd managed to flatten the snow in the crucial places and she'd laid out the chains. She was just getting ready to drive back onto them. He imagined she might even manage to actually get them hooked correctly in place.

But there was no way even properly installed chains were going to get her down the driveway to the road. The snow was just too damn deep. She had to know that.

But then again, she *was* Jillian. And who could ever really know what went on in that mind of hers? Also, who could say how long it was going to take her to face reality and come back inside?

Muttering a few more choice expletives, he went over and shut the door. Then he stuck another log in the wood-burning half of the kitchen stove and stood in front of the heater in the living area until the place began to warm up again.

He'd just settled back into his chair and picked up his book when Jillian blew in again. She went straight to the heater and stood in front of it for three or four minutes, shivering and rubbing her hands together.

Eventually, when she was more or less thawed out, she went looking for the cat.

"Missy," she called softly. "Come on, sweetie...."

She tried the old iron bed in the corner first, where the cat had run to hide after the tail-crushing incident. He could have told her that most likely it wasn't under there, that the last time he'd seen it, it had been shooting off in the direction of the bathroom and the door to the stairs. But if he told her about the cat taking off into the kitchen, she might ask how he, who made a point of paying zero attention to the animal, had even noticed that dear little Missy was on the move. When he answered that one, she'd only start shouting at him again. He could do without more of her shouting.

She got down on her hands and knees and peered under the couch. When she stood again, she made a big deal of clearing her throat.

"What?"

"Missy's not under the couch."

"So?"

"Last night, I saw her coming out of your room. Maybe she's in there now. Do you mind if I...?" She let her voice trail off and gestured at the curtain that led to his bedroom.

"Be my guest." He was already looking down at his book again.

Jilly stared at the top of his bent head, thinking that, really, his very existence annoyed her. She had a distinct and quite powerful urge to say something rude. Somehow, she quelled it. She stepped past him and went through the curtain.

What she saw on the other side made her stomach turn over and the tiny hairs rise on the back of her neck.

Chapter Six

The room was the room of her dream. Everything—
all of it—was just as she remembered it, from the ladder-back rocker under the window to the big dark
dresser against the far wall, the one with the yellowed
runner on top and the streaked mirror above. Jilly
could see herself in that mirror. She looked as if she'd
seen a ghost.

And maybe she had.

Her legs felt shaky. It would probably be a good
idea if she sat down. The bed—honest-to-Pete, the
same bed as in her dream, with the same dark head-
board and faded patchwork quilt—was only a few feet
away. She staggered over to it and dropped to the edge.

She still had her coat and hat on. And it was a good
thing, too, because suddenly she was freezing again.

She wrapped her arms around herself and hunched her shoulders and waited for the shivering to pass.

It did, fairly quickly, thank goodness. She took off her hat, wincing when she bumped the knot on her forehead.

Wait a minute. Gingerly, she touched the injury again. She *had* been knocked out last night. Maybe she'd suffered a minor loss of memory. Didn't people often lose short-term memory after a head injury bad enough to cause unconsciousness?

Yes. Of course. It was all starting to make sense now.

She'd come into this room last night, at some point—maybe doing just what she was doing now, looking for Missy. Then she'd been hit on the head and forgotten all about it. Then, last night, while she was sleeping, the memory had resurfaced and been incorporated into her dream.

It made perfect sense.

Jilly put her hat back on. "Missy?" she called.

She got no response. She looked under the dresser, under the bed, in the crude closet that had been constructed of two-by-fours braced against a wall and hung with more curtains made of that palm-tree-patterned fabric.

When she went back out to the living area, Will glanced up.

"No luck," she told him and then couldn't stop herself from asking, "By any chance, was I in your bedroom last night?"

Now he was looking at her as if she had several screws loose. Not, she reminded herself, that such a look from him was anything all that new or different. "Why the hell would you have been in my bedroom?"

"You know, I was asking myself the same question."

"And what kind of answer did you have for yourself?"

She wondered, Why am I talking to him? It always turns out badly when I do. "I have to tell you, I think this is a subject best not pursued."

"Then why did you bring it up?"

"Now *that's* a good question. Am I going to answer it? I think I'd rather not. I left my car running and I have to find my cat."

He grunted and went back to reading his book.

She realized she needed a little help from him. How unpleasant. She cleared her throat. "Excuse me?"

He let out a big gusty breath. "What is it, Jillian?"

"I hate to put you out, but do you think you could keep an eye on the doorway to your bedroom? Make sure Missy doesn't go darting in there while I'm looking for her in the rest of the house?"

Will seriously considered telling her to forget the cat for now—forget the cat and go out and turn off her damn car, since they both knew she wasn't going anywhere. But that would only inspire more argument. Let her figure it out for herself. She'd have to come to grips with reality as soon as she actually tried to drive off, anyway. "Sure. I'll watch for the cat."

"Thank you," she sneered.

She wandered off, calling, "Missy, Missy, here sweetie, come on…" He heard her footsteps on the stairs. She called the cat as she went. She stayed up there for a while, poking around, calling intermittently, "Missy, baby...come on now, come on..."

She came back down. "Missy? Where are you? Missy, here girl..." She went into the bathroom, still calling. Then he heard her in the kitchen, opening and closing cabinets.

She popped her head around the half-wall and caught his eye, lifting one of those thick eyebrows in an unspoken question.

"Haven't seen it," he said.

She went back upstairs, still calling. It seemed to him he could hear the worry creeping into her voice, becoming more pronounced every time she said the cat's name.

Her concern somehow turned out to be contagious. He was starting to wonder, too, where the damn cat might be, starting to think about how she'd left the door open, how he'd sent the cat flying, how he'd turned his back on the door for several minutes while he peeked out the window to see what she was up to.

And how it *was* Christmas. And at Christmas, if you hung around Will Bravo, bad things seemed to always happen....

She came back downstairs and went out the door, shutting it carefully behind her. He got up, went to the window and lifted the blind. She appeared from the side porch, hunched against the wind. She slogged out to her 4Runner, opened the driver's door and leaned in. The windshield wipers stopped. She pulled her head out and shut the door again.

When she got back inside, she went straight to the heater to warm herself. He was still standing by the

window. She took off her hat and smoothed her hair.
"I don't know what to do next." All the usual ani-
mosity was gone from her voice. "I can't imagine
where she might be."

Will didn't like what he was feeling. Guilt. It tightened his gut and squeezed at his chest. He shouldn't
have shoved the cat off his lap like that—not with the
door wide open, anyway.

"Jillian..."

She made a questioning sound and those dark brows
drew together.

"I, uh, probably should have said something earlier."

"About?"

"The last time you went out, before you came back
to get the cat, you left the door open."

She laid a cold-reddened hand against her throat.
"How...long was it open?"

He hated to see her look so damn stricken. And he
could see it in those gorgeous gray eyes: She was
blaming herself. He couldn't stand that. He liked it
better when she was sniping at him, or chattering away
like Martha Stewart on speed. It was going to be a
relief, he realized, to tell her the truth. Then she could
get mad at him, maybe yell at him and call him a few
rude names. He could take that. He could take just
about anything, if she would only stop looking so worried and scared.

"At least five minutes," he said. "Probably more."

"Oh, no."

"Yeah. And I—" But she wasn't sticking around
for the worst part of his confession. She was already

putting her hat back on, turning for the door. "Jillian, wait."

"I can't. I have to go look for her. She was a stray when I found her, but she's been an indoor cat since then. And she's never been in the wild, that I know of." She pulled open the door and a flurry of snow blew in, borne on a frozen gust of wind. "She won't know how to cope." She went out the door and pulled it shut behind her.

Will just stood there for several seconds, thinking that an outdoor search was an exercise in futility. If the cat had wandered out the door, it was more than likely a frozen cat by now—and if not, it *would* be frozen very soon. And in the meantime, who the hell could say where it might be hiding? It could be anywhere. And he wouldn't put it past Jilly to get herself lost in the woods looking for it.

Will switched from his moccasins to his boots. Then he grabbed his coat off the peg and went after her.

Luckily, she hadn't gotten far. He found her in the woodshed, which was maybe ten feet from the house in the opposite direction from the clearing where they'd parked their cars.

She turned when he came through the open door. "What are you doing out here?" Her breath plumed on the frozen air.

"I want to help."

She didn't argue, only wrapped her coat tighter around her and peered into the gloom. "I should have brought a flashlight."

The woodshed was the simplest sort of structure, a tin roof, a wooden frame and rough plank walls. The wind whistled through the cracks between the planks. For as long as Will could remember, there had always been a flashlight hanging on a big rusted nail to the left of the door. He'd put fresh batteries in it just the other day, as a matter of fact.

"Right here." He grabbed it and turned it on.

They scoured the shed, shining the light in every nook and cranny. There were a lot of those. The wood was stacked three logs deep at the far end of the shed. With slow care, Will ran the flashlight over the rows of logs. They checked out the tool area, examined the big box of rags in the corner, looked over the shelves stacked with dusty jars. He shone the light behind more boxes full of nails and screws.

No Missy.

Will followed Jillian back out into the storm, stopping to pull the door shut and hook the latch. They circled the outside of the shed, to no avail. They checked the perimeter of the house, the two porches and then out behind, where the emergency generator and the propane tank were buried well above their bases in snow. They went on, hoping to find places that a cat might crawl into.

But the snow covered everything, smooth and deep. Once they'd been around the house and the shed, Jillian trudged into the bushes that rimmed the clearing.

Will knew it was pointless to keep at it—that it had probably been pointless from the first—but he didn't have the heart to tell her, so he went with her. For a time, they wandered around in the brush, hunched against the cold, protected a little from the storm by the close-growing trees, as Jillian called the cat and got no answer but the howling of the wind.

Finally, she turned to him, hands in her pockets, bright red nose poking out under the brim of her hat, "I want to check the cars before we go in."

They traipsed to the vehicles. She hauled open the driver's door of her 4Runner and climbed in there to look around, he assumed in the faint hope that Missy might have jumped in while she had the door open. She checked underneath, where she'd had to dig out to get her chains on. No luck either place. His vehicle was buried to the base of the bumper. No way any animal was hiding under there.

The storm had intensified as they searched. By the time they turned back toward the house, it was almost as bad as it had been the night before. Snow and wind buffeted them. The world was a swirling, freezing wall of whiteness.

Back inside, she headed straight for the stairs. She went up and came back down, then she went into the bathroom, and all through the kitchen, the living area and his bedroom, checking every corner one more time, calling forlornly, "Here, Missy. Here, girl…"

Will took off his coat and his boots and warmed up at the heater, waiting for her to stand in one place for a minute or two—at which time he would confess to her that her darling Missy's disappearance was all his fault.

His opportunity wasn't that long in coming. Once she'd gone through the house a second time, she came back to the coat rack by the door. She took off her hat and her coat and hung them up, then unlaced her boots and set them next to his. He stepped aside so she could have the heater to herself for a minute or two.

She took the spot he offered and informed him solemnly, "I'm sorry. I'm not leaving without her."

She wasn't leaving in any case, since they were snowed in. But he decided there was no point in beating her over the head with the facts. If she didn't want to face them, fine. She finally understood that she was stuck here, and that was what mattered.

He shrugged and tried again to tell her what he had done. "Jilly, I—"

She cut him off with a groan. "Oh, this is ridiculous." And then she surprised him by admitting the truth, after all. "As if I ever was leaving in the first place. We both know I wasn't. But I just *had* to make my big scene." She shivered and stared miserably down at her thick red socks. "I'll never forgive myself if I've ended up costing Missy her life."

"Jilly."

She looked up. "Yeah?"

"If the damn cat did run out, it's not your fault."

She scrunched up her nose at him. "Oh, I don't know what's happened to you in the past half hour. All at once, you're just a wonderful, wonderful guy."

He tried to look thunderous. "Don't count on it lasting."

And she actually smiled—though her eyes didn't. "I won't, I promise—and if Missy got out, it *was* my fault."

"No, it wasn't."

"Yes, it was."

"No."

"Will. I was the one who—"

"No. You were not the one. When you left the door open, I should have gone right over and shut it. But I was angry and I figured you could close the damn door yourself."

"Makes sense to me. If our positions had been reversed, I probably would have done exactly the same thing. And if you'd been the one with a cat and your cat had run out—"

"You would have been at fault."

"Oh, please, Will. You're a lawyer. Get real. She's *my* cat and *I'm* responsible for her safety."

This wasn't going the way he had planned. The woman was giving him logic, something he'd never in a million years have expected from her. "There's more. The cat didn't run out. Not at first. It jumped on my lap. I gave it a whack."

Jillian flinched. "You whacked my cat?"

Had he? Whacked it? "Well, it was a good, solid shove, anyway. The animal went flying."

"And she ran out the door?"

"Not exactly. She ran into the kitchen."

"And?"

"Hell, I don't know. I got up to look out the window and see what was taking you so damn long out there, and then it got so cold in here, I gave up and shut the door myself, after all."

"But you never saw Missy run out."

"It's obvious she ran out while I had my back turned."

"No, it's not. The only thing that's obvious is that *I* left the door open."

"I could have closed it right away."

"We've been over that. You were mad and you weren't about to shut the door that I had left open."

What was it with him and this woman? They could argue over anything. They'd even argue over who got to take the blame. "Jillian. I left the door open and I shoved the cat off my lap."

"No. *I* left the door open."

"But I—"

"Will. Could we just not argue? Please?"

"I only want you to understand that—"

"Uh-uh. My understanding is not what you want. What you want is to take the blame. But I'm not going to let you have the blame, because you don't deserve it—not in this case, anyway.

"Oh, Will…" Her voice had gone soft, with a quaver in it. A single tear was sliding down her cheek. "I know you're no animal lover. But you wouldn't hurt Missy on purpose. Smashing her tail with your chair was an accident. And pushing her off your lap wouldn't have hurt her. It was my fault. I left the door open."

"Jilly—"

"There's no point in beating this subject to death. I'm feeling kind of low, and I think I'll just go upstairs for a while."

Chapter Seven

William let her go. He understood that she needed some time to herself.

In an hour or two, he figured, she'd come back downstairs. He was kind of out of practice at consoling people, but as soon as she came back down, he'd try to cheer her up. He knew where to look to find a few decks of cards and a couple of board games. They could play whatever she wanted to play. And he'd let her choose the radio station.

At lunchtime, she was still up there. And she was so damn quiet. He hadn't heard her moving around at all. That didn't seem normal—not for someone like Jilly, who'd almost gone around the bend last night when he'd made her lie still on the couch for an hour.

But he thought he knew how to bring her down. He

had a pretty good idea of her food preferences—and he'd watched her eat. She was a girl with a serious appetite. By now, she had to be good and hungry.

He heated up a big can of Chef Boyardee ravioli. When he put the food on the stove, he opened the door to the stairs good and wide so the smell would drift up to her.

She didn't come down.

Outside, it was still snowing—and still well below freezing. He kept telling himself she'd at least have to come down long enough to struggle out to her car and bring in her champagne, her various vegetables and that free-range organic turkey of hers. But she didn't.

At one-thirty, he decided he'd better do something about her groceries, since it was becoming all too clear that *she* wasn't planning to. He put on his boots and his jacket and struggled through the snow, trekking back and forth from her car until he'd brought in everything—every damn bag of Cheez Doodles, as well as all her other stuff—the rest of the food and the suitcases, the laptop, the boom box. He got it all. Except the cat supplies.

Will was a realist. The cat, he was certain, had gone to that big scratching post in the sky. After all, he thought bleakly as he put her precious perishables in the fridge, it *is* Christmas. In Will's experience, the worst things always happened at Christmas. Little Missy's disappearance and ultimate demise was just one more link in the chain of yuletide disasters Will Bravo had known.

He glanced at the ceiling, wondering what she could be doing up there so *quietly*. It just wasn't like her.

Then again, maybe she was taking a long nap. Sleep would be good for her. And she was bound to come down soon.

Around two-thirty, he heard her footsteps on the stairs. His spirits rose. He set his book aside—but then he heard the bathroom door close. He figured she'd come on in the living area in a minute or two. She didn't. When she came out of the bathroom, she went back up the stairs.

Three o'clock came and went. And four. And five.

At dinnertime, he pulled out all the stops and whipped up a double batch of Kraft macaroni and cheese. Caitlin, who in the past few months had seemed to mention Jillian every ten minutes or so, had told him that she'd seen Jilly eat two huge bowls of macaroni and cheese at the Highgrade one lunchtime when she was in town for a visit with Jane. The Highgrade was the saloon/café/gaming establishment his mother had owned since before he was born.

"That girl can eat," Caitlin had said. "She told me the mac and cheese at my place was the best—next to Kraft." Caitlin had laughed that low, provocative laugh of hers. "Does that sound like anyone you know, my sweet darlin'?" She'd given him a wink, false eyelashes swooping down and fluttering up again.

At the time, he couldn't have cared less that Jillian Diamond shared his fondness for Kraft macaroni and cheese, and he'd told Caitlin as much. But right now, the information could come in handy.

He had the door open to the stairs and he banged the utensils around more than he needed to, trying to get her attention. When the food was ready, he carried the full pan over and fanned the steam up the stairwell.

Then he listened, closely, for the sound of her moving around.

Nothing.

She'd been up there for nine hours—minus that one trip down to use the bathroom. He understood her need to mourn the loss of her cat. But nine hours of silence and stillness from someone like Jilly simply wasn't natural. He mounted one step and then another and then he paused to listen some more.

Still nothing. He didn't like it. It was just too damn quiet up there. And it was dark, too. She hadn't even bothered to turn on a light.

He couldn't take it anymore.

He got a big bowl, filled it with macaroni and cheese and stuck a spoon in it. Then he grabbed two bags of Cheez Doodles and quietly started upward into the darkness at the top of the stairs.

He found her lying on the bed in the room beyond the curtain, fully dressed—or so it appeared, though most of her body was covered by one of his grandmother's old afghans. In the moonlight, the skin of her cheek and throat had the luster of pearl. She'd curled herself up in a fetal press, facing the wall, her tan-and-gold hair—shadows and silver by moonlight—trailing onto the pillow. On the far side of the bed was a snowdrift of discarded tissues. She lay very still.

Too still? A shiver of fear coursed through him.

But no. He couldn't believe that she would end it

all because her cat had wandered outside in a blizzard. Not Jilly. She could drive a man nuts with her constant babbling and her unrealistic, overbearing enthusiasms, but basically, in her own unusual way, she was well-balanced and mentally sound. He would lay odds on that.

Then again, it *was* Christmas Eve. In his experience, at Christmastime, all bets were off.

He leaned in closer. She was breathing—the shallow, even breathing of sleep. He resisted the urge to grab her shoulder and give it a shake just to make certain she'd wake up. Of course, she'd wake up. It was only his own paranoia that had him imagining otherwise.

Taking extreme care to be silent, he set the bowl on the bedside table and tiptoed back the way he'd come, pausing at the low dresser to drop off the Cheez Doodles, trying his damnedest to keep the bags from crackling in the process. He was just about to duck back through the curtain when he heard the bedsprings creak behind him. There was a click—the bedside lamp. A soft glow filled the room.

"Will?"

He turned. She was already sitting up, raking her hand back through her sleep-tangled hair. She had marks from the bedspread pattern pressed into her right cheek and those fine eyes were red-rimmed and puffy-looking, with dark shadows beneath. The puffy eyes and the pile of tissues told it all. She'd been doing some serious crying—and quietly. That really got to him, that she would lie up here for hours, silently crying. It was so unlike the Jillian he thought he knew.

She spotted the bags he'd just set on the dresser, glanced over at the night table and saw the bowl of macaroni and cheese. "Oh," she said, her lower lip quivering, looking so sad and sweet and grateful it cut him to the core. "The two major food groups. Oh, thank you, Will."

"Will you eat?" he asked, more gruffly than he meant to.

Her stomach growled right then, loudly. She put her hand on it and a smile broke across her face. "I guess I'd better." She grabbed the bowl, scooped up a big spoonful—and stopped with the spoon halfway to her mouth. "Did you?"

"What?"

"Eat."

"No, but—"

She dropped the spoon back in the bowl, pushed the afghan to her feet and slid off the bed. "Come on. Let's go downstairs. I can splash a little cold water on my face and you can fill yourself a bowl and pour us two giant glasses of milk."

When they got to the bottom of the stairs, she saw her suitcases, waiting where he'd left them, not far from kitchen door. She gave him another of those heart-twisting smiles. "You brought in my bags. Thank you."

He felt absurdly pleased with himself. "I thought you might be needing them. And you don't have to worry about that expensive fresh turkey."

"You didn't." She turned and pulled open the refrigerator door. "You did. You brought in—"

"Pretty much everything." Except the cat supplies, which he decided it would be wiser not to mention.

She shut the refrigerator door. "I know it's awful out there. Thank you. Again."

"No problem. Go wash up and let's eat."

They ate and cleaned up the dishes without saying much. But the silence was okay, companionable and relaxed.

"For your entertainment this evening," he announced as she was wiping the counter, "you get your choice of checkers or Scrabble. I also play a killer game of Go Fish."

She smiled again. "What about poker? I bet you're good at that."

"Five-card stud, seven-card draw, no limit Texas hold 'em. You name it, I play it. I'm not as good as Cade—but nobody's as good as Cade." His baby brother made his living with a deck of cards. He'd won the World Championship of Poker at Binion's in Vegas a few years back and he had the gold bracelet to prove it.

She was looking at him sideways. "You are being so good to me, it's making me nervous."

"It's my goal to behave like a bona fide human being for as long as we're stuck here together."

"An honorable goal—and do you know what I'd like more than just about anything right now?"

"Name it."

She hitched a thumb toward the bathroom door. "A long soak in that big tub in there."

"Be my guest."

* * *

She was in the bathroom for over an hour. Will tried to read his book, but his mind kept straying to grisly images of potential disaster: a tub drowning, a blow-dryer electrocution...

When he finally heard the bathroom door open, he breathed a hefty sigh of relief. He heard her go up the stairs. Great. Now, at last, he'd be able to concentrate on his book.

He'd read about three interminable sentences when he realized he could smell that enticing perfume she always wore. He set the book aside and followed his nose into the bathroom, where it was warm and steamy and her scent was everywhere.

He stood in there, just smelling the air, for several seconds. Then, feeling vaguely foolish, he flipped on the faucet over the old concrete sinks and washed his hands, knowing he was only doing it so he could tell himself he'd come in here for a valid reason, not just in order to smell Jilly Diamond's tempting perfume.

He dried his hands, pausing in the process to listen. Was she moving around up there? Was she really all right?

She'd seemed okay since he'd gone up the stairs to check on her. She'd even smiled now and then, and teased him about how nice he was being to her. She was fine, he was sure of it. He should just leave her alone....

Jilly looked up from her laptop when she heard Will come up the stairs.

He stopped on the other side of the curtain. "Jilly?"

"I'm decent." She had on her fuzzy pajamas, which

were modesty personified, as they covered more than most of the things she wore in the daytime. She'd pulled on a pair of thick yellow socks to keep her feet nice and toasty and she was sitting on top of the blankets, her computer in her lap. "Come on in."

He parted the curtain and stepped through. "Just checking on you." He looked incredibly handsome— and very concerned for her welfare.

A lovely, warm contented feeling flooded through her. "Well, let's see." She touched the bump on her head. "I think the danger of brain damage is past."

He gave her a gorgeous crooked smile. "I'm glad to hear it. But I was more thinking about…" He seemed at a loss for the most tactful way to phrase it.

"My emotional state?"

"Yeah."

"Let's say I'm a little wobbly, but at least I'm no longer curled in a ball sobbing my heart out."

"Sounds like progress."

"Oh, definitely." She indicated the clear space on the far side of the bed. "As you can see, I've dispensed with my mountain of used tissues. I won't be building another one."

"Very encouraging."

"Yes. I think so, too. And thanks for asking. For…caring."

"If there's anything else I can do, I want you to let me know."

She knew her next line. *Thanks so much, and have a nice night.*

But really, he didn't seem all that eager to get away.

And while she didn't feel much like playing checkers, she wouldn't mind a little company for a while.

She picked up the open bag at her side and held it out. "Cheez Doodle? Hey, if you want to stick around for a while, I'll even turn off the Christmas music." It was one of her favorites, *Aaron Neville's Soulful Christmas.* "As you can see, I've already got it turned down very low in deference to your hatred of all things ho-ho-ho."

He folded those big arms and leaned against the pink Sheetrock doorframe. "I can hardly hear it."

"That's good?"

"It's fine." He was standing up straight again and coming her way. When he got to the bed, she handed him the bag. He took it and stood there, crunching away. "You're working?"

"Just a few notes for a column. I have to turn in five a week now. So I have to keep them coming."

"More advice to the lovelorn?"

She punched the Save icon and arched him a look. "Not at the moment." She closed the file and got out of the program.

"That's your column, right? Helping people work out their love lives?"

"I'll advise on anything—how to get stains out of your carpet, how to accessorize for success *and* how to pull yourself together after a failed love affair. There are those who say I have no shame when it comes to telling people how to live their lives. But I look at it this way. If the people ask, then I'll come up with an answer." She shut the laptop down. "Lately, I've been getting a lot of questions on holiday stress and how to handle it, so I'm working up something on that." She lowered the screen and slipped the computer to the floor, into the space between the lamp table and the bed.

There was nowhere else to sit except the bed and an uncomfortable-looking straight chair way over in the corner. She scooted sideways to make a space for him. He dropped down beside her, shucked off his moccasins and made himself comfortable, propping a pillow behind his back and leaning against the wall beneath the window. It looked as if he might be staying for a while.

Jilly decided that would be just fine with her. She plumped the pillow on her side and leaned back against it with a sigh. He held out the bag, she grabbed a handful. For a minute or two, they sat there, chewing, as Aaron Neville sang "White Christmas," the volume so low it almost seemed to Jilly that the music was only in her head.

She sent him a look.

"What?"

"Well, I can't help but wonder…"

He seemed a little wary, but not dangerously so. "Wonder what?"

"I guess I can just ask and you can tell me it's none of my business—but in a friendly way, okay?—if you don't want to answer."

He actually chuckled. "Go for it."

"Why do you hate Christmas?"

He grunted. "I guess I should have known that was coming."

"Oh, come on." She reached for the bag. He tipped

it her way. She took another handful and popped three or four of the crunchy cheesy morsels into her mouth. "Just tell me. If you don't, I'll only ask Celia or Jane the next time I talk to them."

"You do that, huh? Talk to your friends about me?"

"I haven't up till now. Until now, I've been scrupulously careful never to ask my friends *anything* about you."

"Never?"

"That's what I said."

"Why *scrupulously?*"

"Oh, please. It's obvious."

"Tell me, anyway."

She knew what he was up to. "First, you tell me if you're going to answer *my* question."

"Jilly…"

"Well, are you?"

"The answer to your question is very long and very sad and once you hear it, you'll wish you hadn't asked."

"I'll be the judge of that."

He looked at her for a long time. Then he said, "Cute pajamas. I like the stripes. And the daisies."

"You are not even close to distracting me from my intent."

"I can't believe you've got me considering telling you."

"I'm a very charming woman, once you get used to me."

"Not to mention relentless."

"That, too. Will you tell me?"

"If I do, you have to remember that you asked for it—and kept asking for it—until I gave in."

"Agreed."

He looked at her again—a long, deep look. And for just a second or two, in spite of the fact that he was a young, broad-shouldered, healthy-looking man, she saw a flash of resemblance to the frail old woman in her dream of the night before. It occurred to her that she'd never seen Mavis McCormack—in the flesh or in a photograph. And she couldn't help wondering about the woman in her dream. Did she look even remotely like the real Mavis?

"Have you got a picture of your grandmother around here anywhere?"

He blinked. "Did the subject just change again, or am I imagining things?"

She laughed. "Sorry. I do that. My boss at the *Press-Telegram* calls me the queen of the non sequitur. I think it's something to do with the creative mindset."

"Ah."

"And about that picture?"

He shrugged. "There's a bunch of stuff in boxes and trunks stuck in the crawl space behind that closet." He gestured at another makeshift curtained affair in the corner, similar to the one downstairs. "I'm pretty sure there are some old photographs of her in there. We can look tomorrow, since I'd venture a guess we won't be going anywhere."

"Oh, I would love that. Who knows what we might find?"

"And are you going to tell me why you've suddenly got to see a picture of my Grandma Mavis?"

She thought of her dream—of the two of them, naked and glowing, floating in a soft, warm void, making mad, wonderful, passionate love. No way was she getting into that with him. "Just wondering about her. I mean, this *was* her house...."

He didn't speak for a moment. Jilly couldn't guess what he might be thinking. Then he said, "People said she was crazy, but she wasn't. She was shy, really. Nervous around strangers. Liked to keep to herself. She lived up here, in this house, all alone, for most of her life. She raised my mother up here."

She couldn't resist asking, "What about your grandfather? Where does he fit into the picture?"

He lifted an eyebrow at her. "He doesn't—not in my lifetime, anyway. And not in Ma's either, as far as I know."

"Caitlin never knew her father?"

"That's right. And it's likely that my grandmother didn't know him for very long. McCormack *was* her maiden name. Whoever he was, he hung around long enough to get my grandmother pregnant with Caitlin and then vanished without ever bothering to come up with a wedding band—but you know that, don't you?"

She gave him a half shrug. Of course she knew. They both came from the same hometown, after all. And in New Venice, Mad Mavis and Caitlin and her three wild sons had always been the topic of gossip and conjecture. People loved to whisper about how Mad Mavis McCormack had Caitlin up in that old house of hers, all alone, without getting married first—without even any evidence of a man in her life.

Will made a low noise in his throat. "Around the

Highgrade they always joked about it, called it Mad Mavis's immaculate conception. They said that Caitlin was a product of a virgin birth. The drunks got a good laugh over that one, considering the way Caitlin turned out.''

Jilly took his meaning. Caitlin McCormack Bravo was about as far from a virgin as any woman could get. By the time she was twenty-one, she'd had two sons, Aaron and Will, by the notorious Blake Bravo— and she was pregnant with Cade. Blake had then disappeared, by faking his own death, as it turned out. He'd never been seen by anyone in New Venice again. And after that, for Caitlin, there had been an endless string of affairs. The men seemed to get younger as Caitlin matured. Her last boyfriend had been around the same age as her sons.

Jilly said softly, ''You were close to her, to Mavis, weren't you?''

Will was looking off toward the pineapple-adorned curtain, a musing expression on his face. ''I remember her as gentle. And that she was good to me. Ma always said I was her favorite. I don't know if that's true. But in the summer sometimes, I used to stay up here with her, just the two of us. We didn't talk much. We played checkers and Scrabble and I always felt…at peace with myself here.''

''When did she die?''

''Twenty years ago yesterday.''

Jilly felt a coldness, like a drop of icy water slithering down her spine. She'd dreamed of Mad Mavis on the twenty-year anniversary of the woman's death.

Just a coincidence, she hastened to tell herself. And

surely it was. But that didn't make it any less unsettling.

She asked, "So that's the reason you hate Christmas? Because the grandmother you loved died on December twenty-third?"

He slanted her a look. "Uh-uh. First, you tell me why you think you have to make a point of not talking about me to your friends."

"Oh, Will. Come on. You can figure it out."

"Tell me anyway."

"Because I don't want them thinking I've got a thing for you." She said it, and then couldn't quite believe that she had.

She just knew he was going to ask, Have *you got a thing for me?* What she wasn't sure about was how she would answer him. Now he was being so kind, making an effort, as he'd put it, *to behave like a bona fide human being,* she couldn't help starting to find him attractive all over again.

But he didn't ask. He only said, with a sincerity that melted her heart, "I'm damn sorry about the rotten things you heard me say that night at Jane's. I'm not going to make any excuses for myself. There are none. But it wasn't really about you. You know that, don't you?"

"Yeah. I guess I do."

"You're an attractive woman. You're smart. You're fun to be around. And you *are* charming—too damn charming, in fact, for my peace of mind."

"I am?"

"Absolutely. Maybe that's why I've been so hard on you. To keep you at a distance." Oh, my. She was certainly liking the sound of this. And then he added, "You're something special, Jilly Diamond."

And she realized she was glad she'd come here, in spite of everything, in spite of how mean he'd been earlier, in spite of a big tree limb dropping on her head, in spite of having some kind of visitation from a dead old lady in the middle of the night, in spite of all of it—well, except for Missy's disappearance. She really could have done without that.

"It's just that I'm..." He seemed to be seeking the right words.

She thought maybe she had them. "Not in the market?"

"Yeah. That's it. I'm not in the market—though, when I look at you, I could almost wish I was."

Her throat had gone dry. From the Cheez Doodles, of course. She swallowed.

"Want a root beer?" Will was already swinging his feet to the floor. "I think we really need a root beer." He slid on his moccasins and stood, pausing to hand her the bag before he turned for the curtain.

"Will."

He stopped and looked back at her.

"I haven't forgotten and you're not getting off the hook."

He shook his head. "You really don't want to hear it."

"Yes, I do. I want to hear all of it, the whole long, sad story."

He suggested ruefully, "We could just play checkers."

"Not on your life."

Chapter Eight

"It started when I was little." Will settled back against the pillow and popped the top on his root beer. "My earliest memories of Christmas are depressing ones. Looking back, I don't know how Caitlin managed—three boys to raise, a business to run and my father long gone before Cade was even born. I think, given all she had on her plate, she did a damn fine job. But we had some seriously lean years there at first."

Outside, the wind was up again, making the pines cry. Jilly glanced over her shoulder as a particularly hard gust shook the windowpane behind them. She thought of Missy, all alone out there, and sadness squeezed her heart.

Will was watching her. "You okay?"

She nodded. "Please. Go on."

"Jilly—"

"No. I want you to. I do. You had some seriously lean years…"

After a moment, he continued. "When you're a kid, you don't think of how your mom is killing herself to make a life for you and your brothers. You think, why aren't we like all the other families in town? I didn't get it, you know?"

"You just said it. You were little."

He grunted. "I was little, and I was resentful. Somehow, even from the first, Caitlin always managed to hang a few strands of tinsel downstairs in the Highgrade. She'd stencil grinning snowmen and happy Santas in the windows. She and Bertha—you know Bertha?"

"Of course." Bertha Slider was a big, good-natured woman with freckles and carrot-red hair. She'd been Caitlin's second-in-command at the Highgrade for as long as Jilly could remember.

"Well, Ma and Bertha would put up a tree in the corner of the bar. But Caitlin just didn't seem to have the time or energy left over to get us a tree for our apartment upstairs. Christmas Eve, she'd work the bar, serving up the good cheer to all the sad and lonely types who had nowhere else to go for the holidays. She was always good behind the bar, you know? It's one of the secrets of her ultimate success."

Jilly did know. "She can be so exasperating. But what a heart."

"Yeah. A lot of running a bar is about being ready with a sympathetic ear and a shoulder to cry on. And Christmas Eve, her shoulder would get a major workout. She wouldn't drag herself up to bed until after three or four sometimes. Christmas morning, she'd sleep late. Not that it mattered. There was no tree in the first place and nothing much to put under it, if there had been.''

''Pretty bleak,'' Jilly said.

''From the viewpoint of a seven- or eight-year-old kid, you bet it was. I look back now, I can see she was knocking herself out to make a life for us. But at the time, all I saw was that she wasn't like other moms, that we had no dad. And the only Christmas around our place was down in the bar.''

''So what about Cade and Aaron? Do they hate Christmas, too?''

''Not that I know of. I wouldn't say they're exactly crazy about the holiday season, but they've always seemed pretty much okay with it, as far as I could see.''

''So what makes you different?''

''Maybe it's partly that my birthday is December twenty-sixth.''

''Eeeuu. Tough.''

''I wouldn't call it the end of the world. It only seemed like it at the time. If somehow Caitlin managed to provide some kind of Christmas, no way she had the energy to make a big deal over me the next day.''

''You never had a cake? Or presents?''

''Sometimes. And sometimes everyone would just forget about it—well, except for Grandma Mavis. She would always have something for me for my birthday. She didn't come down into town a lot. Sometimes I wouldn't see her till weeks later. But when I did see her, she'd have something all wrapped for me and it would make me feel good. But a lot of times, on my birthday itself, I'd get nothing—and by nothing, I don't mean so much the cake and the presents. I mean the attention. The right kind of attention, the kind that tells a kid people are glad he's around, happy he was born. On my birthday, as a rule, I either felt forgotten, or I felt like just one more burden, one more job on Caitlin's endless to-do list.''

Jilly was nodding. ''Bleaker than bleak.''

''But on the plus side, it did get better.''

''As the years went by?''

''Yeah. When I was nine, I got a cake *and* a puppy. God, I was happy. I'd been asking for a dog for about three years by then. And I finally got one. He was a lab-and-shepherd mix and he was the sweetest damn dog that ever was. I was crazy about him.''

''Why do I think there's a grim punch line coming?''

''Probably because he was run over and killed two days before my twelfth birthday—on Christmas Eve. Run over and killed by a drunk driver in the parking lot behind the Highgrade.''

Jilly let out a sympathetic moan. ''Oh, Will. I'm so sorry.''

''Pitiful, isn't it? And then, two years later, Ma finally coaxed Grandma Mavis into visiting us for Christmas. By then, well, you know how we were, my brothers and I. Wild, to put it mildly. Cade and Aaron were off God knows where. But I stuck close to home that year, to be with Grandma. I tried to be cool about it, but I was so damn excited that she was there. I knew she'd make Christmas special, and I knew that she'd fuss over me on my birthday, too. She had this old rattletrap Ford pickup and she and I went out together two days before Christmas to cut down a tree.''

''Oh, I don't like the sound of this. Two days before Christmas would be the twenty-third. And the twenty-third of December was the day that she—''

''Who's telling this story?''

''Oops. Sorry.''

''I remember how happy I was, this kind of glowing feeling I had, to be with her. We got the tree and we drove back to town. She parked in one of the spaces right by the back door of the Highgrade and she turned to me...'' His voice trailed off. He sipped from his root beer before he went on. ''That was when I realized something was wrong. She looked so old, I remember thinking. The wrinkles in her face looked deeper than ever before. And the skin around her mouth was dead white. I asked her what was wrong. She forced a smile and said she was a little tired. She thought maybe she'd go on upstairs and lie down....''

Outside, the wind, for a moment, had died. The final Christmas tune had played a few minutes before and the boom box was silent. The room seemed, at that moment, supernaturally quiet.

Jilly heard herself whisper, ''Oh, no...''

Will said, ''What I wanted, more than anything right then, was to believe her. I wanted it to be like she said. That she was just tired and a little rest would make everything better. I helped her up the stairs. She stretched out on the sofa in the living room. She said, 'Yes. Now that is much better.' I said, 'Grandma, maybe I oughtta go and get Ma, don't you think?' She waved her hand at me. She said again that she was fine. She said she wanted me to put up the tree, there by the window, so she could see it. She did seem better, I told myself. A little rest, and she would be fine. I got out the tree stand and put it by the window and went down and got the tree myself and hauled it up the stairs. I was so damn proud to have managed it all on my own. I got it on the stand and I stood back to look at it. I remember what I said. 'So Grandma. Looks good, don't you think?' She didn't answer.''

"She was gone?"

"That's right.''

"Oh, I need a Kleenex and I hate this story.''

The box was on the night table. He passed it to her. Jilly yanked out a tissue. "Here. Hold this." She pushed her root beer at him. He set the box on the bed between them, next to the bag of Cheez Doodles, and took the can from her. She blew her nose and then demanded, "You blame yourself, don't you?''

He gave the root beer back to her. "I tell myself that she insisted she was all right—that I was a kid and I desperately wanted to believe what she said. That she had a massive heart attack and there was probably nothing anyone could have done for her, anyway.''

"But you still blame yourself.''

He leaned close, a sad smile on that wonderful mouth and a teasing look in those blue, blue eyes. "Tell you what.''

She dabbed at her eyes. "What?''

"Just say the word. I'll get the checkers.''

She waved her wadded-up Kleenex at him. "Uh-uh. No way. Tell the rest."

"Jilly—"

"I mean it. I want to hear the rest."

He settled back on his pillow. "Well, let's see…" He shot her a look. "Remember, you asked for this."

"Come on, what next?"

"Next, there was Mitzi Overposter. I think of Mitzi as just more of the same."

"Wait a minute. I know Mitzi. She still lives in New Venice."

He saluted her with his root-beer can. "That's right. Married to Monty Lipcott, with four kids last I heard— Monty junior and three little girls. Monty senior sells insurance now. But back then, he was New Venice High's star quarterback."

"Are you saying Mitzi dumped you for Monty?"

"You got it. I realize now she was not the love of my life, but it certainly felt like she was at the time. I caught her with Monty at Devon Millay's Christmas party. They were making out in the walk-in closet in Devon's mother's bedroom—well, more than making out. It's just possible I witnessed Monty junior's conception. I remember that when I pulled open that closet door, 'Jingle Bells' was playing on the stereo in the living room." Will drained the last of his root beer. "Where's the wastebasket?"

"Over here, on my side." She held out her hand and he passed her the empty can. She got rid of it, along with her own can and her used tissue. "So after Mitzi, you—"

Right then, everything went black.

"Oh, no," Jilly groaned.

Will's voice came at her, disembodied, through the darkness. "It was bound to happen sooner or later, with the storm this bad. I was surprised it stayed on all last night." The bedsprings complained as he shifted his weight. "A few years ago, I put in a generator for situations like this."

"I saw it, on the back side of the house, knee-deep in snow."

"Which is why I don't want to deal with it tonight."

"Smart thinking."

"I'll just get some candles." He was standing by then. She could see nothing, but she'd felt him leave the bed and his voice came from above.

"I'll go with you."

"No need." He was already moving away. She heard his soft tread as he crossed to the dresser. He opened a drawer. A second or two later, a flashlight's beam cut the darkness. "I'll be right back."

When he returned he had a box of votives and a stack of saucers. She helped him put the candles around, several on the dresser, a couple on the night table. They lit them.

"Okay, now," she said when they had stretched out on the bed again. "Tell me the rest."

He laughed. "I think I've told you enough—way more than enough."

"Uh-uh. You haven't. Not near enough."

"Hell, Jilly."

"Please?"

"I'll say this. After Mitzi, I decided I was too young

to get serious over a girl. So I didn't. For more than decade.''

''But then?'' She waited, half expecting him to back out of telling the rest.

But he didn't. ''Five and a half years ago, I met Nora Talbot. And I knew, the first second I saw her, that I would love her. The miracle was, she felt the same way. I asked her to marry me and she said yes. We'd met in February, so we settled on Valentine's Day, which was a few days short of one year from when we met, for the wedding. But the wedding never happened. She was murdered when she stopped at an ATM to pick up some cash. Shot through the head by a two-bit thug who is waiting his turn on death row as we speak, I am pleased to say. It was Christmas Day.''

''Oh God, Will. That's terrible. I am so sorry.''

He'd been looking off toward the curtain, his profile rimmed in gold from the candlelight, but now he turned to her. ''Why do people always say that, 'I'm sorry,' like it's their fault somehow?'' His voice was harsh, his face shadowed.

She didn't shrink from him. ''I guess because there's nothing else to say. It's not about whose fault it is. It's about regret. About how we wish it could have been different, that your Nora had lived, that you'd had a beautiful Valentine's Day wedding, that—''

''Never mind.'' His voice had gentled. ''I get your point—and now I think it's your turn.''

She almost opened her mouth to say something coy—Oh, we're taking turns, are we?—but then she thought of all that he had told her, especially the story of how his grandmother had died and the sad, bare facts about what had happened to Nora. Being coy just wasn't going to cut it. She shivered.

"Cold?"

"A little." She was already scooting down, reaching for the afghan.

He helped her, smoothing it over her, tucking it in around her. "Better?"

"Um-hm." She was thinking that he smelled good, that she could feel his body's warmth.

Oh-so-gently, he brushed the hair back from the bump at her temple. "Still hurting?"

She looked up at his shadowed face and thought of her dream, of Mavis, at the end, tucking her in. And then of the rest of it, of the way he had kissed her. That still remained so vivid, somehow, the power in his kiss....

"Jilly?"

The bump on her head. He had asked how it was. "I'd forgotten all about it until you asked."

"Not hurting, then?"

"Not in the least."

He rolled away from her and stood.

"You're leaving?" She hoped she didn't sound as forlorn as she felt.

"I was just going to get another blanket. But if you want to be left alone...?"

"I don't. I'd rather have company. It keeps my mind off worrying about Missy."

"Okay, then."

With a contented little sigh, she snuggled down and watched him pad in stocking feet over to the dresser.

Pure self-indulgence, Bravo, Will was thinking as he pulled open the bottom drawer and got the spare afghan.

Pure self-indulgence to be here in the candlelight with Jilly now. He ought to be ashamed of himself. Supposedly, he'd come up here to make sure she was all right.

She was fine. So what was he doing, lying on her bed with her, rambling on and on about himself? Just what she needed, after all she'd been through since having the misfortune to be snowed in with him—a chance to hear his long, sad story: Nightmare Christmases I Have Known.

He should go.

But he didn't go. He returned to the bed, stretched out next to her again and settled the blanket over himself.

When he turned to her, those fine gray eyes of hers were soft with understanding. "So you've got issues. Pet issues. Falling-in-love issues. And most definitely Christmas issues."

He really would have liked to disagree with her assessment. However, at that point, after spilling his guts so thoroughly, she couldn't help but peg any denials as outright lies. "You're right, I guess. At least about the pets."

"Oh, right." She let out an exaggerated groan. "Just the pets."

"Hey, I'll admit it. I haven't had a pet since Snatch got his in the Highgrade parking lot."

Her eyes went wide. Even in the warm glow of the candles, he could see that her face had paled.

"What's the matter?"

She blinked. "Nothing. Not a thing."

He didn't buy that for an instant. "Come on. What is it?"

"Really. Nothing."

"Are you sure?"

"Positive."

He wanted to probe further, but the look of shock he'd seen on her face was gone. Whatever he'd said that had rattled her, she'd pulled herself together now. She looked...purposeful. "Let's talk about the Christmas issues, shall we?"

"Let's not."

"You blame yourself for your grandmother's death—which happened at Christmas. You haven't had a pet since your dog, Snatch, died—at Christmas. You're hopelessly scared something awful will happen to you, or someone close to you, when it's Christmas. I'd imagine Nora's death was the final straw. Since you lost her, you hole up here, all alone, and wait the holiday out. You're not willing to try again—to have yourself a decent Christmas, to care for a pet, or to get something going with a woman. You're afraid what happened before will just happen again, that you'll lose what you love. And you're certain that when it does happen, it's going to be at Christmas and you irrationally tell yourself that—"

"Jilly."

"What?"

"You can stop now. You nailed me."

A big, beautiful smile bloomed on that wide mouth of hers. "I did, didn't I?"

"And now, it's time we moved on."

"To?"

"Don't give me that look. I'm not buying."

She groaned. "Oh, Will. You don't need to hear it."

"That's right. I don't. But I want to. And fair's fair. Don't give me any lightweight stuff."

"What does that mean?"

"It means I don't want to know what your sign is. I don't want to know your favorite color or if you prefer jazz or hip-hop or punk. I want the dirt. I want the issues. That way, when we get out of here and we both show up at Jane and Cade's or Aaron and Celia's for some event or other, I'll have as much on you as you have on me."

She let out a loud bark of delighted laughter. He'd always liked that about her, how when she laughed, she really went for it. "Will. You are terrifying."

"No. I'm a lawyer with personal issues, and *that* is terrifying." He realized he was having a very good time. Maybe too good a time.

She craned her head toward him, squinting.

God, she smelled good. He pulled back. "What?"

"You were smiling, and then you stopped smiling. But the light's behind you. It's hard to see your expressions clearly."

"You're evading."

She knew exactly what he was up to. "*Who's* evading?"

"Jilly, we've done me. Now, we're doing you."

"Oh, all right." She huffed and puffed a little, to

show him how unnecessary she thought it was to tell him about herself. Then, at last, she said, "I have a job I love—in spite of how *some* people think that what I do is silly."

"Some people are idiots—and remember, this is about you, not me. And since your job is not an issue, that's enough about your job."

"You are so demanding."

"Issues, Jilly. Issues."

She blew out another huffy breath. "I honestly don't have a lot of them. Nothing earth-shattering, you know? I had a nice, secure childhood. My parents are still married—to each other. I've got two sisters, one older and one younger. They're both happily married and they both have kids."

"And you're not."

"That's right. I'm not married and I don't have kids. However, I *am* happy."

"But your mom and your sisters are always after you. They think you should find a good man, settle down, have a baby."

"Think you're pretty smart, don't you?"

"Would that be a yes?"

"Okay, it would."

"So *is* that what you want, then? To be married, with children?"

"Eventually, yes. Maybe."

"That was an answer?"

"Oh, Will. If the right guy came along tomorrow, who's to say? But if he doesn't, I'm just fine. It's the coupled-up nature of the world as we know it that gets to me. It just gets a little old, that's all. My mom and my sisters and their pitying looks. And now, my best friends are married, too. Celia's pregnant.'' Aaron's wife was very, very pregnant. Every time Will saw her lately, he felt certain she'd be going into labor any minute now. ''Jane's trying to *get* pregnant. Everybody's half of a couple, and all the women are reproducing.''

''You feel left out?''

''At times.'' She frowned. ''But does it amount to an issue? Not really. The truth is, I'm happy just as I am. I'd like someone special in my life, yes. But marriage? I'm not even sure if I'm ready for it. I certainly wasn't the first time around.''

He'd heard from Caitlin that there was an ex, so that information didn't surprise him. As a matter of fact, he'd been waiting for her to volunteer it. ''Now, we're getting somewhere. You're divorced.''

''I was twenty-two. Benny was twenty-nine. I thought it was a love for all time. It turned out to be a love for about fifteen minutes. Benny sold timeshares. He was good at it, too. He was already a millionaire, at least on paper, when we got together. Benny was everyone's best friend. Especially if she was young and good-looking. Jane spotted him for a runaround the first time she met him.''

''Just by looking at him?''

''He made a pass at her.''

''Ow.''

''Yeah. She tried to tell me. But I only got mad at her. I thought she was being jealous and spiteful, after the way her marriage had turned out.'' Jane's first husband had been a born loser. He'd ended up dead early on, and from what Will had heard, he'd deserved what he got. Jilly said, "I didn't speak to her for months after she dared to inform me that my darling Benny had put the moves on her."

"And then?"

"Oh, it's so classic. I walked in on him with someone else. In *our* bed. I divorced him and gave the bed to the Salvation Army. So much for a love for all time."

"I hope you got yourself a huge divorce settlement."

"I probably should have. But I was young and foolish, with a broken heart. All I wanted was out. He was happy to oblige me, since I didn't ask for any of his money." She yawned. "So okay. Is that enough with the issues for now?"

By that time, they were both good and cozy, lying on their sides, face-to-face, pillows tucked beneath their heads.

Time to get up and say goodnight, Will told himself. But he didn't move. It was nice there, in the candle-light. And the storm seemed to have abated a little. The wind no longer cried through the pines or rattled the windows. The snow was still falling, though.

Jilly whispered, "Hear that? No wind, and the snow still coming down. Oh, I love that sound. That soft, soft sound. A kind of hushed sound, you know, with a tiny crackling to it?"

He made a low noise, agreeing with her.

"It's so peaceful...."

"Yeah."

For a while, they just lay there in the candlelight,

wrapped up in their separate afghans, the empty Cheez Doodles bag between them, listening to the quiet sound of snow falling through a windless night.

Will watched as Jilly's dark, thick eyelashes fluttered down. He studied her face. Good, high cheekbones and a very strong chin, that wide mouth and those dark lashes and brows. And a large purple lump on her right temple.

He smiled to himself. She insisted it was all right. He supposed she knew what she was talking about. If that bump was going to give her any problems, there would have been indications by now.

He wanted to reach out and smooth her hair back, ask her if she was feeling any pain at all. But he'd already done that once. If he did it again, she was bound to figure out that he was just using her welfare as an excuse to put his hand on her.

He liked putting his hand on her. He would very much enjoy putting his hand on a lot more than the bump on her head. And now that her continued proximity had forced him to let down his guard and admit that he found her damned attractive, he had to be careful. Or he'd do what came naturally and make a serious move on her.

Yeah, all right. He wanted her. He was willing to cop to that—he *had* copped to it. But he really wasn't up for any lifetime commitment. And it just seemed like a bad idea, to get into something hot, heavy and temporary with a woman who confided in the women who were married to his brothers.

And anyway, who was to say Jilly would even be interested in anything hot and heavy with him—temporary or otherwise? Yes, at one time he'd thought she might be attracted. But he'd taken care of that two weeks ago by opening his mouth and firmly inserting his foot while she just happened to be standing within earshot.

Tonight, they'd come a long way toward mending the breach. But it was a friend thing with her now. Wasn't it?

He should go.

But her face had softened, her lips had parted slightly. She'd fallen asleep. If he got up, the creaking and shifting of the old mattress would probably wake her.

And he felt so comfortable, lying here in the quiet with her.

Will closed his eyes.

Jilly woke to an icy wind blowing through the room. Her eyes popped open and she gasped as the candles, down to mere puddles of wax now, guttered and went out. The mysterious wind died instantly, as if it had only been the cold breath of a merciless giant, intent on putting out the lights.

Alarmed and disoriented, Jilly lay utterly still, the afghan pulled up close to her ears, staring wide-eyed at Will, who was sound asleep on the other pillow. Outside, it was still snowing. She could hear it whispering down. As her eyes adjusted, she could see Will's face more clearly. He looked so peaceful and relaxed.

She dared to squirm a little under her afghan, half

expecting something awful to happen because she had moved. But nothing did.

And Will was still lying there, totally oblivious to whatever was going on. She hated to wake him, but that wind thing had just been a little too weird.

She whispered, "Hey. Will."

He didn't move, didn't so much as sigh.

"Will. Yoo-hoo. Wake up." Nothing. She pushed her afghan aside just enough that she could reach across and shake him. But when she tried to grab his shoulder, her hand went right through it.

Jilly gulped. "Oh, great." She grabbed the edge of the afghan and hauled it over her head. It smelled of mothballs. She didn't care what it smelled like. She was keeping it over her head. No way was she going to look and see if anyone happened to be standing— or hovering—at the end of the bed. She was going back to sleep and when she woke up again it would be real life and it would be morning.

She closed her eyes. "Sleep. I'm going to sleep. I am feeling very, very sleepy...."

Oh yeah, right.

Her eyes popped open again.

"One peek. That's all. I will check and make sure she isn't there and as soon as I do that, I'll be able to sleep again." Jilly edged back the afghan and lifted her head just enough to see over the empty Cheez Doodles bag.

And there was Mavis, floating at the foot of the bed, her blue eyes sad and knowing, her skinny arm outstretched.

Chapter Nine

Jilly sat up. "Okay, Mavis. I've got to hand it to you. That bit with the dog? Inspired. I actually believe now that something really is happening here. What, I'm not quite sure. But something, I'll give you that. However, whatever it is, I don't think I like it. So how about if I just say, no thank you, I don't want to go with you now, I don't want to see whatever it is you've got to show me tonight? How would that be?"

Mavis smiled, her pretty teeth gleaming through the darkness, the wrinkles on her winter apple of a face growing deeper, more pronounced as the corners of her mouth stretched wide.

"Yes? Are you telling me yes?"

Mavis shook her head.

Surely there had to be some way to get through to her. "Look. I know he's your favorite grandson and you love him and your spirit is troubled because he's never found happiness—or when he did, he lost it way too soon.'' Thinking about Will and how he had suffered, Jilly realized she had a thing or two to say to the apparition before her. ''You know, Mavis? As long as you're hovering there, I would like to make one teensy little point.''

Mavis continued floating, looking sad, arm outstretched.

Jilly laid it on her. ''How could you die right in front of him like that? He was just a boy and it broke his heart. Why couldn't you at least let him run and get Caitlin, let him do what he could to save you?''

Mavis didn't answer. She stared and she floated and she held out her hand.

''And Mavis, as far as my making dream-love with Will, I think it's a bad idea. I don't want to do it again. Please don't try and tempt me. Because I won't.'' Did she sound firm enough? Oh, she hoped so. Because when she thought of Will's imaginary kiss, she got that dangerous quivery feeling in her stomach. She stuck out her chin and tried to look unbudgeable. ''Got it?''

Mavis didn't speak, blink, smile or frown. She simply began floating toward Jilly through the bed, just like the night before.

Jilly sighed. ''I guess there's no way to get out of this, is there?''

That skinny, wrinkled hand was right there, waiting. Jilly gave in and took it.

When the walls reformed again, they were outside, in the woodshed.

Jilly groaned. She knew what would happen next: Will, in the woodpile, without a stitch on, beckoning.

"Oh no," Jilly grumbled. "Mavis. Please. Not out here. Not in the woodshed."

Mavis's skinny finger pointed. But not toward the woodpile, toward the rag box in the corner.

"What? By that box? Nope. Sorry. I don't see him."

Mavis only kept pointing.

Jilly floated over and looked in the box, expecting to see a miniature Will, anatomically correct and pleading in a chipmunk voice, "Help me out, Jilly. Help me out, please."

But it wasn't Will. It was Missy.

Her own dear, sweet Missy. Curled in a ball and fast asleep among the rags.

Jilly opened her eyes. The sun shone in the window. The storm had passed at last.

"Omigod!" She bolted upright, pressed her palms together and cast her gaze heavenward. "Please, please, let it be true…"

"What the hell?" Will sat up. His hair stuck out in spikes and he had morning beard-shadow sprouting on that sexy cleft chin of his.

Jilly overflowed with fondness. She grabbed him and hugged him, hard. The empty snack bag, caught between them, crackled in protest as she squeezed.

"Wha…huh?" He was so adorable, so totally at a loss.

She laid her head against his broad chest and heard

the strong, steady beat of his heart. "Will, I just know it. I just know that it's true."

"What? I don't get it. What's the—"

"Uh-uh." She beamed up into his frowning face as a single tear born of hope and joy slid down her cheek. "Not right now."

He saw the tear and rubbed it away with a gentle thumb. "Not right now, what?"

She pushed at his chest. "No time to explain." Windmilling her feet, she got them free of the hampering afghan. Then she threw herself at the end of the bed, scrambled off it and raced for the stairs, which she took two at a time, a neat trick, as the stairs were very steep and very narrow.

Will was right behind her. "What the—?"

"Oh, you'll see. Just wait. You'll see." She hit the kitchen floor at a run and raced to her boots, grabbing one and then the other, swiftly shoving her feet into them.

"I take it we're going outdoors." Will pulled on his own boots.

"Yep. But don't worry. We're not going far." She grabbed her coat and turned for the door.

Outside it was bright and utterly gorgeous, if you didn't mind blinding vistas of sparkling white. Jilly hustled to the end of the porch and then started trudging through the snow, which was several inches deeper than it had been last night. She hadn't laced her boots and the snow came to her knees. She hauled one leg up, shoved it down, and then repeated the process all over again. The snow packed in over her open boot tops. It was cold on her feet as it melted with her body heat. Did she care?

Not in the least. Her heart was beating, loud and hard. Anticipation was an actual taste in her mouth— sharp and tart. "She's there, she's there. She has to be there...." She said it under her breath, a chant, an incantation, a prayer—as she slogged the ten feet from the porch to the woodshed.

She flipped the cracked leather latch. The plank door swung into the shadows beyond, creaking as it moved. The snow had piled up at the sill. Jilly stepped over it and down, onto the packed, cold dirt floor of the shed.

"It's in here? Something in here?" Will was right behind her, so close his warm breath stirred her tangled hair.

All at once, she was frightened. She didn't want to look. What would happen when she looked? Would reality turn sad and empty? Would her dream prove to be just that, nothing more than a transient projection of her hopeful heart?

Will clasped her shoulders with his strong hands. "Hey. You okay?"

It was enough. The sound of his voice, those fine, steady hands. She could manage it now. She could face looking into that box.

"I'm fine." She patted his left hand with her right. He let go. She stepped forward, toward the box in the corner at the edge of the stacks of waiting firewood. One step and then two.

And right then, as Jilly lifted her foot for that third step, Missy rose from the box, good ear first, followed quickly by her sweet little head and her furry kitty shoulders.

"I'll be damned," said Will, amazed.

Missy yawned hugely and lazily blinked her amber eyes at them, obviously just awakening from sleep.

Jilly was on her in two more steps. She reached down and scooped the cat up and buried her face in soft, warm calico fur. Instantly, Missy was purring, her body revving against Jilly's cheek. "Oh, Missy baby," she crooned into her cat's sweet tummy. "Merry Christmas, sweetheart. Merry, Merry Christmas." Overcome with gratitude, Jilly tipped her head back and sent a breathless prayer heavenward. "Thank you, Mavis. Thank you so much...."

Missy was squirming, reaching for Jilly's shoulder. Jilly let her climb up where she wanted to be.

"Thank you, *Mavis?*" Will asked from behind her.

Jilly whirled his way and opened her mouth to tell him everything. But before she let the words escape, she thought again.

The trouble was, he seemed such a practical man— except for his holiday phobia, which, while irrational, was certainly understandable, given all the awful things that had happened to him at Christmastime. If she told him that she was absolutely certain his dead grandmother had dropped in for a visit two nights in a row, she had a pretty clear picture of what would happen next.

He'd figure the bump on her head had scrambled her brain, after all. He'd whip out his cell and dial 911. And most likely, by now, the phone would be working again. He'd have a helicopter full of EMTs and life-support equipment on its way here in five minutes flat.

And Jilly wasn't ready to go. Not yet. At the very least, she wanted her chance to rummage through the boxes in the back of that closet upstairs, a chance to see if the real Mavis had looked anything like the woman in her dreams.

She said, "It was just a little prayer, you know? A prayer of gratitude."

"To my grandmother?"

"Well, this was her place, after all. I kind of feel that she's here, watching over us. Don't you feel it, too?"

He was looking way too skeptical. "How did you know the cat was out here?"

She gave him a huge, bright smile. "Just feminine intuition, that's all. Just a feeling I had."

He wasn't buying. "For plain intuition, you were pretty damned excited to get out here and have a look."

"Intuition's like that sometimes. I have it and I'm just jumping up and down with enthusiasm over it."

He muttered something under his breath. She decided she'd probably be happier not knowing what. "We checked this whole shed, carefully, yesterday."

"And we missed her. Or she wasn't in here yet. I don't know, Will. I told you. It was just a feeling I had, that she'd be here this morning." She knew what he needed. Distracting. She cleared the distance between them and held out her purring cat. Missy purred all the louder and pawed the air, reaching for him. "Here. Hold Missy."

He jumped back so fast, he almost tripped on the snow-packed doorsill behind him. "Damn it, Jilly."

"Aw, now. What kind of attitude is that? You can do it. Come on. Now's your chance to make up for all that meanness yesterday."

"It's freezing out here," he grumbled, shoving his hands in the pockets of his slept-in jeans. "We should go back inside."

"First, you take Missy." She gave him her most serious look and schooled her voice to firmness. "Do it now."

And what do you know? He did. He yanked his hands from his pockets and held out his arms. Missy went to him eagerly, pawing for his shoulder, cuddling close, getting going with an outboard-motor-sized purr.

"Tell her you *like* her. Tell her you'll never reject her affection again."

Reluctantly, happier to see the damn cat than he ever would have admitted to the woman in the fluffy pajamas, the snow-filled boots and shearling coat who was now beaming happily up at him, Will petted the animal and made his apology. "Listen, Missy. It's great to see you. How about we let bygones be bygones?"

Jilly's wide smile got even wider. "Good job. Let's go inside."

"Oh, ye of little faith," Jilly teased when she found out that yesterday he'd left the cat supplies in the car.

Will was only too happy to trudge out there and get everything. While he was outside, they got power again, the old fridge revving to life and the overhead light in the kitchen popping on.

"Ta-da," Jilly sang out when he came through the door, indicating the light above with a flourish. "Now you won't have to fool with the generator."

Once Missy was comfortable and digging into a nice, big bowl of cat food, they made some instant cappuccino and enjoyed their morning bowls of Froot Loops. Will had turned on the radio when they first came back inside, so they already knew that the storm had been a huge one. It was going to be a day or two—or even three—until a county snowplow could possibly get around to that long, winding driveway out there.

That fit in just fine with the plan that was beginning to take shape in Jilly's mind. She ate fast.

Will asked with an amused lift of a bronze eyebrow, "Going to a fire?"

"I want to get upstairs and check in that closet. Remember, you said you thought you could find a picture of your grandmother in there?"

He sipped from his mug. "What I want first is a bath and a shave. That okay with you?"

It wasn't. She was shamelessly impatient to see Mavis. But it wasn't her house and the treasures upstairs were not hers to investigate on her own. "Oh. Well, sure. No problem. I'll wait."

Her expression must have given her away. He suggested, "Look. Why don't you just go ahead and get after it? I think most of the pictures are in a couple of albums in a cardboard file box. You know the kind I mean?"

She nodded, and managed to restrain herself from licking her lips, she was so very eager.

"I'll be up to join you in a while. If you haven't figured out who Mavis is by then, I'll show you."

"Terrific."

"I still don't get why you're so jazzed over this."

"Uh, well, I've been staying in her house. And you've told me so much about her. I'm beginning to feel as if I know her. I want to put a face to my idea of her."

"Whatever." He shrugged and dipped up another big spoonful of cereal. She figured her explanation must have satisfied him, because he didn't ask her any more questions.

Will tried his phone again before he went to take his bath. Same as before. Nothing but static.

"Try yours."

She went upstairs, dug hers out of her purse and pressed Talk.

He was waiting for her at the foot of the stairs. "Well?"

"More static."

"I guess it's you and me and Missy, for now." He gave her the sweetest, most rueful grin.

"Merry Christmas, Will."

"Humph."

"What was that?"

"Do I *have* to say it?"

She just looked at him, patiently.

"Oh, what the hell. Merry Christmas, Jilly." He went in the bathroom and shut the door.

She headed back up the stairs. She was going to get dressed and then she was going to get in that closet and check out those photo albums.

There were lots of boxes and a couple of trunks pushed back in the crawl space behind the closet, between the outside wall and the Sheetrock paneling. Jilly had the flashlight Will had left on the dresser last night, so it didn't take her long to find the file box. She dragged it out into the light. When she took off the dusty lid, she discovered two dog-eared photo albums, a baby book and more boxes full of loose pictures, mostly old, mostly black-and-white.

The baby book was Caitlin's. It had a teddy bear on the cover and the words *All About Baby* in faded pink letters. Inside were all of Caitlin's baby statistics, lovingly entered in a careful, round hand, from birth weight and length to favorite songs of the day—by the Andrews Sisters and Frank Sinatra. There was a lock of glossy black hair. Jilly smiled at that. Caitlin's hair was still glossy black, kept that way, no doubt, with a helping hand from Clairol. Her first word, "No," was noted, and the date of her first baby step. The pages for baby showers and friendly advice were blank, signs of the life they had led, a mother and daughter, up in the mountains, all on their own. There were a few photos glued onto the final pages: baby Caitlin in only a diaper, lying on her back on a bed, and Caitlin as a toddler, holding a toy shovel, standing in the clearing outside with the old house behind her, squinting into the sun.

The two photo albums, on quick examination, appeared to be roughly chronological. The first held very old pictures in sepia tones, carefully posed, of people Jilly didn't recognize. The men wore bowler hats and spats, the women high-necked white shirtwaists with mutton-chop sleeves. The second was page after page of yellowing black-and-whites. Jilly took note of the slim dark-haired girl who appeared about midway through that second album. She thought she could see the resemblance to Caitlin and Will—and to the Mavis of her dreams.

But it was after she moved on to the boxes full of snapshots that she found what she was looking for, shots of an old woman out in the clearing, with three little boys who had to be Aaron, Will and Cade. A picture of that same woman sitting in the chair in the living area, knitting what looked like the afghan Jilly had slept beneath just last night. And another of the woman and Caitlin, standing side-by-side on Main Street in New Venice, in front of the Highgrade. In that one, Caitlin was laughing, dark head thrown back. Whatever the joke was, the old woman seemed to be in on it. Her face was crinkled with humor, but she had her hand over her mouth, as if to keep the laughter in.

Jilly stared from one picture to the next. Her cheeks felt too warm and her heart was racing. She was looking at Mavis, she was certain of it. Because the old woman was the same woman she had seen in her dreams.

Chapter Ten

Jilly's first reaction was elation. She felt lifted up, vindicated. Her dreams were verified as truth.

Close on the heels of excitement, a shiver of dread crawled beneath her skin. This really couldn't be happening. She hadn't *really* been visited by the spirit of Will's dead grandmother two nights running. Had she?

She heard Will's step on the rickety stairs. A frantic thrill raced through her, followed swiftly by the odd urge to toss everything back in the box and shove it into the closet, to pretend she hadn't been looking through it, hadn't found the face from her dreams.

But then again, what was to pretend? Will had no idea of the things she might have seen.

He came through the curtain and she turned, still holding that picture of Mavis and Caitlin on Main

Street. "I think this must be your grandmother. Am I right?"

He crouched beside her and took the picture. He smelled so good and clean. His face was smooth, his hair still wet. "Yep. That's my grandma." He lightly touched the wrinkled face. "She always covered her mouth when she laughed. She had false teeth that never fit right. I think she might have been embarrassed about them."

Jilly was quiet, recalling the beautiful teeth of the Mavis in her dream. It was the first wrong note in this whole symphony of magical happenings. Maybe in the spirit world, you could have the things you'd never had in life, including a set of white, perfect teeth.

Or more than likely, the voice of reason whispered wisely, your dreams were just that: dreams.

It was all rationally explainable, really.

She'd wandered into Will's room sometime that first night, forgotten she'd been in there when that tree branch fell on her head, but incorporated the buried memory into her dream. At some point, she *had* seen a picture of Mavis. Someone at some time or another had mentioned to her that Will Bravo once had a dog named Snatch. After all, she and Will had grown up in the same small town. And now her two best friends had married his brothers. She probably subconsciously knew things about Will she had no clue of at the conscious level.

And Missy in the rag box? Just what she'd told Will: intuition. Nothing more.

Will was watching her. "What's going on?"

"Huh? Oh, nothing."

"You look sad."

Sad? Was she? Maybe a little. She'd grown rather enamored of the whole idea that her dreams might be visions, that Mavis McCormack had come to communicate with her from beyond the grave. It did make her just a tiny bit sad to admit that it all added up to nothing more than her subconscious playing a few cute tricks.

However, she could deal with feeling sad. She wasn't sure how she would deal with having to accept that what she'd seen in her dreams was real.

She smiled at Will. "Maybe I am sad. I've been thinking about your grandmother, wondering what her life was like. It seems that she must have been lonely. So many years living up here, all alone."

His brows drew together. "To me, she just seemed comfortable, at peace with herself and the world she lived in. I was only a kid, though. What did I know?"

He had on a charcoal-gray turtleneck sweater and he'd pushed the sleeves to his elbows. She laid her hand on his forearm. "I'll bet you did know. Better than just about anybody else."

He looked down at her hand and then up into her eyes.

And everything changed. All at once, she was acutely aware of the silky hairs on his arm, the warmth of his flesh, of hard muscle beneath taut skin. She watched his Adam's apple move up and down as he swallowed—and found she was swallowing right along with him.

She dragged her gaze downward and let go of his arm, fast. "Come on," she said briskly, grabbing the scattered photos, dropping them into the open box. "Help me put these away. We have so much to do and only so many hours to do it in."

"Jilly."

She made herself look at him. And there it was again, that burning awareness, that lovely blooming feeling in her stomach, the sense of connection, of being pulled into him, the certainty that something absolutely wonderful was about to happen very soon....

Not.

They'd been over that. He didn't want to get anything started, and that was fine with her.

He was the one who looked away that time. When he looked back, the dangerous moment had passed. He asked, suspiciously, "What, exactly, do we have to do?"

She felt relief—honestly, she did—that they hadn't done anything foolish, like fall into each other's arms and start kissing madly. She had an agenda and making passionate, all-consuming love with Will would only distract her from what needed doing.

Her plan had been formulating since last night, when he'd gotten honest with her and told her all the reasons he had for hating Christmas. It was a good plan, and she wasn't giving up on it just because she'd realized that his dead grandma hadn't been dropping in on her at night, after all. Okay, her subconscious had been playing tricks on her. And why, she asked herself, would her subconscious do that?

Well, because it was trying to tell her something.

What had Will said to her, that first night, in her

dream? *Help me, Jilly. Help me out. God, do I need it....*

It all fit together just perfectly and there was nothing supernatural about it. She had sensed a truth about Will and that truth had spoken to her through her dream.

He needed her help. And she was going to give it to him. By the time the county snowplow got around to clearing the long driveway out front, Will Bravo would be Christmas-friendly. Jillian Diamond would see to that.

"Jilly," he said, when they were back in the kitchen, and she had started assembling the ingredients for dried apple, sausage and toasted pecan stuffing. "Do we have to do this?"

"We do." She opened the fridge and got out the sausage. "You're going to love it. I need a frying pan."

He opened the cabinet in the side of the stove and pulled out a lovely well-seasoned cast-iron one. "You know we'd both just as soon have something simple, something straight out of a nice, big can."

She put the pan on the stove, grabbed a match and lit the burner. "There are times when we are called upon to go all out. Times that demand we sit down to a true feast."

"Times like Christmas," he said glumly.

She blew out the match. "Like Christmas, exactly. Pass me that sausage." He handed it over. She peeled back the label and rolled the meat free of the white butcher paper and into the pan. She held out her hand. "Wooden spoon?"

He turned to the earthenware jar with all the utensils standing up in it, grabbed what she'd asked for and slapped it into her palm. The meat started sizzling.

She adjusted the flame and began breaking up the sausage with the spoon. "Get out the turkey, will you? Rinse it inside and out and wipe it dry with paper towels. Oh, and don't forget to remove the giblets. They're probably in the neck cavity. Wash them, too."

He grunted unwillingly, but he did turn and pull the bird from the fridge.

"I want to get the turkey in the oven," she said. "Then we'll be free to go out and find ourselves a tree."

"My first choice would have to be a silver-tip fir," Jilly announced. "I like the tiered effect of the branches, combined with the lush thickness of the needles. And that silvery-green color. Oh, I do love that." She shivered, mostly from pleasure but partly because it was cold outside. They stood knee-deep in snow at the back of the house, all rigged out in their coats and boots, wool hats and thick gloves. Will had an axe he'd taken from the shed.

"We don't have a permit," he warned, his breath coming out as a white vapor in the icy air. "We can't just wander out in the woods and chop down any tree that catches our eye. We're surrounded by national forest, in case you didn't notice."

"Oh, stop grumbling."

He hefted the axe. "I'm not grumbling. I'm making a valid point."

Jilly brought up a hand to shield her eyes against

the blinding glare of bright sun on new snow. The trees started fifty or sixty feet from the kitchen windows. The land there sloped sharply upward into what appeared to be a mountain. In any case, it was a large hill, covered in evergreens, and it went on for a long way, up toward the ice-blue winter sky. "How big is this property?"

"Why?"

She sent him a chiding look. "Work with me here."

"Ten acres." He pointed toward the hill. "And as you can see, at least half the acreage is on a serious slant. Where we have trees, they're pretty thick. They tend to grow with bare spots and uneven branches, not what you want in a Christmas tree."

Jilly rubbed her gloves together. "Well, then. I guess we'd better start looking."

"Why did I know you were going to say that?"

Right then, Jilly thought she saw movement—in the trees at the base of the hill. "Do you see that?"

He squinted toward where she pointed. "I see trees. A lot of trees."

"No. Something moving. An animal, I think."

"I don't see anything now. Probably a deer."

"No, it was smaller than a deer."

"Jilly, around here, we've got deer and raccoons and brown bears and mountain lions. And that's just for starters."

"It's gone now, whatever it was." Jilly shivered— and not from cold. "I hope it wasn't a lion. They scare me. You never know what they'll do."

"You want to forget the tree?" he suggested hopefully. "I could go get my hunting rifle and we could track the unknown animal instead."

"Not a chance."

It took about a half an hour. By then, Jilly was cold enough to compromise a little. The tree they found was in the woods on the side of the house where they'd trooped around calling for Missy the day before. It was a Douglas fir, about six and a half feet tall and a little sparse on one side.

"But we'll put it by your chair, in front of the window in the living area," she said, "with the bad side turned so we can't see it."

"You're saying I should start chopping, right?"

"Yes. The quicker we get it cut down and put up in the house, the quicker we can start figuring out what to do for decorations."

His expression turned especially bleak. "We're going to decorate it."

"Oh, come on. It's a Christmas tree, remember? You put it up in the house and then you *decorate* it. Now, just cut it down, will you? It's cold out here."

"Okay, stand over there."

"Because?"

"Can't you ever in your life just follow instructions?"

"You know, I could ask you the same question."

"Jilly. If you stand over there, you won't get hit by flying wood chips and the damn thing's unlikely to fall on you."

"Well, all right. That makes sense." She trotted over to where he'd pointed. He raised the axe. But before he struck the first blow, he lowered it and turned to her.

"Oh, Will," she moaned. "What now?"

"In a couple of days, we'll be able to get out of here. You're not just going to drive off and leave me with this thing in the living room, are you?"

"What are you after?"

"A commitment to tree removal. From you."

"Since we'll be making the decorations, everything should be disposable. Taking it down won't be a big deal."

"We're *making* decorations?"

"You have a better suggestion?"

"Let's get back to my original request. Are you going to help me take this damn thing down?"

"Okay, no problem. I'll help you take it down before I go."

"Thank you very much."

"Start chopping."

Under ordinary circumstances, Jilly would have put the tree in water with tree preserver to keep it green. But they were improvising here, with the equipment on hand. No tree stand presented itself, and they'd be taking it down in a day or two anyway. So Will nailed on a wooden stand of two-by-four scraps he found in the shed. They carried it inside and stood it up in front of the window next to the easy chair.

Jilly stepped back and drew in a big breath through her nose. "Oh, smell that. I love the smell of evergreen, don't you? And it looks great. You can't even see the uneven part." Will's radio was still playing, softly, in the kitchen, still tuned to NPR, which was cooperating nicely now, with a program of Christmas tunes in honor of the day. One of her favorites was on right then, "Holly, Jolly Christmas," a real classic, sung by Burl Ives. She turned to Will.

He was watching her. And he was almost smiling. Was that admiration she saw in those beautiful deep-blue eyes? She got those lovely flutters in her stomach again. Her cheeks felt warm, her heart beat faster. She was maybe four steps away from him. She wanted to close that small distance.

She could see it, just how it would be.

He would hold out those strong arms to her and she would move into them. He would wrap her close in his warm and cherishing embrace. She would offer her mouth. He would claim it.

Oh, yes. A long, sweet Christmas kiss. In front of the tree they'd just cut fresh, themselves.

"Does your enthusiasm ever flag?" His voice was rough—and soft at the same time, one notch above a whisper. He wasn't smiling anymore. He was looking at her mouth.

What was she *thinking?* She shook herself. Firmly. "Don't tell a soul, but now and then, I can get a little down."

"Like yesterday?"

She glanced at the old sofa bed. Missy was curled there, asleep on one of the thin throw pillows. Safe. "It hit me hard, her disappearing. Mostly because I knew it was all my fault."

He started to argue. "It wasn't your—"

"Will."

"What?"

"We've already been through that. Let's not start on it again."

After a moment, he nodded. "Good idea. So. Decorations are next, right?"

"Good gravy, you should see yourself. For the first time, you mentioned decorations without scowling."

"You'll have me singing 'Jingle Bells' before we're through."

That brought on a clear visual of a teenaged Will opening a closet door and finding Monty and Mitzi in flagrante delicto. He was remembering the same thing. His devilish smile told her so.

"Well, it's Christmas," she said. "Anything's possible, right?"

"So you keep telling me."

They were doing it again, staring at each other. She had that dizzying, falling feeling as if she were drowning deliciously, right there in his eyes.

Speak, she thought. Say something *now.* "I did come prepared for tree decorating."

"You were going to cut down a tree all by yourself?"

"You don't think I could have managed it?"

"I'm sure you can do anything you put your mind to."

She gave him a slow smile. "That's what I like to hear. And I brought construction paper and scissors, glue and glitter. It's upstairs in my suitcase. I'll just—"

"I've got a better idea."

The way he said that sent a lovely, warm shiver quivering all through her.

He said, "Upstairs, in that closet where you found the pictures, you'll also find a couple of big boxes of Christmas stuff."

The lights were the old-fashioned kind, heavy black wires with big multicolored bulbs. There was rumpled gold garland and a variety of dime-store glass ornaments, most of them faded with age.

"This stuff is a little the worse for wear," Will said when they opened the dusty boxes and had a look inside.

"I love it. All of it. Every last inch of ragged garland, every ancient ornament."

He looked hopeful. "That means no craft projects, right?"

"Let's haul it all downstairs."

By one in the afternoon, they had the lights, the garland and every last faded ornament hanging on their tree. They took a break to share a can of Campbell's tomato soup. They wanted to eat light, because dinner was going to be a feast and it was only a few hours away. Over the soup, she convinced him to turn up the radio a little so she could hear her Christmas favorites while they cooked.

As the savory smell of cider-glazed roasting turkey mingled with the piney scent of the tree, they got to work on the big meal. There was to be pumpkin soup with sage and crème fraîche for starters. With the bird, they'd have gingered cranberry sauce, roasted root vegetables, the stuffing, corn strips with chives and cheddar, green beans with sherry vinegar and soft wheat rolls. She'd planned for two desserts: apple tart with tangy cranberry swirl topping and chocolate pecan pie.

Will was an angel. A miracle. A total surprise. He chopped and sliced and diced and shredded, whatever she asked of him, he did. He found a yellowed linen tablecloth in the bedroom bureau and he spread it on the table. He polished up the mismatched flatware, brought a couple of pewter candle holders down from a top shelf and stood two white household emergency candles in them.

At a little before five, they were ready to eat. Will carved the turkey. He did a fine job. Then he poured the wine—they made do with a pair of juice tumblers for wineglasses.

Jilly lit the candles and they sat down. They raised their juice glasses and toasted each other, the season—and Mavis, for the use of her fine house. Then they ate. For a very long time.

When they were both sure they couldn't eat another bite, they cleared off the table and put away everything but the tempting desserts that still waited untouched on the counter. They played Scrabble for a couple of hours.

Jilly won.

Will was sure she had cheated. "Do you know how many times I've played this game?" He answered his own question. "Hundreds. Thousands. Nobody takes me at Scrabble."

"Oh, stop beating your chest or I won't let you have any chocolate pecan pie."

"Just admit it. You cheated."

"I do not cheat at board games. I'm above such things."

"When I went to the bathroom, you—"

"No. I didn't. Wrong, wrong, wrong."

"But…*zestfully,* on a triple-word score, the Z on a double? I don't think so."

"I beat you fair and square. Live with it. And come on, let's get some water boiling so we can have a little instant cappuccino with our pie and apple-cranberry tart."

He tried to keep scowling, but he was having too much fun. "All right. I concede victory to you."

"There's nothing quite so admirable as a graceful loser."

"Do me a big favor. Don't rub it in."

They put the game away and served themselves dessert. Then they turned off all the lights except the ones on the tree and they sat together on the old sofa bed, sipping instant cappuccino, eating apple tart and pecan pie.

"The tree is beautiful," she said. The old-fashioned lights reflected off the faded bulbs. Those bulbs gleamed and twinkled just as brightly as they must have when they were new.

"God. This pecan pie…"

"Will. You're groaning."

"I can't help myself. I'm amazed and humbled. You beat me at Scrabble. You appreciate franks and beans. You love mac and cheese. But when you set your mind to it, damn it, can you cook."

"Amazed and humbled. I really like the sound of that."

"But maybe I'm just relieved."

"I like amazed and humbled better. But I'm interested. Why are you relieved?"

"You didn't insist on a gift exchange. I think I hate that part the most. It's so over the top anymore. Stores start pushing you to buy, buy, buy before Halloween."

"I really wanted to do gifts."

"And here I thought you'd risen above the crass and commercial aspects of the holiday."

"No way. I'm as crass and commercial as they come."

"So what stopped you?"

"I just couldn't think of what to give you on such short notice. And then there was the little problem of the limited shopping opportunities up here on your grandmother's ten acres. I did consider making them. I could have gotten us into the craft project you managed to avoid when you came up with the boxes of decorations—origami, maybe. Or macramé."

"Some things you shouldn't do to a man."

"So true. I was afraid if I tried it, you might become violent."

"So you're saying, you ordinarily do all that? You go all out with the gifts?"

"That's right. I shopped and wrapped for everyone before I left Sacramento. Bought for my folks and my sisters and all their little darlings, for Janey and Cade and Ceil and Aaron."

"You send cards?"

"I do. Over a hundred now and the list is always growing."

He was shaking his head. "Sorry. I don't get it. It's too much work, and for what, really? People get crazy during the holidays, you know damn well they do. Expectations get too high. The suicide rate soars."

"Oh, relax. Nobody's making you do anything you don't want to do. All I'm trying to get across to you is you don't have to hide out here until the season is past. You could come down from the mountain, you know? Join your family for Christmas dinner. Expect a miracle, instead of disaster."

"If you're cooking, I might come."

"You are being altogether too appreciative." She took his empty plate and mug from him, set it, with hers, on the table at the head of the sofa bed. "I keep waiting for you to get mean again."

"I won't. On that level anyway, I'm a changed man. I've accepted the fact that I really do like you. And your damn cat, too."

"And next year? Will you be holed up here all over again?"

He faked a frown. "What do you want from me?"

What she wanted, she was trying very hard to keep remembering, she wasn't going to get. But he did look fabulous by tree-light. And here they were, all alone, with all this time on their hands, getting along so well, enjoying each other in *almost* every sense of the word.

And he was single and she was single and they were both adults and sometimes the best way to get rid of a big appetite was to simply go ahead and eat. Indulge yourself. Worry about paying the price later—if there was even going to be any price.

Certainly, it had to be possible for two reasonably mature adults to have a lovely, romantic, sensual interlude and remain on good terms when it was over. Who could say? Maybe it wouldn't have to end. Maybe they'd discover they were meant for each other. Like Jane and Cade—and Aaron and Celia.

Stranger things had happened.

Okay, okay. She could see the writing on the steamy window. Will Bravo was *not* going to suddenly realize she was the woman for him. He'd already found the woman for him. And she had died. He hadn't really gotten over her, and he wasn't looking for anyone to take her place.

And that was fine. Jilly wasn't looking for anything permanent either. Necessarily.

Jilly sighed. "What was the question?"

He had leaned in closer. He was looking at her mouth again. "I really want to kiss you."

She was looking at his mouth, too. Such a fine and tempting mouth it was. "I can't believe you said that."

"It would be a mistake, huh?"

"Probably." Her voice came out sounding so husky. She was thinking, *Probably, but do I care?*

And the answer? Less and less as each second ticked by.

"We could call it my Christmas present." He was whispering now. No need to speak louder. His mouth was just inches from hers, his breath warm on her lips, smelling of apples and chocolate and coffee.

"You want a kiss from me for Christmas?"

"I do. I want it a lot."

"And we *are* trying to build you some positive Christmas memories, now aren't we?"

"It's in a good cause."

"Oh, yes. I think so."

He lifted a hand and oh-so-tenderly smoothed her hair, following the line of it along the side of her face and under, until his palm lay curved, warm and encompassing, against the back of her neck. He pulled her toward him, that crucial last inch or so.

And at last, she felt his lips touch hers.

Chapter Eleven

It wasn't like her dream. He didn't burn her lips off.

He melted them.

Jilly sighed in pure pleasure, parting her lips slightly, just enough to tempt him to slip his tongue inside. He did.

Oh, yes. Oh, yes, yes, yes...

She slid her tongue along the bottom of his. He moaned. She liked that. She moaned right back and reached up a hand, clasping that hard, muscled shoulder of his, then caressing her way up, over the soft wool of that charcoal-gray sweater until she could slip her fingers into the silky hair at his nape.

He moaned again. And he guided her down against the skinny little pillows at the head of the sofa bed. He kissed her mouth for a long time and she kissed him right back, their tongues sparring and sliding, occasionally pausing to share a smile, mouth-to-mouth, and then delving in again.

Oh, it was lovely.

When he finally opened those deep-blue eyes and looked down at her, she found herself thinking how really great it was to be alive. You never knew what might happen. Someone mean and awful could decide to make a little effort to be a decent human being and then, before you knew it, you might find yourself discovering he was the best kisser you'd ever met.

"Merry Christmas, Will."

"Merry Christmas, Jilly. Thank you for my present."

"My pleasure." And it had been. Her pleasure in the extreme.

"I'd like to do a lot more than kiss you."

"I kind of picked that up. But you're conflicted, right? I mean, my best friends, your brothers, all that. Not to mention your mother."

He gave her a crooked smile. "See what you're doing to me? For a minute there, I actually forgot all about her and the trouble she can make."

She reached up and ran a finger along the fine, manly line of his nose. It was so nice. To touch him. To have him looking at her the way he'd been looking at her for most of the day. With admiration. With kindling desire. She was sorely tempted to explore this situation further, to get into it in delicious detail.

And anyway, why keep denying it? They were past the denial stage. He wanted her. She wanted him. Oh, yes. She did. She really, really wanted him.

But then again, she was like that. When Jilly really

wanted something, good sense flew right out the window. It shamed her to admit it now, but she had really wanted Benny Simmerson. And look where that had gotten her.

"I hate to be the voice of reason," she whispered. "It's so totally *not* me."

He looked gorgeously rueful. "You think we'd better sleep on it, don't you?"

"Yeah. I do. I think we'd better sleep on it *alone*."

Jilly had just climbed between the cool sheets of the bed upstairs when her phone started ringing. The bleating sound took her totally off-guard. After all, it hadn't rung for over two days now.

She grabbed it off the night table.

"Merry Christmas, darlin' girl." Caitlin's voice was husky and low and way too sexy for a woman who would be a grandma any day now. "We ought to put in a land line up there. I tried to call yesterday. And twice earlier today. I couldn't get through."

"No kidding. I guess you tried Will's phone, too?"

"He doesn't much like to hear from me this time of year. He doesn't much like to hear from anybody. But I guess you've figured that out by now."

"Well, Caitlin. I can't say about the phones. I'd imagine the storm knocked them out."

There was a tiny pause, then Caitlin asked sweetly, "Jilly honey, you mad at me?"

"Now, why would I be mad at you?"

"Oh, come on. You're mad. You are. But look at it this way, I never lied to you, now did I?"

"Yes, you did."

"You didn't ask. I didn't tell. That's not a lie."

"Have you ever considered running for public office?"

"With my past? Are you crazy?"

"Caitlin, I'd really like to know, was Celia in on this with you?"

"She was not. You know Celia. Not a tricky bone in her whole body. It was just one of those things."

"Just one of *what* things?"

"Things that happen. Things where everything works out all by itself. You needed a house in the mountains and you called Celia. She thought of my ma's house and said you ought to call me about it."

"And when I did call you, you lied."

"Sweetie. Face it. If I'd told you he was up there, would you be there now?"

"Of course not."

"Well, okay then. What else is there to say?"

"A lot. You've got to start reining yourself in a little, Caitlin, you've got to stop treating people as if they're pawns in some big chess game you're playing."

"Havin' a good time?"

"Well, I wasn't at first."

"But you are now, right?"

"Caitlin, I know that whatever I say to you is likely to come back to haunt me at a later date. So I think I'll just keep my mouth shut."

"Now, Jilly. Is that any way to be?"

"Are you at Jane's?"

"I got back to the Highgrade about twenty minutes

ago. My newest daughter-in-law can cook. What a meal. I won't have to eat for a week, at least. Why?''

"Maybe I'd like to say Merry Christmas to my friends. Maybe I'm concerned that they've been worried about me. For all they know I've been stuck alone in an old house way up in the mountains in a blizzard, with the phones on the blink. Maybe they'd like to hear that I'm all right.''

"Well, yeah, they were a little worried. But they put their heads together and figured out pretty quick that you weren't alone up there. And then, over dinner tonight, they got on me until I confessed that I sent you to Ma's house without mentioning that Will was going to be there, too.''

Missy jumped up on the end of the bed. She was looking only slightly sulky to be locked away from Will for another whole night.

"Jilly, you still there?''

"Barely.''

"I thought for a minute you'd hung up on me.''

"I have to admit, I'm tempted. So you told my friends how you tricked me.''

"*Tricked* you? I never used that word.''

"I'd better call them.''

"Whatever you think.''

"Maybe *you* ought to call Will.''

"And have him shout at me on Christmas? I'll pass.''

Jilly thought of the kiss they'd shared not too long before and smiled to herself. If Caitlin did call him, she might be surprised at how well he was taking being snowed in with the woman he had claimed to despise.

Not that Jilly would even hint at such a thing. It would only encourage Caitlin to keep on with her meddling.

Caitlin was still talking. "In years to come, you'll thank me. And look at it this way, all I did was give you an opportunity. And then along comes that big storm. Now, nobody could call that my fault. So in the end, what you two do with bein' stuck there together is completely up to you."

"You played me, Caitlin. You know that you did. All that stuff about how *primitive* it was going to be, on my own here in this isolated house, all the tips on how to start the stove, how to work the generator in case the power went out."

Caitlin laughed that husky, pure-sex laugh of hers. "Had you goin' there, didn't I?"

"Did anyone ever tell you that you are absolutely shameless?"

Caitlin sighed. "Well, sure. All the time."

"I have to go. I need to call my friends and let them know I'm all right."

"Jilly?"

"What now?"

"If you run into my ma's ghost, you be sure to tell her hi for me."

Jilly could hear the laughter in Caitlin's voice, but a cold shiver skittered up her spine anyway. "Very funny. Good night." She hung up before Caitlin could say another word and immediately dialed Jane.

Her friend answered on the second ring. "Jilly. Thank God you're okay."

"I'm fine. It's been…an adventure. The phones have been out."

"I know. I called and called."

"Well, they're working now. I didn't even realize they were back on until I got a call from Caitlin and—"

Jane cut her off. "Hold on, okay?" She spoke to someone on her end. Jilly recognized the other voice. Jane came back on the line, "Now, where were we?"

"Is that Celia?"

"It is. She and Aaron are staying the night. She wants to talk to you."

"You sound so serious. Honestly, I'm perfectly safe."

"We're just so relieved to hear from you—and you'd better call your mother. She's about to send out a posse."

"I will, I will."

"You said Caitlin called you...."

"That's right, a few minutes ago."

"We had it out with her at dinner tonight. We told her she had to stop manipulating people. You know how I adore her, but sometimes I think she needs a good spanking. Ceil's mortified, since she was the one who suggested you call Caitlin in the first place. She's sure you're going to think—"

"Put her on."

"I will. Jilly?"

"What?"

"You're *sure* you're all right?"

"Oh, Janey. You know me. Nothing gets me down for long."

"And Will?"

"He's fine, too."

"You're getting along?"

"Yes. I'll tell you all about it later. Maybe."

Jane laughed. "Miss you. Wish you were here."

"Merry Christmas."

Celia came on the line apologizing. "Jilly, I swear to you. I didn't know that Will would be up there. I assumed he'd be here, with the family, for Christmas. Turns out Janey knew, but I didn't get the story from her until after you'd left Sacramento."

"How did Jane know?"

"When she asked Cade to invite Will for Christmas dinner, Cade told her why there was no way Will would come, about he goes up to Mavis's old house every year now, since Nora died—and wait a minute. Do you even know about what happened to Nora? Am I making any sense at all?"

"You're making perfect sense. I do know about Nora. Will told me. And I don't blame you for a thing, so get that thought out of your mind."

"Oh, good. I'm so relieved."

"How are you? How's the baby?"

"Oh, pu-lease. You saw me two weeks ago. The words *elephantine* and *enormous* should come to mind."

"You look great."

"Right. Jilly, I am so sorry about all this."

"Don't be. Truthfully, everything's worked out fine. Will and I are getting along great. We've…made the most of an uncomfortable situation."

"But he wanted to be alone and so did you." Jilly heard Jane's voice in the background. Then Celia said, "Jane wants to know where you'll go when the roads are cleared. She says you should come here, stay with her and Cade for a few days.''

Jilly hadn't a clue right then what she would do when the roads were passable. Originally, she'd intended to stay at the old house until the second of January. And then, when she found Will here, she'd wanted to get out as soon as she possibly could.

But now?

She thought of his kiss again, felt her midsection melting. At this point, it was anybody's guess what would happen once she was free to go elsewhere. She had no appointments scheduled for another whole week. And her columns were no problem. She turned them in via e-mail, anyway.

"Tell Jane I'll give her a call."

"I will. And Jilly?"

"Yeah?"

"Merry Christmas."

"Merry Christmas to you, Ceil. Get your rest. Take your vitamins."

Jilly's sisters were in Reno with their families, at her mother's for the night. She called them all there. After she'd reassured them she was fine, she listened to a chorus of thank-yous for the gifts she'd sent.

Once she said goodbye to her family, she checked her e-mail. Incredible, the amount of mail that could pile up with just two days of down time. A lot of it was junk mail, links to her favorite on-line shopping sites where after-Christmas sales were already in progress. She grinned to herself. She ought to buy something—just so she could tell Will that she'd been to the after-Christmas sales and she hadn't had to jump over a single dying man to do it.

She went to sleep around eleven. If she dreamed of a certain man's exquisite kisses, that was her business. But in the morning, when she woke, she had no memory of any visits from Mavis.

Jilly raised her mug of instant cappuccino high. "Happy birthday, Will."

He grinned at her, a shy grin that tugged at her heartstrings, reminding her of the boy he must have been once, the boy whose birthday was too often forgotten. "You remembered."

They shared a long look. Jilly felt warm all over. Will had already been outside and come in to report he'd seen no sign of the snowplow. On the radio, all the talk centered on what had happened during the recent storms. "The worst in two decades," one announcer kept declaring. There were tales of people trapped in their cars, people stranded, digging snow caves, somehow surviving in spite of the terrible cold. And now it was over, not even the experts could say for sure how long it was going to take the Tahoe area to dig out from under.

Jilly figured they'd be stuck here at least till tomorrow. Possibly till Friday.

The thought sent her pulse pounding. Another day, at least, alone with Will, another day where she didn't have to make an actual choice to be here. Right now, the only decision before them was how intimate they would be while they remained snowbound in this house together.

"My phone's working," she told him. "I got a call last night."

He knew instantly. "Caitlin."

"I told her she ought to call you—but don't worry. She said she wasn't up to listening to you shout at her on Christmas."

There was a pause. It was a lovely one—but then, lately, all the pauses were lovely ones. They sipped from their mugs and they looked at each other and the morning sun shone through the window, bringing out the gold lights in his brown hair.

Finally, Will said softly, "I wouldn't have shouted at her."

"I know. But I didn't tell her that."

"Good thinking. If she knew how much I'm enjoying your company, I'd never hear the end of it."

"Your secret is safe with me."

"I didn't say it was a secret. I just said I'm not in the mood to discuss it with Caitlin."

Was that good news? Oh, she didn't know. She didn't care. She was feeling just a tiny bit addled, a little goofy, a tad confused. And very, very excited.

"After I talked to Caitlin, I called Jane. We wished each other a merry Christmas. I talked to Celia, too. She and Aaron were staying there for the night."

She waited for him to respond to that, thinking maybe he'd remark on how everyone would razz them now, about being snowed in here together for days and days. But he didn't say anything. He just looked at her, a slight smile curving his mouth. As if he liked looking at her, as if he liked it very, very much. As if he'd like to look at her with all of her clothes off.

As if he planned to do just that, very soon.

She set down her mug. "You should have a birthday cake. I'm pretty sure I can fake it with the ingredients on hand."

Now he was looking at her mouth. He seemed to really like that—to look at her mouth. He certainly did it enough.

He said, tenderly, "We've already got desserts running out our ears."

That warm, melting feeling was spreading—out from her stomach, down low in her belly, along her legs, up through her chest and down her arms. "Admit it," she said. "You'd like a cake."

"Well. Maybe a small one...."

"With a candle in it."

"Jilly, you think of everything."

"I try."

Right then, she was thinking that there was absolutely no way they would make it through the next night in separate beds, and she was wondering if she would live to regret what she was thinking.

Then again, maybe she was just thinking too much.

After they cleaned up the breakfast, Will said he wanted to put in a little effort at digging out the driveway. "There's no telling when the plow will get around to us. Might as well get a start on it."

Action. Yes. Fresh air and exercise. Ordinarily, Jilly wasn't all that big on physical fitness, but today, well, she had an excess of energy and clearing the driveway seemed as good a way as any to work some of it off. "You have two shovels?"

"There's no need for you to—"

"I want to. And I've certainly got the time. It's not going to take me all day to bake you a cake."

So they piled on their outerwear and got the shovels from the shed and spent the morning shoveling—well, to be strictly truthful, Will spent the morning shoveling. Jilly shoveled, too, but she took a break now and then— a bathroom break, a cup-of-cappuccino break, a stand-in-front-of-the-heater-until-the-shivering-stops break.

Even with breaks, it was hard work. And Jilly thought she saw that animal again—it was a flash of brown and white, sliding through the trees at the edge of the clearing. She stopped shoveling to watch for another sight of it, and Will teased her that she was daydreaming on the job. She shrugged and went back to work.

When they put the shovels away at noon, she was sore and sweating beneath her heavy coat. And for all the work they'd done, there was still a lot of driveway buried in three feet of snow.

"Every little bit helps," Will said. "Tomorrow, we'll get farther. And maybe the plow will show up."

Jilly's shoulders and arms were aching. "Tomorrow, I may not be able to move. What I want right now is a long, hot bath."

"The bathroom is at your disposal."

When they got inside, she made him go first. She knew he'd be quick and then she could relax in there, take her time, lolling and lingering. There were few things Jilly enjoyed quite so much as a long soak in a scented tub. And today, after doing all that shoveling, she really needed it.

But somehow, once she took off her clothes and climbed into the lovely fragrant water, she couldn't relax, couldn't tune out the fact that Will was on the other side of the bathroom door and as soon as she got done in there, she could be with him.

"That was fast." Will pulled the platter of sliced turkey from the fridge. "Want a sandwich?"

"I would love one."

He sent her what he clearly intended as a quick, affectionate glance. But then he must have seen it, right there in her eyes—what she really wanted, and how powerfully she wanted it. He turned to her fully and held out his hand.

She needed no further urging. She ran to him.

Chapter Twelve

Will gathered her into his arms.

Was there ever a woman who smelled this good? He buried his face in her fragrant hair and breathed deep. She nuzzled his shoulder. He kissed the crown of her head, loving the feel of the silky strands against his lips.

"You want this, right?" He cradled her face in both hands and made her look at him. "You've made up your mind. Is that the message I'm getting here?"

She pressed those sweet lips together and nodded.

He couldn't help smiling at her expression. "Scared?"

She stuck out that obstinate chin. "Are you kidding? Me?" Then she sighed. "Well, all right. Maybe a little." She held up her thumb and forefinger, with a quarter inch of space between them. "This much. No more."

"If you want to back out—"

"Uh-uh. I'm up for this."

"You're sure?"

She giggled up at him. "Are you trying to talk me out of it, now?"

"No way."

It was probably foolish and they'd both live to regret it, but hell. She was willing. And he ached to have her. And maybe, in the end, there were just some things even a man who wasn't in the market for a woman couldn't turn down.

But there was a problem. One that had only occurred to him when he saw she'd decided to carry this thing between them to its natural conclusion.

He'd brought no contraceptives. He never did, not to his grandmother's house. He always came up here on his own and no one ever dropped in for a visit. Opportunities for sexual encounters were nil. Or they had been.

Until Jilly.

And that had been fine with him—until Jilly.

He touched the bump on her forehead. "This is looking pretty good."

"You have an inordinate interest in the bump on my head."

"I'm just glad, every time I look at it, that it isn't any worse."

"It looks like hell, and you know it. But the good news is, I think I'll still be able to lead a full and productive life."

"It would appear so."

"And you're stalling."

"Maybe."

She kissed his chin. "Why?"

"Because right now, under any other circumstances, I'd be begging you to hold it right there while I ran down to the corner drug store."

The light dawned in those gray-blue eyes. "Better safe than sorry, you mean?"

"That's right." Now he couldn't read her expression. "What, exactly, are you thinking?"

"Well, it's like this," she said, and then wrinkled her nose at him in lieu of finishing her sentence.

"Jilly. Spill it."

"Okay, okay. I've got them."

He blinked. "Condoms? You've got—"

"Yes." She tipped her head back and let out a groan. "Oh, I just know what you're thinking. That I came up here to hook up with you, after all, that your original suspicions about me were true."

"That's not what I'm thinking."

"Right."

"Jillian. I swear to you I'm thinking nothing of the kind. And anyway, at this point, I don't give a damn why you came up here. In fact, if you *had* come up here because you just couldn't wait any longer to make mad, passionate love with me, you wouldn't hear me complaining. The only thing you'd hear from me would be, 'Hey, let me help you with that.'"

She turned her head to the side and slid him a look. "Really? You're past caring why I came up here?"

"Past it? It's so far behind me, I don't even remember anymore that I ever did care."

"And you're not thinking that I planned to seduce you?"

He cupped her face again, and lowered his mouth to brush a kiss against those sweet, sweet lips. "No, I'm not. But please. Don't let that stop you from going ahead and seducing me anyway."

She smiled against his mouth—and then pulled back enough to announce, "It's a matter of principle."

"I understand completely."

"Oh, you do not."

"Yes, I do." She started to argue further. He put a finger against her lips. "Wait. Listen." He tried to remember, to get the wording exact. "'Our bodies—and our health and well-being—are our own responsibility. Too many women aren't prepared when the moment comes. Or they tell themselves they plan to say no—and then find themselves changing their minds, saying yes. The point? Say no. Say yes. As a grown-up self-sufficient woman, it's your choice. But no matter what you plan to say, be ready to be safe.'"

Her cheeks were adorably flushed. "Will Bravo. You've been reading my column."

"I remembered that one in particular. I thought it was right on the money."

"But you...I mean, you, I..."

He grinned down at her. "Jillian Diamond at a loss for words. This has to be a first."

She made a face at him. "Treasure the moment."

"I am—and I'll admit, you were never supposed to know. No one was ever supposed to know. It was my guilty secret that 'Ask Jillian' had become every bit as much a part of my morning routine as Froot Loops and Belgian Crème cappuccino. That's why I made such an effort the other night, asking you those questions about what you put in your column.''

''You were hoping I'd never guess that you already knew?''

''You got it.''

''You don't seem especially guilty about it now.''

''All that's behind me. Somewhere between when you blew in the door Sunday and that kiss last night, I've given up trying to resist you.''

She sighed. He felt her soft, small breasts rise and fall against his chest. Her eyes were gleaming. She slid her hands up over his shoulders and her fingers brushed the back of his neck, threading up into his hair. ''You're surrendering totally?''

''Yeah. I'm gone. There's no turning back. I think it's only fair that you kiss me now.''

She obliged, lifting that incredible mouth and parting her lips beneath his.

He loved the way she tasted. It was every bit as good as how she smelled. He slipped his tongue inside, swept it around in that wonderful wet, slick heat. He could kiss her forever. That would be fine with him. They could stand there, in the kitchen, with the warm steam from her bath all around them, kissing until the rest of the day went by and the night came, and then just kissing some more.

It would be better, though, if they were both naked. And then, eventually, he was going to have to do something about how powerfully he wanted her—so much that it hurt.

But in a good way.

She'd come out of the bathroom in a red fleecy sweater that ended just above her waist. She also wore tight jeans that rode her hips and flared at the ankles. And red socks. Big, heavy, bright-red socks.

The sweater made things easy. No problem at all to slip his hands under there, to touch her bare skin, which was warm and so incredibly smooth. She shivered—and then she sighed.

They went on kissing. Her mouth invited him. Her slim, soft body pressed close.

He caressed the silky skin at the small of her back, followed the bumps of her spine upward. He already knew that she wore no bra. No red-blooded male could miss that, pressed as close as she was. Still, it was a delight to discover the fact all over again with his hands.

The sweater was in his way. He took the bottom of it and gave an upward tug. She helped him, lifting her arms. They had to break the kiss when the sweater got to their lips. But not for long. He pulled it over her head and tossed it behind him and pressed his mouth to her mouth again, gathering her close, feeling her tremble a little, smiling to himself.

In their time here together, he'd come to understand her—maybe better than she really wanted him to. Jilly had it all figured out—except when it came to herself. She was very tender at heart. Woundable.

He cupped her face again, made her look at him. "I won't hurt you, Jilly." He said the words and then he wondered why he'd said them. If he really meant to be certain of not hurting her, he shouldn't be doing what he was doing now.

Sex in the new millennium might not carry all the freight it once had. But there was still plenty of baggage around it. You got naked with someone and it could end up opening doors, setting off charges neither of you had expected. It could blow up in your face, and anybody who said they could guarantee otherwise was either a liar or a fool.

Jilly swallowed and nodded, her eyes wide. Wounded already. And sweetly dazed with desire. And right now, well, he was throwing good sense out the window and not caring in the least.

He wanted her. A lot. And her smooth, slim body was his for the taking.

He kissed her some more, daring to cup her small breasts, to play with the nipples, feel them pebble and harden. He pulled free of her mouth, only to kiss that wonderful chin of hers, to scrape his teeth on the stubborn tip of it, to slide his tongue along the satin skin of her throat.

There, he paused. He pressed his lips to the side of her neck, down low, just above the rise of her collarbone. He opened his mouth enough to draw on the thin, tender skin of her throat, sucking it against his teeth, raking it with his tongue. He would a leave a mark, and he knew it. He didn't care.

And neither did she, it seemed. She arched her throat to him eagerly. He eased the hard, drawing kiss, made it brushing, tender...

She said his name, on a whimper. He liked that, the

sound of his name from her mouth while he kissed the bruise he'd brought up on her throat.

He kissed his way downward, capturing one pretty, hard little nipple and sucking it into his mouth. She moaned and he sucked harder, slipping a hand down, finding the buttons at the front of her jeans and releasing them, one by one.

He slid his hand in there, under the elastic of her silky little panties. Yes. Wet. Creamy. So good....

It had been such a long time since he'd felt that. The silky curls, the soft mound, the wet readiness, growing wetter at his touch.

He cupped her, and then dared to slide a finger into that waiting wetness, to rub the tiny, swollen nub while he continued to kiss her breast, to lick circles around the nipple, to close his mouth over it, to draw long and deep...

She was moving now, pushing herself against his hand, making sweet, hungry noises low in her throat, clutching his head to her breast. That gold-streaked brown hair dragged, feather-soft, against his cheek.

She whimpered his name again. And then again and again. Her movements grew more frantic. She held him closer, urging him to drink from her, while at the same time, below, she moved, riding his stroking hand.

And then it happened. She stiffened and cried out. He felt her release, the tender pulsing against his fingers, the spill of wetness, the hard shudder that ran through her and then the low, purring moan. She curved herself around him, sighing, her hair falling in a veil over his face.

He took his mouth from her breast and, very carefully, drew a long, steadying breath.

He was right at the edge, and it was taking all he had to keep from going over. The scent of her, the silky wetness against his hand, the way she had shuddered as she came, all that had swept him dangerously close to the breaking point.

"Oh," she said. "Oh, Will…" And she slid one soft hand down and laid it over his hardness, cupping him so lovingly.

It was too much. He lost it. He ground his teeth and held on tight as a shattering climax ripped through him.

Chapter Thirteen

After a minute or two, Will chuckled softly. Then he groaned. "You'd never guess, would you, that it's been a while for me?"

Jilly wanted to kiss him all over. She settled for lifting his face, cradling it tenderly and kissing his lips—a long, deep, wet, very thorough kiss.

When she finally pulled her mouth from his, she whispered, "We never even made it to a prone position. But I have to tell you, I feel just great."

"*Yet*," he said low. "We haven't made it to a prone position *yet*."

She really did like the way he said *yet*. "Ah. I stand corrected."

"You certainly do. And I think I need a towel."

A few minutes later, they went upstairs to the bed they'd slept in beneath their separate afghans just two nights before. Jilly got the condoms from her suitcase and set them on the table by the lamp. Then she took off the rest of her clothes. Will took his clothes off, too, and put them on the straight chair in the corner of the room.

She gulped when he came toward her, so fine and strong, with those wonderful broad shoulders and powerful arms—and ready for her all over again.

When he reached her, he wrapped his arms around her, but not tightly, just resting them, clasped, at the small of her back. Below, she could feel him, nudging her belly, causing that giddy lightness in her chest, that wonderful weakening at the knees—and that delicious melting sensation within.

He kissed the tip of her nose. "Who would have thought it—the two of us, together like this?"

She felt a smile break across her face. "Well, Caitlin, of course."

The corners of his mouth turned down in a frown—but a playful one. "You *would* have to remind me."

"You know what I think she needs?"

"Hit me with it."

"A new boyfriend."

He considered, then nodded. "It's a thought. She obviously needs more leisure-time activities. But on the other hand, I have to say…" He brushed a finger up and down her spine, leaving lovely goose bumps in his wake.

Jilly sighed and almost forgot what they were talking about. But then she saw the teasing gleam in his eyes. She asked, "You have to say what?"

"Well, if it hadn't been for Caitlin, you wouldn't be here now."

"Too true." She could top that. "And neither would you—in the most basic sense."

"You have a point. It's one I should probably try to keep in mind whenever I get that urge to do her serious bodily harm. She was, after all, the one who carried me around for nine months, the one who gave birth to me and then fed me and clothed me until I was old enough to do it for myself."

"And loved you. You know she did—she *does*—in her own unusual way."

"Yeah." His voice was rough—and tender, too. "You're right. I know she does."

Jilly looked up at him, thinking that she'd never felt quite this way before—and then thinking, Omigod, what am I *thinking?*

She did have to watch herself. She could end up in big trouble.

I've never felt this way before was the kind of thing a woman tended to think before she started telling herself she'd found her one and only—otherwise known as *a love for all time.*

And *a love for all time?*

Well, that was what Jilly had told herself she'd found when Benny came along.

And let us never forget where it ended with Benny: divorce court—and having to give a perfectly good bed to the Salvation Army.

Therefore.

If perhaps it was true that she'd *never felt this way*

before, she was not moving on to believing that this just might be *a love for all time.*

It wasn't. It was a love for this moment. This magical, wonderful, tender, sweet moment. And for this moment, she was going to enjoy herself. Thoroughly.

She whispered, "Happy birthday, Will."

And he nodded, dark lashes low and lazy over those matchless blue eyes. "It is. One of the best. Maybe *the* best."

Now, that did sound lovely. But did she buy it? "Be honest, now. Nothing could top the year you got Snatch."

"This is pretty damn close—and you're not going to start in on me again about how I should get myself a pet, are you?"

"I never said you should get yourself a pet."

"Admit it. You thought it."

She fluttered her eyelashes at him. "Well, all right. Now that you mention it, I do think that a pet would be good for you."

"Now that *I* mention it?"

"You did bring it up, Will."

He made a low, disbelieving noise.

Which forced her to insist, "You did. You brought it up. You said—"

"I'm not going to argue with you, Jilly. I'll never win."

She smiled then. "Now you're learning."

"You know just what I need, huh?"

"Hmm," she said.

"Hmm, what?"

"Nothing. Just hmm..." She laid her hands against

his chest, where silky hair grew in a T pattern, across and then down in a trail to his navel—and below. With a sigh, she let her eyes drift shut. "Nice. The feel of your heartbeat..."

His fingers had gone wandering again. He was tracing little circles up the curve of her back. "Am I going to live?"

"Oh, I think so. Your heart is very strong. A good, even beat." She teased the small, tight masculine nipples, rubbing them lightly with her flattened palms. "You'll live a very long time. And you'll be happy."

"You not only give advice, you tell fortunes?"

She slid her index finger down that tempting trail of hair in the center of his chest, over his stomach, his navel...

He gasped as she encircled him.

"Yes," she said, gasping a little herself. "It's true. I can see the future. I have...connections in the spirit world." She thought of Mavis, shivered, put that thought away.

He tightened his arms around her. His eyes had changed. The teasing light was gone. He groaned. "Kiss me, Jilly...."

She was stroking him—long, slow strokes. He felt so silky, so hot, so good.

His mouth closed on hers. Jilly kissed him eagerly, hungrily. She was thinking in a dazed, half-formed way that she wished this pleasure could go on forever, wished the plow would never come, the snow would never melt. That it would be just the two of them, snowbound for eternity, warm and close, naked together.

They fell across the bed, arms and legs all tangled up, in another of those endless, bone-melting kisses. When at last they broke for air, she tried to slither down his body, to taste him in the most intimate, encompassing way.

He laughed—a laugh that got caught on a needful groan. "No, you don't." He took her arm and pulled her up so they were face-to-face again. "You'll finish me, like you did in the kitchen. I'm not letting that happen this time."

"But—"

"No." He put a finger to her lips and he whispered, "I want to be inside you...."

And she felt his other hand, moving down her body, finding the feminine heart of her, parting her. She cried out and pushed her hips toward him, eager and ready for the pleasure he would give.

"So wet," he murmured against her hair. "So sweet..."

She made a low, urgent sound—of agreement, of excitement, of yearning. Of joy.

And then he rolled away from her. She let out a whimper, a tiny cry of need and loss. But in no time he was close again, with one of the condoms she'd left on the table. He quickly unwrapped it. She reached out, helped him slide it down. And then he was rising above her, slipping a knee between her thighs.

The old bed creaked in complaint at all the activity—not that either of them cared in the least.

She looked up at him, braced on his hands, staring down at her, the whole wide sky right there, in his eyes. A sky she was falling through, endlessly, joy-fully.

She felt him, a touch of silky hardness, at her thigh and then right there, where she wanted him.

Needed him.

He came into her slowly, by aching, sweet degrees. She burned where he touched her. She went up in flames. Inside and outside, it was all one.

And she was falling, forever falling, through the endless blue depths of his eyes.

It was dark and they were still in the bed, though they'd crawled under the covers by then, when Jilly's phone rang. They looked at each other. And then they both laughed.

Jilly reached over and picked it up.

"Darlin' girl, let me speak to the birthday boy."

"Hold on." Jilly punched the Mute button. "You'll never guess who."

"Why didn't she call me on my own phone?"

"You want me to ask her?"

He swore and sat up. "Give it here." She handed it over. "What?" He listened. "Yeah?" He was silent. Caitlin, as usual, must be holding forth.

Jilly dragged herself to a sitting position, raked her love-ravaged hair out of her eyes and winked at Missy, who sat on the end of the bed giving herself a leisurely bath.

At last, Will said, "All right, Ma. Thanks." He pushed the end button and handed Jilly her phone.

She set it back on the table. "Let me guess. She wanted you to know how much this day means to her, the day you came into her life. She may not have always told you this, but she loves you with all of her heart and she's so grateful that you are her son.''

He made a growling sound. And then he smiled. ''Believe it or not, you're right. More or less.''

''In her own words, of course.''

''Of course. She also said I should be gentle with you, that you're a sweet, shy girl at heart.''

She dipped a hand under the covers and ran her fingernail up his beautifully muscled hairy thigh. ''She must be talking about some other girl you had up here once.''

He held her gaze. ''I never had any other girl up here. Only you, Jilly.''

She thought, *Not even Nora?* But somehow, she didn't quite have the nerve to ask. Nora seemed, somehow, a special being. His one true love, lost forever, but forever in his heart....

She cut her eyes away—and then looked back, grinning. ''And really, you didn't even have me up here on purpose, now did you?''

He didn't grin back. ''Not at first, no. But now, as far as I'm concerned, I've got you here on purpose. I'm glad you're here, Jilly. Very, very glad.''

She didn't know what to say to that. She felt...revealed, somehow. And that made her just a little bit nervous.

He seemed to understand, because suddenly he turned teasing. ''Is that your stomach I hear growling?''

She laughed and put her hand on her tummy. ''And

here I thought it was an earthquake. Pass me the Cheez Doodles.''

''Uh-uh. Let's go down and raid the refrigerator.''

Right then, she remembered what she'd forgotten to do. ''Oh, Will. I never baked your cake.''

''As if I noticed.''

''I could still do it. Why not? It's not like there's anything else we just have to get done.''

''Jilly, stop. The last thing we need around here is another dessert.''

''You're not *too* disappointed?''

''I am not in the least disappointed.'' He grabbed her by the shoulders and kissed her. Firmly. ''Now, is it all right if we eat?''

They threw on their clothes—well, Will did. Jilly put on everything but her red-fleece top. It was still downstairs on the floor where Will had tossed it when he whipped it off over her head. When they got down there, she picked it up, shook it out and pulled it on. They heated up what they wanted to eat, after which they sat at the table and didn't speak to each other until they both had empty plates.

Jilly pushed back her chair. Will started to rise, too.

''Sit right there.''

''You are the bossiest woman.'' But he didn't try to get up again.

She took their plates to the sink. And then she went around turning off lights—all except the one overhead. That accomplished, she got out the chocolate pecan pie, which only had two slices missing from it and would do just fine for a stand-in birthday cake. She found a candle in the candle drawer and stuck it in the center of the pie. There were kitchen matches in the old-fashioned dispenser on the back of the stove. She struck one and lit the candle.

Will chuckled as she flew over to douse the one remaining light.

"No laughing," she commanded. "This is serious business."

"Ah. Forgive me."

"All right. Just this once."

She returned to the pie, scooped it up and marched solemnly toward him, singing the birthday song. She set the pie before him and she sang the song all the way to the end. When she was done, he looked up at her, candlelight casting the planes and angles of his fine face into sharp relief.

"Well, what are you waiting for?"

"I thought maybe you'd have more instructions for me."

"What instructions? You make a wish. You blow it out."

"Gotcha." He tipped his head to the side and furrowed his brow, making certain she'd understand that he was doing the wish part. Then he closed his eyes, drew in a breath and blew out the candle.

She turned on the light.

He looked her up and down. "You've still got your clothes on."

Now, what was that supposed to mean?

He took note of her puzzled expression. "You said make a wish."

She understood. And groaned. "You're kidding."

"Uh-uh. I'd like you to do it now."

"You are getting awfully pushy."

"We're trying to give me good birthday memories. One way to do that is by seeing that my birthday wish comes true."

"Me naked? That's your birthday wish?"

He nodded.

"You should wish for something you haven't already had."

"Jilly. It's *my* wish. I think you should be nice and grant it." As if she could refuse him when he was looking at her like that. "And Jilly...."

"What?"

"Do it slowly, okay?"

After she finished her striptease, Will shoved back his chair, grabbed her and lifted her high against his chest. She squealed in surprise and then wrapped her arms around his neck and tucked her head into the curve of his shoulder. "You didn't eat your birthday pie."

"Later for that." He strode boldly across the cracked linoleum of the kitchen floor and up the stairs.

It was a long, heavenly night. They made love and they dozed, they woke up and talked for a while, shared a bag of Cheez Doodles, made love some more.

Very, very late, Jilly woke and could have sworn she saw Mavis at the foot of the bed—not reaching out, not floating toward her. Just standing there, a soft smile on her wrinkled face.

But maybe not.

When Jilly blinked, Mavis was gone. Jilly reached

for Will and her hand met warm, solid flesh. He opened his eyes, lazily murmured her name.

She whispered, ''Kiss me?''

He answered by opening his arms.

In the morning, after breakfast, Jilly told him she really had to spend some time on her column. So he kissed her and went out to shovel snow.

By a little before one in the afternoon, she had four days wrapped up, pieces she'd been working on that just needed a decent concluding paragraph or a snappy intro. She zipped them off. That put her well ahead of schedule. She wouldn't have to get anything more in until after New Year's, which made her feel very smug and self-satisfied.

And how was Will doing outside? A delicious shiver slid through her and warmth pooled low in her belly, just at the thought of getting out there and shoveling alongside him. She put her laptop away and rolled her shoulders, which were a little bit achy from the shoveling she'd done yesterday. But not bad. Not bad at all. She threw on her coat and boots, gloves and hat, and went out through the kitchen door, detouring to the shed to grab the second shovel.

Out in the clearing, she discovered he'd made some serious progress. She couldn't even see him when she stood by the cars. She hurried along the path of frozen ground he'd made, toward the close clumps of brush and trees that lined the twisting driveway, aware of a sad, sinking feeling in her stomach, a dragging heaviness in her feet.

The time was coming, and it wouldn't be long now.

Choices would have to be made—to go or to stay. And even if she stayed, how long would it last?

A few brief, lovely days. Then she'd return to her life and he'd go back to his. They'd meet periodically, for dinner at Jane's, a party at the Highgrade, some event in Las Vegas that Celia might organize.

Jilly's steps slowed to a stop at the top of the driveway. She looked down at the shovel in her hand. She wasn't going to like it much, having to be at get-togethers where Will would show up, too, where he'd smile and say hi, where they'd try to act normal and friendly, like casual acquaintances, after all that had happened here in the last few days. She had a feeling that was going to be pretty bad. Awful, even.

From somewhere far above, she heard a bird cry. Jilly lifted her head and sucked in a deep breath of bracing winter air. She could smell woodsmoke. And pine. She looked back at the old house, at the sparkling snow on the roof, the smoke from the chimney pipe trailing up toward the clear blue sky.

Winter in the mountains. Nothing like it in the world.

And as to her and Will…

Hey, the good part wasn't even over yet. She'd do well to remember that, to enjoy every last lovely second of the time they did have together. And who was to say that it had to end when they left this place? Okay, Will had told her that he wasn't in the market for a serious relationship. Did that mean there was some hard-and-fast rule that he could never change his mind?

People *were* allowed to change. And Will *had*

changed. They had both changed. Since they'd been snowed in here together, they'd gone from mutual dislike to friendship to becoming lovers.

Who could say what might happen next? Sometimes you just had to forge ahead and deal with whatever was around the next turn when you got there.

Jilly did forge ahead.

And around the next turn, from the bushes, a flicker of movement caught her eye.

It was a tail, wagging back and forth. The tail was hooked to a dog and the dog was staring right at her.

He was so *cute*. A brown-and-white shorthaired hound, nearly full-grown, but still with that soft, sweet puppy look about him. He had knobby, gangly legs and floppy ears and big, soft, lonely brown eyes.

But he was much too thin. His ribs stuck out.

"Oh, you little sweetheart...."

The dog let out a small, lonely-sounding whine, and then started backing deeper into the brush.

"Stay. Stay, boy. It's okay...."

The dog wagged his tail.

"Good boy." She took a step toward him.

The movement must have spooked him. He whirled and ran for the trees.

Jilly dropped her shovel and went after him, plunging hip-deep in just-cleared snow as soon as she stepped beyond the path Will had made. Ahead of her, at the edge of the brush where the trees started, the dog had paused to look back at her, tail low, but still wagging—hopeful, but not quite sure if he ought to trust her.

"Hey," she said softly, holding out her hand, palm up. "Come on. It's all right."

The dog perked those silky brown ears, tipped his sweet head to the side and whined again.

Jilly dared to haul her booted foot up and put it down into the knee-deep snow beyond the shoveled pile. Another step. And then another.

The dog whined once more and took off.

"Wait! Here boy, it's okay...." Jilly pushed on, snapping bushes aside, plowing through the snow. Behind her, she heard Will call her name.

But she didn't turn. She staggered on. She knew the dog was the animal she'd spotted yesterday and the day before, the shy creature she'd seen skirting the clearing. The poor guy was hungry. The poor guy needed help.

At last she reached the trees, where the snow was patchier than in the bare brush, making it easier to struggle ahead. But the tall pines not only made the way clearer, they also cut off the sun. Jilly shivered at the sudden drop in temperature—and kept going, fast as she could, following the tracks the dog had left, though by then the animal itself was nowhere to be seen.

From behind her, Will called again. "Jilly! Jilly, stop!"

She turned to look for him and saw him, just ducking under the thick cover of the trees. She waved at him, but kept on moving. She just wasn't ready yet to give up on the poor, lost mutt.

It was a big mistake—that she turned to wave and took her attention off the ground before her. She compounded the error by spinning quickly to the front again, rushing ahead without really looking where she was going.

It was one of those slow-motion moments. She put her foot down just as she registered that she'd stumbled onto a ravine. She tried to yank her foot back.

Too late.

She teetered. Gravity won.

With a sharp, startled cry, she fell, rolling. And then she hit her head on something hard. Lights seemed to pop and flash before her eyes. She was still rolling...

And then everything went black.

Chapter Fourteen

Will had tried to warn her. He'd shouted at her to stop. He should have known that wouldn't work. Jilly, after all, was one of those women who could be counted on *not* to do what a man told her to do.

She went over. It was terrible to watch. She was there, twenty yards in front of him—and then she toppled from view into the ravine his grandmother had always called the Dead Drop, the one that seemed to be there out of nowhere if you didn't know to look for it.

Will raced for the spot where she had vanished, his heart beating out a rhythm of doom, her name a desperate litany scrolling through his brain.

Jilly, Jilly, Jilly, Jilly...

At last he reached the edge. He looked down. She was at the bottom. Curled in a ball.

Not moving.

He swore, a harsh string of very bad words. And then he started down, sliding, stumbling, almost falling, keeping his feet by some dark miracle, willing her to be all right.

Maybe two-thirds of the way, he lost his footing and went rolling. Fine, he thought, perfect. It would get him to her faster.

He hit the bottom and crashed to a stop against the trunk of a tree. With a groan, he surged to his feet. He'd landed close. Good. Two steps and he was standing over her.

"Jilly…" He knelt beside her and reached out, oh-so-carefully smoothing the hair, sticky with blood, away from her forehead.

And there it was, another bump, rising on the left side, exactly opposite the one she'd acquired the other night. It was bleeding, but not too badly. If he hadn't been so starkly terrified for her, he might have smiled.

She wouldn't like it, another bump like that. The good news was it didn't appear that any of the blood had gotten on her coat this time.

He was not a man who prayed—but he did then. He prayed that she would come to, look at him, for God's sake, that she was going to be okay. He prayed and he tried not to think that it was Christmastime, that bad things—the worst things, the horrible, ugly things—always happened at Christmastime.

"Jilly…" Very gently, smoothing more hair out of the way, he put two fingers at the side of her throat.

Yes! A pulse—a strong and steady pulse.

And right then she groaned and batted his hand

away, sucking in a deep breath, which caused her to groan again. She touched her head, whimpered, and rolled to her back, groaning some more as she did it, her sweet face scrunched up in an expression that told him rolling over had not felt good.

He ripped off his coat, wadded it in a ball and gently eased it beneath her head.

She moaned some more and touched the new injury a second time. "What...?" Her eyes popped open as she pulled her hand away enough to see the blood on her fingers. "Oh, no. Not again...."

"Jilly. Jilly, can you hear me?"

She blinked, focused on him, blinked again. "Will?"

"Yes. That's right. It's me, Will."

She lifted her head, looked around, then let it drop back to the pillow of his jacket again. "What happened?"

She knew who he was. She knew she'd been injured. What she'd said when she saw the blood on her hand led him to believe she even remembered that a tree branch had dropped on her a few nights ago.

The tight bands of dread and terror that had clamped around his chest eased a little. He realized he'd hardly been breathing and let himself suck in a long, hungry gulp of freezing winter air.

"Jilly, you fell. Into a small ravine not far from the driveway at my grandmother's house."

"I fell?" She was scrunching up her face again. And then her eyes widened. "I remember. There was a dog. Oh, Will. He was the sweetest thing. The way he looked at me, through those big, soulful brown eyes. I just loved him on sight, I swear I did.''

What the hell was she babbling about? He couldn't begin to guess. ''Listen. Concentrate.''

''Concentrate,'' she repeated, as if the meaning of the word eluded her. Those heavy brows drew tightly together and she squinted up at him. ''All right. What?''

''Are you hurt anywhere else, other than where you hit your head?''

''Oh, come on. I hurt *everywhere*.''

He chuckled at that, though the sound had a frantic, strangled quality to it. ''I know you do, sweetheart. What I mean is, do you think anything's broken or sprained?''

She closed her eyes. For several seconds she was very still. Then, slowly, she moved her head from side to side.

''Is that a no? Are you giving me a no?''

She made a low noise in her throat. ''Yes, Will. I am giving you a no. I don't think anything's broken. Or even sprained. I honestly don't. I think that I have bruises on my bruises and it's not going to be fun to drag myself out of here. But I'm okay.'' And then she smiled. He'd never in his life been so grateful to see a woman smile. ''Hey, pretty good, huh? I roll down the side of a rocky ravine and the worst I get is another whack on the head. Do I lead a charmed life, or what?'' She started to sit up.

''Uh-uh. Better not.'' Gently but firmly, he guided her back down. ''Rest a few more minutes.''

''It's cold out here. I'm not lying out here for long,

I'm warning you—and where's your jacket? You've got to be freezing.'' She frowned, felt behind her head. "Oh. Here it is. I want you to—''

"Jilly, damn it. Lie still.''

"But you need your—''

"I'm fine. I don't want my coat.''

"You don't have to shout.''

She was right. She was hurt and the last thing she needed was to hear him barking orders at her. "Sorry. Just…keep the coat. Please.''

"I won't lie here forever.''

"Just for a few minutes.''

"Oh, all right.'' She closed her eyes—for maybe thirty seconds. Then they popped open again. "Where's my hat? I'm not wearing my hat.''

"I'm sure it's on the hillside somewhere. We'll find it. Relax.''

She sighed. "Will?''

"Yeah?''

"Did you see the dog?''

She was back to the mysterious dog again. He shook his head.

She insisted, "There was a dog. Honestly. The cutest thing. Brown-and-white spotted. Shorthaired. I'm sure it was the animal I saw before—remember, yesterday when we were shoveling, and then also Christmas Day when we—''

"I remember.''

"He looked so sad and hungry.''

"You're saying you were chasing a dog just now?''

"Um-hm. But I lost him. He disappeared into the trees.''

The last thing she needed to worry about at this point was some stray mutt. "Well, the dog is gone now."

"There were tracks. I'm sure if you—"

"Jilly. Are you listening?"

"I hate it when you treat me like I'm brain-dead."

"Forget the dog."

"But—"

"Please. Forget the dog."

She looked at him with the dangerous gleam of impending mutiny in her eyes. "I just think—"

"*Please.*"

Finally, she sighed. "All right. I'll forget the dog. For now."

"Thank you."

Gingerly, she poked at the new lump on her forehead again. "Ugh. I do not believe this. One lump on each side." She shivered. "And I'm cold. *You* must be freezing." She lurched to a sitting position so fast, he didn't have time to make her stay down. "Ow. It hurts to sit up."

"I could have told you that."

"But it's manageable." She was already drawing her legs under her.

He grabbed her shoulder. "No, you don't."

She batted at his hand. "Oh, stop that. I'm fine. And we can't hang around down here all day. We'll freeze to death."

"You really believe you can make it back up that hill?"

"What else is there to do?"

"You can stay here. I'll go up and get—"

"Forget it."

"You didn't let me finish."

"You don't need to finish. You already said the part I don't like, which is that I would stay here."

"It's only until I can—"

"No way. I can make it. I know I can."

She seemed pretty sure of herself. And if she got a few steps and realized she'd overestimated her current capabilities, they could always do it his way. "All right. Let's go."

She flashed him a big smile to show how game she was. "Give me a hand, will you?"

He slid in close and she wrapped her arm over his shoulder. "Ready?" he asked.

"As I'll ever be."

"Here we go." He levered her upright.

She groaned, but she got there. "Oh, my poor head is spinning...."

"Want to lie back down?"

"Not on your life. Put on your coat and let's go." She looked so damned adorably determined.

He warned, softly, "I'll have to let go of you to do that. You'll have to stand on your own."

"Got that. Let's try it." Her cheeks were bright red and so was her nose. Her breath came out as a white cloud. Her forehead looked like a topographical map. He'd never seen anyone so beautiful in his life.

She nudged him with her hip. "Hey."

"Yeah?"

"You're still holding on."

He was. It had just occurred to him that he didn't want to let go. Ever.

Now, how the hell had that happened? It wasn't *supposed* to happen. This was an interlude they were sharing, wasn't it? Something sweet and passionate, tender—and temporary. She was helping him with his Christmas issues and they had become lovers. For a time.

He'd given up thinking about how they'd deal with what had happened between them when it was over. Maybe he'd been avoiding thinking about that. But one thing he'd been sure of. This wasn't going to be permanent.

So why, he wondered, was it suddenly so damn difficult to imagine letting go?

"Will? Are you all right?"

"Yeah. Fine." He stepped away from her.

She wobbled a little, but then she pulled it together. "See?" Her smile was smug now. "What did I tell you?"

He scooped up his jacket. "Okay, let's start climbing."

She stumbled more than once on the way up. But she didn't complain about it. She just went to all fours until she found her footing again. Whenever he offered a hand, she waved it away.

"Fine so far," she told him, and "I can do it," and "I'm okay. Really." And she was, as far as he could see. She was doing just fine.

She found her hat about halfway up. "You were right." She beamed him one of her beautiful smiles. "Here it is." She shook off the snow and pulled it on her head.

At the top, she let out a big breath. "Whew." She looked down to where they had been. "We made it." And then she veered off to the left.

He caught up with her in two strides and grabbed her arm. "Not that way," he said gently and tried to turn her toward the driveway.

"Will, look." She pointed at the snow, at a set of animal tracks leading along the rim of the ravine. "The dog."

"What about it?"

"He went that way. We can follow him and maybe we'll find him, after all."

He wanted to shake her. And he wanted to protect her. And the desire to grab her and hold her and never let her go seemed to keep getting stronger as each minute ticked by.

"Come on. Let's find him." She tried to shrug off his grip.

He held on. "Listen to me."

"You know, you're squeezing my arm really hard."

He loosened his grip, but he didn't let go. "Say that we caught up with the dog."

"Okay, great. Say we did."

"If we caught up with the dog, then what?"

She looked at him, so hopeful, so determined, her forehead all bumps and bruises, blood in her hair. "We would bring him back to the house."

"How? The animal wouldn't come to you before. What makes you think it's going to be different now?"

"Well, but we can't just—"

"You've been hurt. The last thing you should do

right now is to go trooping off into the woods after a stray dog.''

''But what if he meets up with a mountain lion, what if he—''

''Jilly.'' He took her by the shoulders and turned her so she faced him fully. ''You can't save every stray creature that runs across your path.''

She glared at him. ''I can try, damn it.''

He cast about for the words that would get her to do what was best for her. ''Look. You said you think this dog was the same animal you've seen twice before.''

''I know it is.''

''Then have a little damn faith, would you? The dog's lasted this long. Maybe it knows what it's up to. And there *are* other houses in these mountains. It probably belongs to someone who lives in one of them.''

''But he was so skinny. And he didn't have a collar....'' Her mouth twisted. She looked up at him, pleading with her eyes. He refused to give in. At last she let out a long sigh. ''All right. I'll go inside.''

He barely had time to enjoy his relief before he realized there was a bargain coming.

''But,'' she said.

''Hit me with it,'' he muttered bleakly.

''*I'll* go on inside. *You* follow the tracks and see if you can find him.''

No damn way. Now she'd managed to get out of that ravine, he wasn't taking his eyes off her until he was certain she was going to be all right. She must have picked that up from his expression, because she came up with another idea.

"Well, then, how about this? We'll go in together. I'll behave myself for a while. You'll see that, once again, I have escaped the looming specter of brain damage."

"Brain damage is nothing to joke about—and how long is a while?"

"An hour."

He scowled at her.

She offered, "Two?"

He said nothing.

Her mouth went tender—and her eyes knew way too much. "Oh, Will. I know you're scared. Since it's Christmastime, of course you're expecting the worst. But it's not going to happen. I'm going to be fine. How about this? I'll do what you said. I'll have some faith that the dog will survive another day. But then, tomorrow morning, when it's been over twelve hours and I'm still fine, we'll go out together. We'll see if we can find him."

It was all these damn conflicting emotions that were doing him in. She'd been hurt and he wanted to take care of her. But she wouldn't let him take care of her. She wanted to go traipsing off on a wild goose chase after some lost dog. And that made him want to shout at her. And then, he couldn't stop asking himself, how could any injured person be so damn sexy, standing there, shivering, at the edge of that ravine?

"What do you say?" she asked softly.

He swore. "All right. It's a deal." He grabbed her arm again.

And he refused to let go until they were back in the house.

Chapter Fifteen

Jilly meant to be a model patient, she truly did. But she'd never been all that good at being sick even when she really *was* sick. There was just too much to do to waste time lying around getting well. And to have to rest and be still and try to be quiet when there was nothing wrong with her beyond a few bumps and bruises, well, it was a lot to ask.

But she'd made an agreement. And she would try to stick by it.

Will insisted on tending her injury. After she rinsed the blood from her hair, he made her stand by the sink while he used a pad dipped in peroxide to clean the bits of dirt and debris out of the abrasion that crowned her newest goose egg.

"Oops," she couldn't help teasing him, "looks like death by infection is outta here."

For that, she got a scowl and a grunt.

"Will you stop worrying?" she implored.

"Yeah. Eventually. For now, lie on the sofa. Rest."

"For how long?"

"Jilly, you promised you'd behave."

"I'm behaving. I just want to know how long I have to lie down."

"At least an hour."

"Oh, great. It's not bad enough I roll into a ravine. I have to lie down for an hour. You know I really hate that. Just lying there, with nothing to do."

He only looked at her, the way a put-upon parent might look at a recalcitrant child.

She asked, sheepishly, "So would you mind if I got my laptop first?"

"I'll get it." He had the ice pack all ready. He handed it to her. "You lie down."

Carefully, she pressed it to her left temple. "And bring both of the pillows from my bed, will you? The ones on the sofa are too skinny."

He was already at the stairs by then. He signaled he'd heard her with a wave of his hand.

Jilly trudged into the living area and plunked herself down on the edge of the sofa bed. She pulled the ice pack away and prodded her new bump a little. Then she put the pack to her temple again and looked at her heavy green socks for a while, noting the way her head pounded when it was lowered, acutely aware of all her new aches and pains—at her left hip, the small of her back, her right shoulder. Those areas would probably be black and blue by tomorrow.

She sighed. Oh, well, at least it was overcoat

weather. To the world at large, the damage wasn't even going to show—well, except for the disaster that was her forehead. Hmm. Maybe what she needed was one of those slouchy Ralph Lauren straw hats.

She heard him coming back down the stairs. "Oh, thank you," she said, her heart melting a little when he appeared around the corner from the kitchen, carrying everything she'd asked for—and a bag of Cheez Doodles, too. He helped her to get comfy sitting up against the pillows, her snack beside her and her laptop on her knees.

The hour started out fairly well. She spent a few minutes fooling with her e-mail correspondence. But that was awkward, since one hand was occupied holding the ice pack in place. Next she went to the Web to get in a little research on a possible future column. But then she made the mistake of looking up.

Will sat in his easy chair, cell phone in hand, his face a grim mask. He stared straight at her, clearly awaiting the first sign of coma or convulsion so he could dial 911.

She laid the ice pack aside long enough to shut down her computer. "All right, Will." She set the laptop on the floor. "We need to talk."

He frowned. "About what?"

Where to begin? "I'm fine. Can't you see? Nothing terrible is going to happen to me. And all the progress you've made in the past few days is going to be worth exactly zip if you refuse to give up all these irrational fears."

His lip curled—and not in a smile. "Irrational."

"Don't sneer at me. I said your fears are irrational.

And I think, if you'll examine them a little, you'll see that I'm right.''

He sneered some more. ''In the past five days— since you've been around me—you've had a tree limb fall on your head, your cat has disappeared, and you've fallen down a ravine.''

She readjusted her ice pack. ''So?''

''So, I don't like it. It gives me the creeps. It's as if I'm a jinx or something.''

''Will Bravo.''

''When you say my name like that, I know damn well a lecture is coming.''

''Listen to me carefully. You are a reasonable man. And as a reasonable man, you have to know that there's no such thing as a jinx.''

''Sure. I know that. It doesn't change the way I feel. And I feel that I'm a jinx. People and animals get hurt when they hang around me at Christmastime.''

''Oh, that is crazy. You know that it is. You can't blame yourself because a branch breaks off a tree and falls on my head, because a cat runs out a door you didn't even leave open, because I don't look where I'm going and end up falling down a hill. None of those things was in any way your fault.''

He set the phone on the chair arm. ''Look. You're supposed to be resting, not arguing with me.''

She was not getting through to him and she knew it. ''Will, you're worrying me.''

He made a low, growling sound. ''*I'm* worrying *you?*''

''Yes. Oh, don't you see?'' She waved the ice pack, a wild gesture in the general direction of the tree they'd put up two days before. "We were tricked into being here, together, for the holiday. You despised me and I couldn't stand you. But look what happened? It's turned out so beautifully, in the end. We made a real Christmas, just the two of us. And you said yourself that yesterday was one of the best birthdays you've ever had."

Right now, he was saying nothing. He only stared at her, his jaw set and his eyes unreadable.

"Oh, Will, why not look on the bright side? Sometimes bad things happen, but on the whole, life is really something. You said it yourself, out there in the woods a little while ago. You just have to have a little faith. You have to trust, to believe that things will work out all right in the end."

"And what if they don't?"

"Well, then, you pick yourself up off the floor and you try again."

"And if trying again means that other people will get hurt or die?"

"Oh, listen to yourself. You can't possibly believe what you're saying."

She waited for him to tell her that she was right, of course he didn't believe such a crazy thing. But the seconds crawled by and he didn't answer. He only looked at her, stone-faced and brooding, like the doomed hero of some tragic nineteenth-century romance.

At last he shrugged. "You're right. It's not logical. Let's drop the subject."

"But—"

"Damn it, Jilly. I mean it. There's no point in talking about this."

Jilly looked down at her socks. There was something about the way he'd said *Damn it, Jilly* that let her know the subject was closed—for the moment, anyway.

Maybe later she could get him to talk about it some more.

She put the ice pack down, opened her bag of Cheez Doodles and held them out to him.

"No thanks."

So she took a handful for herself and picked up her laptop again. She worked for the remainder of the hour she'd promised to rest, crunching her cheese snack, taking care not to look up at him. She really didn't want to see him sitting there, watching her like a hawk, ready with gruff denials if she dared to suggest he ought to lighten up and stop waiting for her to keel over dead.

For the rest of the day, Will was tender, solicitous—and emotionally about a million miles away. Once he'd begun to believe that he wouldn't have to call in the paramedics after all, he dared to leave her alone long enough to go outside and put the shovels in the shed.

When he back came in, he looked at her probingly. "You're feeling all right?"

"I'm feeling great." It was a slight exaggeration—but in a good cause.

"Will you be okay on your own if I have a quick bath?"

"I'll be fine."

He was in and out of the bathroom in record time. When he emerged, she was standing at the refrigerator trying to decide what to whip up for a very late lunch.

"You okay?" he demanded, as if he suspected she might have been temporarily comatose when he wasn't looking.

She bit back a flippant reply, shut the refrigerator door and sauntered over to him. He eyed her with a wariness she didn't find flattering.

However, nothing ventured, as the old saying went.

And he really was such a gorgeous example of the male gender. How could a girl resist? All shaved and smelling so clean and good. She put her arms around him and laid her head against his shoulder. Those strong arms encircled her and held on tight. For a minute, she almost dared to hope that things were going to be okay.

But then she lifted her head and tried to kiss him.

He took her by the forearms—and gently pushed her away. "What's to eat?"

So they ate. After that, he suggested a game of checkers. She almost said she'd prefer that they take off all their clothes and do naughty things to each other.

But no. A remark like that was a little too risqué for the mood he was in. He seemed to see her as an invalid who refused to admit she was sick. And he was hardly the kind of man who did naughty things to invalids.

She gave him her most cheerful smile. "I'd love to beat you at checkers."

She didn't. He won. Five times running.

When he took her last man for the fifth time, she wanted to demand a kiss as consolation for the trouncing she'd endured. But then she looked up from the checkerboard. He'd been watching her—and the minute she caught his eye, his gaze shifted away.

This was awful. It felt as if they were back at square one. They might never have been lovers, the way he looked at her now.

A new approach was needed. Maybe, since none of her attempts to get close to him seemed to work, she'd be better off to surrender the field for a while. Give him a little private time.

In fact, she could do with some private time herself. Some time to relax without the constant pressure of his worried gaze tracking her every move. Time to try to figure out how to bridge this chasm that seemed to have opened up between them.

He was putting the game away. She suggested, "I think what I could use is a long, hot bath."

"Help yourself."

In the bathroom, while the tub filled, she shucked off her clothes and examined all her bruises in the cracked mirror on the back of the door.

Ugh. Not a pretty sight. The one on her right shoulder was especially large and purple and shaped roughly like the continent of Africa. And her forehead was a mess. Aside from the gruesome bruising, she looked as if she was about to sprout a pair of horns.

Ah, well. She had no broken bones. Yes, it was ugly, but it wasn't *permanent* ugly. In a few weeks, it would all fade away.

And also, she did have one *good* bruise—the tiny

one at the base of her throat, where Will had marked her with a passionate bruising kiss the first time they made love.

She climbed into the bath, shampooed and then gently washed her poor, battered body. After that, she lay back and drifted. She shut her eyes and drew in deep breaths, setting her mind on peaceful thoughts.

Until Will pounded on the door and she lurched upright, sending water sloshing everywhere.

"What!"

"Are you okay?"

"Fine."

"Are you sure?"

"Will."

"What?"

"If I'm about to die, I'll let you know."

"Is that supposed to be funny?"

"Go. Away."

A silence. Then she heard his footsteps moving off. She spread her wet washcloth over her face, sank back into the cooling water, and wondered what she was going to do about him.

It got worse.

He went to bed with her, yes. But she should have known what he was up to when he climbed between the covers wearing a T-shirt and sweats.

Determined to give it her best shot, she cuddled up close and lifted her mouth for a kiss.

She got a quick, dry peck.

"Goodnight, Jilly." He reached over and flicked off the light and settled in on the other pillow with his back to her.

She lay there, staring into the darkness. She was starting to get angry. "Will?"

He made the kind of noise that was probably supposed to make her think she was waking him up. Right. No way he was sleeping. He was lying there, listening, waiting for something terrible to happen to her so he could take steps to save her.

"You only came to bed with me to keep an eye on me, didn't you? If you weren't set on protecting me from whatever awful thing you're just sure is going to happen to me, you wouldn't be here now, would you?"

He sat up and turned on the light. "You want to fight, is that it?"

"No. I don't. I promise you, I don't."

"You sound like a fight just before it happens."

"I admit, I'm getting close. And you just avoided answering either of my questions."

He raked his hand back through his hair. "Jilly…"

She waited. But he didn't say anything else. Only her name in that sad, unfinished, trailing-off way.

"Are you going to talk to me, Will?"

"Sure. What do you want me to say?"

Be calm, she told herself. Do not start shouting at him. "You're just so far away. I don't know what to do, don't know how to get through to you."

There was a pause, endless and awful. Then he said, quietly, "Maybe you should just let it be." He sounded so…weary. So completely resigned.

Her anger fizzled and died.

She was tired, too. It had been a tough day. Right

now, she simply didn't have the energy to keep struggling to scale the wall he'd put up between them.

Maybe tomorrow...

"I guess so," she said softly. He said nothing, so she whispered, "Turn off the light."

He reached for the lamp. The room went dark again.

They lay down, not touching, facing opposite directions. After a while, Missy jumped up between them and settled in, purring.

At least the cat's happy, Jilly thought. She closed her eyes. And for the first time, she actually found herself hoping for a visit from Mavis. She could certainly use a little advice from beyond the grave concerning what to do about Will.

When Jilly woke in the morning the only dream she recalled was a long, rambling one where she'd gone to a party of strangers. Once she realized she didn't know a soul at that party and no one wanted to talk to her anyway, she kept trying to leave. Too bad every door she opened only led to another room full of people she didn't know who had no interest at all in talking to her.

She could not remember seeing Will's grandmother in the dream. Where were the spirits of the dead when you needed them?

And where was Will? She reached out, touched the wrinkled sheet on his side of the bed. Cold.

She got dressed—moving a little stiffly due to her various bumps and bruises—and went downstairs. He was sitting at the table, eating his breakfast. He looked up and smiled at her, a friendly smile.

But cool. And distant. A smile that told her the wall between them was still firmly in place.

She had the most awful, hollow sort of feeling right then. She thought, *It's over. What we had is all we're going to have. He's going to get up and go outside and get the driveway cleared so that I can go.*

"Good morning," she said and smiled back at him. Then she made her instant coffee and poured herself some cereal.

He was done eating before she finished. He went into the bathroom. She heard the water running. When he came out, he headed straight for the coat rack and started putting on his boots.

"What's up?" she asked, her voice falsely bright.

He pulled on his jacket. "I'm going to get out there, get to work on the driveway."

Her heart felt as if some cruel hand had wrapped around it and was squeezing hard. Oh, yeah. He needed to get that driveway cleared. No way to get rid of her until he did.

And then she remembered that poor, lost dog. And Will's promise of the day before.

She said, "I'll be out in a few minutes. We can look for the dog."

He was on one knee, tying his bootlace. He glanced up. "Do you really think there's any point in that?"

"I don't know. I just want to try."

"I'd say it's pretty unlikely we'll find the animal now. You realize that, don't you?"

There was a traitorous tightness at the back of her throat. She came very close to hating herself for that, for the urge to shed her tears of hopelessness right there in front of him. "I just want you to keep the promise you made to me yesterday."

"Jilly…" There it was again. Her name. Trailing off into nothing. "Listen, I—"

"No." She swallowed, pulled her shoulders back. "*You* listen. If you don't want to look for the dog, fine. I'll look by myself." She had him there and they both knew it. No way he would let her go off by herself—except when she left him, which would be very soon now.

"All right," he muttered, rising. "I'll help you look for the dog." Instead of turning for the door, he went through the living area. He disappeared into his bedroom and when he came out, he had an old rifle with him.

She'd lived in the mountains as a girl. She knew that it was wise to have a weapon if you planned to traipse around deep in the woods. But they shouldn't be going that far from the house. "I don't think you'll need that."

"Maybe not. Better safe than sorry, though." He grabbed his gloves from the shelf above the coatrack and went to the door.

"Will. I'd like to make one other point, if you don't mind."

He paused with his hand on the knob. "Go ahead."

"Other than this, to help me look for that poor lost dog, I am not asking for anything you don't want to give. I don't *want* anything you don't want to give. Is that clear to you?"

"Perfectly." His voice was soft and utterly flat. He

pulled open the door and went out, closing it quietly but firmly behind him.

A half an hour later, she got the second shovel from the shed and went to find him.

He was a good two-thirds of the way down the driveway. She felt it again—that infuriating tightness at the back of her throat. He looked so strong and purposeful, rhythmically shoveling, his hair gleaming bronze in the thin winter sunlight, working hard to clear the way for her to leave him.

He tossed a final shovelful off the driveway. Then he stuck his shovel in the high bank of cleared snow and turned to face her, panting slightly, a dew of sweat on his brow. "Ready?"

She stood her shovel a few feet from his. "I'll help you with the driveway once we've looked for the dog."

His gaze swept over her, from her battered forehead to the toes of her boots. "It's not necessary. I'm sure, after yesterday, you've got some serious aches and pains."

"I'm all right. A little exercise will loosen up the stiffness."

He looked as if he would argue, but then he pressed his lips together and gave her a curt nod. "Suit yourself. I left my rifle on the porch."

She resisted the urge to argue again that they didn't need a rifle. She knew it was an argument she'd never win. "I'll go with you."

They walked back to the house together. He got the rifle and they set off, Jilly in the lead.

"This way," she said, when she found the spot where she'd first seen the dog the day before. They slogged through the piled-up snow at the bank and then into the bare brush, following the tracks from yesterday, widening the path their own boots had already helped to flatten. Quickly, they reached the cover of the trees and soon after that, the edge of the ravine.

The dog's tracks were still recognizable. They followed them along the rim of the ravine for perhaps two hundred yards, and then away from the edge. Once, as they began to climb the hill behind the house, Jilly lost the trail. But she picked it up again several yards on. That happened a number of times. She'd lose the tracks only to find them a few minutes later. They were descending by then. After a time, they ended up on level ground once more. About then the tracks just petered out to nothing.

Jilly was still in the lead. She stopped beneath a tall cedar and admitted, "I don't know where to go from here. I can't tell where he went."

She expected Will to shrug, turn around and head straight for the driveway—wherever that was. She'd lost track by then of how to get directly to the place where they had started. However, she felt reasonably certain she could get them back to the ravine, and from there, retrace their steps along it until they reached the place where she had fallen. Once she got to that point, it should be a simple task to find the way back to the driveway through the trees.

But Will didn't do what she expected. "Over here."

He had picked up the trail. He took the lead and they were on the move again.

Maybe fifteen minutes later, she heard what she thought was water—a creek or even a river, rushing fast. But then they came out to the edge of a cliff—a high embankment, really. She looked down and saw the road below them. It was clear of snow. The whooshing of the cars going by made that sound that she'd mistaken for rushing water.

Will went to the edge. He was frowning. "Wait a minute."

She stayed there while he backtracked along the route they'd just taken. When he returned to her, he was shaking his head. She knew what he'd tell her before he spoke.

"I'm sorry, Jilly. I've lost the trail. I don't know where to go from here."

She met his eyes then. "Neither do I."

He waited. She felt tenderness for him rising, soothing the hurt in her heart. He wanted to keep the one promise he'd made her. He had tried to keep it. But the dog was nowhere to be found.

And Will Bravo wasn't ready to love again. She had to accept that. It was time they both moved on.

She sent a brief prayer heavenward, that wherever that sweet, shy mutt might be by now, he was safe. And well.

And then she gave Will a real smile, one that was a little bit sad, but also one-hundred-percent sincere. "We haven't seen a single bear or mountain lion. I don't think you'll have to use that rifle of yours, after all."

He looked vaguely abashed. "You're right. I probably should have left it at the house. I'm a little on edge, that's all.''

''Positive that some other bad thing is bound to happen?''

''You got it.''

She opened her mouth to promise him that she was not allowing any more bad things to happen. But then she realized it would only be one more promise destined to remain unkept. Another bad thing *was* going to happen: the end of their time together. A hundred rifles couldn't protect them against that.

Jilly set her mind on the business at hand. ''I'm completely turned around. I hope you can get us back to your grandmother's house.''

He nodded. ''No problem. This way.'' He began trudging through the snow along the rim of the embankment.

As they moved along the edge, the embankment sloped downward. About twenty minutes after they first came out above the road, they were walking on the shoulder, single-file, sticking close to the dirty ridge of snow pushed aside by the plow. Cars and trucks and SUVs, crusted with road salt, snow piled high and white on their roofs, rushed past them, sometimes too close for comfort.

They came around a curve and Will pointed at a narrow driveway that met the road and wound off into the trees maybe thirty yards ahead. ''There. That's it.''

Jilly stopped where she was. ''The driveway to your grandmother's house?''

''That's right.''

"But it's been cleared."

"The plow must have—" He cut the sentence off himself. There was no need to go on. As they watched, the snowplow emerged from the driveway. The driver turned onto the road and saluted them with a mittened hand as he rolled by.

They got their shovels and went inside.

"Well," she said, "Let's get that tree taken down."

He shook his head. "Leave it."

"I promised you I would—"

"Leave it. Please. I'll handle it myself."

"You're sure?"

"Positive."

An hour later, with Will's help, Jilly had taken the unneeded chains off her 4Runner and cleared the windshield of snow and ice. She'd packed up her stuff and stowed it in back. Missy was safe in her carrier, already complaining from the passenger seat.

Jilly made one more pass through the old house. But there was nothing she had left behind.

Well, maybe her heart. But, hey. She was a strong, self-reliant and self-directed woman. She knew her own worth and her single life was a good life. She had no doubt she'd get over Will Bravo.

Eventually.

He went out with her to see her off. The sun was directly overhead by then, the sky ice-blue and clear.

They stood by the driver's door of her car and looked at each other for longer than they should have.

He was the one who broke the silence. "You know I'm going to miss you." It wasn't a question. He added, low and rough, "I'm going to miss you really bad."

She knew exactly what he meant. But she couldn't have said a word right then if her life and his life and Missy's life depended on it. So she swallowed and she nodded and she found her throat had loosened up enough that she could speak, after all.

"What I'd like to hear you say right now is that next year you'll be with your family when Christmas comes around."

He stuck his hands in his pockets and looked down at his boots. "I'll work on it, Jilly."

It wasn't the answer she'd hoped for. But it was something. And she might as well put a good spin on it. She sucked in a big breath of freezing air and let it out in a rush. "Well, okay. What more could I ask?"

Lots more. And they both knew it. But there was no point in asking for what you weren't going to get.

"Goodbye, Will." She turned to reach for her door.

Before she got it open, though, she heard him swear low. And then he was grabbing her by the arm, spinning her back around to him and yanking her close.

He looked down into her startled face, his eyes blue shards, two flags of color staining his beard-roughened cheeks. And then his mouth swooped in and closed on hers.

It was the kiss of her dream.

The one that burned her lips right off.

His hands ran down her back, pressing her close to him so she could feel how much at least one part of him wanted her to stick around. She kissed him back, as hard and hungrily as he was kissing her.

And then he pulled her closer still, so close that the savage kiss was broken. They breathed together. She could hear his heart beating, right in time with her own. Twin tears slid down her cheeks. She moved her head just a fraction, enough to wipe them away on his jacket, so he would never have to know they had fallen.

From some unknown reserve she hadn't realized she possessed, she found the strength to pull away. Still held in his arms, she looked up at him.

"This isn't going to be one of those steamy relationships that never really goes anywhere, but doesn't quite go away, either, is it?"

He gave her that wonderful, wry smile of his. "No. I swear to you. It was only that it hit me all over again. You're really going. And I couldn't stand it, not without one final kiss."

"So when we see each other—and you know we will—at Jane and Cade's, or the Highgrade, or at Celia and Aaron's, or maybe just coincidentally, on the street…"

He made a low sound in his throat. "I get the picture. Smile. Say hi. Walk on by."

"It probably won't be a whole lot of fun."

"I hear you. But we'll manage it."

"And right now, you'd better let go of me."

He released her. Damn. She hated that.

"Do me one last favor?" he asked, so softly.

"Anything." And she meant it.

He took her hand, turned it over and folded a piece of paper into her palm. "That's my cell phone number.

Call me when you get home. I just want to know that you made it safely.''

She snatched both hands behind her back—quickly. Or else she would have reached for him. ''Oh, Will. How can I convince you I'm going to be just fine?''

''Just call.''

''All right.''

She forced herself to turn again, to grab the door handle and pull the door wide. She hitched herself up and slid behind the wheel, setting the scrap of paper with his phone number on it in the little niche beneath the ashtray and hooking her seatbelt in place.

Will shut her door for her. He stepped back, mouthed, ''Drive carefully,'' at her through the window.

She gave him a jaunty wave, started up her car and headed down the driveway, taking extreme care not to allow herself so much as one glance back at him, or the clearing, or the old house where she'd found love so unexpectedly—and then, just as suddenly, lost it again.

Chapter Sixteen

Jilly got home without incident. She dialed the number Will had given her as soon as she pulled beneath her carport and turned off her car.

He answered midway through the first ring. "Jilly?"

She ached for him, picturing him in his easy chair, the phone in his hand, driving himself a little nuts with his usual expectations of disaster as he waited for her call. "I'm here. I'm fine."

"Thank you."

"Goodbye, Will."

She heard a click and the line went dead.

Jane called her on her cell the next day. "Well, are the roads cleared?"

It took Jilly a second or two to realize that Jane assumed she was still at the old house high up in the mountains. "Yes, they are. As a matter of fact, I'm home."

Silence echoed down the line as Jane digested that piece of information. "Home? In Sacramento?"

"That's right."

"But I thought you said you would call me before you left, maybe come on in to New Venice and stay with Cade and me until New Year's."

Jilly cast about madly for a way to explain herself. Nothing came to mind except the truth, which was a long story with an unhappy ending and would entail spilling the beans about Will—something she really didn't want to do. She and Will were nobody's business. They'd had a beautiful time together and now it was over and telling his sister-in-law all about it wouldn't help the situation one bit.

Jane prompted, "Jilly?"

At a loss for what to say, she found herself launching into a verbal tap dance. "Oh, that's right. I did say I'd call. I'm sorry, it's just that something came up. I had to get home."

Jane cleared her throat, pointedly. "Jillian. Please. I've got my bull-detector set on you and it is beeping. Fast and loud. What's going on?"

"I just wanted to come home, that's all."

"You mean that whatever it is, you're not going to tell me."

Jilly wondered what could have possessed her to try being evasive with Jane. With Jane, it was always better to come right out with it when you didn't intend to tell her something. Jane could get ugly if you lied to her.

"You're right, Janey. I'm not going to tell you."

"Was it Will? Did he—?"

"Will was a perfect gentleman. I just wanted to come home."

"Celia said he told you all about poor Nora. Evidently, he gets very weird over the holidays."

"We worked everything out. We had a fine time." Oh, yes they had. They really had. "And I'm very sorry I didn't call you. It was rude. I just had a lot of things on my mind."

There was another silence—but not such a strained one as before. "There's no need to apologize. You know that. I only wish you would tell me what's bothering you."

"I'm all right, Janey. Truly."

"You sure you won't change your mind and come on up to visit, anyway? We would love to see you."

No, you wouldn't.

Jilly was standing by the brass-framed mirror in her apartment's small entrance hall and what she saw reflected there wasn't anything anybody else needed to see. She'd stopped for gas at a convenience mart yesterday and made the mistake of going inside. The clerk had looked up from the register and gasped.

"My God, lady. Are you okay?"

That was when Jilly decided she'd avoid leaving her apartment for a while—until the bruises went away and the bumps went down or until something came up where she had no choice. And if she did go out, she'd have sense enough to wear a hat pulled low on her forehead.

"Jilly? What do you say? Why don't you come on up?"

"Thanks bunches, Janey. But I just can't make it right now."

They said goodbye a few minutes later. Jilly punched the button to end the call and then had to stop herself from dialing Will's number. It was a problem she had now. Every time she had a phone in her hand, her fingers just itched to call him.

She'd torn up the paper with his number on it and flushed the pieces down the toilet. But that hadn't helped. Somehow, that number had managed to burn itself into her brain. She'd forget her own name before she'd forget that number.

Oh, what was she going to do with herself? Maybe she ought to sit down and write a letter to "Ask Jillian." She could give herself the answer to all her troubles and print it in her column.

Dear Jillian...

What? She didn't even know where to begin.

She put the phone down and went to make herself a double batch of Kraft macaroni and cheese. As she sat down to eat, she told herself she was not even going to think about what Will might be doing right now....

Will had made himself a double batch of Kraft macaroni and cheese. He took his place at the table and picked up his fork and dug in.

A few minutes later, he realized he'd stopped eating.

He was just sitting there, his food growing cold in front of him, staring at the kitchen door, wishing a certain gray-eyed woman with gold-streaked brown hair would come bursting through it, that mouth of hers going a mile a minute....

He picked up his fork again. He had to stop that, getting lost in thoughts of Jilly. She was gone and it was for the best.

He was just tired, that was all. He'd had a rough night last night, missing the warmth of her beside him.

And his dreams had been unsettling.

In one, he saw his grandma Mavis standing at the foot of the bed, shaking her head at him, her blue eyes so sad. And in another, he saw Nora, standing a long way off, in some misty nowhere place, waving, calling to him. But he couldn't make out what she said.

Both dreams had left him feeling bleak and depressed. And then he got up in the morning and went out to the living area and the first thing he saw was that damn tree of Jillian's. He couldn't take looking at that tree until New Year's.

So, before he even allowed himself a cup of instant cappuccino, he'd taken the thing down and tossed it out in back to chop up for firewood at some later date. He'd packed up all of Mavis's old decorations and put them where they belonged, in the crawl space upstairs.

And then, damn it, he found himself missing the tree after it was gone. He had this feeling of an empty space, there, by the window, where the tree ought to be.

Will shook his head. He forked up a mound of macaroni and cheese and shoved it into his mouth.

He chewed, stolidly. Life was just that way sometimes, bad dreams and memories. Restless nights and lonely days.

Outside, it was near dark. The wind was up, whistling through the trees, making the old window frames rattle, whining at the door....

Will set his fork down again. He listened intently. That wasn't the wind.

Yes. There it was again. It sounded like...

Will got up and opened the door.

Jilly had had a couple of consultations scheduled for the first week in January. Friday, when she got home, she'd managed to reach those clients and move them both to a later date. Her column was no problem. She did that from home, anyway. She planned to really churn them out while she was stuck at home, estimating that by the time she was ready to show her face in public again, she'd be at least a month ahead. And that, as the divine Martha would say, was a good thing. In the end, the way Jilly saw it, everything had its upside—even hiding out in her apartment in order to spare other people the horror of having to look at her.

Saturday, a few hours after Jilly spoke with Jane, Caitlin called. Correction, Jilly thought, when she heard that low, sexy voice. *Almost* everything had its upside.

"Sweetie, I called Jane and I asked if she'd heard from you and she said that she'd talked to you and you were at home. I couldn't believe it. Tell me it isn't so."

"It's so, Caitlin. I'm at home."

"I don't get it. What the hell's the problem now?"

"There is no problem. Everything's fine."

"Where's Will?" Caitlin demanded, in a tone that seemed to hint that Jilly must have done something criminal with her middle son.

"The last I saw him, he was up at Mavis's place. I think he plans to be there until the second of January—and Caitlin, Will and I talked about you. We decided that what you need is to find yourself another boyfriend."

"Don't try to switch subjects on me, darlin' girl. When I want a new boyfriend, I'll find one. And when I go after information, I don't quit until I get it. Did you two have a tiff? Is that what you're telling me?"

"Caitlin, let me give it to you straight."

"Go right ahead. Hit me with it. I like it straight."

"There is nothing going on between Will and me. We're…friendly acquaintances. And that's all."

Caitlin made a snorting noise. "Well, that is a great big load of stinkin' you-know-what if I ever heard one."

"Caitlin. I have to go. Have a happy New Year." Jilly hung up and turned off the phone.

"Omigoodness, Jillian. What *happened?*" Jilly's neighbor, Orlene Findley, gaped at her, horrified.

Jilly had made the mistake of stepping out to get her Monday morning *Press-Telegram* without checking first to see if anyone was going to have the misfortune of getting a look at her. She'd just bent down to scoop up the paper when Orlene popped out of her own apartment across the breezeway.

Jilly tried for a lighthearted tone. "Just a couple of accidents up in the mountains."

"A *couple* of accidents?"

Right then, from inside, Jilly's house phone started ringing. She waved her paper at Orlene. "Phone. Gotta go. Take care." She backed up and shut her door on her staring neighbor, leaning against it briefly, promising herself that she would never so much as poke her head out that door again unless she had on a hat or a minimum of a week had passed. She figured by a week, the two goose eggs would have gone down and her bruises should yield, at least somewhat, to a heavy application of foundation.

Then again, maybe she was handling this all wrong. Maybe she should simply go boldly forth, let people gasp and exclaim over her all they wanted. They'd get over it. A lot sooner than she was going to.

Missy sat on the floor a few feet away, glaring up at her. The cat had yet to forgive her mistress for spiriting her away from Will.

And the phone was still ringing.

"Hello?"

"Happy New Year's Eve, Jilly."

"Ceil. How are you?"

"In labor."

At first, Jilly thought it must be a joke. "You're kidding, right?"

"No. My contractions are coming five minutes apart and Aaron and I are on the way to the hospital."

"Omigod. You mean you're in the car?"

"That's right."

"How are you? Are you—?"

"I'm fine. Poor Aaron, though. I don't know if he'll survive this."

Aaron said something at Celia's end of the line, but Jilly couldn't quite make it out.

Jilly smiled. "Tell him to take slow, deep breaths."

"I have. It didn't seem to help much—Janey's coming, with Cade. They're on their way."

Jilly clutched the phone a little tighter. She knew what her friend would say next.

"Oh, Jilly. Could you come, too?"

The problem was, she wanted to. She really, really wanted to. But Will might be there. And certainly Caitlin would. She didn't know if she was ready to deal with either of them just yet.

Celia coaxed, "I know you don't have much on your schedule till after the first, since you'd planned to stay up at Mavis's house until then. And it would be my treat. Just say yes and get to Sacramento International ASAP. We'll have a ticket waiting in your name for the next Las Vegas flight. And Aaron will send a car to pick you up at McCarran."

"Oh, that's crazy. You don't have to—"

"I want to. Every time I think of this baby, of how happy I am, I think of the three of us sitting by the fire at Janey's last February. I think of how I might never have had the nerve to go after what I wanted, if it hadn't been for you two."

"Ceil, I know you would have gone after that man on your own eventually."

Celia was laughing. "Sure, in another decade or two." Then she sighed. "It would mean so much to me—to have you here for this. Since the first day of kindergarten, whenever something major happened in my life, you and Janey were there. This is pretty major, you know? And I have to admit, I'd just like to see you. I've been a little worried about you since that mix-up last week over that old house of Mavis's.''

Jilly winced. It was the problem with having really close friends—somehow they always sensed when something was wrong. ''Oh, Ceil. Why? I really am okay. And the last thing you need right now is to be worrying about me.''

''I can't help it. Janey says you never called her back about visiting her and Cade.''

''She called me. We worked it out.''

''I know. But you haven't called *me*.''

''Ceil. Come on. It's only been a few days.''

''Something's bothering you. I can sense—'' Celia gasped. And the gasp became a low groan.

''Ceil. Are you okay?''

''Damn it, Jillian.'' Suddenly, it was Aaron growling in her ear. ''She's having another contraction. Say you'll come so she can get off the phone and concentrate on having this baby.''

When he put it like that, what else could she do? ''All right. But I'll get my own flight.'' He started to growl some more. She said firmly, ''I don't want you worrying about me. What hospital?'' He told her. And she said, ''Okay. Tell Celia I'll be there as soon as I possibly can.''

''She's coming.'' He was talking to Celia now, his voice low, tender. And urgent. ''Don't worry, my darling. She's on her way....''

* * *

Orlene promised to look after the sulking Missy. Jilly threw what she'd need for a couple of nights into a carry-on and found a cute, slouchy gray wool hat that covered most of the train wreck formerly known as her forehead. She locked up and went out and jumped in her 4Runner.

At the airport, the terminal smelled of Cinnabons. Jilly was practically salivating as she took her place in a very long ticket line, not holding out a lot of hope for getting a ticket at the last minute like this, on New Year's Eve. She was already resigning herself to calling Aaron back to report that she'd be driving in, after all.

But an hour later, when her turn came, she managed to get a flight with only a two-hour wait till takeoff. She couldn't believe her luck. And it wasn't even standby. She bought some magazines and an intriguing looking paperback mystery and then she surrendered to that delicious aroma and bought herself a huge, delectable cinnamon roll. She was just sitting down to devour it when the phone in her purse rang.

She checked the display before she answered. Great. "What do you want, Caitlin?"

"Hey, don't bother with a friendly tone. After all, it's only me."

"What do you want?"

"Aaron says you're on your way to Vegas."

"That's right."

"You got a flight?"

"I did."

"Way to go, sweetie pie. Listen, I want to be sure you get to the hospital in time to see my grandchild born. Give me your flight number. I'll have a car waiting to pick you up.''

''Oh, Caitlin. I can see you coming a mile away.''

''Now, darlin' girl, what is that supposed to mean?''

''You're up to something.'' Jilly didn't know exactly what, but it was Caitlin, so there had to be some kind of scheme going on here. Maybe she planned to trick poor Will into being the one to meet her at the airport. It seemed like a stretch, but with Caitlin, anything was possible.

''Jilly, sweetie, how come you're so damn suspicious lately?''

''Oh, puh-lease.''

''Now, hon.'' Caitlin had put on a wheedling tone, one Jilly found particularly grating, given Caitlin's basic nature, which was brash and bossy in the extreme. ''You just be a good girl and give me that flight number, now.''

''Thanks, but I'll rent a car.''

''That could be a problem,'' Caitlin advised in a sweet, husky singsong. ''Darlin' girl, it's New Year's Eve.''

''I'll manage. And I have to go. My Cinnabon is getting cold. Bye, now.''

Caitlin was still wheedling away as she disconnected the call.

Jilly's flight took off on time and landed at Mc-Carran right on schedule. She ran into a snag at the rental car booth. She'd called to reserve a car before her flight, but when she got there it turned out that available vehicles were nil. She thought of Caitlin, wondered if Will's manipulative mother could possibly have done something to keep her from getting her rental car.

But then how would Caitlin Bravo, who ran a saloon and café in a tiny town east of Tahoe, have that kind of influence with a Las Vegas rental car outlet? And why would she even want to do such a thing? Jilly must be getting paranoid. She'd have to watch that— though it was difficult to keep suspicions in check after you'd been dealing with Caitlin for a while.

Finally, about an hour after Jilly showed up at the desk, someone turned in a no-frills compact. Jilly snapped it up.

It took her forty-five minutes to reach the hospital from the airport. By then, it was three in the afternoon. She raced inside, stopped at the front desk for directions and then headed straight for the maternity ward.

When she stepped off the elevator, which opened right on to the waiting area, she knew she was in the right place. Celia's mom, Maggie Tuttle, sat in one of the gray chairs, wearing her usual sweetly distracted expression. Celia's oldest sister, Annie, sat beside Mrs. Tuttle, holding her mother's hand. Caitlin sat two chairs down from the Tuttle women. She was thumbing through a dogeared magazine, her hard black hair gleaming, her black satin shirt spangled with sequins that perfectly matched her skin-tight turquoise jeans. Cade and Jane were there, too—Cade in baggy cargoes and a leather jacket, Jane in one of those Eddie Bauer jumpers that always looked just right on her, her coffee-colored hair a wild mass of cascading curls.

Oh, yes. Everyone who should be there *was* there.

Except Aaron, who had taken labor classes with his wife and was probably with her right now. And Will…

Caitlin looked up first. "Darlin' Jilly. It's about time—and what's with the hat?"

"Hello, Caitlin." Jilly tipped her head back slightly so she could see beneath the hat's low brim and gave Will's mother a big, defiant smile.

"Hey, there," said Cade.

Celia's mother let out a tired littler chirp of greeting, and Annie gave Jilly a nod and a smile.

Janey jumped from her chair, arms outstretched. Jilly rushed to her. They met in a hug. "I was getting worried," Janey whispered once they had their arms around each other.

Jilly gave her other best friend one more good squeeze and stepped back. "Nothing to worry about. Here I am, safe and sound."

"Is this some hot, new look?" Janey brushed the low brim of the hat. "How do you see?"

"I tip my head back. Tell me. How's Ceil? Has the baby arrived?"

"Not yet."

"Is everything going okay?"

"So far as we know. Evidently, things have slowed down. But there's nothing to worry about. The baby's fine and Ceil is, too."

Maggie Tuttle sighed. "First babies. They always take forever." Celia's mother ought to know. She'd had six babies herself.

Caitlin stood. "Jilly honey, it'll be a while before we get anymore news. And I'll bet you're dyin' for a snack about now. I've checked out the cafeteria and they've got bacon burgers and fairly decent fries. It ain't the Highgrade, but it'll do in a pinch. How about if you and me head on down to the cafeteria?''

Jilly grabbed Jane's hand. There was no way she was letting Caitlin Bravo corner her alone. "Thanks so much. But Janey'll take me. We have some catching up to do, anyway.''

Jane was a champion. She didn't miss a beat. "Do we ever. This way.''

"Don't you leave me alone with her," Jilly said desperately.

Jane had led her to a quiet corner, where they could talk undisturbed. Jilly had her bacon burger and fries in front of her and her head tipped way back so she could see her friend across the table.

"I'll do what I can." Jane tore the top off a container of strawberry-kiwi yogurt. "And I am sorry. But she really thinks you're the one for Will, and when Caitlin decides you're right for one of her boys..." Jane's voice trailed off and she shook that cloud of thick, dark hair. "She'll get over it. In time. And Jilly, come on. What is going on with that hat?''

It was one hat comment too many. Jilly gave in and took the hat off.

Jane said, "My God."

"I think of it this way, in six or eight weeks, who's gonna know I ever looked this bad?''

"How did it happen?''

"Got a month?''

Jane leaned closer, dark eyes shining with love and concern. Jilly felt a little better, just to have so much caring coming her way. "I want to hear," Jane said. "Everything. Please. It's what friends are for, you know?"

"We should get back soon. Ceil might—"

"If they need us or she wants us, they know where to find us."

"It seems...I don't know, like a bad idea, to tell you about it."

Janey had no trouble understanding why. "Because it's about Will, right? And his brother is my husband."

Jilly felt her face turning red. "Yeah, 'fraid so."

And Janey said, "I'm your friend. It feels to me that we've *always* been friends. You know in the end you'll have to come to me or to Ceil—and Ceil is married to one of Will's brother's, too. So what can you do?"

Jilly picked up a French fry and set it down without eating it. "Oh, Janey. I just don't know...."

A sudden frown drew Janey's brows together. "You're not trying to tell me...Will didn't...?"

"What?" Jilly pointed to her forehead. *"This?"*

Janey now wore a look of pure horror. She gulped. Nodded.

Jilly cried "No! Of course Will didn't do this to me." It hurt, she realized, just to say his name out loud. Tears tightened her throat. "He only *thinks* that he did."

Jane set down her yogurt and laid her hand over Jilly's. "Come on, now. You'd better explain."

So Jilly did. She told it all. How she and Will despised each other at first, how the tree branch fell on her, how she told Will she'd overheard him saying rude things about her, how Mavis appeared in her dreams. She included the part about how Missy went missing, and the night Will told her about Nora and then the lights went out. She explained how Mavis showed her where to find Missy. And then she shared a little about the best times—the Christmas she and Will had made, just the two of them, his birthday the next day....

Jane leaned close across the table. "You became lovers, then?"

"Yes." And Jilly told the rest, about the lost dog they never found and how she fell into a ravine chasing after him. How everything changed after that. How Will sent her away—but then had to go and give her that one last incredible kiss, out in the clearing, as she was leaving. How he insisted she call him to say she'd made it home safe.

When she was done, Janey said, "So what now?"

"I don't have any idea."

Janey was smiling. "I think you do. I think maybe Caitlin's right about you and Will. I think maybe you think so, too."

"Oh, God. You think?"

"How could I not? Look at all that's happened. Even Mad Mavis is trying to get you two together."

"Don't even joke about that. I mean, that is seriously creepy. I sincerely did feel that she really *was* there, that she was trying to help Will, you know, from beyond the grave?"

Jane shrugged. "Maybe she was. And if she was, well, isn't that kind of wonderful?"

"Oh, Janey. You think?"

Jane leaned close again. "Maybe you just have

to…accept it. Just take whatever lesson you believe you were supposed to learn from it and go with it.'' She picked up her yogurt and sat back in her chair. ''Eat your burger.''

''I will.'' Jilly reached for it. But before she took a bite, she set it down again. ''Where *is* he? Do you know? Is he still up at Mavis's house? Did anyone call him? Does he realize that his first niece or nephew is, at this very moment, being born?''

Jane spooned up more yogurt. ''I assume he's still at the cabin. And yes, he's been told about the baby. Aaron finally got hold of him. I think Caitlin called him about a hundred times. She left message after message. She finally badgered Aaron into calling and that call, Will answered.''

''But he's not coming?''

Jane gave her a patient look. ''Jilly, think about it. A baby's birth is not really the kind of thing bachelor uncles feel obligated to attend—especially not when they have to get to the hospital from high in the mountains five hundred miles away.''

''Not coming…''

Jane gave her a sympathetic look. ''No, I don't think so.''

Oh, why did she feel so deflated and sad? She'd been telling herself that what she wanted most was *not* to have to see him.

Jane was leaning forward again. ''Jilly…''

''Is this advice I'm about to get?''

''Yes, it is. Are you listening?''

''Oh, yes. Yes, I am.''

''When it comes to love, *somebody's* got to go for

it, to stand up and say, 'This is what I want and I intend to fight for it.' Caitlin told me that.''

"You're kidding."

"No. My mother-in-law does have her honestly insightful moments."

"You're saying I should fight for Will?"

"I'm saying you two won't work anything out if you never see each other. I'm saying if you have something to say to him, you ought to track him down and say it. You can't allow yourself to imagine that the opportunity to work things out with him is somehow going to drop into your lap."

David Aaron Bravo, ten pounds, three ounces and twenty-one inches long, was born at ten minutes past midnight on the first day of the New Year. After mother and child were cleaned up and settled in their own private room, the anxious visitors who'd waited all those hours for the baby's arrival were allowed in to see them, one or two at a time, for only a few minutes each. The new mother asked to see Jane and Jillian together.

Jilly's first thought when she entered that hospital room was that Celia looked awful. She had dark circles beneath her eyes. Her red hair, hanging lank and oily on her shoulders, cried out for a shampoo and some decent conditioning. The hideous floral hospital gown had to go.

Ungroomed, exhausted and unattractively dressed, Ceil also somehow managed to look luminous. She gazed down at her child with so much love and pride on her heart-shaped face, that Jilly found herself gulping furiously to keep from bursting into tears.

Celia glanced up and a sharp cry of distress escaped her. "Jilly. What's happened?"

Jilly touched her forehead. "Oh, this? It's nothing. A tree branch fell on me and I rolled down a ravine."

"But you're okay?"

Jilly shared a look with Jane, then announced, "Never better."

"And we'll only stay a second," Jane vowed.

Ceil was smiling again. "It's so good to see you both." And then she whispered, "Triple threat."

Jane and Jilly repeated the words in unison. "Triple threat."

It was what they used to call themselves, way back when, as kids. In reality, of course, they'd been no threat to anyone. They were three nice girls who, for the most part, had spent their lives behaving themselves.

Jane and Jilly moved in to get a closer look at David Aaron.

"Oh, I cannot believe those tiny hands," Jilly whispered. "That incredible perfect little mouth...." She offered her index finger and one of those waving hands wrapped reflexively around it.

Ceil said, "Janey, did you talk to her?"

Jilly caressed the baby's gripping fingers with a brushing motion of her thumb. "She did. I told her everything. And as usual, *she'll* tell *you* everything I said."

Jane chuckled. "But later. After you've rested."

Ceil said, "Jilly, you *could* just tell me yourself."

And Jane said, "She can't. In a few minutes, she's leaving."

Reluctantly, Jilly pulled her finger free of David Aaron's grip.

"Leaving?" Celia adjusted the blanket around her new baby's darling wrinkled face. "Where is she going?" And then she looked up and grinned. "Never mind. I think I can guess."

Caitlin caught up with her as she was heading for the elevators. "Jilly. Hold up. Don't even imagine you're getting away from here without—"

Jilly turned and grabbed Will's mother and hugged her for all she was worth. "Gotta go. See you soon."

For once in her life, Caitlin Bravo actually seemed a loss for words.

The elevator door was already open. Jilly stepped through. The door closed just as she turned and gave Caitlin a wave.

Outside it was sixty degrees. A beautiful winter's night in Las Vegas. Jilly sucked in a big breath of the balmy, smoggy air and headed for her car.

But there was a problem. The space where she'd left her no-frills compact rental had a huge midnight-blue Chevy Suburban in it now.

Was it possible that someone would actually go to the trouble of stealing a car like the one she had rented?

Maybe this was just a mistake. She'd been careful to write down the level and row number on a piece of paper, since more than once in her life, she'd lost track of where she'd parked her car in the first place.

But not this time. Right level, right row.

Wrong vehicle.

She heard a car approaching, rolling slowly her way. She turned and put up a hand against the glare of the headlights. The car kept coming, slowing to a stop right beside her.

She saw that it was a Mercedes. G-Class. Very dirty, a car that had recently covered a lot of distance on muddy roads. But underneath the mud, it was silver.

Will rolled the driver's-side window down. ''Need a lift?''

Chapter Seventeen

Her heart was doing impossible things inside her chest. And the world was suddenly so vivid. So beautiful. The parking garage seemed to shimmer with loveliness.

Yet she spoke quite calmly. "What are you doing here?"

"Aaron said you would be here. I came to find you."

She stared at him, narrow-eyed. Then she blinked. "You're serious."

"As a blow to the head. As a long roll down a steep ravine."

"That's pretty serious." She looked at him sideways. "Would your mother go so far as grand theft auto, do you think?"

"Hmm," he said. "We *are* talking about Caitlin, which means anything's possible."

She saw movement behind him. She blinked again. But the brown-and-white spotted dog on the seat beside him was still there, ears perked, panting contentedly. "Oh, Will. You found him...."

There was a moment. A shimmering, private, perfect moment. Will looked at her and she looked back. It was magic.

It was love.

Finally, Will said, "The truth is, *he* found *me*. I opened the door. There he was. I started calling him Snapper, for no reason in particular. He didn't object, so that's his name."

She had never been quite this happy in her life. "You mean—you're keeping him? You've got a dog, at last?"

"I would have to say it's more that *he's* keeping me. He's why I *drove* down. Hard enough to get a flight at New Year's without a dog to worry about."

She thought of David Aaron. "Did you hear—about the baby?"

He shook his head. "I've been leaving my phone turned off a lot. Caitlin's always calling. I get sick of hearing it ring."

She told him the news.

"Well," he said, a musing half smile on that wonderful face. "What do you know? I'm an uncle."

They looked at each other again, just stared and grinned until a car drove up behind him and honked to let them know they were blocking the flow of traffic.

Will said, "Let's go."

She rushed around to the passenger's side. Snapper jumped in back without even having to be told. "Where are we going?" Not that she really cared.

"Some place where we can talk."

In Las Vegas, finding a decent hotel in the middle of the night presented no problem. They paid a hefty extra fee in order to be allowed to have Snapper in the suite with them.

Once the three of them were alone, Jilly fussed over the dog for a few minutes, then Will ordered him to go lie down. Snapper trotted right over to the sofa against the far wall and made himself comfortable.

Will took her by the shoulders. "You won't believe this. I keep having these dreams. Of my dead grandmother. Of Nora. Last night, I finally put it all together. My grandmother wants me to be with you."

"I *do* believe it. I had a few nighttime encounters with Mavis myself."

"You're not serious."

"Oh, but I am. And I have to admit, the whole experience had me seriously spooked. But yesterday I talked to Janey about it. She said what I needed to do was to accept it, to learn whatever lesson I thought Mavis might be trying to teach me."

"I always did like Jane. She's woman with both feet firmly on the ground."

"Not silly and flighty like some of us."

"Silly and flighty? No damn way. Lighthearted. Eager. So very, very *alive*." He had her face cradled in his hands. He kissed her. A kiss that burned her to a joyful cinder and melted her into a puddle of love and desire. Simultaneously.

But there was still more to talk about before they could make use of the big bed a few feet away.

She broke the kiss. "And Nora?"

He gave her a crooked, musing grin. "It took me a while to get what she was trying to say to me."

"Because?"

"I kept dreaming of her off in the distance, waving, telling me something I couldn't make out. And then, last night, I got it. I understood she was saying goodbye. She was saying—"

Jilly knew. "That her dying was not your fault."

He grabbed her close again, his strong arms banding tight around her. "I did know it." He whispered the words into her hair. "In my mind. It's just...taken a while for the knowledge to settle into my heart."

Jilly hugged him as hard as her arms could hug.

And then he was taking her shoulders again, holding her away enough that he could see her face. "Luckily, this Christmas, I got professional help."

She laughed at that. "It was a hell of a job, but somebody had to do it. And for my fee..."

"Anything."

She laid a finger against those warm, tempting lips. "Don't say that until you've heard what I want."

He grabbed her hand, kissed that finger. "Anything," he repeated. "Name your price."

So she did. "I love you, Will. Marry me."

He said, "You're crazy."

"No. It's time for the big leap of faith. For both of us. I'm scared to death and I know you are, too. But

I think that you do love me. And as I've just told you,
I love you. So…''

He grabbed her close again, even tighter than before.
''But what if—''

''No. None of it, none of the bad things that have
happened in the past were your fault.''

''But you have to admit—''

''I admit nothing, not when it comes to this. I
messed up once, badly, when I chose a man to love.
But I'm not letting that wrong choice keep me from
making the *right* choice now. And *you* can't let the
bad things that have happened to you keep you from
reaching out and grabbing hold when a good thing
comes your way. Oh, Will, there's just no way for us
to know how it's all going to turn out, what will happen next year, tomorrow, an hour from now. All we
can do is live for all we're worth, from minute to minute.''

''You seem so damn sure.''

''I *am* sure. About this, anyway. You are no jinx,
Will Bravo. You are the man that I love.''

''I really like the sound of that.''

''I'm glad. Because it would take a lot more than
your bad luck to do me in. I lived through this holiday
season at your side. And I intend to live through a
lifetime more of them.''

''Is that a promise?''

''It is a vow.''

''I love you, Jilly. Marry me.''

She sighed. ''Missy is going to be so very pleased.''

''Kiss me, damn it.''

Jilly did. With tenderness and heat, sweetness and sizzle. And with all the love in her heart.

They ended up in the bed for several long, lovely hours.

But luckily, it was Las Vegas. They got up at noon and called Jilly's mother to give her the news. Next, they called Aaron, who put Celia on to congratulate them. Then they tracked down Jane and Cade to be their witnesses. Caitlin got wind of a wedding in the works. She insisted on being there, too. She also swore she'd had nothing to do with the disappearance of Jilly's rental car, which turned up a few days later— in Winnemucca, of all places.

Thus, in a very short time, everything was arranged. And at six in the evening, on the first day of January, Jilly Diamond and Will Bravo exchanged their wedding vows at the Chapel of Love Eternal in the heart of Las Vegas, right on the Strip.

Epilogue

On December twenty-second of that year, Jillian and Will Bravo put their cat and their dog and a whole lot of groceries into Will's Mercedes and drove up into the mountains.

The old house seemed to be waiting just for them. They cut down their own tree and decorated it with all the wonderful faded ornaments in Mavis's attic. Will read the first two hundred pages of *The Brothers Karamazov*. Jilly got in a little work on some future columns. She beat him at Scrabble and he trounced her at checkers. They listened to NPR and Christmas carols. For the most part, Missy and Snapper got along.

There was Dinty Moore chili and Campbell's tomato soup, Kraft macaroni and cheese and bags and bags of Cheez Doodles. For Christmas, they prepared the kind of meal that would have made the divine Martha proud.

And they made love. Frequently. With great joy.

If Will seemed reluctant to let Jilly out of his sight, she tried to be tolerant of his not-quite-banished fears. Life, after all, was a work in progress. And old ways of thinking sometimes died hard.

As midnight approached on December thirty-first, they filled their juice glasses with the finest champagne. When the clock on the old desk in the corner said the New Year had come, they raised their glasses high.

Will proposed the toast. "To us, to our first anniversary. And to one entire holiday season injury-free."

"I'll drink to that."

They drained their glasses.

She put her hand over his. "It's going to get easier as every year goes by."

"Is that a promise?"

"It is a vow. Now, kiss me, damn it."

And he did.

* * * * *

Look out for Christine Rimmer's
From Here to Paternity, *out in June 2008, and*
The Man Who Had Everything, *out in*
July 2008, only from Special Edition!

THE ROYAL HOUSE OF NIROLI

...*International affairs, seduction and passion guaranteed*

Volume 5 – November 2007
Expecting His Royal Baby by Susan Stephens

Volume 6 – December 2007
The Prince's Forbidden Virgin by Robyn Donald

Volume 7 – January 2008
Bride by Royal Appointment by Raye Morgan

Volume 8 – February 2008
A Royal Bride at the Sheikh's Command by Penny Jordan

8 volumes in all to collect!

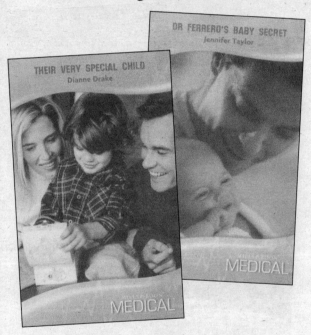

MILLS & BOON®

MEDICAL™

Proudly presents

Brides of Penhally Bay

A pulse-raising collection of emotional,
tempting romances and heart-warming stories by
bestselling Mills & Boon Medical™ authors.

January 2008
The Italian's New-Year Marriage Wish
by Sarah Morgan

Enjoy some much-needed winter warmth with
gorgeous Italian doctor Marcus Avanti.

February 2008
The Doctor's Bride By Sunrise
by Josie Metcalfe

Then join Adam and Maggie on a 24-hour rescue mission
where romance begins to blossom as the sun starts to set.

March 2008
The Surgeon's Fatherhood Surprise
by Jennifer Taylor

Single dad Jack Tremayne finds a mother for his
little boy — and a bride for himself.

*Let us whisk you away to an idyllic Cornish town —
a place where hearts are made whole*

COLLECT ALL 12 BOOKS!

Available at WHSmith, Tesco, ASDA, and all good bookshops
www.millsandboon.co.uk

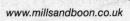

They knew what they wanted for Christmas! *

Two powerful and passionate festive novels:

* ## The Sicilian's Christmas Bride
by Sandra Marton

The Boss's Christmas Seduction
by Yvonne Lindsay

Available 2nd November 2007